the HOLIDAY clause

A HAWTHORNE BROTHERS NOVEL

LYDIA MICHAELS

WWW.LYDIAMICHAELSBOOKS.COM

The Holiday Clause
The Hawthorne Brothers Series
A Christmas Romance Novel
By Lydia Michaels

For Michelle Windsor—
A Christmas gal who loves to ho-ho-ho with the best of us!
#Idontcarewhetheryoulikemeornot
#ofcourseyoudo
#SFP

Listen as you Read

To the holly jolly jams that inspired this

holiday romance!

PROLOGUE

"Dashing Through the Snow"

"There I was," Wren began the story as dramatically as she always did, "fumbling for my keys as cats coiled between my legs on the cabin porch, their urgent mewing echoing in the frigid air."

"Here we go…" Logan rolled his eyes.

She ignored him, sitting up to better reenact the chaos that unfolded one year ago, the absolute insanity they put her through that led her to this very place. She didn't care that they heard the story a hundred times before. She lived it.

So did they, of course.

But she would never let them forget what they put her through. And each time she made them sit through the recap, she added more flourish and dramatization than the last.

"I bit the tip of my glove, precariously balancing my grocery bags in one arm, so I could dig through my purse," she continued, still able to hear the rock salt crunching underfoot. "It had been a frigid day. I still remember my breath clouding as I spoke to the cats."

The rescued strays were why people once assumed she was Hideaway Bay's unofficial cat lady at thirty. That was back when she was still single. A lot had changed since then.

"Your stories take forever."

"Shut up, Soren."

"Get to the point, Wren."

She shot Greyson a threatening look, warning him to hush. "The metallic bite of wind promised more snow, and we already had a foot from the storm that rolled in before Thanksgiving that year."

"There was a northern wind, and the temperature was a biting seventeen degrees. Two blue jays sat on a branch," Logan mocked.

"Patience, guys." She narrowed her eyes at the men. "That's what I remember saying to Figgy and the other cats as they perched on frost-dusted chairs. Then, suddenly, the roar of a motor exploded through the silence! I spun, keys tumbling from my grasp as a black super-duty pickup rocketed over the snowdrifts—an avalanche of ice and slush erupting in its wake as it plowed straight toward me! I screamed, and the cats scattered like buckshot."

Greyson's deep chuckle rumbled as he lounged by the fire.

"I don't think it was all that dramatic," Logan mumbled.

"Get to the good part," Soren urged.

Wren continued, "Out of nowhere, a snowmobile buzzed from the woods behind the cabin! I plastered myself against the front door in a sorry attempt to avoid a collision as claws scraped wood and the cats scrambled up the walls in sheer terror! My groceries crashed to the ground, eggs exploding, as I threw my hands up to shield my face. The truck slammed on its brakes, spraying snow all over me and my midnight blue siding as it skidded to a halt mere inches from my step. I was terrified. The engine growled like a caged beast as the driver's door burst open, and I screamed, *'What the hell is going on!'*"

"Whoa, whoa, whoa. Even I know that's stretching the truth. The snowmobile totally got there first."

"False." Logan laughed. "And you can't start the story there anyway." He sipped lager from a pilsner glass. "That makes us sound like maniacs."

Wren scoffed. "You are maniacs."

"She has a point." Greyson stretched his thick denim-clad legs toward the raised hearth of the massive fireplace.

"That's exactly how it started," Wren continued. "I'm telling the non-fiction version."

"Your version might be true, but that's not how it started." Soren brushed a piece of non-existent lint off his knee onto the oak floor. "You've got to give a little background to accurately portray the emotion."

Wren pursed her lips. "The emotion was fear."

"Nah, that kind of unhinged urgency can only be provoked by love." Soren flinched as a balled-up copy of *The Beacon* pegged him in the head. "What? Love can make a man do crazy things."

"You're an idiot." Greyson rolled his eyes.

Logan settled into the empty chair on the other side of the fire. "I'm with Soren. If you want to tell the story right, you have to go back to the beginning."

"Fine. You guys tell it."

The rocks in Soren's glass clinked as he sipped slowly, his eyes watching Wren like a predator watches prey. "All right. It was the weekend after Thanksgiving. Dad insisted we all come to the big house to celebrate. We'd just finished feasting on leftovers and were delving into Dad's bourbon collection as we pilfered his humidor when he dropped the bomb of the century on us."

"He always was a master of manipulation."

Wren cast an empathetic look at Logan. Of the three brothers, he'd had the least time with their father, so his grief always rang closer to anger and resentment than his older brothers'.

The loss of Magnus Hawthorne impacted all three of his sons

differently—in ways they would likely unpack for years to come. Grief was funny like that. It didn't arrive all at once in a tidy package. It stretched out over time and seeped into unexpected crevices of life, showing up when you least expected it and teaching lessons that pushed a person to feel things no one would willingly choose to feel.

Heartache moved in phases, and over the last year, she'd watched all three brothers process the stages differently at different times. Denial, anger, bargaining, depression, every phase played a part until they finally reached acceptance. Some were getting there slower than others.

"He really was a prick when he wanted to be," Soren agreed, never one to sugarcoat the truth. "Dad came into that study knowing exactly what he was doing. It was never about the business. It was always about controlling us from the grave."

"I think you're being a little harsh." Wren tucked her legs under the fur blanket as she nestled into the corner of the sofa with her mug of cocoa.

"You weren't there. I'm telling it exactly as it happened." Soren swept up the wood shavings by his feet and tossed them into the fire. "There we were, actually believing Dad wanted us there for some quality time that Thanksgiving. Then he dropped the bomb."

"I still remember the sound of that massive file hitting his leather-topped desk." Logan laughed without humor. "He shoved Soren's feet right off the edge and gave us a look of pure disappointment."

Greyson grinned and quietly recalled, "He always got pissy when you stole his cigars."

"Well, I still have the one I nabbed that day. A nice Cuban. Never even got it lit."

Wren looked at Greyson, noting the introspective way he stared into the fire. As the eldest of the three and by far the most reclusive, he never followed his brothers' lead. But he observed everything, depending only on himself, his presence like a silent shadow in the background of all their family drama. Of all the boys, Magnus had the least control over Greyson.

Soren retrieved the bottle of bourbon from the thick oak mantle. "Dad thought he was so slick, dangling that carrot over our heads only to snatch it away as a last hurrah."

Logan laughed bitterly. "He always knew how to tease the line to get the fish to do exactly what he wanted."

Staring into the flames, Soren shook his head. "He loved finding his opposition's Achilles heel."

Another gruff, humorless laugh escaped Logan's throat. "Opposition's the perfect word."

"Your dad loved you," Wren reminded.

"Sure—in his way. But he still saw us as the enemy."

"No, he didn't."

"You weren't there, Wren. There were times—after Mom died —that I swear he wished we'd been in the car with her."

Her heart clenched. "That's not true, Logan. Your dad, just like mine, never expected to be a single father. He did the best he could with what he knew."

"He knew how to pit us against each other."

"Well, lucky for the three of you, he wasn't very good at it."

Few brothers could claim the loyalty Greyson, Soren, and Logan shared. Sable Hawthorne would have been proud of the men her sons had become.

Soren refilled his glass at the wet bar. "The company was the perfect bait to get one last emotional response from us. He lured us in, and once he knew he had our balls in a vice, he couldn't wait to tighten the crank."

"You gave him that power." There was something primal about Greyson, something wild and wise his brothers lacked. Maybe it was because he was older, or maybe it was his years at sea that had hardened him.

Not to say Logan and Soren weren't formidable—they were. But Greyson was different. He didn't need anyone.

Wren smiled at his stubbornness. Magnus could never manipulate Greyson the way he manipulated his brothers.

He didn't need his father's wealth to feel content. He didn't crave his father's approval like his brothers, nor did he waste time antagonizing the man over their endless differences of opinion. Greyson created his own security and kept to himself most days, so it made sense that he hadn't reacted when his father dropped the ultimatum that fateful Thanksgiving.

As if sensing her thoughts, he met her stare, flames flickering in his dark blue eyes, his mouth a flat, unreadable line hidden by the stubble of his beard. Those devilish blue eyes smoldered, and Wren dropped her gaze—familiar heat spreading through her belly the way it always did when he fixed her with that knowing look.

All of the Hawthorne men possessed a potency that was impossible to ignore. It wasn't easy sitting in a room surrounded by such raw masculinity, but she'd been around it her entire life. Despite their history, when any one of them drilled into her with that shameless Hawthorne stare, she was as defenseless as every other redblooded woman. Even now, after everything they'd endured together, that intensity could still overwhelm her.

Mercifully, Greyson turned his attention back to the fire.

Wren faced Soren. "Finish the story. What happened next?"

"He laid down the law," Soren said with a gruff laugh. "Told us we'd been invited to Thanksgiving only to help him decide who would inherit the family business. We'd always assumed it would be divided among the three of us, so you can imagine our surprise when he suddenly changed the game."

"Not all of us wanted it," Greyson said, his stare turning pointedly toward his brother.

Soren scoffed. "How can you say that?"

"Because if you wanted it, you'd have it. Hawthorne men get what they want. And they own their mistakes."

"Fuck off." Ice rattled in Soren's glass. "It was never about who wanted it most."

"Wasn't it?"

Logan stretched out his legs on the ottoman, mimicking Greyson's radiated confidence. "As his sons, we all deserved an equal share."

Soren's eyes narrowed on his brothers. "But we're not talking about the company, are we?"

Together, they all turned to her, each wielding that penetrating Hawthorne stare. "Don't look at me! I had nothing to do with this."

"Wren," Soren smiled wickedly, "you had everything to do with it. You were the true prize."

She rolled her eyes. "No, I wasn't. It was always about the company. I was just a means to an end."

Logan laughed, the sound a little lighter now. "Dad wanted one last hurrah—one last chance to pit us against each other—and he got his wish, just not the way he expected."

"I was never part of Magnus's plans."

"But you were always part of ours."

"Take it easy." The low warning was enough to defuse any flirtation sizzling in the air.

The room fell silent. Even the crackling fire seemed to quiet as Greyson met his youngest brother's stare. "You never showed any interest in running the company back then, so stop acting like you did."

"How the hell would you know what I wanted? All you cared about was keeping to yourself in that secluded cabin of yours, chopping wood at all hours of the day and night."

"All right, Logan, keep it civil."

"Grey's right," Soren agreed. "You never said anything about wanting it until Dad said you couldn't have it. On paper, the fishery might look good, but you never cared about the actual work that went into managing the fleet or making sure the captains had everything they needed to keep the crews safe. You were too impatient to sit through quality control meetings, discuss logistics for managing the supply chain, or build relationships with our overseas buyers."

"Because I was never given the chance."

"Bullshit."

"Here we go," Greyson mumbled, rolling his eyes.

"Boys!" Wren snapped, slapping her hands against the fur blanket covering her lap. The muffled sound didn't have quite the effect she wanted, but it got their attention. "We were reminiscing, not having an argument. Stay on topic, or I'm going to bed."

"Maybe we all wanted the prize," Soren admitted, meeting her stare from the shadows. "At least on some level."

Greyson and Logan glared at Soren. Wren dropped her gaze to the contents of her mug, afraid to meet any of their stares in that moment.

"Dad did what he did best," Logan said, disrupting the tension. "He reminded us how much we disappointed him and leveraged his stingy affection to create a competition between us."

"Not all of us were starved for his affection, Logan."

"Shut up, Grey. I guess it was just about the money for you then."

"Watch it."

Wisely, Logan withdrew his challenging words and continued with the story. "What choice did we have? We either grew up, settled down, and acted like responsible adults, or he was selling off the company and giving the profits to the board and share-holders."

"He loved being a prick." Soren sipped his bourbon and stared into the fire.

"Maybe his actions weren't malicious at all. Maybe this was his way of making sure you boys would be okay in the end."

"There she goes, romanticizing things again," Soren grumbled. "Sometimes, people are just shitty, Wren."

She adjusted her blanket. "Everything in nature has duality, Soren. Even Magnus Hawthorne. If he could feel anger, he could feel peace. And if he was capable of happiness, he also knew sadness. I know for a fact your father loved you."

"You guys ever see Dad happy?" Soren joked, and his brothers chuckled.

"Couldn't even tell you what his laugh sounded like."

"Did Dad even have teeth?"

They all chuckled, but then the mood sobered as they each recalled a personal memory with Magnus that—despite his gruff and direct manner—brought a soft smile to their faces.

"He laid down the law before we'd even digested our Thanksgiving turkey," Soren recalled, his gaze unfocused as he seemed to relive the whirlwind of the past few months. "The doctors gave him weeks, and he wasted no time meeting with his attorney to permanently change the will."

"It was a pointless clause," Logan grumbled. "How did he expect any of us to actually change our lives that much before Christmas? His expectations were always unrealistic."

A strange mixture of guilt and relief flooded Wren as she kept her gaze down. That holiday clause was where she came in.

Magnus had changed his will just before the holidays to include a section stating that the lion's Hawthorne Fishery of the family business would be inherited by the son who married first. None of the men had been thinking about marriage until Magnus dropped that bomb. He'd wanted a reaction, and he'd gotten one.

Hawthorne Fishery wasn't just some rinky-dink, small-town operation. It was a billion-dollar, global-scale company with astronomical expenses and hundreds of vessels in each fleet built to travel deep international waters. There were inland processing plant stations off the coast, and the board wielded government-level influence when it came to ocean-related legislation and the country's environmental laws. There was an entire world of capitalism out at sea, and the Hawthornes were one of the oldest family-run fisheries still in existence.

The boys had a right to be disgruntled. It wasn't just Magnus's legacy—it was their birthright. The thought that the company could have been divided into shares and sold to the highest bidder or passed down to the board was simply unthinkable. Hawthorne Fishery needed to stay in the Hawthorne family.

"As always, Dad got his way."

Like a magnet, she felt Logan's dark stare pulling at her senses. Wren lifted her eyes and met cold obsidian. The year had changed him in ways she was still trying to figure out. Gone was the sweet companion she'd grown up alongside, and in his place sat a cold-hearted man desperate to hide all the gentle qualities he now believed made him weak.

He held her stare. "Didn't he, Wren?"

Logan had a gift for unnerving others with that penetrating glare, but she'd learned how to deflect it long ago. Despite the way her breath grew shallow, she held her body perfectly still. "I suppose he did. In a way."

Logan's cold stare slowly warmed when he smiled at her. With a past as long as theirs, every glance carried language outsiders couldn't decipher. Her tangled history with the Hawthornes harbored more secrets than anyone would guess, and their silence spoke volumes.

When the four of them were together, it was impossible not to feel the pull of nostalgia. Their shared past could be as over-whelming as their masculine intensity.

"Don't give me that look." She turned back to Soren. "Finish the story."

Soren sighed and sipped his bourbon, shifting to get more comfortable in his seat. "So he dropped the bomb on us, and we all knew he meant business. None of us woke up that morning with a single thought about marriage, but that all changed when we under-stood what was at stake."

"It's a big company," she agreed, and they all chuckled.

"Yeah, that's what this was about."

Her cheeks flushed. She couldn't fathom a reality where she wielded that much influence over men as unapproachable as the Hawthorne brothers. They might not intimidate her as much as they did outsiders, but that came with a lifetime of knowing each other.

Despite playing together in diapers when they were young, she still recognized the potent breed they were. She preferred to believe their actions were motivated by money, but when she found herself at the center of their family feud, she learned there was more to the story. Much more.

Logan chuckled. "There was no way you were beating me to her."

"I guess not when you stole my fucking keys."

"I didn't steal them. I relocated them into a snowbank."

"Prick." Soren reclined in the wooden rocker and stretched out his legs. "We all had the same thought. If we had to pick a wife in a pinch, there was only one choice."

All eyes again turned on her, and her cheeks burned. "Okay, take it down a notch." The testosterone radiating from the three of them was thinning the air and making it hard to breathe.

They smirked with Neanderthal-like male satisfaction.

"So Logan steals my keys, leaving me with whatever was left in Dad's garage. I grabbed the first set I could find—"

"To the snowmobile."

"Correct. Next thing you know, I'm blasting through the woods —without proper gear—in my socks—getting blinded by the snow." He shot his brother a pointed look. "I could have died."

"Don't be such a drama queen." Logan rolled his eyes. "The whole time I was driving, he wouldn't shut up on the two-way radio. It couldn't have been that treacherous if you had the ability to use the radio."

"Talking shit was my only defense! You were in a truck!"

Logan snickered. "And I got to her first."

"Which brings us back to where I left off." Wren set her mug aside and sat up. "I was carrying in my groceries—swarmed by cats —when you two maniacs barreled in like a landslide and almost killed me."

"Now who's being dramatic?"

"My whole life flashed before my eyes!"

"And like I said, that's not where the story starts."

She frowned at Logan. "If not there, then when?"

"You have to go back. Way back, to when we were kids."

"He's right," Greyson agreed, watching her with that quiet attention that missed nothing.

Wren frowned, oddly feeling as if they harbored secrets that—for once—didn't include her. "How far back?"

Soren shrugged. "Probably to the Christmas after Mom died."

The room grew silent as it usually did at the mention of Sable Hawthorne. As always, any reference to their mother reminded Wren of her own.

Haven Wilde and Sable Hawthorne had been lifelong best friends. Losing them at the same time was a sort of poetic tragedy that further sealed the bond she shared with Greyson, Soren, and Logan. Their mothers' connection had been stronger than marriage. The expectation that the four of them remain friends had been instilled from birth. Therefore, Wren's life had always been entangled with the untouchable Hawthorne brothers—even when she'd tried her best to detach herself.

As she stared at the lapping flames in the hearth, she tried to recall the fading memory of her mother's hair. It had been blonde, like hers, but with fiery copper undertones. The crackling wood put her in a trance as she fixated on the flames, searching for the exact shade of red she sometimes glimpsed in her mother's highlights when she stood in the sunshine.

A gentle hand closed around her shoulder, startling her. She closed her eyes, able to recognize and differentiate each brother's touch. The grief in her chest instantly eased as she pressed her cheek to his familiar fingers and sighed.

Their silence spoke volumes. After their mothers passed away, birthdays, holidays, and ordinary Mondays were never the same. Nothing was. They'd somehow managed to stick together.

The Christmas Magnus died was, by far, one of the most challenging, but, as always, the challenges they faced together only made them closer in the end. And, what was one of their hardest holidays, somehow also ended up being one of the most memorable and cherished.

"Fine," she eventually conceded. "If that's not where the story starts, then you tell it from the beginning."

The men shared a knowing grin. "For that, we're going to need a refill and another log on the fire."

CHAPTER 1

"On The Naughty List"

Sixteen Years Earlier

THE FIRST CHRISTMAS after Mom passed, Dad went overboard with gifts, but none of them captured the holiday spirit. An impenetrable, dull haze had lingered over all of them since the funeral. Everything felt hollow without Mom.

It had been forty-one days, six hours, and roughly thirty minutes since their world shattered. The shock lingered, but they each performed a masterful job of hiding their grief.

Greyson spent most days in the shed, building God knew what out of wood he'd salvaged from last winter's pile. Soren self-medicated by drinking in the woods with friends. And Logan stayed up all night playing video games.

Their father didn't want to face reality, so he drowned out the emotional fallout with gifts, games, and investments in youth clubs and sports. They all feared being sent away to boarding school, so they suppressed any grief that threatened to escape.

Once all the overcompensating presents had been opened that Christmas, none significant enough to penetrate the numbness left in their mother's absence, they drifted off to various parts of the house.

It didn't feel like Christmas. There was no tree, no cookies, no Mom.

Their father had left the house before dinner, claiming he had business to handle. The three of them returned to the den and sprawled out on the furniture, silent but together. At least they had their newest distraction to keep them occupied—state-of-the-art laptops.

Logan could use his for gaming. Soren would likely use his for school. And Greyson, well, he didn't really see much use for technology until...

A breathy, female moan broke the silence.

Logan's head snapped up in confusion, and he frowned. Another soft sigh keened through the silence, and Logan's eyes widened. "What is that?"

"It's not me." Soren slammed his laptop shut and leaned over to peer at Greyson's screen. "Holy shit."

Logan rushed to stand behind the couch. His eyes—and other things—bulged at the sight of long legs and pink lips. "Whoa! Is that allowed?"

Soren shoved Logan's head out of the way and moved closer to get a better look at Greyson's screen. "How'd you find that?"

"It's called a search engine."

More moans filled the room, now accompanied by staccato masculine grunts. Greyson lowered the volume as they all stared in awe at the beautiful woman getting railed on the screen.

Nothing could have prepared Logan for what the male actor did to the female actress next. "Doesn't that hurt?"

Greyson laughed. "She seems to be begging for it."

Logan's jaw unhinged. "But... what's he doing?"

"What do you think he's doing?"

As the youngest, Logan knew less than his brothers but still more than most boys his age. He wasn't disgusted by what they were watching. He just didn't expect it to look so... aggressive. His stomach tightened, and his cheeks heated when the man on the screen pulled the woman's hair.

Was this what moms and dads did?

What if their mom was watching them now—watching them watch what they were watching? "Turn it off."

"No."

"Grey, I'm gonna tell."

"No, you're not."

"If you don't want to watch, go do something else." Soren edged closer to the screen.

Grey shoved him. "Back up."

Soren hardly moved, his jaw unhinging at the sexual display on the screen. "Look how her tits bounce!"

"You guys are gross," Logan's interest gave way to shame. He was curious, but guilt kept his eyes partially averted. "That chick's older than my teacher."

"Your teachers aren't this hot."

"Or this naked."

"You're going to get a virus on your computer."

"No, I won't."

Logan rolled his eyes and went back to configuring the settings on his own laptop, ensuring all the firewalls were in place since his brother was corrupting their network.

"Logan, you're missing it. Her friend just showed up." Soren teased. "Is it just me, or does she look a little like Tammy Reynolds?"

"Yeah, maybe if Tammy had boobs."

"She's got boobs."

"Hardly."

"You know who's got big ones? Jenna Blackwell. She was flat as a board last spring. Then she came back in the fall with cannons the size of grapefruits."

"She's probably stuffing."

"No way. At the last pep rally, she was bouncing around like crazy. Tissue doesn't do that."

"I'm more of a leg man."

Logan rolled his eyes. "You're not a man. You're seventeen."

The moans and grunts coming from Greyson's laptop grew ridiculously dramatic. Real people didn't actually make those sounds during sex, did they?

Greyson hit a few keys and shut his laptop.

"Hey, I was watching that!" Soren snapped.

"Drool on your own screen. I need a shower."

Soren snickered and reopened his own laptop. "I will." He typed something in on the search bar. "Hey, you know who has nice legs?"

Greyson paused at the door. "Who?"

"Alison Jenkins."

"Her sister's annoying." Now that the moans had stopped, Logan could rejoin the conversation.

"What the fuck's her sister got to do with anything?"

Logan shrugged. "She's in my grade."

Greyson tilted his head. "Alison doesn't do anything for me. Now, Ashley Stables, on the other hand—"

Soren groaned. "That hair."

"I know."

"How do girls do all those waves and clips? She sits in front of me in Chemistry, and I can smell it. She must use strawberry shampoo. It gives me an instant hard-on."

"You should ask her out."

"Nah. She's still with Jace."

"I thought they broke up."

"Even I know Jace and Ashley break up every week—and I

don't even go to the high school." Logan considered all the girls they knew. "If you ask me, Wren's the prettiest girl in Hideaway."

The room fell silent, and his brothers fixed him with cold stares. "We don't go there," Greyson warned, blue eyes stern.

"Why not? Wren's just like any other girl in town, only cooler."

"Because she's not like other girls. She's like a sister to us." Tension coiled in Greyson's shoulders as he slid his laptop into its sleeve case.

"But she's not our sister. There's no real blood between us."

Soren lifted a dark brow. "He's got a point."

"No, he doesn't. Now, drop it."

"She's not the same Wren we used to chase barefoot at the docks. Have you seen her lately?"

"Yes, dumbass. At the funeral."

"Oh. Right." Soren glanced away in shame but quickly recovered. "That black dress looked hot—*ouch!*"

Greyson scowled, his hand still in a fist. "What did I say? We don't look at Wren that way."

"Dick." Soren rubbed his sore arm. "Who made you her keeper?"

"She's got enough on her plate right now. The last thing she needs is you sniffing around like some junkyard dog."

Soren's stare hardened. "Did you ever consider that Wren and I might have something special that you don't understand?"

"No, because you don't."

"You don't know that. She's closer to my grade than yours. I know her better."

"No, you don't."

"Oh, please. You barely said two words to her at the funeral."

"So? Maybe there was nothing worth saying. She barely spoke to anyone."

"That's not true," Logan corrected. "I talked to her."

Logan had been hiding in the sitting room when Wren found him. He'd been crying and embarrassed. It was a well-known saying that Hawthorne men don't cry, but he couldn't seem to stop his tears that day.

When she found him, she took his hand and talked about how they used to catch frogs by the creek when they were young. It was so random, but somehow, it was precisely what he needed in that moment to distract himself from the pain. Wren always had a gift for putting others at ease.

"What did she say?"

Logan's mouth opened, his words catching in his throat. Something inside of him warned not to share that private moment. "None of your business."

"Tell me."

Soren frowned at Greyson. "Since when are you so protective of Wren Wilde?"

"Since her mom died. Don't you get it? Mom would have wanted us to look out for her, not ogle her. Without Haven around, she's got no one to protect her."

"Uh, she still has her dad, dumbass."

Greyson rolled his eyes. "Bodhi Wilde's never been reliable. He disappears for days and leaves her all alone."

Logan frowned. "Protect her from what?"

"Anything could happen in those woods."

Soren snickered. "Is that what all those nature walks have been about? I think you have protector confused with stalker."

Greyson's jaw ticked, but he didn't deny it. Had he been watching over Wren in the woods? Their house was secluded enough that no one would know.

"I don't see what any of this has to do with the fact that Wren's getting hot." Soren instantly drew back at Greyson's icy stare. "Chill, dude! My arm's already bruising from your last punch."

"Then watch your mouth."

"I'm just saying, even if we agree not to look at her that way, we can't stop everyone else from noticing her. Wren's always been beautiful. We're not the only ones with eyes."

Finally feeling like he had helpful information to share, Logan sat up. "I heard Travis Whitaker plans on asking her to the Winter Formal."

Greyson's stare snapped to him. "Who told you that?"

"Chelsea, Travis's little sister. She said they went for pizza last week and Travis kissed Wren."

Soren gaped. "You're lying."

Greyson's jaw locked.

"Why would I make that up?"

"Aw, man," Soren clicked his tongue against his teeth. "Travis is such a player. He got in Becca Reese's pants the day after he did the deed with Addison Levy."

"He's not touching Wren," Greyson growled through gritted teeth.

"According to Chelsea, he already did."

"Did you hear me?" Greyson snapped. "No one lays a hand on her. She's going through something massive. She's vulnerable and not thinking clearly. One wrong move with an asshole like Travis Whitaker could destroy her future. It's our job to make sure that doesn't happen. Mom always said we should watch over her like a sister."

"Maybe she likes Travis."

"Like I said, she's not thinking clearly. Travis is not getting near her. And that rule goes for everyone. Anyone who thinks of laying a hand on her will have to get through us first. Understand?"

Logan frowned. "I don't think Wren's going to like that."

Greyson leveled his brother with a hard stare. "Tough. It's for her own good. From here on out, we protect her like one of our own."

After that Christmas, any guy who got within two feet of Wren got his ass kicked. Greyson was such a force to be reckoned with that it didn't take long for other guys to get the hint. No one touched Wren Wilde. And soon enough, no one even looked at her.

CHAPTER 2

"Out Jumps Good Old Santa Claus"

Fifteen Years Later

Wren screamed as the cats bolted for cover. Her groceries scattered across the porch as she threw her hands up to shield her face. The moment Soren sprang off the snowmobile, her terror transformed into rage. "Are you trying to kill me?"

"I have to talk to you."

"Don't listen to him, Wren!" Logan launched out of the black super-duty truck and rushed up the porch.

Soren grabbed him by the back of the shirt and tugged. They stumbled down the steps and scuffled, tripping into a snowbank and grunting like idiots as they peppered each other with pathetic slaps.

"What the hell is going on?"

Logan shot to his feet, but Soren yanked his pants down. "Damn it, Soren! Get off!"

Soren fumbled his way out of the snow and clambered up the steps, scooping up her spilled apples as he rose. "You dropped these."

She scowled at him through wide eyes. Her eggs lay shattered. "What the hell is wrong with you two?" They weren't even wearing coats. She looked down at Logan's feet. "Where are your shoes?"

"There wasn't time." He panted.

"You're terrifying my animals." The cats hissed and bolted off the porch.

"Sorry. Here, kitty, kitty—*umph!*"

Logan checked Soren, knocking him into the railing.

"Stop!" Fanning away the exhaust fumes, Wren coughed. The truck pinged continuously with the door ajar. "Are you just going to leave those running?"

Both men looked at each other and then rushed to turn off their vehicles. The silence deafened. She still didn't know what the hell could cause them to show up like that.

When they offered no explanation, she swung out her arms. "Well? Is someone going to tell me what's going on?"

They looked at each other again but said nothing.

"Great." She bent to collect her spilled items, stuffing them angrily into her torn grocery bags. "Just another day of inexplicable Hawthorne behavior."

"We didn't mean to scare you," Logan said, passing her the carton of dripping eggs. "Sorry. We'll replace them."

She pursed her lips. "If you don't want to scare people, don't drive like psychopaths." She shoved the bag into Logan's arms and searched the porch for her keys. When she finally unlocked the door of her cabin, the men lingered at the threshold, looking contrite.

Wren sighed. "Come in and dry off before you catch pneumonia. Leave your shoes at the door and lay your socks on the hearth."

The cabin was small and toasty from the logs in the woodstove she'd left burning that morning. She moved through the open-concept layout to the small kitchen as they swept snow chips off their jeans. Even with the tall A-frame roof, they looked too big for her tiny home.

When she'd had her house built, they'd made fun of its size. She didn't mind that it was small. She lived alone, and it met all her needs. She especially loved the east-facing window where she practiced her sun salutations each morning in the natural light.

Only her bedroom and bathroom had interior walls, but even they didn't reach the cathedral ceilings. Wren hated feeling boxed in and preferred to spend time outdoors in nature. Unfortunately, Hideaway Bay endured its long winters, so the icy seasons were tough. By the end of the colder months, her cabin fever peaked through the roof. If she had to be indoors, she at least wanted to be somewhere she loved, and she adored her little home.

Soren looked around as if the locally sourced custom cabinetry his brother built offended him. "It always feels like entering a dollhouse whenever I come in here."

"Don't start." She unloaded her damaged groceries on the island. They still hadn't told her why they were there. "Is your dad okay?"

"He's the same."

"Didn't he have an appointment this week?" One of the many joys of small-town life meant that no one's business stayed private, and HIPAA laws didn't apply to neighborly gossip.

"Yeah, but nothing's changed," Soren said, helping her unload some of the groceries. "They're still saying he has months. Maybe weeks."

She stilled. Sometimes, they acted so cavalier about their father's health that she wondered if they lived in denial. Bodhi might be an unconventional father, but she couldn't imagine losing him. After losing her mom, he was all she had left.

Magnus Hawthorne was far from what anyone would call pleasant or easy, but like her, they'd lost their mother, and Magnus remained the only parent.

She rested her hand on Soren's. "I hope he has more time than the doctors expect."

Christmas was difficult without their moms. They all knew Magnus faced terminal illness, but she really hoped the boys could have at least one more holiday with him.

Soren turned his hand and laced his fingers with hers, meeting her stare. "Thanks. That means a lot, Wren."

Logan cleared his throat, his sad expression mirroring his brother's. "Yeah. It's been really hard."

She glanced at them and frowned. What were they up to? It might be normal for sons of a dying man to express concern, but the Hawthornes weren't wired that way. They seemed to be working extra hard to fish for sympathy.

She changed the subject. "How was Thanksgiving?"

Soren continued looking at her with puppy dog eyes. "It's been really hard…"

She withdrew her hand from his and crossed her arms over her chest. "All right, what's going on?"

"Well, it's funny you mention Dad." Soren's voice softened. "He's actually why we're here."

"Uh, hold on, now." Logan shoved his brother behind him with a silencing glare. "Let's not go rushing into anything."

Wren's frown deepened. "You're both being super weird. Either tell me what's going on or I'm throwing your asses out into the snow." She looked expectantly at Soren, but his lips seemed sewn shut. She stepped closer to Logan. "I know you can't keep a secret."

His jaw trembled.

"Logan," Soren warned, but it was too late.

"Dad changed the will."

"Damn it, Logan!" Soren pivoted out of the kitchen and paced. "Of all the places to start!"

"What do you mean he changed his will?" And why would Magnus's will and testament bring them here? She fixed Logan with a penetrating stare.

"He's no longer leaving us the company."

"*What?* But you're his sons!"

"Hold on," Soren objected. "He's not leaving it to Logan."

Logan shoved his brother. "He's not leaving it to you either. It's going to the board and shareholders unless..."

She leaned forward, waiting for him to finish. "Unless what?"

Logan shifted and shoved his hands in his pockets. "Unless one of us proves we're responsible enough to take it over."

She frowned. "How does he expect to measure that?"

Again, they clammed up.

"Somebody better start talking. You came here for a reason, and I want to know why."

Her mind went to the property, and her curiosity morphed into panic. The Haven, named after her mother, sprawled across a private retreat of more than fifteen thousand acres of woodland, but it also bordered the Hawthorne estate.

"Is this about the occupancy permit for the new lodges?"

"No, it has nothing to do with your plans for the retreat."

"Then why are you here?"

They both looked uncomfortably at each other.

"Enough with the weird looks!"

"He added a clause."

"A clause?"

"Some minor new requirements," Soren explained.

"Such as...?"

"He wants us to take more interest in our positions on the board and show up for more meetings."

"Well, that seems fair. If you guys are going to run the company, you'll need to stay informed."

"But that's not all he wants."

They both stared at her, and she instinctively stepped back like cornered prey. "Why are you looking at me like that?"

And where was Greyson? Wouldn't this affect him, too? Leave

it to Greyson to remove himself entirely from any emotional situation.

"He, uh…" Logan cleared his throat. "…wants us to settle down."

She laughed. "Yeah, right."

No resident in Hideaway Bay would classify any of the Hawthorne boys as settled. They were as untamed as the seas and as unruly as the wind. Even a patriarch as powerful as Magnus Hawthorne the Third couldn't control such wildness.

"Good luck with that."

Soren met her stare. "He wants us to find a wife."

She stilled. "Excuse me?"

"He thinks getting married will calm us down."

Her laughter doubled. "That poor woman, whoever she is! Getting married isn't going to tame you boys." Suddenly, her laughter stopped, a foreboding queasiness creeping in. "Wait…"

Soren glanced at Logan. "I think she's getting it now. Give her a sec."

"You're not here because…"

They both looked at each other then at her.

She took another step back. "Absolutely not! *Are you insane?*"

"It's not that crazy of an idea, Wren."

Frantically, she stowed groceries in the cabinets and fridge, shoving items onto the wrong shelves, too distracted to achieve any organization. "Whatever crazy ideas brought you here, forget it! My God, there are three of you! What did you expect to happen?"

"Forget the fact that there are three of us and only one of you. You're the only woman any of us would ever consider marrying."

She spun and gaped at them. "*Us?* What the hell are you suggesting, Logan?"

"No, it wouldn't be like that. You would pick."

"Pick what?"

He shrugged. "Whichever one of us you liked most."

Her jaw unhinged. "You've lost your mind."

Wren pushed past them and carried her new shampoo into the bathroom. When she set it down and turned, they were right behind her—cornering her again and sucking all the air out of her little house. She wedged between them and went back to the kitchen.

"Come on, Wren. We'd let you choose."

She stilled then pivoted to face them. "Oh, I get to choose? Well, how lucky for me! Whichever one will it be? Let's see. Considering that I've never had a single romantic interaction with any of you, I guess my answer is none."

"Come on, Wren—"

"No!" she snapped, stepping away from Soren's cajoling touch. He could be quite convincing when he turned on the charm, and she wasn't falling for that. "Did you actually think you could come here and talk me into marrying one of you? What kind of woman do you think I am?"

"The marrying kind."

Her stare snapped to Logan's. "Don't be a smartass. If I ever do get married, it's going to be to someone who loves me. Not someone who views me as a means to an end." She didn't know why her voice cracked. "I think you both should leave."

"Hey." Soren closed the distance. "We didn't mean to upset you."

Again, she shrugged off his touch, unsure how such a ridiculous proposition could trigger this much turmoil. "You're supposed to be my friends."

"We are your friends. Wren, we love you."

She scoffed and flung away any attempt to comfort her. "If you loved me, you'd want the best for me. Did my feelings even cross your mind when you rushed over here?"

They shot each other a sidelong glance, and she had her answer.

She shoved both of them in the chest. "Jerks!"

"Are you mad because you don't think we'd make good husbands?" Logan asked defensively.

"*Husbands?* We live in America, Logan. Bigamy is illegal!"

"To be clear," Soren chimed in, "we aren't asking for anything polyamorous. We're just trying to keep Hawthorne Fishery in the family. We need your help, Wren. Could you imagine if the company were sold off and divided? The Hawthorne name would mean nothing after that."

"And let's say you chose me," Logan chimed in. "You know I'd treat you better than Soren or any other man could. I'm a lover."

She blinked up at him, wondering if he actually heard how idiotic he sounded.

"There's no way you're winning this," Soren growled.

"This?"

"Not this. You."

"Ah, so much less offensive when you say it that way." Her eyes narrowed. "How about I talk now?" She took a step forward and scowled at both of them, putting the two idiots on the defensive. "Since I was sixteen years old, you did everything in your power to keep every guy in Hideaway Bay away from me. For a time, I figured you might actually like me, but it turned out none of you had a single romantic interest in me. You just wanted to screw up my life and make sure I stayed single."

"That's not—"

"I'm not finished!" She took another step, forcing them to stagger back. "You stand here, in my home—where I live alone thanks to years of your ridiculous, territorial crap—telling me you could treat me better than any man. Well, I'd hope so! I deserve that. But with all this crazy talk of marriage and wills, neither of you has made a single mention of love. Why is that?"

They looked dumbfounded.

"It's because you don't love me!"

"Wren, how could you say that—"

"I'm still speaking. You see me as a little sister. Is that what you want in a wife?"

"We were only trying to protect you."

"You punished me! By the time I was a senior, no one would even ask me to prom."

"I offered—"

"That's not the same!" Her eyes prickled with unshed tears. "You've never actually thought about my feelings or what I might need. You all just did whatever the hell you felt like doing, and today is no different." Her anger left on an exhalation. "Maybe your dad's right. You boys need to grow up. But I won't be the woman who makes that happen for you."

"Give us a chance."

"No." She blinked rapidly as her eyes blurred. "I've waited years to fall in love. You think I'm going to settle now? Whatever pathetic impression of love you're offering doesn't interest me. I think you both should leave."

"You're offended—"

"*Yes*, I'm offended! As my friends, you should want the best for me. This has nothing to do with me. This is about you. It's always been about you—your feelings, your insecurities. Well, I'm not a kid anymore. All your games of *'Keep the Boys Away from Wren'* made me the independent woman I am now, so you can blame yourselves for getting kicked out."

"You're really kicking us out?"

"Yes." She snatched their socks off the bricks and flung them at their chests. "This is the last I want to hear about any of this. Now, you both need to leave." When they just stood there, she snapped, *"Go!"*

They quickly hopped into their socks and grumbled apologies as they rushed to the door. Not a single tear fell in their presence, but when the truck engine roared to life and the snowmobile buzzed off in the distance, she lost her composure.

Wren locked the door and pressed her back to the wood, sliding all the way to the floor. Her vision cleared as soon as she stopped fighting her tears. She searched the rafters for any sense of her mother's presence and sighed.

"Tell Sable her sons are morons."

CHAPTER 3

"It's Coming On Christmas"

Thirty Minutes Prior

"Aren't you following them?"

Greyson leaned quietly against the bookshelf in the shadows, still processing everything his father had just shared. "I was never much of a follower."

"No, you weren't." Closing the revised will into the folder, his father reflexively groaned as he shifted back in his seat. "She's not the answer anyway."

Greyson's gaze snapped to Magnus, personally taking umbrage at the slight against Wren. It bothered him that his father's disdain for Haven carried over to her daughter. Wren had suffered. Girls needed their mothers. His father never cared about any of that.

"In truth, I'd hoped you'd be the one to take over, Greyson. But I've never been able to make you do anything you didn't already want to do, so I've accepted that loss and learned to sit with my disappointment peacefully."

Peacefully, but not quietly. "If you insist on dividing us, we all know it should be Soren. He wants it the most."

His father scoffed. "Wanting something and being able to handle it are two different things."

"Then give it to Logan."

"Logan's a child. I can't predict the final outcome, but I can guarantee he won't be the one to take over Hawthorne Fishery." He coughed and withdrew the silk handkerchief from his pocket to cover his mouth.

Men like his father didn't wear illness well.

Magnus was a man of small stature with astounding presence. His bearing carried specific gravity, and despite Greyson towering over him by at least a foot, he never underestimated the damage a man like Magnus Hawthorne the Third could inflict.

He'd been such an overbearing presence in their lives that imagining a world without him was difficult. They knew this moment approached, and they'd all had time to prepare. But it still didn't feel real.

Greyson thought reality might set in when the treatment started, but his dad walked in and out of those appointments like ordinary business meetings. And when his skin showed bruises that refused to heal, Greyson somehow overlooked those symptoms as well. Even when his dad's bones protruded through his clothes, he pretended not to notice a difference. It was how his father wanted it. No emotion. No fuss.

His father tucked the silk handkerchief away and shook his head. "I can only imagine what kind of fools your brothers are making of themselves right now."

Greyson didn't want to think about it. He didn't want to think about any of this—not his father's inevitable demise or the selling off of their family's company, and certainly not Wren.

Of course, she'd been the first thought for all of them. But she would never go for that sort of arrangement. Wren embodied emotion and wouldn't settle for anything short of love. She deserved the absolute best. None of them were good enough for her.

Soren was as deep as a puddle and far too self-involved. Logan stayed too oppositional. And Greyson... Well, he just never wanted to disappoint her.

Wren needed a talker, someone who loved all that spiritual nonsense she practiced down at the retreat. She had so many remarkable talents. She needed someone who would listen to her and not try to change her. Someone with above-average emotional intelligence who would spend every day making her happy.

He frowned as he considered the qualities of a decent man for Wren. As much as the idea sickened him, he'd prefer his youngest brother over Soren. There was just something less threatening about Logan.

"You know, it could actually be Logan." Saying the words out loud turned his stomach. But Logan always shared a special bond with Wren. Of the three of them, his youngest brother was by far the most sensitive. She deserved sensitivity.

A gruff laugh left his father's throat. "The day that boy sees anything through is the day I start believing in Santa Claus."

His father had a point. But if Logan or Soren truly wanted this badly enough, they could make it happen. Wren wasn't the only single female in town.

"Our name's worth something, Dad. They could go on any dating app and find a wife in a matter of weeks. The clause only states that we have to get married before the holidays. It says nothing about love."

His father's eyes narrowed. "Marriage is a contract. Only a fool would enter one with a stranger."

"You're sort of forcing our hands."

"Am I? Or am I validating that none of you are ready to take on this responsibility?" He shook his head. "Three sons, and not a single one of you—"

"Stop." Greyson held up a hand. "You invited us here, pretending it was for Thanksgiving when it was only one more way to express your disappointment. We get it. We got it when we were teenagers. You can stop hammering us with all your grievances."

"And why do you think I grieve, Greyson? Boys are supposed to grow up into men. The three of you are now in your twenties and thirties and still acting like boys."

As if it had only started in their teens.

"Just because we're not making a living according to your expectations doesn't mean we're not living respectable adult lives."

Magnus waved away his words. He appeared tired, as if dressing after breakfast and having one short meeting with his sons had worn him out. He probably stayed too prideful to rest as long as others remained at the house.

Greyson withdrew the keys to his truck. "Do you need anything before I take off?"

"I need you to do the right thing, Greyson. One of you has to step up to the plate, or everything I've worked for—the sum of my existence—will all be for naught."

Crossing the room, he dropped a hand on his father's narrow shoulder and gently squeezed. "We can't control everything, Dad. The day you accept that, things will become easier."

"I'm running out of days," he grumbled, shouldering him off. "For once, you could do as I ask instead of doing what you damn well please."

On the drive home, Greyson's two-way radio was silent. His dumbass brothers probably sat at Wren's, receiving an earful for even thinking she'd go for such a ridiculous plan.

Wren didn't care about money like some women, but she valued integrity. She'd never settle for some sham of a marriage simply because of a clause in a contract.

"Morons," he grumbled, shoving all thoughts of his brothers and Wren away.

Turning down Main Street, he slowed his truck as holiday

tourists flooded out in full force, catching all the post-Thanksgiving Christmas sales. Hideaway Bay was renowned for its winter festivities. The anticipation of Hideaway's influx of visitors reminded him to stock up on essentials for the month so he didn't have to venture into the crowds. Once the Christmas countdown began, it wouldn't ease up until the following year.

Like a bear, Greyson preferred to hibernate in his own little hideaway deep in the woods rather than sip hot cocoa, sing carols, or shop the freshly painted window displays like the rest of the townies and guests. Since his mother died, Christmas just wasn't his thing.

Once the holiday season kicked off with the tree lighting, it meant full speed ahead into Christmas with nonstop events—ice carving competitions, parades, endless caroling, festivals, and firework displays. There was never a dull moment in their little coastal town around the holidays, which was precisely why Greyson treasured his secluded cabin in the woods, far removed from all the chaos and noise.

Just as he pulled onto the private dirt road leading to his hidden home, the two-way radio chirped, and he glanced at the dashboard.

"Well, that didn't go as planned."

Greyson shook his head at Soren's comment and mumbled under his breath, "Dumbasses."

How the hell did they expect it to go? And what exactly had they done—blown into Wren's retreat, interrupted her yoga class, and launched into a marriage proposal?

The walkie-talkie chirped again. "Could have gone a lot better if you didn't get in the way."

"I was there first!"

"Only because you cheated!"

"Bullshit. Fair is fair," Logan's taunting voice chirped over the airways. "Hundred bucks says I get her to agree to a date by the first of December."

"You're on. And when she turns you down because she's already out with me, I'll take my hundred in tens and twenties."

Greyson twisted the dial on the radio, turning the volume off so he didn't have to listen to their bickering. This far up north, there wasn't much of a cell signal, so the two-way was necessary, but over the years, he'd definitely overheard his fair share of personal business. Soren and Logan should know better than to air their laundry on a public channel.

Most Hideaway Bay locals still used the rotary phones installed during Nixon's term because cell signals were unreliable unless standing right below the towers up on Make Out Point, so two-ways and landlines it was.

Recalling those times he'd spent at Make Out Point had him shifting uncomfortably. It had been too long since he'd had a woman wrapped around his body. The radio continued to chirp as his idiotic brothers rambled on, and Greyson's mind returned to Wren. She likely sat at home. Probably pissed off. Definitely alone.

One turn, and he could be there in two minutes.

What excuse could he use today?

His stare assessed the cloudy sky, but rather than give in to temptation, he blew out a frustrated breath and turned down his long drive.

Shoving the truck into park, he swiped the key out of the ignition. The stillness contrasted sharply with his brothers' blathering idiocy. He flicked off the radio and paused to savor the silence.

His dad was right. They needed to grow up.

On the other hand, he knew lots of immature married people. Having a wife didn't make someone a man. Nor did inheriting a billion-dollar company. This nonsense about wives and wills was just his father's last desperate attempt to control everyone around him.

Despite years of fixating on all their shortcomings, Magnus had never been able to change the nature of his sons. Logan would always be the intense, overly sensitive one. And Soren would remain surface-level as long as he deflected anything real with a joke. Greyson wasn't as easy to pigeonhole. He intentionally lived on the outskirts of town to avoid expectations, specifically those of his father.

Isolation suited him, and he preferred the quiet over the chaos. Sure, it got lonely on occasion. A warm female body could make the coldest nights tolerable. But Greyson lived by his own rules, the way he wanted, and nothing would ever change that.

Looking up as clouds gathered in ripples of grey like woolen blankets covering the sky, he closed his eyes and breathed deeply. The scent of wood smoke and damp earth permeated the truck. He cracked the door, noting the tension and salt in the wind as it flicked at the frost-bitten leaves.

The pressure had dropped, making everything feel crisper. If he listened closely, he could hear the creak of bare limbs in the forest and taste the bitter metallic bite of the coming snow.

Before going inside, he checked the woodshed and restocked the timber rack on the porch. Like most Hideaway residents, he depended heavily on fire for warmth.

Once the rack was loaded up, he kicked the snow off his boots and damp cuffs, then carried a few logs inside. The house was cold because he'd crashed at his dad's the night before. He twisted up the latest issue of *The Beacon*, the town's weekly paper, lit it, and left the woodstove open so the fire could breathe.

While the hearth warmed, he stripped out of his clothes and headed for the bathroom, his body accustomed to the bite of cold that came with living in these parts.

As the heater kicked on, the pipes squealed, water rushing past a few ice chips in the line. Then steam billowed from the showerhead in a welcoming spray. The hot water soothed the tension in his back and loosened his muscles.

Lathering the soap, he washed and mentally reviewed the preparations for the day ahead. Roads would need to be salted. Rivulets of suds spiraled into the drain as his hand drifted lower. His fist tightened around his flesh, washing and tugging through his daily routine.

He should check on Wren before the storm hit to make sure she had enough supplies. He braced his weight against the wall, resting his head on his forearm as he stroked. How long had it been since he'd sharpened Wren's shovels?

His gut tightened with his fist as he tugged in smooth, gliding strokes. He'd check in on the elderly neighbors to make sure they were stocked up with everything needed to stay warm, then he'd salt a few sidewalks while he was in that area.

His breath quickened with each tug. He should also refill the bird feeders so the wildlife had enough food to weather the storm.

"Fuck," he growled low, his muscles stiffening as each nerve fired along his spine.

Glimpses of her flickered in his mind, but he never lingered on a single vision long enough to truly feel guilty about it. It could have been any woman's hair he imagined. Any woman's eyes. But it wasn't. It was always her. Always Wren.

"Damn it," he growled through gritted teeth, trying desperately to picture a brunette or a woman with more curves. But his mind always went to Wren.

Fuck it. With a harsh exhalation, he gave in and trembled through his release. Panting, he let his shame wash down the drain and turned the water to scalding.

Once rinsed off, he dressed for a long, cold day.

CHAPTER 4

"ALL I WANT FOR CHRISTMAS IS…"
SHARP SHOVELS?

"LET YOUR BREATH DEEPEN LIKE SNOW GENTLY GATHERING ON THE earth—slow, steady, quiet." Wren soundlessly weaved her way around the yoga mats and bodies stretched out across the studio.

Sunlight filtered past the tall pines and warmed the hardwood through the floor-to-ceiling windows. The overcast skies looked as though they would flurry.

The pale sun-bleached white oak floors were warm underfoot despite the cold outside. "Wake up those hands by gently wiggling your fingers."

Her toe ring caught the light as she wove softly around her students as they rested on their backs in the savasana pose. With every gentle step, her mandala tattoo peeked out from the ankle of her cocoa brown harem pants.

"Now, wiggle your toes."

A subtle blend of palo santo, cedar, and eucalyptus drifted from the clay diffuser in the corner.

"Invite sensation back into the body. And when you're ready... roll gently to one side."

One by one, her students shifted and turned.

Ambient Nordic folk music played softly as the gentle wind chimes trilled outside. Her fingers twirled the delicate moonstone pendant resting on her collarbone.

"Press up slowly, no rush. Find a comfortable seat. Palms together at heart center."

Wren returned to her mat at the front of the room, where she kept the sound bowls and gong. She sat cross-legged in front of the class, their eyes half-lidded and peaceful as they awaited her guidance.

She matched their poses and took a moment to bask in her gratitude. "Thank you for choosing stillness today. For choosing presence."

A few relaxed sighs met her ears, and as the class became more alert. She bowed her head slightly. "*Namaste*."

"*Namaste*," the class responded in unison.

"I hope The Haven gave you something you needed today. The kitchen has warm herbal broth and fresh rye crackers waiting if you want to linger. Don't forget to grab a flyer on your way out. It has our full holiday schedule and details about next month's winter solstice flow, which will be by candlelight."

Pleasant sounds of interest accompanied the rustling of people packing up their mats and slipping into their snow boots. Wren retrieved her water from the shelf and took a long sip.

"Great class today."

Swallowing a gulp, she capped her bottle and faced Noah. "Thanks."

"That crow pose didn't totally destroy me this time. I think I hovered for a full three seconds before the face-plant."

Wren laughed. It wasn't quite a face plant, but it wasn't graceful either. "Practice makes perfect."

Noah trailed her steps as she wandered around the room collecting blankets to hang on the driftwood ladder. "Your alignment's come a long way."

"Thanks to you."

Noah was one of her most devoted local yogis. "It's wonderful how dedicated you are."

"Well, I enjoy the class—and the teacher—so it's a rewarding hobby all around."

Realizing he was waiting for some sort of reaction, she laughed nervously. "That's sweet. I really appreciate devotion."

"I've been telling people around town they should try a class."

"The more locals who sign up, the more classes we can offer." When she lifted the stack of folded blankets, he took them from her.

"I can carry those. Where do they go?"

"Oh, just over here." She really didn't need help, but he literally took the choice out of her hands. She neatly hung the folded wool over the wooden rungs as he handed them off.

"I was wondering if you would be interested in something more one-on-one."

"Oh. You can schedule a private session at the front—"

"I was thinking more along the lines of dinner."

She stilled, wondering how she hadn't seen that coming. "Like a date?"

"Could be nice. No breathwork, no balancing on one arm. Just good food. A firepit. Maybe even a glass of wine—if that's not too scandalous for a yogi master."

Caught off guard, she smiled nervously. Noah was a transplant she didn't know much about, but he seemed nice and looked about her age. "I'll... think about it."

He grinned and handed her the last blanket. "Just don't make me hold a crow pose until you decide."

A shadow passed by the door, and stilled. Her gaze shifted over Noah's shoulder. Greyson stood in the empty doorway of the studio.

What was he doing here? As always, he glared at any man within ten feet of her.

"Well, it was great seeing you, Noah." She didn't know why she made the effort to touch Noah's arm, but something inside her liked provoking Greyson. She supposed he was the bear she couldn't resist poking.

Noah's smile widened, and Greyson's frown deepened. "Yeah, you too, Wren. See you tomorrow."

"I look forward to it." He turned and paused when he noticed Greyson watching them. Stowing his rolled yoga mat under his arm, Noah gave the other man a nod. "How ya doin'?"

In typical Greyson fashion, he didn't say a word. He took Noah's measure and barely moved out of the doorway when the other man exited.

Wren rolled her eyes, and as soon as Noah was gone, she turned her back on the entrance, on him. "What do you want, Grey?"

His cold stare followed Noah until the other man fully left the building. "Who was that?"

"A student. Why are you here?"

She typically wasn't so short with him, but she'd had her fill of Hawthorne men today.

"What's up your ass?"

"Can't a girl be busy? Believe it or not, I am trying to run a business on my own." Under her breath, she grumbled. "Not everyone has an inheritance waiting for them." The moment the words left her mouth, she grew sick with regret. "I'm sorry. I can't believe I just said that."

"It's fine."

"It's not—"

"Drop it."

She looked up at him, hating that she said something so cold to her friend who could lose his father at any moment. Pressing a hand to her stomach, she looked up at him apologetically. "That was a terrible thing for me to say."

"It was true."

The way Soren and Logan made it sound that morning, she wasn't so sure. "How is your dad?"

"The same."

How foolish to think Greyson might actually open up to her. Same old games. Same old Greyson. Her regret faded. "Well, if there's nothing you need, I really have to get back to work." Without waiting for approval, she pushed past him to collect the rest of the blankets.

SHE WAS ANNOYED. Greyson could blame his brothers for that. But this visit had nothing to do with their bullshit. "I came to get your shovels."

She paused and glanced back at him, a divot forming between her brows. "My shovels?"

"Yeah. They're overdue for a sharpening."

"Shovels need to be sharpened?"

"It helps." The automatic doors chimed as another guest left through the main entrance at the end of the hall, letting another draft into the building. "Aren't you cold?" His gaze drifted to the hem of her cropped top that hung slightly off her shoulder, and tied at the waist. He fixated on that sliver of tan skin and frowned. "You're dressed for summer. Where are your shoes?"

She patted his chest as she breezed past him to the closet. "It's a yoga class, Grey. What I'm wearing is perfectly normal."

"So…who was that guy?" The front door chimed again, and another draft curled past his legs.

Wren pulled a broom from the closet and started sweeping the studio. "What guy?"

"The one who walked out of here like he just found religion." He nodded toward the hallway, jaw tense.

"Noah?" She laughed, light and dismissive. "He's harmless."

Greyson glared at the empty corridor and walked further into the studio. His eyes didn't leave her body as she swept the sunlit sprinkle of dust into a pile.

A flicker of heat crawled up his spine. He really needed to get laid. Jerking off wasn't cutting it anymore.

Clearing his throat, he forced himself to look away. "Where did you say the shovels are?"

"I didn't. I'm sure my shovels are fine, Grey."

"We've got another eight inches of snow coming. It'll make cleanup easier."

She stopped sweeping and hung her weight on the broom handle. "My shovels aren't your responsibility."

A muscle in his jaw jumped. On some level, he always felt responsible for Wren—and her shovels. "It's no trouble."

"From what I hear, you've got problems of your own to deal with. Your brothers told me all about your situation when they nearly ran me over this morning." She moved closer and lowered her voice. "You sure you're here for my shovels, Grey? Or are you looking for something else?"

His cock twitched and he took an intentional step forward, close enough that her head had to tip back to look at him and looming enough that there was no mistaking his position.

"Just the shovels," he said, his voice a low rumble.

She held his stare, wisps of sandy blonde hair framing her face. How the hell did she get all that hair into that knotted chaos on her head she called a bun? A faint sheen of sweat clung to her skin, and he breathed deep, resenting the scent of eucalyptus and cedar coming from the steaming diffuser in the corner that masked her familiar fragrance.

The tiny brown flecks in her blue-green eyes mesmerized him as they stood, locked in a challenging stare. Too close. He stepped back and he swore a look of disappointment flashed in her eyes.

"The shovels are in the shed." She tipped the broom handle against his chest and let it go. "I'll grab them."

"I can get them." He was at the back door in two strides, propping the broom against the wall.

"I said I'll grab them."

He scowled at her tiny feet. "You're not wearing shoes."

"So."

"So, have a little common sense."

"The ground won't hurt me. It's actually good for you to stand barefoot outside."

"Maybe in summer."

"In any month."

He was not falling for her nature mysticism. "It's twenty-six degrees out, Wren. That's how people get sick."

She groaned and pushed past him, but he yanked her back before she could set foot out the door. Her eyes narrowed and locked with his.

"Greyson."

He wasn't thinking about the shovels anymore. "Don't be stubborn."

"*I'm* being stubborn?" She laughed. "Isn't that the pot calling the kettle black?"

They didn't always bicker, but when they did, she could drive him up a wall. Distracted again by that wisp of hair, he reached forward to tuck it behind her ear, sliding his fingers down to the fine tip. She wore tiny jade earrings, the subtle kind that dangled. He pictured her putting them on, and something shifted in his gut.

Startled, she stepped back. "What are you doing?"

What *was* he doing?

He released her hair. Shit. "I…" He unlocked the exit reserved for staff only and barked, "Stay here."

Making a beeline for the shed, he found three shovels. Rather than return to the studio, he carried them to his truck and set them on the open tailgate. Once he dug the file and oil from his toolbox, he got to work. Good thing he'd stopped by because the edges were dull and in need of attention.

Ignoring the guests who came and went from the main building, he kept his head down and focused on his task. Several cats circled his feet as he worked. One even jumped into the bed of his truck.

"I don't have food," he told the old, patchy tabby missing an ear.

When the cat meowed back, it sounded like its trachea had gone through a garbage disposal. Greyson reached into his toolbox and rustled around.

A slender calico jumped onto the tailgate next, twirling around his arm as it purred. More cats wandered from the reflection garden, where their shelters had been built.

"You're lucky I'm nice."

Of course, he kept a jar of cat treats on him. Whenever there was a stray in town, it was captured and brought to Wren. She and Bodhi had made a sanctuary for the animals, and the town included the cat care as part of their ongoing fundraising efforts. Over the years, he'd brought several strays to Wren. Damned if he knew which ones, but she always took them in and loved them equally, no matter how battered or mangy they were. She was kind like that.

He slipped each one a niblet—not the kind they sold at the pet stores. These were homemade treats Wren had made from dehydrated whatever the hell cats ate.

He sniffed the jar and drew back. They smelled like rotten fish food, but the cats loved them. "That's it. Go play."

They ignored his command in true cat fashion but eventually lost interest when he started filing the edges of the shovels.

"I was wondering when you'd stop by."

Greyson glanced over his shoulder at Bodhi as he wandered from the Zen garden. "What's your family's issue with boots?"

Wren's father looked down at his bare toes peeking through his Jesus sandals and shrugged. He looked like he'd escaped from a commune in that silk kimono hanging out from under his Big Lebowski sweater.

Leaning against the truck with a steaming cup of something green that smelled like dirt, Bodhi glanced at the clouds overhead. "Wren told me we're expecting more snow."

"Another eight inches."

Bodhi rubbed his straggly grey beard, contemplating the flurries as they fell. "Feels more like three inches."

"That's what she said."

Bodhi laughed. "I hope not." He drew in a deep breath as flurries drifted through the air. "This isn't the sort of snow that sticks. It'll melt as soon as you're done plowing. See, big flakes. Big flakes always lead to a small accumulation. It's the little flakes you gotta worry about, Greyson."

He didn't trust old hippie science, which was roughly based on joint pain, astrology, and the taste of air.

"Three inches or eight, you're gonna need salt and shovels, Bodhi." Finished with the last blade, he switched to oiling the metal. "You have enough supplies?"

"We've still got a pallet of salt from last year."

Greyson nodded. "Good. But you should order more. That's not going to be enough to get you through winter."

"I'll make a call."

"Ask the receptionist to place an order online—"

"Those Wi-Fi waves alter the aura, Greyson. Fastest way to misalign the chakras. Not to mention the declining bee population."

"Right," Greyson said slowly, learning long ago that debating with people like Bodhi was not a constructive use of his time. "Well, I'll swing by with the plow once the ground's covered. That way, you just have to worry about the walkways. If you can, ask the guests to move their cars to the far side of the parking lot."

The wind picked up, and the scent of patchouli oil wafted from Bodhi's clothes. "I'll try. But first, I should see to the elders." The elders were what Bodhi called the cats.

"Sounds good."

Wren's father scooped the mangy tabby with one ear off the hood of the truck. "Come on, Nog." As he passed Greyson, he used the cat's paw to wave. "You know, a cat who naps in sunlight knows more about life than a man who checks his phone."

Greyson lifted his eyes from the screen, where he was waiting for the weather app to load. Accumulation had dropped from eight inches to six, but who knew how up-to-date that report was? The satellites hit Hideaway Bay on sporadic waves, so their headlines weren't always current.

As soon as Bodhi disappeared down the gravel path, Wren appeared. Like her father, she only wore sandals. At least she had the sense to throw on a sweater. "You told me to wait and then never came back."

He used a rag to oil down the now sharp edge of the shovel. "I didn't tell you to wait. I told you to stay."

"Ah, this must be why I flunked collie training."

He met her dry stare. "Smartass."

She lifted the canister of mineral oil and read the label. "Thanks for taking care of my shovels. I never would have thought to sharpen them or even known how."

He meant to say welcome, but only a grunt of acknowledgment escaped.

When her hand rested on his arm, he paused but didn't take his gaze off the blade. "Greyson, you can talk to me. I know what Magnus did this morning."

"I've got nothing to say about that."

Her touch fell away. "Are you upset about what he plans to do with the company?"

He shrugged and continued oiling the metal. "His company, his choice."

"You have a right to be angry. He promised Hawthorne Fishery to you guys since you were children."

"Well, he changed his mind."

There was a time Greyson thought he would follow in his father's footsteps. He loved fishing and being out at sea, but it had been decades since his father set foot on one of their boats. Crews managed everything, and with so many vessels in the fleet and captains handling the details of each expedition, his father hadn't been on a boat in years.

Being the CEO of a billion-dollar fishery had very little to do with actual fishing. Greyson liked being out at sea but CEOs rarely saw the coastline. They were too busy trapped inside corner offices looking at numbers. He had no interest in a life like that.

"Do you really think he's going to sell it off?"

"Magnus doesn't make empty threats."

"What about Soren and Logan?"

"What about them? You gonna marry them?"

She pursed her lips. "Don't be ridiculous."

He shrugged again. "If they want to keep the company, they need to find a wife."

"You all act like I'm the only single woman in town."

He finished with the shovels and turned to lean against the truck. "You're not at all tempted? You'd be set for life."

She rolled her eyes. "Don't insult me. You know money doesn't motivate me like it does others."

"Money's a necessary evil. It's freedom."

"Says the reclusive billionaire living off the land in the woods."

He chuckled. Money didn't motivate him either, but he did respect all that it could achieve. Speaking of which... "The studio looks good all finished."

When she smiled, her entire face lit up. Wren didn't cake on makeup like some women. He wasn't even sure she wore any. She spent so much time outdoors, taking retreat guests on nature walks and doing weird hippie shit in the woods. She always had a sun-kissed glow and cinnamon sprinkle of freckles over her nose.

"I love it," she admitted. "You did an incredible job on the beams."

He'd spent a year harvesting the perfect lumber and shaping those beams exactly as Wren had described. "I'm glad you're happy with it."

An oversized flurry fluttered onto her lash, and she flicked it away. "I guess you want the guests to move their cars."

"It would help."

She sighed. "Make sure you keep track of your hours."

"Don't be dumb."

"It's not dumb. People pay good money for snow removal."

"I don't do it for the money."

"Well, you're still paying for gas and salt. Don't be a stubborn jackass about it."

He scoffed. "You're the only person who gets away with talking to me like that."

"You don't scare me, Greyson *Elowen* Hawthorne."

His mouth firmed into a flat line, and his eyes widened. "Keep it down." Very few people knew his middle name.

She snickered. "You either let me pay you or I tell everyone that you were named after your mother's mother."

He leaned over her, purposely crowding her as he narrowed his eyes. "Try, and there will be consequences."

She jutted out her chin. "No there won't."

She was right. He talked a big game, but he never followed through on his threats when it came to Wren. She was *one of them*, which was why she was everyone's first thought when their father made that ridiculous proposal. She'd fit right in as a Hawthorne.

He recalled the guy she was talking to when he arrived. He didn't look like her type. Or maybe he did. It was hard to tell, considering that Wren never really dated anyone. The guy had been holding a yoga mat. Greyson didn't even know where they sold such things.

The wind picked up, and she drew the lapels of her sweater together. He frowned. "Don't you own a coat?"

"I can't find it."

He rolled his eyes and went to the cab of his truck where he had an extra flannel jacket with a quilted lining. "How Darwinism hasn't taken out your line is beyond me." He draped the flannel over her shoulders, dwarfing her by its size, and she smiled.

"Thanks. And evolution can't touch us. We were the gatherers and shamans."

"You better not be eating those mushrooms in the woods again."

"Lion's mane is not poisonous."

"Wren, stop eating shit from the dirt!"

"Everything comes from the dirt."

He'd heard enough. "I'm sure you and that yogi will have tons of fun foraging from the trees and chanting in drum circles."

"What yogi?"

"The guy from your class."

"That's the third time you've brought him up. Do you want me to get his number for you?"

"Very funny."

"I don't know if you're his type. He asked me out."

Greyson's shoulders tensed, but he played off his concern. "You should go."

All bravado left her face and her cocky expression fell. "Are you serious?"

"Why not?"

"Since when are you supportive of me having a love life?"

"I've never been unsupportive—"

She scoffed. "Bull. Shit. It's your fault I'm single!"

He drew back. "You can't pin that on me."

"Oh, yes, I can. All my life, you've scared off anything with a penis that tried to get within two feet of me."

"That's not true."

"Greyson, you know that's one hundred percent true. Even today, when Noah tried to get by, you barely moved in an attempt to intimidate him."

"Who's Noah."

"The guy from my class!"

"If he can't figure his way out of a door, he's probably bad at other things."

"You know what? Forget it. You're right. The only reason I'm single is completely my fault. You had nothing to do with it."

"As if anyone could have that sort of control over you, Wren."

She gaped at him. "You're unbelievable." Reaching into her back pocket, she pulled out her phone.

"What are you doing?"

"Calling your brother."

"For what?"

She waved her phone around, trying to find a signal. "Maybe I will take them up on their proposals."

She was bluffing.

"You should."

"You're right. I mean, if you guys sell off the company, the estate could go next. Where would that leave me? The Haven needs to be surrounded by nature. I can't have a bunch of box stores and cookie-cutter houses cropping up in my backyard."

Shit. That was a good point. He didn't want that for her either. Most of the backwoods acreage was Hawthorne land, but they gave The Haven full access to the trails, allowing the guests to do whatever tree-huggers did out in the woods.

"You wouldn't lose the woods," he promised. No matter what happened with the fishery and his family, he'd make sure her woods were safe.

"Still, a girl needs to protect her interests." She swiped her thumb over the screen of her phone. "Who should I call, Soren or Logan?"

She was still at this? Fine. He could play along with her little charade. "Does it make a difference?"

"Not really, since this is all about money and contracts. The sex should be interesting." She flicked her thumb over her contact list.

Greyson's mind flashed to an image of Wren naked. *Fuck no.* He was not picturing his brothers in that scenario.

"Oh, lucky Logan. His name comes first alphabetically. This should only take two seconds."

His hand closed over the phone before she could hit send. "Enough."

She smirked. "Is this more of you not interfering in my dating life?"

This wasn't about that. They both knew she wasn't going to date Logan. "Don't mess with him like that."

"Like what?"

Logan got way too sensitive when it came to relationships. Plus, he'd always had a soft spot for Wren. "Don't lead him on."

She laughed. "This morning, he proposed marriage, Greyson. He's too far ahead for me to lead."

Had the dumbass actually asked her to marry him? "We both know you're not into Logan, so maybe leave him out of it."

"And what is *it*?"

"It's nothing. You and I both know that nothing's going to change."

"Do we?"

Of course they did. They'd always had a hard limit regarding Wren. His father's ludicrous proposal might have slightly disrupted that, but at the end of the day, right was right, and she wasn't marrying any of them.

"You and I both know you're not going to date my brothers."

"Oh, I don't know. Those winter nights can get awfully chilly."

He growled, not wanting to imagine his brothers near her any more than he wanted to picture her frolicking in his woods with that limp-dicked yogi dork. But he wasn't going to give her a reaction.

"Do whatever you want." He released his hold on her phone.

She raised a brow. "Thanks. I was hoping for your permission."

"You're welcome."

Her eyes narrowed, and she paced, searching for a signal. "It gets damn lonely on those cold nights, all alone, in my little house."

"Get a dog."

"The cats won't like that."

"Then get a fish."

"I have a feeling I'd enjoy Logan more."

His jaw tightened, but before he could respond, she pulled the phone to her ear and held up a silencing finger.

"Hey, Logan." She pivoted and wandered toward the hedge of arborvitae to talk in private.

What sort of game was she playing? Was she actually considering getting involved with his brother? She could do so much better.

Her laughter carried like a soft breeze, and he irritably reorganized his toolbox, making as much noise as possible. He should get moving. He still had several more stops to make, and regardless of Bodhi's predictions, the flurries were starting to stick to the trees.

Setting her shovels aside, he gathered up the file and oil to put away. When she returned to the parking lot—still on the phone—he busied himself by checking the cab of his truck, not really sure what he was looking for.

"Perfect. Can't wait. I'll see you Wednesday." She ended the call just as he returned to the back of the truck and smiled up at him. "Soren says hi."

He did a double-take. "Soren? I thought you were calling Logan."

"I did. Then I called Soren. I agreed to go out with both of them. Figured I might as well play the field and test out all my options."

His irritation bubbled but he didn't understand why this was pissing him off so much. "Have fun."

"Oh, I plan to."

He slammed the tailgate. "Shovels are done."

"Great."

He carried them back to the shed. The gravel crunched behind him as she followed.

Bodhi kept all the brooms, rakes, and shovels upside down in a metal trash can. It was a stupid, top-heavy system that spilled whenever anyone touched it. Greyson cursed and fumbled with the shovels until he was sure they wouldn't topple over. When he pivoted, Wren crashed into his chest.

She looked up at him, her features slightly shaded by the shadows. Her soft jasmine fragrance filled the cramped space, despite the fading scent of drying herbs and fertilizer.

"If you don't want me to date your brothers, Greyson, say the word and I won't."

He didn't want her to date his brothers.

The statement rang like a gong through his mind, rattling his skull, but he remained outwardly silent.

There was no logical reason for him to keep her away from his brothers or anyone else at this stage. She was thirty years old and free to see whoever she pleased.

"Date whoever you want."

It was such a subtle shift but he swore her shoulders sagged. He needed to get out of this shed. The longer she cornered him, the more he felt like prey.

She bit her plump lower lip and nodded, her gaze skating off into the corner. "Okay, Greyson. If that's really how you feel, I will."

How else should he feel? If his father wanted to throw down ultimatums and sell off his legacy, that was on him. He was staying out of it. Maybe she and Logan could actually make this work since they'd always shared a special bond.

A bad taste filled his mouth. "I have to get going."

"Right. More shovels to sharpen." She met his stare and took a small step forward. "I'm seeing Logan Tuesday night."

"Busy week. Don't forget Nate."

"Mature. You know his name's Noah." The wind blew, and the

wooden door to the shed swung closed, cutting away the light. "If you're jealous, you could add your name to my dance card?"

"Wren." He gave her a warning look.

"Greyson?" She used to tease him like this when they were young, but it had been years since she'd played these games. She took another step toward him. One deep breath and they'd be touching.

He tried to shift back, but there was nowhere to go in the cramped shed. "There's not enough room in here for two people."

"Is it too tight?"

His breath caught in his throat as he cocked his head. What had gotten into her? Did she think she could push his buttons without consequence? Did she want to see how far she could go without crossing that line? It had been a damn long time since he'd felt the touch of a woman. They were alone. It was dark. Who would know?

He would.

He grabbed her shoulders to move her aside so he could leave, but she contorted her body and slipped out of the flannel, suddenly behind him. *Damn yoga.* She was as bendy as a coil.

"Aren't you curious?"

"No."

"I don't believe you."

"Damn it, Wren, we're not doing this."

"Logan and Soren would."

His molars locked, and he took a threatening step toward her before catching himself. She gasped but didn't back up. Her eyes dilated, and her breasts lifted. She was enjoying this.

"What is it you want from me?" he asked through gritted teeth.

Arched back so she could meet his stare, she blinked up at him. "Honesty."

"I'm always honest with you."

She settled her hands on his arms, and a zing of electricity shot to his cock. "You're not even being honest with yourself."

Her hand squeezed ever so slightly around the girth of his arm, and he imagined her grip elsewhere. He caught her wrist. "There are rules, Wren."

"What rules? I never made any rules."

First, the dates with his brother, now this? "Whatever game you're playing, knock it off."

"Or what?"

Did she have to move like that? Arched back as she was over the work table, he could see every way her body shifted and twitched. "You shouldn't play games like this with men."

Her gaze dropped to his mouth. "Why? Are you afraid I'll spoil your delusions that I'm still a little girl? Sorry to disappoint, Greyson, but I'm a grown ass woman. Your brothers realize it, why can't you?"

"I'm aware you're not a child anymore."

"Haven't been in some time."

"If you want to be recognized as a woman, act like it."

"What does that even mean?"

"It means, quit it with the games." The tension coiled tighter as he held her challenging stare.

"No."

His nostrils flared at the defiant way she whispered that word. He snatched her hand and pressed it to the bulge at his crotch.

"Greyson!" When she tried to pull away, he tightened his grip.

"Is this what you want?" He stepped forward, still holding her hand to his cock. "You want to play games? Fine, let's go there. I could have you against that wall in two seconds flat and fuck you right into next week." He flung her hand away and growled. "I don't like games, and you should know better than to taunt anything twice your size."

When he turned, she said, "I'm not the one afraid here, you are."

"That's it." He shoved her into the wall and gripped the back of her neck. The second she gasped, he took her mouth in a hard, punishing kiss, shamelessly grinding his body against hers, showing her exactly what a man like him could do to a tiny little thing like her.

Her fist tightened on his jacket, and she moaned, soft and needy. He backed her into the wall, his feet tripping over the pots and bags of soil on the floor. Something heavy hit the floor with a thud, but he was in too deep to stop himself now.

"Who the fuck taught you how to kiss like this?" he growled against her soft lips.

Her fingers forked into his hair, jerking his head to the side to tease him with the tip of her tongue. "I don't kiss and tell."

The thought of anyone else touching her made him rabid. He cupped her jaw, taking back control, and she gave it over to him. Her leg hooked around his, and he lifted her.

His hips flexed as she moaned into his mouth, and he yanked her sweater aside, spreading open-mouthed kisses down her shoulder.

"Grey," she breathed his name like a plea, and his cock pulsed.

Her shirt drooped low. One little nudge and—

"Fuck." He paused and panted, his stare fixed on her breasts. The cotton sports bra was the only thing stopping him.

"Greyson?"

"Shut up."

"Hey."

"Sorry. I… I need a second to think."

What were they doing? He was kissing Wren. They didn't do this. This was dangerous. Too far, and there would be no undoing it. But she felt perfect in his arms, and he had a slab of granite in his pants. He could take her right here, and no one would ever need to know.

No.

He couldn't.

Not with her.

Panicked, he tried to step back, but she caught him by the shirt.

"Greyson, you can't leave me like this."

His gaze snapped from her bra to her face, and his heart jolted. She appeared on the verge of an orgasm, but from what? They'd only kissed.

"Please. Don't stop. Not yet."

His cock twitched. He was so screwed. "Wren—"

"Just…pretend it's not me."

He frowned. As if that could ever be possible.

Slowly, she reached behind her neck and loosened the clasp of her bra. "Oops."

What was she doing to him? This was insane.

Her hand dragged slowly between her breasts, pulling the loose cotton lower until the pink crescent of her areola showed. "I want you to do it…"

"Fuck me." Yanking down the front of her cotton bra, her breasts popped free—nipples tight and stiff. He closed his mouth over one tip and sucked hard.

She arched into him and gasped, scraping her nails over his shoulders. He ground his hips against her, pushing her into the wall.

"Take this off." One quick move and her arms were free, breasts fully exposed.

Her breathing turned erratic when he cupped her possessively. "Is this what you wanted? To see me lose control?"

"I don't know."

"You know."

"Yes. Maybe." She gasped when his teeth scraped over the sensitive tip.

"I'm not someone you should taunt." He sucked her nipples harder, darkening the tips. Part of him wanted to punish her for making him lose control.

His hand shoved into those ridiculous harem pants she wore to teach her yoga classes. Wet heat met his fingers as he parted her folds, sliding into her slit until she made a sound of distress, and he stilled.

"What's wrong?"

Her confidence vanished and her words came out in a stammer. "N-nothing."

Suddenly feeling like a monster, he pulled his hand free. "You did this on purpose."

"No, Greyson—"

"Damn it, Wren!" He dragged a hand through his hair, angry that she would be so reckless. "What were you thinking?"

"Me?"

"Yes, you. I told you there are rules. We don't do this. Ever."

"Those are your rules, Greyson. Not mine."

"What are you trying to prove? You think because you can get a man to fuck you that somehow changes the situation? I told you no and you pushed anyway."

"I guess you had absolutely nothing to do with this." She waved a hand at her bare breasts.

"Cover yourself."

She lifted her chin in defiance. "No. Not until you admit that you liked putting your hands on me."

What he liked was irrelevant. "We're done here."

"Greyson—"

"Wren, we're done," he snapped, once again facing her. "This was a mistake."

She flinched, and tears sprang to her eyes. Her nipples were still wet from his mouth, and her breasts were rosy from the scruff of his beard.

"For the love of God, fix your shirt."

With shaky hands, she righted her clothes. "You don't have to be such an asshole."

"I told you not to push me. Why do you do that?"

"I barely did anything."

"Bullshit. You followed me in here and purposely provoked me. What did you think would happen?"

Her lips firmed into a flat line, and she narrowed her eyes. "I guess I thought you might be honest for once."

"I'm always honest."

"Not with me. Not about your feelings. We're not little kids anymore, Greyson. I just celebrated my thirtieth birthday."

"I'm perfectly aware we're not children and I bought your damn cake candles so I know how old you are."

"Then act like a man and admit there's something happening between us."

The breath in his lungs turned chilled. She'd never actually called him out like that.

When he remained silent, she frowned. "Do you hate me so much?"

"Hate you?"

"When you like someone you don't punish them this much."

Is that what she thought? "I've only ever wanted to protect you."

"From what? We live in one of the safest towns on the planet. I don't need protection. I need affection. Are you honestly going to act like you don't want the same?"

Of course, he wanted it, but not with Wren. If they crossed that line, they'd never be able to uncross it. He'd inevitably screw it up and then she'd hate him for disappointing her. "Sometimes, it doesn't matter what we want. It only matters that we know what's right and what's wrong and choose correctly."

She gaped at him. "Was it right for you to chase away every guy who ever showed interest in me?" She shoved his chest. "Was it?" Her brows pinched. "Answer me."

"Wren..." He was speechless. "I'm not..." Words evaded him. He checked his motives, but quickly grew frustrated with all that deep reflection. *"You're the one who followed me in here!"*

She scoffed and looked away. "You should go."

"Don't get upset."

"What do you care anyway if I'm upset?"

"I care."

She scooted around him and adjusted her clothes. Her voice contracted as if she were holding back tears. "No, you don't."

"Wren..." He reached for her, but she drew back and knocked into the trash can full of rakes and shovels.

"Ouch!"

"Shit." He shoved the falling tools, but not before more crashed into her and clattered loudly to the floor.

She cupped her shoulder protectively.

"Let me see."

"Don't." She curled away as he tried to move her hand.

"Knock it off. Let me look at it." He pulled her fingers away, revealing a surface scratch. "It's just a graze." Nothing that would scar, but it probably stung like a son of a bitch. He scowled at the spilled trash can. "Bodhi needs a better system. You're lucky it didn't leave a gash."

She glanced over her shoulder and met his stare. They were too close.

Stepping back, he said, "You should still clean it out."

She pointed to a small metal box hanging on the wall by the door. "There's disinfectant in there."

He looked at the little vintage box and frowned. It looked like a prop from *MASH*. "Do you have anything from this century?"

She rolled her eyes. "I keep it stocked with up-to-date supplies."

He pulled down the box and sorted through the gauze and tapes until he found alcohol wipes. "This should work. Sit here." He cleared an empty stack of flower pots off the work table and lifted her onto the surface.

She turned her shoulder and lowered her shirt. There was something so elegant and feminine about her body. Every inch of muscle seemed honed to perfection, like a natural work of art.

She gasped when he touched the alcohol-soaked towel to the cut.

"Sorry. Does it sting?"

"It's cold." She shivered.

"There. Good as new." He pulled her shirt and sweater into place and stood silently for a moment. "About what happened—"

"It's fine. We don't have to dissect it."

"I should have had more control."

"Greyson, I said it's fine. Besides, you were right. I started it."

He still felt guilty. He didn't want her to feel embarrassed. "It's my fault. It's been a long time since I..." He cleared his throat. "You know. Not that that's an excuse. But I'm usually not so..."

She laughed. "No matter how long it's been for you, I'm sure I've got you beat."

"I wouldn't be so sure. I remember it was snowing the last time I... so that means it was either last winter or the one before."

She tipped her head forward, dropping her chin to her chest as she stared up at him. "Like I said...I've got you beat."

He arched a brow, dangerous curiosity pushing him to ask, "Really? How long?"

She scoffed, then searched his confused stare and laughed. "You do realize..."

He frowned when she didn't finish her statement. "Realize what?"

Her lips twisted. "You're not seriously going to make me say it?"

"Wren, I have no freaking clue what you're trying to tell me, so yeah, using words would help."

She rolled her eyes. "Fine. It's been forever for me."

"Feels like that sometimes," he agreed.

"No, Greyson. I'm saying that literally."

His entire body stilled. No breathing. No blinking. For a moment, he even lost his hearing. "What's that now?"

"You know my relationship history."

"Yeah, but..." Dating had nothing to do with sex. Just because Wren never had a long-term boyfriend didn't mean she didn't have... "You've had..."

"Never."

"Shut the fuck up."

"Okay. But that doesn't make it any less true."

"Wren, you're thirty years old."

"I know my age, Grey. But thanks for giving me more of a complex than I already have as Hideaway Bay's spinster cat lady."

"You're not a spinster. Spinsters are old and frumpy."

"Old like thirty?"

This didn't make sense, yet it made perfect sense. He stepped back, tripped over a rake handle, and stumbled into the wall. "God damn, Bodhi and his stupid fucking system!"

"Careful!"

He angrily picked up the shovels, rakes, and brooms and shoved them back into the trash can. "I'm building you a wall rack tomorrow."

"Why are you so angry?"

"Because Bodhi puts shit away in the dumbest places!"

He couldn't think. She wasn't actually saying what he thought she was saying. Was she?

"Greyson, what's with you today?"

"What's with *me*? What about you? You don't normally lie—"

"Who said I was lying?"

"Wren, you honestly expect me to believe you're a thirty-year-old virgin?"

"Of course not. I lost my virginity years ago when I bought my first vibrator."

"Jesus, Wren!" His skull practically cracked as a thousand unwanted erotic images burst through his mind. "Don't tell me stuff like that!"

"Like you don't masturbate."

"We're not discussing this."

"Except we are. It's a perfectly natural use of time. It releases endorphins and improves mental wellness. But, to clarify, no, I've never actually slept with a man. I assumed you knew."

"Why would I know that?"

"Because you're always the one scaring men off."

"Well, I didn't know and now I wish I could go back to not knowing."

"It's not that big of a deal."

He glared at her. "It's a huge deal."

She rolled her eyes. "Maybe it was back in the day. But in this century... no one cares who I'm fucking."

He gave her a stern glare. "I don't like this side of you."

Or maybe he did, and that was the problem.

His mind was blown. Was this common knowledge? Did Logan and Soren know? Was she planning on screwing the yogi?

He scowled. Absolutely not. A girl's first time should be with someone meaningful, not some twerp wearing a bracelet of lava rocks.

"Forget I said anything." She snicked her tongue against her teeth. "I can see you're making way too big of a deal out of this. Just pretend I've had tons of sex."

His brain short-circuited.

She scooted off the table. *"Ow!"*

"What now?"

"Nothing." She rubbed her ass and winced. "I think I got a splinter."

They needed to get out of this damn shed. "Let me have a look."

"No, it's in my butt cheek."

"Are you going to be able to get it out?"

"Yes." Then she twisted but couldn't see the area where the splinter went through her pants. "Maybe."

He rolled his eyes. "Turn around." Before she could object, he spun her to face the work table and pressed a calming hand onto her spine, bending her forward. "Which cheek?"

"The left."

He lowered her pants and stilled at the sight of emerald lace flossing her plump ass-cheeks. How the hell did he get here?

Keeping it clinical, he cleared his throat. "I see it. Hold still." He squeezed the skin around the splinter.

"Ow, ow, ow!"

"I have to get it out."

"Can't you use a pin or something?"

"It's almost there." He pinched the area, loving the way her juicy flesh filled his hand.

"Son of a nutcracker!"

"Got it." He plucked the shard of wood free and held it up for her to inspect.

She rubbed her butt and frowned. "It's so tiny."

When she tried to pull up her pants, he stopped her. "Hand me another alcohol wipe."

She passed him a packet, and he tore it open, then disinfected the area. "Good as new."

"Thanks." She pulled up her pants and blushed.

He tucked that unruly strand of hair behind her ear. "One more injury, and it's a helmet and a bubble for you."

She laughed, sounding slightly embarrassed, which was unusual for her. When she finally looked at him, she asked, "Are we okay?"

He nodded, but this couldn't happen again. Wren was too important to risk losing. After the storm, he'd hit up a local bar and work out his issues elsewhere. "For what it's worth, I'm sorry I crossed a line."

"For what it's worth, I'm not."

He did a double-take, and she grinned. That's when he knew he was in trouble.

CHAPTER 5

"The Season Doesn't Hit
The Same As It Did Before"

The tree lighting ceremony kicked off Hideaway Bay's holiday festivities the first Saturday after Thanksgiving. Wren hated attending annual events alone because they served as a painful reminder that another year had passed. She'd grown another year older, spent another year alone.

So, like any cool person would, she took her dad as her date.

Her dad enjoyed the town events, as they gave him a chance to catch up with the locals and visit with his sister Astrid.

Once the speeches started, the mayor would undoubtedly mention the recent fundraising efforts for the cat sanctuary at The Haven, and everyone would stare at her—the local cat lady. But Bodhi would be by her side, making that unwanted attention a little more bearable.

She appreciated the townspeople. Without their help, the cats wouldn't have heat and shelter for the winter, but being known only for cats really wasn't the vibe any woman of thirty wanted to achieve.

By the time they made it into town, it was dark. She hadn't meant to run late, but she was so flustered from her encounter with Greyson that morning that she'd forgotten to remind her dad the tree lighting was that night. Then she had to wait for him to get ready.

Not knowing when the snow would start, she decided to take her Jeep rather than walk. Bodhi always preferred being on foot and complained the entire two-minute drive into town.

"We could have walked," he said, as Wren struggled to find a close parking space. "At this rate, we'll park farther away than home."

"Enough, Dad." She spotted a small opening by the bank. "I didn't want to walk home in the snow."

"You act like we're getting a blizzard. It's only going to be three inches."

"Greyson said eight."

"He's wrong."

She wasn't getting caught up in another one of their silly debates. For some reason, Greyson always took issue with the way Bodhi did things, predicted the weather, and didn't show up for events in her life. With only one parent left, she tried not to dwell on the negative and simply focused on the things she and her dad shared.

"Astrid's probably already there."

Astrid, her eccentric aunt on her dad's side, was extremely close to Bodhi and equally strange to outsiders. Wren was used to both of them and hardly noticed their quirkiness. It was likely that the locals found Wren just as odd.

She didn't expect the Hawthornes to attend the tree lighting. Losing their mothers during the holiday season always made the sweetness of Christmas a bit bitter.

The anniversary had already passed, but for some reason, they all associated the loss with the holidays. That first Christmas without their moms had been the absolute worst. Something Wren didn't like to think about. But unlike the Hawthornes, she tried to rewrite the sad memories with new traditions. It didn't always work, but when it did, she remembered for a split second just how magical Christmas could be.

When she and Bodhi reached the crowded end of town with the enormous tree, it was hard to hear anything over the speakers blasting Christmas carols. Her father smiled and pointed as they worked their way through the merry crowd.

The music swelled with holiday cheer, and the locals gathered like toys on a shelf, beribboned in festive scarves and hats, bouncing anxiously for the show to begin.

The stage beside the tree had bleachers for the local choir. Uplights illuminated the podium where Mayor Quimby would make his speech.

As soon as they reached the front, Mayor Quimby appeared with a big smile and waved as the crowd cheered. Every year, he grew out his full white beard for his upcoming role as Santa Claus. The carolers, dressed in robes and elf-ear headbands, gathered behind him.

"Happy holidays, Hideaway Bay!" Mayor Quimby bellowed, and the crowd echoed his enthusiasm with a great big cheer. It took a few moments for the mayor to gain control of the pandemonium, but it was all in good fun. "Alright, alright," he said, raising his gloved hands to settle the crowd, his cheeks red from the cold or, more likely, the cider. He flashed a wide grin and clutched the podium. "Settle in, folks. I promise to keep this short and sweet."

Wren tucked her hands deeper into the wool-lined pockets of the shirt Greyson had loaned her as snowflakes floated like confetti beneath the glow of the harbor lights. The scent of the nearby bakery mingled with the warm, cinnamon-spiced aroma of pecans roasting at a vendor cart nearby.

The music lowered, but the crowd hardly quieted as children

laughed and played underfoot. For some, it was the first time they'd caught up with neighbors since October's pumpkin carving contest.

Parents hushed their children and looked up at the stage expectantly, waiting for the main event.

"I want to start by thanking each and every one of you for your incredible generosity during last week's fundraiser," the mayor continued. "Because of your kindness—and a shocking amount of hand-knit cat blankets—we raised over two thousand dollars for the sanctuary at The Haven."

A cheer erupted, followed by a few "meows" from the teenage boy Wren recognized as the drama club president. He was wearing reindeer antlers and elf ears.

Wren smiled, and Bodhi waved over a paper cone of roasted nuts.

"The sanctuary's new outdoor *catio* will be built next week, the lowest contract bid going to none other than Greyson Hawthorne." The mayor paused to look for Greyson, but when he didn't see him in the crowd, he continued speaking. "Let me tell you, these kittens and cats will be living their best life come spring."

The locals laughed.

"Now, as for what's ahead—brace yourselves. Keeping with Hideaway Bay tradition, our goal is always to upstage the prior year's festivities."

The crowd cheered and whistled with abundant town pride. Mayor Quimby grinned, his pearly teeth flashing within his thick white beard.

"Local author, Jocelyn Collins, is hosting a ticketed event at Vine & Barrel next Thursday, and she's requested all of Hideaway Bay's brave—or foolish—single men to sign up. In hopes of raising money for the upcoming library renovations, Jocelyn has arranged for fifty romance readers from her local chapter to come to Hideaway Bay to find their holiday hero. Where is Jocelyn?"

A sharp whistle belted through the crowd as Wren's best friend pulled her fingers from her mouth and waved. "Over here!" Of course, Jocelyn didn't need a microphone to be heard. She waved a clipboard and a long tail of raffle tickets in the air. "Tickets are available, and signups are open! Who wants to be on the naughty list?"

"Thank you, Jocelyn," the mayor said, clearing his throat. "And good luck to all of you who sign up for her *Raiders of the Lost Heart* fundraiser event. That brings us to our next charity, the Winter Festival fund, which, as you all know, supports our world-famous caroling division, the Santa Fun Run championship, and, of course, the lobster trap tree lighting, where Captain Claws will make his shining debut..."

Wren shook her head fondly. Hideaway might be slightly unhinged around the holidays, but that was part of the charm.

Mayor Quimby grinned proudly and tipped his hat. "And now, the moment we've all been waiting for. It is my honor to introduce a woman who can out-charm Santa Claus himself—Vivienne Pike!"

Uproarious applause erupted as the famous actress took the stage and waved. Her red, plaid flannel coat and shearling collar paired perfectly with her lumberjack hat. Even with the earflaps, she was stunning in that effortless way she always seemed to pull off.

"Vivienne Pike will be lighting the tree tonight and officially kicking off this year's Winter Festivities!"

Children bounced on their toes to see what the fuss was about, appearing somewhat disappointed when it wasn't the big guy in a red suit causing all the excitement. Wren smiled when she heard a little one ask in a whiny, bored voice when Santa would get there.

Parents pulled out their phones to take pictures as Vivienne Pike took the official plug in hand. The towering tree was wrapped in thousands of lights, and Wren's heart pinched slightly at the fact that another year had passed.

Here she was, alone again.

"If not for my sweet tooth, I'd skip this barbaric tradition," Bodhi said over a mouthful of honey-roasted nuts. "Tree's probably at least fifty years old."

"Dad, don't ruin their fun."

He shook his head in disapproval and licked the sugar off his lips. "They could at least bring back the Yule log and get the most out of their kill."

Wren rolled her eyes just as the crowd roared. The enormous tree glowed in a mixture of colorful lights. She felt sorry for the tree, but she still loved this part of their town's traditions. If not for Hideaway Bay's relentless cheer this time of year, she'd most likely spend each December depressed and overwhelmed by memories of her mother.

The music turned up, and people returned to mingling about the square, where the local shops showcased their merchandise and tempted guests inside with delicious winter treats.

"I see Astrid over there."

"Go ahead." She waved at her aunt and urged Bodhi to go to her. "I'll walk around for a while."

Wren wandered through the crowd, not stopping at any of the stores, but enjoying the ambiance nonetheless until she lost her vision to a set of cold hands.

"Guess who?"

She stilled and caught his wrists. "Soren?" she teased, knowing perfectly well it was Logan.

"Brat." He uncovered her eyes and tugged her braid, then tipped a paper cone in her face. "Nut?"

Warm cinnamon sugar wafted to her nose. "No thanks."

"You sure? My nuts are delicious."

She rolled her eyes. "What are you doing here?" Typically, the Hawthornes sat out the big holiday festivities.

Logan laughed. "I signed Soren up for that *Raiders of the Lost Heart* thing Jocelyn's running. He's gonna murder me when he finds out."

"Uh, yeah, he is."

He snickered and popped a honey-roasted nut into his mouth. "Where's Bodhi?"

"Off with Astrid."

"You free for the night?"

"I'm his ride."

"Oh. Bummer." He pulled her toward a line for hot cider. "I guess we'll just have to make the best of the Christmas cookies and chaos while I have you."

Of all the Hawthornes, Logan seemed to process his mother's absence the easiest. Maybe because he was the youngest and therefore got away with actually crying when he was sad, unlike his older brothers, who were encouraged to bottle up their grief and never let it show.

Townspeople bustled around the square as kids darted past in brightly colored hats and scarves. The playlist blasting from the speakers shifted to a less polished version of holiday music sung by the local choir, which was mostly comprised of holiday enthusiasts and longtime carolers.

Now that the speeches were over, Mayor Quimby held court by the bonfire, probably retelling the time Captain Claws' claw short-circuited the whole harbor.

"How long are you sticking around?" she asked Logan as they moved up in line.

"Not long. Too many humans. You want to hang out after you drop Bodhi off at home?"

She raised a brow. "Depends what you're offering."

"We could watch one of those weird old Christmas movies you like. The ones where nothing happens, but everyone contemplates the meaning of snow and somehow the crooner's the hero."

She chuckled. "So basically every movie I've ever loved."

"Exactly."

"Perhaps." It was their turn in line and she waited as Logan ordered two hot ciders.

"Here we go a' wassailing. Cheers."

He handed her a cup, and the nutmeg-spiced steam warmed her face.

Sticking by her side, Logan led them down the main drag. "So, what do you say? Candles. Blankets. Fire. Socks are mandatory, of course. And I'll insist the phone goes off."

The boys always gave her grief about her phone, but she liked to keep it on at all times in case Bodhi needed something—not that calls ever went through in their part of town.

"I don't know."

"Please." He pouted. "I have two new puzzles for approval—a nature scene and one full of cuddly woodland creatures."

She shook her head, grinning. "You know my weak spot for puzzles."

"*Yassssss!*" he hissed victoriously like an evil mastermind and sipped his cider.

"Fine. After I take Bodhi home, I'll meet you at your place in an hour."

"I'll have the movie cued up and the good fuzzy socks waiting."

By the time she dropped her dad off and got to Logan's it was almost ten. She'd regret staying up late tomorrow, but old Christmas movies were her weakness.

She walked in without knocking and slipped off her shoes. "Logan?"

"In here." He appeared with a bowl of popcorn, already in his pajama pants and hoodie. "Classic holiday movie or heartwarming drama?"

"Oooh, tough choice." She debated for a moment. "The classic."

"Really? I was almost positive you'd pick the drama."

"It's the first movie of the season, and not even December yet. We don't want to peak too soon."

"Gotcha." He cued up *White Christmas* as Wren made herself comfortable under a blanket on the couch. Logan was a cuddler, so she didn't find it strange when he sat beside her and snuggled close.

She nibbled on popcorn as the opening scene unfolded. Later, when the female leads performed their musical number, Wren smiled. "We should choreograph this for our next town fundraiser."

"Only if I get to hold a big blue feather fan like that."

"Obviously."

Within minutes, Wren was utterly charmed. "Bing was the original golden retriever."

"No comment."

She gave him a sidelong glance. "Fine, who do you find more attractive, the blonde or the brunette?"

"Hands down, the brunette."

"Because she's the curvier one?"

"No, because the blonde looks like she could mess a man up. I don't trust her."

Wren took the bowl of popcorn back and giggled. "Can you imagine someone just being like, 'Hey, let's go to Vermont,' and you actually go?"

"We could go right now. It would probably be more entertaining than this movie."

She elbowed him in the side.

When the characters reached the inn in Vermont, Wren sighed. "Tell me this doesn't scream Hideaway Bay."

"Meh, there's not enough coastal charm. Throw a few *lobstah* traps in there, more alcohol, and a sea breeze, and then we're talking."

The general appeared. "He reminds me a little of Magnus."

"Yeah, right. Maybe if Magnus discovered emotions."

"Your dad has feelings, Logan."

"Agree to disagree. Besides, Magnus would never allow Christmas music. Too much joy."

By the final scene, she was nearly asleep. Or maybe she had already drifted off. Logan pulled the covers over her and shut off the lights. "You need anything?"

He'd set her up with a pillow from his bed and put a glass of water on the coffee table for her. "I'm good. Thanks, babe."

He kissed his fingers and touched her forehead. "'Night, Wren."

She turned into the cushions and fell right to sleep.

CHAPTER 6

"Out of All the Reindeer, You Know You're The Mastermind"

Wren paced by her front window, chewing her fingernail to a nub. How could she have agreed to this? She should have canceled.

Lights panned across the snow, and Logan's black truck came into view. Too late to cancel now.

She meant to get out the door as soon as he pulled up, but she needed a moment to calm her breathing. It took longer than usual to pull herself together. She flinched when he knocked.

With a shaky hand and an unsure belly, she pasted on a smile and opened the door, doing her best to play it casual. "Hi."

"These are for you." He revealed a stunning bouquet of sunflowers and eucalyptus branches.

"Oh, Logan, they're beautiful." She took the flowers inside, and he followed.

"I remember you telling me once that sunflowers were your favorite."

She looked back at him, surprised. "You do?" He was right, of course, but Wren had no recollection of that conversation.

"Yeah. Sometime after our moms died. You said lilies used to be your favorite, but there were so many at the funeral that you no longer liked them. I asked what your second favorite was, and you said sunflowers."

She was speechless. She hated the scent of lilies now, but had forgotten why. He was right. She associated the smell with sadness.

"Well," she breathed in the sunny blooms. "These are beautiful. I don't even know where you find sunflowers this time of year."

"I have my ways."

"I'll just put them in a vase and then we can go."

"No rush. How was your day?"

She wasn't used to anyone asking her about her day and it caught her off guard. "My day was good."

"What did you do?"

She searched for a vase. "I, uh, taught my noon class, helped my dad mend a few of the cat houses, and did the kitchen inventory with Freya. She's talking to Mia about having a photoshoot for the new menu. Mia's also been photographing content for all our social media. Things are really coming together."

"Freya's the new chef you hired?"

"Yeah."

"How's she working out?" He pulled out a stool, making himself comfortable at the counter.

"I like her a lot. And the guests really like her style of cooking. She specializes in traditional Nordic dishes. I mean, right now, she's only doing breakfast and afternoon teas, but I hope to get her on special event dinners soon. We have one planned for the winter solstice."

"I love how your face lights up when you talk about The

Haven." He caught her hand and squeezed. "Your mom would be proud."

Something heavy shifted in her chest. "Thanks, Logan. I hope so."

The Haven was named after her mother. She'd been the one who taught her how to do yoga, garden, and appreciate the seasons for the lessons they taught. Everything about her business was inspired by the way her mother lived. In a way, it kept her alive and present in Wren's life.

"You should probably put those in water."

Realizing they were still holding hands, she let him go and unwrapped the paper from the bouquet. "Oh, what's this?" It looked important, a stiff envelope with a candy cane taped on top, so she passed it to Logan.

"Nope, it's for you."

She turned the small vintage Christmas card over, and read, *"Go where you were when Wendy first met Pan."* She frowned. "I don't get it."

"It's a clue."

"A clue to what?"

"Our date. I made us a scavenger hunt."

"Really?" She beamed, curious excitement overtaking the nervousness that had first filled her belly. "That's so clever. And thoughtful." She couldn't believe he'd planned something so extravagant. Looking back at the clue, she reread it and tried to put the pieces together. "Neverland?"

"Close. You have to think back to our childhood. Don't take the story reference so literally."

"So you're talking about the book, not the movie."

"Correct."

She set the flowers in water and arranged the blooms. When they were younger, Magnus used to make the boys go to the library to do their homework. She and Logan would pass the time reading fiction in the children's section while they waited for his older brothers to finish their assignments. That was where she first read J.M. Barrie's Peter Pan.

"The library?"

He lifted his keys. "Only one way to find out."

Giddy to play this game with him, she grabbed the flannel by the door.

Logan stilled. "Is that Greyson's?"

"Oh." She looked down guiltily. "He loaned it to me when I lost my coat. If it bothers you, I don't have to wear it."

"No, it's cool. When did you see Grey?" He held open the door and waited as she locked it.

She didn't want to think about the other day when Greyson came by because she was still embarrassed. The longer he avoided seeing her again, the worse she felt about the things she'd done and said.

"He stopped by about the snow."

"Of course he did." Logan rolled his eyes and opened the passenger door for her—something he didn't typically do.

"Why do you say it like that?" She hauled herself onto the seat.

"That's just typical Greyson. Disappears three seasons of the year and shows up like a hero whenever there's snow. It's how he ensures people don't give him grief about his disappearing act."

"I see him in the other seasons."

"That's because you're a little forest witch and he lives out in the woods like he's Bigfoot's long-lost cousin."

She laughed. "He has a nice place out there."

He paused from buckling his seat belt. "You've been to his place?"

"Of course. I was there as soon as he finished construction, just like I came by all of your places when you moved out on your own."

He started the truck and was quiet for a moment. "I just don't understand how anyone could be that introverted. Grey never used to be like that."

"Maybe he just likes his privacy."

"I'd go out of my mind. All he does is make furniture all day and cut wood. He doesn't even have a television."

"He reads, and when he wants to watch a game, he usually goes to The Chowder House Rules."

"You defend him too easily."

"I defend all of you boys."

"I guess." He glanced at her as he drove toward the library. "And we're not boys anymore, Wren."

She shrugged. "You'll always be my boys."

"Well... we're men now."

She smirked at his need for validation. "Fine. Men it is."

When they parked, there was only one other car in the lot. She hoped to see Mrs. Zian, the old librarian who used to run the library when they were kids, but a younger woman with glasses sat behind the counter. Logan said hello as they walked past, and the woman smiled. She looked about their age, but Wren didn't recognize her.

When they got to the children's section, everything was much smaller than she recalled. The old, braided rug had been replaced with a large, circular rug that resembled a globe. The shelves were shorter than she remembered, and the walls were painted a different color.

"Wow. It looks so different."

"Still smells the same."

Wren breathed in the scent of paper, ink, and pine cleaner, then grinned. "It does." She scanned the shelf and spotted a red envelope. "Oh!"

Stuffed like a bookmark inside Peter Pan, she tipped the spine and withdrew the clue, pulling out another vintage postcard with a Christmas scene on the front tied to a candy cane and a long string.

She opened the card and read, *"Put this on."*

Pulling the string, a pair of mittens tugged free of the bookcase. When she stuck her hand in the mitten, she found another clue, this one written on an old holiday recipe card.

"I hope you're feeling lushy because we're off to get some slushies." She smiled and looked at him expectantly. "The corner store?"

"Only one way to find out."

She put on her hat and waved with an almost giddy bounce to her step when they passed the librarian. "Have a nice night!"

When they reached the corner store where they used to get slushies after school, Logan let her lead the way. She walked in and out of the aisles but found no clue. When she asked the clerk if he had a clue, he looked at her like she was insane.

"Are we in the wrong place?"

"You haven't checked everywhere yet."

She remembered they used to sit out back on the palettes and boxes with their slushies, so she went around back. "Oh, my gosh!"

A bottle of wine waited on a stack of palettes with a quilt draped over them. Two milk crates were flipped over as chairs.

"Table for two?" He waved his hand like a maître d'.

Once she sat down, he uncorked the wine and lit the small candle in a mason jar. "I can't believe you went to all this trouble."

"We spent a lot of time here back in the day."

"I remember." She turned the bottle and snorted. It was the swill they used to steal from her Aunt Astrid's house. "I didn't know they still made this."

"I wanted to be nostalgic." He poured them each a glass. "Cheers."

"Cheers."

They each took a sip and winced. "Oh, God."

He gasped. "I don't remember it burning like that."

She gagged. "Maybe it's an acquired taste." When she sipped again, her eye twitched.

"You looked so nervous when I showed up."

She blushed, now feeling silly for ever being nervous about Logan. "I was."

"Why?"

"I don't know. This is... weird. We're friends."

"So? Sometimes friends date."

She still wasn't comfortable calling this a date. "Some friends aren't as close as we are."

"True. I was surprised you changed your mind. What made you call?"

She'd called to goad Greyson, but she didn't want to bring him into this. "I don't know. I'm still not sure this is a good idea."

"Is that because you still see me as the kid brother? Because I haven't been a kid in a long time, Wren."

She looked at his defined jaw and five o'clock shadow. Meeting his dark eyes, she agreed, "No, you haven't."

He refilled their wine. After the first glass, it went down a little easier. He studied her for a long moment, and nervousness crept in again.

Sipping the unpalatable wine, he asked, "What's something you used to believe about love that you don't anymore?"

His question cut to a hidden part of her she didn't easily expose. If he was trying to knock her off balance with his emotional maturity, he succeeded.

"Um…that's a deep question." She laughed and tried to think of a truthful answer. "That there's someone out there for everyone—like a perfect soulmate."

"You don't believe in soulmates?"

"Not anymore. How about you?"

He shrugged. "Hard to say. I've never actually been in love, but I think it's possible to meet someone who fits your personality so well they complement your soul and fill in all the missing pieces."

"That's really sweet. What's something you stopped believing in?"

He took a deep breath and smiled softly, staring into the murky wine. "I used to think love was something you had to earn. Like, if you worked hard enough, stayed out of trouble, did everything right, eventually, the payoff would come."

"What do you mean? Of course love begets love."

"Not always. I think some people are incapable of deep emotion."

She wondered if he was referring to romantic love or his father's approval. "Maybe you're trying to win the hearts of the wrong people."

He shrugged. "People are too self-centered to care about love anymore. Nobody pays attention. Everyone cuts corners, and cheaters end up at the top."

But Logan paid attention. He remembered the books they used to read and the flowers she no longer liked. He knew things about her that other men never could know, things that came from sharing a long history with someone. "Are you saying you don't believe in love?"

"No, I believe in love, but love isn't a paycheck. It's not some reward for good behavior. It's a choice. You either show up for someone or you don't. You either pay attention, or you don't." He finally met her stare. "I pay attention, Wren. I see you."

Her breath turned shallow, and she sank a little on her milk crate. "I know you do, Logan. And I've always loved you for it."

"I'd make a good husband."

Worry crowded her thinking. Although he'd not pushed the subject, she felt the pressure of the other day return. "Logan."

"Take my dad out of it. I'm just talking right now. It's just us. You know I've always supported your vision for The Haven. I love watching you follow your dreams. I have security and enough money that—if we were married—you'd be able to streamline your plans and get them finished in a fraction of the time—"

"Logan."

"I'm just saying, even without Hawthorne Fishery, I have a lot to offer."

"I know what you're saying, and I want you to stop."

"But it makes sense."

"Logan, I can't marry you."

"Why not?"

"Because I'm not in love with you." She winced as her words came out harsher than anticipated. "And you're not in love with me."

"Love takes time. I know I could love you, Wren. And you could fall in love with me if you'd just be a little open-minded about it."

"That's not fair."

"Why?"

"Because you're putting too much pressure on me. This isn't about your feelings for me. This is about your dad—"

"It's not."

"Logan, it is. You never would have even asked me out if he hadn't changed his will and added that silly clause requiring one of you to marry someone in a rush."

"I always expected to get married, Wren."

"But now? With me? Come on. You're with a different woman every other week. I'm not saying you won't make a great husband someday, but you're not ready to settle down right now."

"You don't know that."

Despite the truth, he was taking great offense at her appraisal of the situation. "Don't be mad at me."

"You just called me a player with daddy issues."

"You are a player. And you do, in fact, have issues with your father. But that's okay. Anyone would in your situation. Magnus has never been easy."

His jaw ticked, and he looked away. "We should go."

"What about the next clue?"

His mouth formed a flat line. "This was a dumb idea."

Unease tightened her shoulders. She hadn't meant to hurt him. "Logan, you know I love you. I'd do almost anything for you and your brothers. But what you're asking—"

"Forget it. I get it." He twirled the stem of the wine glass and wouldn't meet her eyes.

She hated leaving like this. The night had started so pleasantly, and now he was upset with her. "Do you want to take me home?"

"That's probably best."

She stood from the milk crate and pulled on her mittens, a lump of regret tightening her throat. He dumped the last of the cheap wine on the pavement, blew out the candle, and gathered up the blanket. He didn't say a word as he stashed everything in the back of the truck.

They couldn't leave things like this. "I'm sorry."

"It's cool."

None of this was cool.

A gold-edged paper blew from the pallets through a hole in the chain link fence. That was her clue, and now it was gone. Game over.

She grabbed the sleeve of his jacket. "Look at me, Logan."

When he did, it wasn't with the eager inquisitiveness she was used to from him. His eyes darkened, and there was an intensity about him that hadn't been there before. Or maybe it was, but she continued to see him through layers of memories, unable to wash away the recollections of the sweet young boy who was one of her best friends.

"Can I have a hug?"

He hesitated, but then he saw her regret and sighed. "Yeah."

His arms closed around her and a sense of safety enveloped her. She rested her cheek on the cold wool of his coat.

"You aren't allowed to get mad at me. Ever."

His arms tightened. "I can't stay mad at you anyway."

She smiled and looked up at him. "One day, you're going to make an amazing husband for a very lucky woman."

He studied her, their faces only an inch apart, and his arms still hooked snugly around her back. When he leaned in, she drew back but could only go so far. "Logan—"

His hold tightened. "Just let me try something." His lips pressed to hers, and her eyes went wide.

His kiss was soft and sensual, the slow kind that begged to go deeper. But she couldn't go deeper with him.

Turning her cheek, she looked away. "I can't."

Neither of them moved for several long seconds as they died in the awkwardness and had to wait to be reborn.

His arms loosened, and she pulled away as soon as he unhooked his hands from her back. Wind whipped at her face, but she was too embarrassed to feel the cold.

"Just tell me one thing, Wren."

She nodded, her voice having disappeared.

"Would it be any different with Soren or Grey?"

She thought back to the shed and the weight of Greyson's mouth on her. She recalled how her body responded to his touch, shivering at the memory of him pressing her into the wall. Her cheeks burned when she remembered the way he'd forced her hand over the bulge in his pants. No one had ever been so aggressive with her before. Even now, her body clenched at the intense memory.

But Greyson didn't want intensity. He regretted touching her at all.

"My relationship with each of you has always been different, but I love each of you equally."

He glanced at her under a firm brow. "Now, who's in denial?"

"Soren and I are just—"

"I'm talking about Greyson."

She couldn't argue that she and Grey had always had a complicated relationship, but that didn't make them more than friends. "He doesn't see me that way."

He laughed without humor. "If you really believe that, you're blind."

CHAPTER 7

"Meet the Stranger Who Has Saved Your Life"

Greyson slammed the ax down, splitting the log in two. Breath gathered into vapor as steam rose from his shoulders. The prior night's events played like a loop in his head, and he couldn't figure out where things went wrong.

He'd gone to The Chowder House. Run into Sarah. Had a few drinks. Bought her a round. The chemistry was good and still familiar enough that they knew where the evening would lead. All systems were go, until he paid the tab.

"You wanna get out of here?" she'd asked, leaning in as if to show him the offer on the table. "I'm free all night."

With a nod, he threw some money on the bar and grabbed their coats. Once outside, he walked her to her car.

"Meet you at my place?"

Where else would they meet? He never brought women back to his cabin because he preferred an exit strategy.

She'd leaned against her car door, waiting for confirmation. He needed to work out his tension, so he was ready to go. But when he kissed her, something felt off. She was too tall, and her hips didn't fill his hands the way he wanted. Her lips weren't soft enough. Her perfume was all wrong.

"I can't. Not tonight," he said, and she stared up at him in confusion.

Greyson wasn't one to explain his decisions, but he couldn't if he wanted to. He needed to get laid. He and Sarah had been down this road several times before. There was no reason not to go home with her. He didn't even have to stay the night.

But she wasn't Wren.

Another log split and clattered to the frozen ground. The snow had melted. The storm was a bust. Bodhi was right about the snow predictions. They got three inches, and it melted shortly after it stopped coming down. Crazy old coot.

This was the nonsense that drove him nuts. Science had a purpose, but not to the Wildes. No. They relied on nature's vibrations, the phases of the moon, and how a leaf might curl when clouds rolled in.

Perhaps Greyson was more like his father than he wanted to admit. Wren's mother, drove Magnus insane. She'd change vacation plans because Haven pulled a worrisome card from a tarot deck.

Some days, they'd come home from school, and the entire house would be filled with smoke because Haven convinced his mother that negative energy filled the walls.

They were kids back then, so these strange tendencies didn't concern him, but his father would become enraged, threatening their mother with ultimatums if she didn't cut off her friendship with Haven.

But no force could come between the women. They had been best friends since childhood. And the more his mother chose Haven over his father, the worse their marriage became.

Greyson set up another log and split it in two, recalling how loud their fighting became at the end. Wren didn't have any of that at home.

Bodhi loved Haven. She was his entire world. And when she died in the same accident that took their mother, he was never the same. Wren not only had to deal with her own confusing grief as a child, but take care of her father as well.

Giving his muscles a break, he set down the ax and carried the split wood to the woodshed. Despite how different the Wildes were, there was something to envy about their closeness.

Wren never complained about taking care of her father. She'd been a kid—just fifteen—and become responsible overnight. After Haven died, Wren took over cooking and shopping while Bodhi disappeared for days to sleep in the woods, alone with his grief. He used to tell Wren that's where he felt the most connected to her mother.

Greyson understood. While he felt no presence of his mother anywhere, he took a great deal of peace from the woods. He enjoyed the silence and preferred keeping his distance from the rest of the world. Very few people knew where his cabin was located, since it didn't come with a traditional address and all his mail was sent to the post office. Only a select few knew how to get there, which was exactly how he preferred it.

Maybe he and Bodhi were more alike than he wanted to admit.

When he finished with the wood for the day, he removed his work gloves and dragged the soles of his boots over the mat. Tonight, he'd head back to town and try to patch things up with—

Greyson stilled as something quiet squawked nearby. The leaves rustled in the breeze as he concentrated on the sounds of the wildlife creeping around him.

Another peep, and he turned to locate the source of the sound. Possibly a field mouse. At least he hoped that's what it was.

Tracking the soft cry to the porch steps, he crouched low. "Please don't be another—Fuck my life."

Blue eyes and a tiny black face stared back at him from the shadows. It chirped the second they made eye contact.

"Where did you come from?" Were there more? He kneeled on the cold ground and stretched out his arm, but the little kitten clumsily stumbled away. He grabbed it by the scruff and rescued it from under the porch.

Drawing it to eye level, his stern tone demanded honesty as he asked, "Are you alone?"

The little rat didn't answer.

It was a tiny thing, but not newborn. Its ears were up, and its eyes were open. Specks of dirt clung to its downy grey fur. When he cradled it in his hand, it barely filled his palm.

"You're a complication I didn't need today."

The kitten mewed, and he carried it inside. The drill never changed. Find a box, grab an old towel, and give it a saucer of cream. The little guy wasn't the most agile, but once he stumbled up to the milk and realized it was food, his little motor started to purr.

"You're lucky I found you." The poor thing wouldn't have lasted one night once the temperature dropped. Greyson stared down at the dirty little rat. "Where's your mother?"

The cat was occupied with the milk, so Grey went to the kitchen to call Wren. She answered on the first ring.

"Thank you for calling The Haven, where stillness begins. This is Wren. How may I help you find your reset today?"

"Hey."

"Greyson?"

"Yeah."

There was a long pause. "Hi." She sounded unsure. "I'm glad you called."

Was she? He frowned. "I, uh, have something for you."

"You do?" The curiosity in her voice drove his mind to places he shouldn't go, but he liked when she got inquisitive.

Maybe that was why he didn't tell her what it was. "Yeah, you might want to get here soon."

"I can be there in five minutes. Is everything okay?"

"Everything's fine. See you in five." He hung up the landline and stared at the retro receiver.

He should have told her it was a cat.

It wasn't right to play games with her. That's what got them into trouble the other day. If he didn't want a repeat, he needed to be straight with her. No more wavering or mixed messages no matter how good her attention felt.

He picked up the phone and called her back. "Thank you for calling The Haven, where stillness begins. This is—"

"Wren."

"Grey?"

"Yeah. I, uh, just wanted to be clear. It's a cat."

"Oh." She sounded disappointed, but quickly recovered. "Is it one of ours?"

"I don't think so. He's small. I don't recognize him."

"It's a male?"

Craning his neck over the box, he lifted the cat and took a quick peek at his undercarriage. "Yes. He's dirty and probably needs a trip to the vet."

"Is he injured?"

"No, just cold."

"Okay. I'll be right there. Keep him warm and give him some milk if you have it."

"Already done."

When he hung up the phone, he felt better about clearing up any mixed messaging. "Your new mom's going to be here in a minute. Hang tight."

It chirped at him, droplets of white sprinkled over its tiny muzzle.

Greyson lifted it to eye level. "You're a mangy little thing."

Despite how dirty it was, he held it as he waited for Wren. The little guy vibrated happily as he hunkered into the crevice of

Greyson's elbow. When several minutes passed and Wren still hadn't arrived, he stopped pacing by the window.

The kitten was sound asleep, so he tucked it into the front pocket of his flannel shirt, allowing him to use his hands for other things while keeping an eye on the little guy. It also served as a good reminder that her visit to his home was about a cat. Only about a cat.

By the time Wren arrived at Greyson's, the sun was setting. She hadn't meant to take this long, but on her way out of The Haven, one guest after another stopped her for help. None of that mattered, however, as she pulled up to Greyson's cabin.

When he called, she'd suffered a surge of relief, only to deflate when he confessed he was only contacting her about a stray.

That was her! Hideaway Bay's official cat lady—spinster for life.

With a sigh, she grabbed the basket of supplies off the passenger seat and went right into Grey's house, only to pause when everything was silent. "Greyson?"

A low rumble stirred from the next room, where she found him sitting up and sleeping, his hands folded over his chest as he softly snored. She took a moment to just watch him.

Regret and confusion surfaced as she once again recalled his hands on her. The thought of him never kissing her like that again left her hollow.

She couldn't think like that.

Setting the basket down, she scanned the room for the cat. When she saw a box on the counter, she peeked inside only to find it empty.

"Uh-oh."

Searching the kitchen, she found no trace of the kitten anywhere. Making soft little cat calls, she whispered about the house, looking for the stray. When she returned to Greyson, she debated how he'd react to a possibly feral cat being lost in his house.

He looked so peaceful, she hated disturbing him. An open copy of *Walden Pond* rested over his chest. That was Grey. He always preferred the quiet classics, like Thoreau and Rilke. She closed the book and set it on the table.

"Grey." She tapped his hand. "Greyson, I'm here."

He drew in a deep breath and stretched his legs before opening his eyes. When he saw her, he smiled. "Hey."

"Where's the cat?"

He sprang up and scrubbed a hand over his face, then searched the cushions. He didn't seem to be fully awake yet, but the moment his brain roused, his panic disappeared. "He's here." Reaching into the front pocket of his shirt, he withdrew the tiny puff of grey.

"Awww." She took him into her hands and cradled him close. "He's precious."

"I call him Rat."

She frowned at him. "That's horrible."

He shrugged. "He looks like a wet rat."

She clicked her disapproval and spoke to the cat in motherese, "I won't let him name you after a rodent." It was a tradition at The Haven to name all the rescues after holiday words. That was why they had Figgy, Nog, Snowball, Garland, Spruce, and Sugarplum. "You look like a Tinsel to me."

"You can't call him that. He needs a manly name, or the others will bully him. He's already got a size disadvantage."

The kitten was definitely the runt of the litter. "There weren't any others?"

"Nope. Found him shivering under the porch."

"Thank goodness you heard him." She gave the kitten a nuzzle and then drew back. "First things first, you need a bath." She looked over at Greyson. "You probably want to throw that shirt in the wash. Chances are he has fleas."

She carried the cat to the kitchen and got to work. First, she set out a towel, soft washcloth, mild, unscented baby shampoo, and a small plastic cup, then she filled the basin of the sink with an inch of warm water.

From the corner of her eye, she caught Greyson stripping out of his shirt and tossing it into the wash closet down the hall. Her lips parted as he reached for the laundry detergent, thick ropes of muscle twisting along his arms as sinew stretched and rippled down his back with every turn. There wasn't an ounce of fat on him.

Her stomach dropped as he bent over. The curve of his spine and those exposed muscles were not something the average man could claim. She swallowed and removed her jacket, suddenly warm.

Greyson turned—caught her staring—and she dropped her attention back to Tinsel.

"Well," she said, forgetting for a moment what she was supposed to be doing. "How about some Enya to set the vibe. This is your first spa visit, after all."

She tapped her phone and pulled up one of the playlists she used at The Haven for various treatments. Enya's crooning voice paired perfectly with the trickling water. Tinsel sidestepped her fingers and stumbled along the counter, chirping away like a little cricket.

"What did he put in that milk? You're walking like you're drunk."

"He's probably feral," Greyson said, sneaking up behind her.

Her spine stiffened when his bare arm reached past her to scratch the kitten, and she realized he hadn't put on a fresh shirt.

"Possibly." She kept her eyes on Tinsel. "Kittens need socializing until about seven weeks. He looks younger than that. The fact that you found him alone is a little concerning."

"Nah, Rat's tough. He'll be just fine once he gets a good night's sleep and a good meal in him."

"His name is Tinsel." She shut off the faucet and prepped her washcloth with some shampoo, then sloshed it around the warm water. "He doesn't look like any of ours, which means there's another female out there needing to get spayed."

"You're dunking him in there? I thought cats don't like water."

"Older ones don't. It depends on how they're brought up. But, no, he's too young for a full bath." She cradled Tinsel to her chest, holding him close so he felt safe and secure. "You're okay, baby." Using her wet fingers, she gently stroked between his ears. His feather-like fur was fine enough that he was wet in only a few soft pets.

"I don't think he likes that."

The kitten chirped and squawked, its little needle claws pawing at her as he desperately sought escape. "Squirt a dab of shampoo in my hand." She held out her palm and Greyson gave the bottle a squeeze. Using the sink water, she formed a lather and stroked Tinsel, making sure to get all his hidden crevices.

"He hates it." Greyson frowned, hovering every step of the way.

Wren was careful to avoid the kitten's ears, eyes, and mouth. Once he was covered in suds, she held him over the sink and used the cup to rinse him off gently, shielding his face and making sure the water was warm, but he cried the entire time.

As soon as the water rinsed clear, she pulled him back to her chest. "Hand me the towel."

Greyson was already unfolding it. She swaddled Tinsel up like the world's smallest burrito, and he finally stopped crying. A second later, his eyes were closed, and his motor was softly purring again.

"I think we tired him out."

Greyson stepped closer to peek at the little bundle. "I still think he looks like a rat."

"He'll be cuter when he dries." She tipped her chin toward her basket on the counter. "There's a heating pad in there. Can you set it up in his box?"

While Greyson prepared the kitty condo, she rocked and hummed softly to Enya. Once he was done, she laid Tinsel inside and nestled a fresh towel around him to keep him warm. He was out cold.

"Sweet little feral gremlin."

They both reached out to pet him at the same time and stopped when their hands accidentally touched. Greyson pulled back first.

Great, back to awkwardness.

Wren cleaned up her supplies and pulled out the canister of kitten formula and a bottle. "He's still too small for solid food, so he's going to need formula for a while longer."

Greyson cleared his throat and looked up at the rafters. "Your, uh, shirt."

She looked down and gasped. The entire front of her T-shirt was soaked, her nipples pressing noticeably against the wet cotton. She grabbed a towel to cover her chest then decided not to.

"You act like you've never seen my boobs."

"Jesus, Wren." He still wouldn't look at her.

"Oh, come on, Grey. You're being ridiculous. I'm wearing more clothes than you."

He glared at her then, his gaze shifting to her chest and back to her eyes. Every shift of his breathing was evident in the rise and fall of his chest.

He acted like he hated the sight of her this way, but he obviously didn't. She couldn't understand why he'd fight something he so clearly wanted. Or, at least she thought he liked it. She wasn't entirely sure, since she didn't have much experience with men. And Greyson was unlike every other man she'd ever met.

With an unsteady breath, she met his stare and said, "I could... take it off."

"Don't start."

"Don't start what?" She took a step back, gathering the hem of her shirt and twisting it around her fingers.

"Wren."

The corner of her mouth curved upward. He could try to play the serious grump with her, but she knew him too well and couldn't resist teasing him when he got all stern and bossy.

Pushing her mouth into a pout, she held his stare. "But I'm all wet, Greyson."

He sprang for her. "Brat—"

She laughed and bolted, rushing around the rustic farm table, laughing as she zigged and zagged out of reach. When he finally caught her, they were both out of breath.

Something about being captured in his strength caused her insides to melt. She closed her eyes and sank into his hold. Her softness curved into his hardened body, and she savored the rightness of being in his arms.

Time stilled. Was he feeling it too? How could he not? Or, perhaps this was what it felt like for him with every woman.

The thought turned her stomach. She didn't want to picture him with other females, even though she was sure he'd had his fair share of experiences.

Panting softly, she carefully turned to face him without untangling from his hold. His grip tightened, his calloused palm dragging slowly over her hip. She arched back to look him in the eye, her back pressing against the edge of the table.

No matter what he said or how deeply he frowned, he wasn't unaffected. His lips parted as his gaze drifted to her chest.

Slowly, as if approaching a skittish wild animal twice her size, she leaned up and gently brushed her lips over his.

He stilled. Even his breathing seemed to stop. But he didn't pull back.

Softly, she whispered, "Did you want to take it off for me?"

The catch of his breath sent more heat rushing to her core. "You're out of control."

"Am I?" She purposely went languid in his arms, and he tugged her closer.

His knee wedged between her thighs, forcing her to straddle his leg. She showed no resistance, and his grip tightened. "What are you doing, Wren?"

"Giving in."

"To what?"

"You." The tension in her body went slack, and his gaze again dropped to her chest.

The heat of his calloused palm rode over her hip to cup her ass. He studied her face as if waiting for her to object. When she didn't, he slid his hand under the hem of her shirt. In the silence of the house, she could hear every ruffle of fabric and every intense breath.

Chills raced over her flesh as his rough fingertips treaded slowly against her skin. Higher. *Higher*. The anticipation was a drug that instantly addicted her but might also kill her. She needed his hands on her, rough and strong. She wanted him to grab her and pull off her clothes in a fit of madness, but Greyson was a master of control, and all she could do was wait, praying sensibility didn't return and scare him off.

Heat engulfed her damp flesh, and her lips parted when his warm palm finally cupped her breast. This was what she'd spent the last several days fantasizing about, unsure if she'd ever experience his hands on her again. It was slow and possessive, overwhelming her with a sense of safety that somehow felt equally dangerous.

"We're not doing this," he said as he proceeded to peel down the cup of her damp bra to drag the side of his thumb over the turgid tip of her nipple.

If he needed her to lie, she'd lie. "Of course not. That would be bad."

"Very bad."

"Horrible."

He paused, then leaned down slowly, angling his head as if to kiss her, but not closing the distance. Instead, he dipped his mouth close to hers and pulled away, teasing her with an almost kiss.

Her breath hitched as he coaxed her mouth open without even touching her lips. His fingers pinched her nipple and her spine arched. Licking swiftly across her open mouth, he got her to stretch toward him.

The side of his mouth curved with cocky satisfaction. He was a puppet master pulling her strings.

"Tease."

"Stay still."

At first, she tensed, unsure why he'd give such a command, then she realized he wanted control. He withdrew his hands, and she tried not to show disappointment. Patience was the key with Greyson, and she'd waited an eternity for him to touch her like this.

He looked down at her body, his large fingers framing her ribs and then dragging slowly to her hips, where he squeezed and pulled her more firmly onto his thigh. She moaned softly at the pressure of him, hard and hungry. Proof he was not unaffected by her.

He was starting to realize she wouldn't stop him. He could do whatever he wanted and she would let him. She knew this infuriated him, but she didn't care. His control was equally maddening, and she wanted to see him snap.

Her hands gripped the edge of the table, pushing her breast out in invitation. His gaze roamed over her like a hungry caress. He teased the hem of her shirt, longing in his touch as much as it rested in his eyes.

"Tell me to stop, Wren."

She shook her head. She wouldn't. She wanted this too much.

His eyes met hers in silent warning.

"Do it," she whispered, and he shoved the shirt up, exposing her breasts, and pulled down her bra as far as it could go without coming off. Exposed and constricted, she gasped.

He cursed under his breath. "Tell me to take my hands off you."

She met his stare, making it perfectly clear that she had no intention of stopping him. "Or... you could kiss me." She slowly trailed her fingers between her breasts. "Here."

He grabbed the back of her neck and jerked her close, sealing his mouth to hers. Demanding and deep, he took possession of not just her mouth but her entire being as he yanked her down on his thigh so her body throbbed against his muscular leg. Her fingers curled into his bare, broad shoulders.

"This is the last time this happens, you hear?"

She caught his face and pulled his mouth back to hers. "You don't make the rules."

He broke the kiss, hauling her onto the table. "I mean it, Wren. This goes no further than this."

"Since when are you such a prude?"

He snatched her arms, pinned them on the table above her head, locked tightly in his one-handed grip. "I mean it. No more poking. No more teasing. And no more coming over here all done up."

She laughed. "All done up? Grey, this is what I put on in the morning. There's nothing special about what I'm wearing."

He growled. "You look... hotter."

Something inside of her clenched. The furthest Grey had ever gone with his compliments was to tell her she looked nice. He thought she looked hot? No, not hot—hotter.

Something was definitely going on between them, and she didn't think it had to do with wills or weddings.

"You make me feel hot." The confession cast a moment of intense silence.

Everything stilled.

She swallowed, breathing in his familiar scent, a mixture of cedar, the outdoors, and pure masculinity. This close, she could see the tiny scars that nicked his skin from labor and woodworking over the years.

His hand tightened around her wrists. "Grey, if it's just tonight, make it count."

"What are you doing to me?" His fingers traced slowly down her throat, as if he were testing his limits and hers. She didn't move her hands from where he'd pressed them into the table.

Lifting her chin, she gave him full access to anywhere on her body he wanted to touch. The drag of those slightly calloused, work-roughened hands sent a shiver through her as they grazed slowly beyond her collarbone to hold her breasts possessively.

Her gaze softened to a half-lidded stare as she let the sense of his touch wash over her.

Greyson never spoke unless he had something meaningful to say. But when he looked at her like he was looking at her now, a thousand unspoken words were exchanged between them.

Need. Want. Lust. Hunger. Obsession. Denial. Anguish.

Fantasies from the last fifteen years flooded her mind as she waited for him to lose control and finally take what he wanted.

His fingers, reverent and gentle, whispered desires over her skin as his eyes spoke of longing. The intensity of his stare set a claim, and the energy radiating from his body left no argument about what he considered his territory.

But when he spoke, he said the opposite. "This is wrong, Wren."

"It's not."

"It is. We have too much history. I don't see you…like this."

He was a flesh-and-blood contradiction, but, in the end, actions always mattered more than words. When his warm palm, again, cupped her breast possessively, she arched into his touch, and his gaze filled with panic.

The moment held, like a silent negotiation that hit like a reprimand. "You can't expect me not to respond when you touch me, Grey. It feels too good."

His nostrils flared as the internal debate ticked across his stern face. His hand shifted, and she caught his wrist, stilling him before he could pull away.

"Please."

He studied her through a veil of doubt and confusion. They'd never done anything like this before—not until recently in the shed —but she'd be lying to say she hadn't imagined it a thousand times. However, nothing compared to the reality of his hands on her.

She pressed her body into his touch, so there was no misunderstanding. "Please, Greyson."

His silence was torture.

Again, he captured her hand, returning it to the table, above her head, with an unmistakable press that warned her to keep it there. She feared he'd fix her shirt and end whatever this was.

Instead, he trailed his fingers down her front, between her breasts. She closed her eyes, lost in the teasing sensations, achingly turned on by every torturous caress. When his tongue traced the tip of her nipple, she gasped.

His grip closed around her hips, wedging her against him with a deliberate tug. Only, this time, it wasn't his thigh he pressed against her.

The firm friction was so precisely placed. Heat rushed past every nerve ending along her spine, tickling the hairs at the nape of her neck. Pressure built at her core as dark wanting flooded her insides.

His mouth closed over her nipple and more pressure built as he sucked and teased. Her body rocked against his, riding out the friction he created with slow, grinding thrusts of his hips.

His hands were quick and accurate, flicking open the button of her jeans and sliding his hand over the lace of her panties. She was soaked and had no doubt he felt her arousal through the damp silk.

His fingers rubbed over her and she moaned at the exquisite contact. His body rocked the table beneath them as he ground into her, his palm pressing against her throbbing clit, edging her toward a point of no return.

He pinched one nipple while his mouth suckled at the other. She'd never experienced something so comprehensive. Pleasure overwhelmed her. She became a raw nerve of sensation and then...

Her back bowed, and the sound that escaped her was nothing like the sounds she made in private. He didn't let up. Hand stuffed in the front of her jeans, he rubbed and sucked and worked her higher and higher until reality blurred into a haze of pleasure and sin.

"That's it, baby" he rasped against her flesh. "Come all over your pretty panties."

Her lips parted in shock. His words, his touch, it was so much more than she expected from him. An exquisite gift that left her trembling in shock as the pleasure rolled through her.

She shivered as he slowly withdrew his fingers. Panting in awe, she waited for the world to return to its axis, and looked up at him. He leaned down to kiss her, but the moment she moved to meet him, he drew back, teasing her again.

Was that the deal? He didn't trust his control and needed her to remain still? She rested her head back on the table, surrendering to his command. Slowly, he traced his soft lips over hers, rewarding her with a gentle kiss.

"So pretty," he whispered over her mouth. "So pure." He dragged his lips over her cheekbone until he was nibbling her ear. "Did you like coming on my fingers, Wren?"

She whimpered, arousal soaking her once more as she discovered this new side of Greyson. Rather than answer, she kissed him in a way that left no room for mistaking her satisfaction.

He cupped the back of her neck and lifted her in one fluid shift. She turned her face into the shelter of his shoulder. Her legs wrapped around his waist as he rubbed those calloused fingers down her spine. No one had held her like this since she was a child. It seemed strange to feed such a juvenile part of her moments after he'd treated her like a flesh-and-blood woman, but somehow the way he pleasured her and then protected her went hand in hand. It felt—

Enya cut off. The sweet moment interrupted by the obnoxious ring from her phone on the counter.

"Ignore it." He seemed reluctant to put her down, but her father was usually the only one who called her cell and only when he needed something that couldn't wait.

"I can't." She didn't want him to let go, but there could be an issue at The Haven or something might be wrong with Bodhi.

She wanted to stay in this moment as long as possible, fearful that life would permanently throw them back into a reality of denial and longing.

What would happen next? Was this the end or were they just getting started? "Let me just see what he wants." Then maybe they could come back to this and take it into his bedroom.

The ringing stopped and then the phone instantly rang again. They both sighed, knowing that if someone was calling twice, something was probably wrong.

"I'm sorry," she said, sliding her legs down his body to put her feet back on the floor.

Heat rushed to her head the moment he let go. She blushed as she adjusted her bra and shirt. Disoriented and unsteady, she rushed to the kitchen and grabbed the phone, caught off guard when Soren's name flashed on the screen, and a hundred realizations hit at once.

"Shit." She pulled the phone to her ear and answered. "Hey."

"Where are you?"

"I'm, uh, right around the corner."

"Did I get the time wrong? Tonight's our date, right?"

"Yes. I mean, no, you didn't get it wrong. Sorry. I just got tied up with..." She looked at Greyson, who watched her with an unreadable expression.

He knew her too well and instantly realized she wasn't speaking to Bodhi.

Regret flooded her as she met his stare. "I can be there in ten minutes."

"Okay. I'll wait for you."

"See you soon." She ended the call and looked at Greyson apologetically. "I'm really sorry."

"You have to go." His disappointment quadrupled her own.

"I wish I could stay."

"Who was that?"

This mess was her own doing. She didn't want him to change

his mind or regret anything they'd done, nor did she think bringing his brothers into the conversation would help matters. "A guest."

"Don't lie to me, Wren."

Her eyes pleaded for understanding, but too much reality was returning. "It was Soren. I told him I'd hang out with him tonight."

If he had an internal reaction, she couldn't tell. His expression was unreadable and his tone indifferent. "You better get going then."

"Grey—"

He turned away and walked down the hall to his room. Very aware of the time, she looked at the cat box and the front door. Soren was waiting. She went after Grey anyway, unable to leave things on a bad note.

He slipped on a sweater. His sandy blond hair stood on end.

"We're just hanging out, Greyson."

"Let's not have lies between us, Wren. I was there when you called him to arrange a date."

That was true, but that was before she and Greyson kissed. "I can cancel—"

"Don't."

Taken aback that he'd tell her not to cancel a date with his brother after what they just did, she blinked at him in confusion. He said no lies, but he seemed to be avoiding the truth.

"But... what about everything that just happened?"

"I told you that was the last time. We both know anything between us is wrong and it won't work out."

She didn't know that, and neither did he, but she was too hurt by his indifference to say that to him.

Then he looked back at her, as if surprised she was still standing there. "You're gonna be late."

She closed her mouth to stop her chin from trembling. It was stunning how much his apathy hurt. She blinked away the sting and swallowed, not even knowing how to respond to such a comment.

He brushed past her and left the room. She needed a few

seconds to find her bearings before she could follow. When she returned to the kitchen, she picked up the canister of kitten formula with shaky hands.

"He'll need a bottle of formula four times a day." She rattled off directions as a weak defense mechanism so she didn't humiliate herself even more. "Once we see how he adjusts, we can wean him off slowly and introduce solid foods."

"What?" He turned and frowned. "I'm not keeping the cat."

"He's too small to live outside on his own with the others. This is only for a couple of weeks."

"Wren, I don't have space in my life for a kitten."

"Finders keepers, Greyson."

Maybe she wanted to punish him. Why should he get away from every situation without taking responsibility? He was going to take accountability for something, at least for a little while.

"I can take him to the sanctuary once he's a little bigger, but it's too cold to put him out there now. He doesn't have a mother to feed him, so it looks like the universe picked you. Congratulations. It's a boy." She pressed the canister of dry formula into his chest and let go so he had no choice but to catch it. "Directions are on the back."

She was losing her battle with her emotions and needed to get out of there. Gathering the basket of supplies, she bundled up without meeting his eyes.

"Wren—"

"I have to go, Greyson. I'll check in tomorrow to see how Tinsel's doing."

It would be awkward to see him, but she had a responsibility to the cat. When she reached the door, she looked back, giving him one last chance to apologize for being so dismissive.

He said nothing, so she swallowed down her hurt and accepted that he'd rejected her yet again. Somehow, this time hurt more than all the times that came before.

CHAPTER 8

"More Than Just a Mistletoe Moment"

Soren's fingers drummed against the heated steering wheel, restless energy coursing through him. Wren had slipped by the car to ask for a few more minutes so she could change. Nothing like an afterthought at the start of a date.

This had to be a date, right? She'd been the one to call him and suggest they see what happened. He assumed that meant she was considering his proposal to take their friendship to the next level.

Glancing at the rose sitting in the cupholder, he flicked the switch to heat her seat. This was definitely a date.

Adjusting the wool lapel of his coat, his attention fixed on the front door of her tiny house. The interior lights went out, and she appeared, much more put together than she had been ten minutes ago.

He climbed out of the warm SUV to get her door. "Your chariot awaits."

"I'm so sorry I was late."

"It's okay."

"There was an issue with one of the cats."

"It happens." He pulled the seatbelt over her and clipped it, breathing in her familiar, delicate scent—something between vanilla and winter air. "You smell nice."

She laughed nervously. "Thanks."

Shutting the door, he rounded the car, returning to the driver's seat. Soren expected a little awkwardness tonight, at least at the start, but he knew what he wanted and he wasn't holding back. He planned to prove that their connection was enough of a foundation for a good future. It might be strange at times, but he intended to break down any polite barriers quickly and get her accustomed to his touch and attention, so any unease would fade quickly.

It shouldn't be too difficult. They were already familiar with each other. This was just a different sort of familiar, one he'd considered many times before but never honestly thought she'd be down for exploring.

"Ready?" He put the car in reverse.

"Where are we going?"

"I reserved the private dining room at Salt & Ember." When she did a double-take, he knew he'd impressed her.

"How did you do that with such short notice?"

He shot her a cocky grin. "I have my ways."

Salt & Ember booked up months in advance. She didn't need to know he had a table on retainer. That was a perk of good tipping and frequently impressing women, which guaranteed he only dined with those who were sure things. He took care of others, and others took care of him, but Wren wasn't like the others, so he needed to go above and beyond for her or she'd call him out on his bullshit.

"You deserve the best and I wanted to treat you."

She shifted uncomfortably. "Soren, I'm underdressed for Salt & Ember."

Shit. He hadn't thought about that. Glancing to his right, he could only see her coat, which was a man's flannel. *Greyson's*. A spike of irritation through his chest at the sight of his brother's oversized shirt draped across her shoulders. "What are you wearing?"

She glanced down and frowned. "Jeans and a shirt. Soren, I can't eat there in this."

He checked the time. "I have an idea." He veered off course to take a detour down Main Street and parked in front of the local boutique, House of Pearl. "We've got a few minutes."

Before she could object, he hopped out and went to her door. "Soren, wait. I have clothes at home."

"Don't be ridiculous. It was my mistake not to give you a heads up about the dress code. Now, I get to treat you like a queen before I sweep you off your feet."

He led her into the boutique and held the door. They were immediately greeted by a well-dressed woman whose eyes lit up with recognition.

"Mr. Hawthorne, welcome to House of Pearl. Can I help you find something special this evening?"

"We're in a bit of a rush. Is Liza around?" Liza was the manager.

"She's in the back. I can get her for you."

"Please do. Tell her Soren Hawthorne is here with a guest."

The woman glanced at Wren, who fidgeted uncomfortably in her understated clothes.

A moment later Liza appeared, her heels clicking against polished marble. "Soren, to what do I owe the pleasure?" She kissed his cheek and smiled at Wren.

"Slight oversight. Wren and I have a reservation at Salt & Ember, but I sprung it on her last minute. She needs a complete wardrobe change."

"I'm sure we can manage that." Liza smiled at Wren with the practiced warmth of someone accustomed to last-minute transformations. "I'll need your sizes and an idea of your style."

The women disappeared to the back while Soren found a seat.

The floor attendant brought him a glass of sparkling water with a twist of lime while he waited. They always took good care of customers, but Wren would get the elite treatment. Not only did the Hawthornes own the building, it was their fisheries that sourced the pearls used in all the jewelry.

"Liza asked me to give you this." The store attendant slipped him a folded piece of cream linen paper.

"Thanks." He unfolded the note and read.

She's insisting on a budget.

He rolled his eyes and suppressed a growl of frustration. "Tell her I said no prices. She gets whatever she wants. I'll handle the bill."

"Yes, sir."

The floor attendant disappeared, and a moment later, Wren appeared, no longer in her street clothes and her expression far from happy. A sapphire silk dress clung to her curves like liquid starlight.

"Soren, this is too much."

"I don't want to hear it, Wren."

"Well, you're gonna. I'm not letting you buy me clothes."

"Why not?"

"Because! I have my own money and my own dresses at home."

Even barefoot, she looked ethereal—all long legs and graceful curves. "You don't own anything like that."

"Either I'm paying or the date's off."

He stood and closed the distance, surprise flashing in her eyes when he boxed her in at the counter. The scent of her skin mixed with expensive fabric and his pulse hammered against his throat. "No. You're not. You're going to get your sexy ass back in that dressing room and find some shoes. Then, you're going to pick out a necklace, earrings, and a decent coat, and not say another word about the cost."

"No, I'm—"

He leaned in and lowered his voice, close enough that his breath ghosted across her ear. "Don't fight me on this, Wren. You won't win. Not this time."

She appeared stunned that he could be so firm and unbending, but he refused to pussy-foot into this territory with her. If she wanted to experience what it was like to date him, he planned to hold nothing back.

"You can't—"

"I just did." He gently took her wrist and gave her a nudge toward the dressing rooms. "Go."

Her lips firmed, but she didn't argue. Stomping off, she grumbled, "I'm not happy about this."

He only replied, "You're beautiful."

When he paid the bill, slipping the black card across marble with practiced discretion, he made sure Wren didn't see the cost. It wasn't about the price. It was about showing her that he enjoyed treating her.

The clothes she'd arrived in were carried out in a boutique gift bag. He glanced at the quilted flannel shirt she'd worn as a jacket, fighting the urge to toss it into a bonfire when he got home. Leave it to Greyson to mark territory he never planned to occupy.

When they reached Salt & Ember, Soren didn't wait for a valet to help her out. He opened her door and enjoyed the sight of her toned legs turning toward him in those sexy gold heels. The cool harbor breeze carried hints of salt and winter pine, mixing with the warm glow spilling from the restaurant's windows. He took her arm and nodded to the attendant.

"Keys are in the console."

A doorman stood at the entrance, his breath visible in the frigid air. "Good evening, Mr. Hawthorne."

Soren kept a hand on Wren's lower back at all times, getting her accustomed to his touch. The hostess recognized him as soon as they set foot in the foyer, and had their coats collected with efficient grace.

Salt & Ember sprawled like a gilded fortress on the coast, its stone facade weathered by decades of sea spray and winter storms. It had three floors and enclosed balconies that overlooked the harbor where the lighthouse illuminated the rocky banks. Fireplaces crackled in every dining room, casting dancing shadows that warmed the air with hints of vanilla and cedar. Candles flickered in the intimate ambiance, creating amber reflections across crystal stemware.

Despite the bitter cold, they lit the lanterns lining the stone path that led to the cliffs every night. He'd typically suggest a walk to the banks after dinner if not for the ice coating the ground like a treacherous mirror. As it was, the lanterns still made an elegant picture from the sweeping view they had on the third-floor enclosed balcony.

A waiter approached in black livery with a linen cloth draped over his arm. "May I start you off with something to drink?"

Soren suggested their finest champagne. Once the waiter retreated, he settled into the high-back velvet chair to study Wren. "Are you still mad at me?"

She pursed her lips. "I don't like high-handedness."

He smirked playfully, enjoying how the jewels she picked elongated her neck and caught the candlelight. She was far sexier than she realized. "Was it high-handed, or was it charming? I think charming."

"Don't try that flirty stuff on me. I'm immune."

"We'll see about that." His gaze dropped to the deep V of her dress, where silk clung to curves that had haunted his imagination. "You're stunning. Blue suits you."

"Thank you."

"See how easy that was?"

The waiter appeared with the champagne, condensation beading along the sleek bottle. He described tonight's menu in reverent tones. Soren studied Wren as she listened attentively, admiring her unique beauty that seemed to glow brighter in the intimate lighting.

Bohemian yet statuesque, Wren possessed the sort of body any man would have no trouble worshipping. Her skin glowed with health, just like her glossy blonde hair, thick and wavy, with natural sun-kissed highlights that caught the light. She'd truly grown into a gorgeous woman who didn't seem to realize her own power.

"I'll give you some time to decide."

When the waiter quietly backed away, she rolled her eyes at Soren. "You're over the top."

"What can I say? I like to put on a good show."

"Well, it's enough already. I haven't been this pampered..." She laughed, the sound like wind chimes in the warm air. "Ever."

"That, beautiful, is a shame." He laced his fingers with hers, and she stilled, her gaze dropping to their entwined hands as her smile slightly faltered.

"Soren." Disentangling her fingers from his grip, she tucked her hands in her lap and sat back. "Um, I think we need to slow down."

"Why?"

"Because it's a lot. First, the dress and the shoes and the jewelry. Then this place. You're opening doors and holding my hand. Things are moving too fast for me."

"I warned you I wasn't going to waste time."

"And I'm warning you to slow down. This is... weird. We're friends."

She didn't understand, so he made himself crystal clear. "I've pictured you naked a dozen times, Wren. And that's just today."

"Soren!" she hissed, glancing around nervously, but they were alone, at the best seat in the house.

"What?" He shrugged. "We're more than friends. I'm done pretending I don't see you. I'm not immune to you, and you're not immune to me. No more polite lies for whatever bullshit reason we had for taking so long to get here."

She looked like she wanted to call for help, but they were

completely secluded on the enclosed balcony. "Don't say stuff like that."

"Why? You'd rather I lie and pretend I've never thought of you in a sexual way? I'm a man, and you're a beautiful woman."

She sipped her champagne and flushed, the darkening of her cheeks adding to her natural glow. "It's a little too much."

"Fine. I'll tone it down. But I've given this a lot of thought, Wren. I want this. And I go after what I want in life."

THE CHAMPAGNE in Wren's stomach fizzed wildly as she recognized the determination blazing in Soren's dark eyes. It wasn't that he studied her like prey. He studied her like a challenge. And Soren hated to lose. If anyone were going to inherit the Fishery, it would most likely be him.

"Does it scare you to realize that I want you?"

Her heart stuttered as nervous energy made her reach for her champagne flute again. "You have to stop."

"What am I doing? We're just talking."

This was more than talking. He was never so explicit or direct with her, saying such blatantly flirtatious things. No one spoke to her with such shameless intentions, and she didn't know how to respond. There was no way to shield herself from his directness, especially when he looked at her like she was something he planned to devour.

She took a long swallow of champagne, bubbles dancing on her tongue. "What scares me is that determined expression in your eyes. I'm not that easy, Soren. Just because you want something doesn't mean you automatically get it."

"We'll see. I can be very persuasive."

"Obviously. But I'm not like other women. As much as I appreciate your generosity, I'm not used to being spoiled. I don't think you're going to get the outcome you're hoping for."

"Give it time." He leaned back and studied her with predatory focus. "You'll learn to like being taken care of, Wren, maybe even expect it over time. I enjoy treating you."

She frowned, unease prickling along her spine. "It's a little intense." She was used to Soren's confidence, but she'd never been the sole target of his relentless pursuit.

"That's because we can be real with each other. We're past the point of fake, Wren. We've been through too much together."

She shifted in her seat to reach the champagne. Soren beat her to the bottle and refilled her glass with practiced grace.

She took a sip. "Okay, let's say this works out. How do you see it going between us?"

"Well, I think we both want to stay in Hideaway Bay."

"Especially if you inherit the company," she said with a bite of condescension.

"That might be the catalyst that got us here, but it's not the only reason I'm interested."

"No?"

"It's not an unpleasant predicament, Wren. We'd make a decent couple."

"Mmm, decent." She sipped her champagne, annoyed by the cold calculation silently surrounding his motives.

"You understand what I mean. We get along. I make you laugh. You'd want for nothing."

"Yes, I'm so tired from all the wanting."

"Make jokes all you want. But I mean it. You'd literally want for nothing." His gaze deliberately dropped to her chest.

"Stop it, Soren," she hissed, covering her cleavage with her hand.

He chuckled and sat back. "I'm just saying I'd take care of you financially and in other ways. We can leave it at that for now."

Soren wasn't one to brag. He simply demonstrated. He'd spent his whole life being underestimated and proving people wrong. She understood him well enough to be intimidated by the determined expression burning in his eyes.

She searched her mind for any argument that might throw him off course. "What about kids?"

"What about them? I've always pictured myself with a family."

"You have?"

"Of course. I'd like four."

"Four?"

"Sure. Or three." He shrugged. "Two seems too few, and five might be pushing it."

"You think?" Maybe she needed something stronger than champagne for this conversation. "So, let's say you get the company—"

"Only one way for that to happen." His gaze dropped possessively to her lips.

"Don't stare at me like that. This is a hypothetical."

"Fine. I get the company—and a hot wife."

"Give me strength," she mumbled into the champagne flute. "Who's taking care of all these children you plan to father?"

"My wife. I want a traditional dynamic. I'll be the provider. She'll be the nurturer."

"See, we're already having issues." She reached for the bottle, swatting his hand away when he tried to beat her there. Dumping more champagne into her glass, she swirled it under her nose before sipping. "I've got The Haven."

"Yeah, but you'd be in a different position. Once you have the capital backing, it wouldn't take long to finish the property plans. Then you could hire people to run it for you. You'd have plenty of time to do the things you really love."

She scowled at him. "I'm already doing the things I love. I like being the manager, Soren. The Haven is mine. I don't want someone else to run it."

"Fine, you could stay involved, but you'd have enough staff to delegate the parts of the job you don't enjoy. No one loves their job one hundred percent, Wren."

She did. Even the challenging parts, like investing in ads and figuring out how to get a lucrative return on her investment. Every challenge motivated her to some degree. It was hard, but that made it that much more rewarding.

"Listen, Wren, I love seeing your dreams come to life. We all knew this was your vision since our moms passed. You've done what you said you would and made an incredible tribute to honor her life. People from all over the country travel to Hideaway Bay just to stay at your place."

"Thank you."

His praise meant more than he realized. The Haven wasn't only named after her mother, it was designed to share all the things she loved with the world. She'd lost her life too early and hadn't had time to create a legacy, but Wren created one for her.

"I respect that you're an independent woman, Wren. But, if we were to actually do this, nothing would stop me from spoiling you."

"I don't need to be spoiled."

"I realize you don't. No one does." He took her hand again, this time not letting her go when she tried to pull away. "I know you can handle the work. But that doesn't stop me from wanting to make your life a little easier."

Thankfully, the waiter returned before she figured out a response.

After placing her order, she excused herself, needing a few minutes to find her bearings. Unfortunately, the champagne was already hitting her, making the world softer around the edges. By the time she wobbled back to the table in her fancy gold heels, she acknowledged she should probably stop drinking, but there Soren sat, waiting with that same intense stare, so she decided to have another glass.

Soren continued to push her boundaries throughout the meal, holding her gaze a few seconds too long, unapologetically flirting, taking any chance he got to brush his hand over hers. The more the champagne went to her head, the more she found herself enjoying his uninterrupted attention, basking in the heat of his focus like a cat in sunlight.

By dessert, she was completely drunk. "I think I drank too much cham—" She hiccupped. "—pagne." She giggled and wagged her finger at him. "Don't try anything funny on the way home."

"I make no promises."

"You better. I need you to be Protective-Soren, now." She cupped her hand at the side of her mouth and whispered a fake cry for help, "Save me! I'm smashed, on a date with a very determined man who thinks I'm pretty."

Leaning back in his seat like a king occupying a throne, he chuckled. "Very pretty." Holding his jaw in the V of his forefinger and thumb, he eyed her carefully. "Don't worry. I'll always protect you from bad boys."

"Including yourself?"

"I'm not one of the bad ones."

She smiled, her face warm and pleasantly numb. "No, you're not."

The waiter returned for one final lap to ask if they wanted coffee. Soren lifted a brow in question and she figured why the hell not.

"Two coffees."

The waiter disappeared, and they fell into a comfortable silence broken only by the distant crash of waves against the cliffs below.

"This is nice," he commented, studying her the way he had most of the night.

"Yeah. The food was outstanding."

"No, I meant this—being here with you."

She smiled as her vision wavered around the objects on the table until it settled unsteadily on him. "I'm actually having more fun than I thought I would."

"See? We're good together. Familiar."

They were familiar with each other, but she didn't know if she could do this again. The weight of her guilt pressed against her conscience. "You're really special to me, Soren."

"I have the same feelings."

"So special that I don't think we should go on another date."

"Wren—"

"Just hear me out." She splayed her fingers to hold back his objections. "I only have Bodhi and you guys. You're my entire world. If we go there, and it doesn't work out, I lose a quarter of my world."

"You'd never lose me."

"You can't say that. People fall in and out of love all the time. Divorce happens, and it can get really nasty."

"Do you honestly think I could ever be nasty to you? My brothers would skin me alive."

"Or, they'd take your side, and I'd lose even more of the people I love." There was just too much to risk.

Once again, he took her hand, his thumb tracing circles against her palm. "That's not going to happen. I swear to you, Wren. Even if things don't work out between us, I give you my word that I would never disrespect you in any way."

She sighed, doubt churning in her stomach like acid. One way or another, someone was going to get hurt. And despite all of his well-intentioned promises, Soren had a short temper and he was known to be a poor loser when he didn't get his way. "You realize I had a date with Logan."

"I'm aware. He said it didn't go well."

She still carried guilt about the way she and Logan left things. All the Hawthornes had short fuses and regardless of how much they believed they were in control of their emotions, she'd seen each of them lose that control from time to time.

Unfortunately, she was drunk, and that meant her words weren't as accessible as she'd hoped. She could only come up with temporary excuses at the moment. "I have to think about this."

"But you'll consider it?"

She hesitated. Was she actually willing to cross so many invisible lines? No, but maybe she already had. Logan tried to kiss her. Greyson touched her. And, now, she was on a date with Soren.

"I don't want anyone to get hurt." Protecting them was her primary concern.

"I don't want that either."

"And I'm not making any promises. I don't want to be rushed into anything."

"No one's rushing you."

"What about the stuff with Magnus?"

"Leave him out of this. I understand that's part of how we got here, but it's not my motive."

She frowned in confusion, champagne making her thoughts sluggish. "What is?"

"You, Wren." He laughed softly, the sound warm and intimate. "I want this. I want to see what it can be like with us."

"Really?" He spoke as if he'd thought about this much longer than she expected.

"Yeah. When my dad made his ridiculous announcement, of course, you were the first thought that came to mind. Not because I thought I could get you to agree, but because I realized this is our time. There's a peacefulness about you. It's easier to breathe when you're nearby. You've always helped me find a sort of calm I can't find with anyone else. You're the one, Wren. You're the woman I'm meant to be with."

"Soren..."

"I understand I'm saying too much again, but it's the truth. You're the only person I've ever been able to picture a future with. You've always been with us. Why not make it official?"

She stared down at the table, as candlelight danced across the white linen. "I have to tell you something."

"What?"

She swallowed and forced the confession out. "I've been seeing your brother."

"I'm aware. We just talked about this—"

"Not Logan."

The air stilled and a chill slipped in. "You've been seeing Greyson?"

Maybe seeing wasn't the right word. "Not officially. But there have been some moments." Despite the chill, her skin burned with shame. "Does it seem hot in here?"

"Wren, look at me."

She didn't want to. What kind of woman dates three brothers? She was making a mess of things. How could she sit here and claim she didn't want to risk what they shared when she was risking all of it?

"Wren."

"What?" Concern flashed in his eyes when she looked up at him with regret. "I didn't pick any of this. You all came to me."

"Greyson came to you?"

She shook her head, embarrassed. He knew Greyson wouldn't do that. Which meant he probably also knew she threw herself at him. Her vision blurred, as he spread his hands in a calming gesture.

"Okay, okay. Don't get upset. I was just taken off guard. I didn't think Grey was in the running. He showed no interest in taking over the company when Dad—"

"It's not about the company with him."

Soren laughed, but the sound held an edge. "Wren, if you think the company is the prize here, you've seriously misinterpreted the situation." He took her hand. "I told you. You're the real prize."

Now, she felt like prey. Soren was just one Hawthorne. How would she ever deal with three of them? Even if she fell for one, others would get hurt. Someone was going to lose. Maybe all of them.

The moral dilemma became less complicated as she reminded herself of the only promise that mattered—she would only marry for love. As long as she kept true to her promise, she'd figure the rest out eventually.

Looking back at her friend, she smiled awkwardly and

confessed, "I had too much to drink and it's making me say things and think things that…" She shrugged. "I don't know. I'm drunk."

"It's okay. You never have to be embarrassed in front of me."

She squeezed his hand. "Thanks, Soren."

The drive home was quiet, filled only with the hum of the engine and the distant sound of waves crashing against the shore.

"Tired?"

She turned to watch him as his eyes focused on the road. "A little."

"When can I see you again?"

"My schedule's usually the same most days."

"How about Saturday night?"

That constituted prime real estate, and she wondered if she was making decisions too fast. She also realized Soren wasn't planning on backing off any time soon. Maybe if she gave in, he'd realize they were better off as friends. They were, weren't they?

"Sure. Saturday works." It wasn't like she had a demanding social calendar to check.

"Great. I'll make all the arrangements."

Of course, he would.

When they got to her house, he shut off the car and walked her to the door. She dreaded any awkwardness and worried how far he might go to prove this was a date.

Unlocking the door, she turned to him with uncertainty. "Thank you for a beautiful night and the clothes."

"It was my pleasure."

"Well…" Moments like this were so painful. She just wanted to get through it. "Goodnight." She hugged him, but he caught her hips, then slowly moved his hands up her back, fingers trailing through the silk.

"Goodnight, Wren."

"Soren…" She feared he wasn't going to let her get away without a kiss.

"Do I scare you?"

"Of course, not."

"You're not trapped here."

Although he held her intimately, she was free to leave. With an awkward smile, she said, "Well, goodnight then."

They broke apart, and she took a step, but Soren caught her hand and tugged her back. It was just enough to set her off balance as he backed her into the wall and caged her in with his body.

"Did you honestly think I'd let you get away without a kiss goodnight?"

She sucked in a breath as he gave her a moment of warning, his body radiating heat in the cold night air. Her heart raced as he closed the distance.

"Tell me that you're not the least bit curious and I'll stop." He framed her face with his hands, tucking her hair behind her ears with gentle reverence. "Last chance to push me away, Wren."

She had plenty of time to tell him no, but she was silent, caught between terror and anticipation.

"Don't be scared."

Her breath hitched as soft lips glided over hers. Slow and seductive, teasing her mouth open with practiced skill. It was nothing like Greyson's hungry, desperate kisses, and she immediately felt guilty for thinking of Greyson at a time like this.

"You're not kissing me back," he whispered, as his hand slid into her hair.

Slowly, she traced the tip of her tongue against his, and he groaned, taking control and deepening the kiss. He was measured and deliberate, the kind of kisser who had so much skill one could never get bored.

Enjoying the feel of his mouth on hers, she leaned into him, looping her arms over his shoulders. His hand tightened at her hips as the other threaded through her hair. He kept her on her toes, and when he pulled away, she swayed, warm and slightly disappointed to see it end.

He touched her lower lip with his thumb. "I knew it would be like that—kissing you."

"Like what?"

"Life-affirming."

She might have rolled her eyes if she weren't still reeling, her pulse hammering wildly against her throat. Who knew one kiss could confuse her so much?

"You're dangerous, Soren Hawthorne."

"Never to you, Wren Wilde. Never to you."

CHAPTER 9

"Oh, Damn, Look What I Forgot"

THE MOMENT WREN STEPPED OUTSIDE, TWO THINGS BECAME CLEAR. Her aunt had arrived at The Haven sometime that morning, and snow would follow. Both left their mark on the atmosphere—one scientific, pressure dropping like a stone, the other wafting a trail of patchouli and rosemary like breadcrumbs from a fairy tale.

She smiled and sought out Bodhi, who would undoubtedly be sharing time with his sister, Astrid. The Sol Room drew Wren like a magnet—that sun-drenched sanctuary where retreat guests found a peaceful place to sip tea and reflect in quiet, but also where Bodhi often liked to sit and read.

"There she is!" Aunt Astrid rose the instant she spotted her, arms opening wide and disrupting the morning peace like a whirl-wind in silk scarves. "Oh, would you feast your eyes on this glow? You're absolutely luminous!" She pulled Wren close, whispering against her ear with breath that smelled of ashwagandha and echinacea tea, "Only two things paint a woman with such radiance. You're not carrying a child, are you, pumpkin?"

"No!" Heat climbed Wren's neck as her eccentric aunt's smile widened with knowing satisfaction.

"Then it's a man. I demand every delicious detail."

"Sorry to disappoint you, Aunt Astrid, but my love life is as mundane as ever." Certain secrets deserved protection when Aunt Astrid entered the picture with her uncanny ability to read people like open books.

Wren's aunt frowned, her wooden bangles clacking as she gestured dramatically. "Really, I was so certain I sensed a shift in your aura. I hope my vertigo's not coming back. Damn inner ears can give the third eye such problems."

"Sorry. Any glow I have comes strictly from daily yoga and a plant-based diet."

Astrid's brow furrowed as she shook her head, clearly unconvinced. "My intuition's getting worse with age." Reaching into her blouse, she withdrew a satchel of herbs and tossed it onto the table like dice, the dried leaves rustling with aromatic promise. "Brought this for you. Last season's lemon balm. It eases tension and digestion. Steep it for ten minutes with honey. It pairs beautifully with hibiscus."

"Thanks." As the town apothecary, nothing surpassed one of Astrid's freshly ground teas.

"Too long since I've read your tea leaves, Wren. Maybe we should brew a cup now."

"I can't. I promised Jocelyn a visit this morning."

"How is Hideaway's bestselling author? I devoured her latest series. Who knew I harbored such an appetite for Viking smut?"

"Viking smut, you say?" Bodhi raised an eyebrow with genuine curiosity as he sipped his tea. Her father devoured anything printed, but she wasn't sure Viking smut was up his alley.

"Devastatingly sexy," Astrid informed him with a knowing nod.

"Magnificent braids and you wouldn't believe the size of the Vikings—"

"Weapons," Wren interrupted, shooting her aunt a warning look.

Experience taught her to derail such conversations before they careened off track. Other guests lingered nearby and Viking anatomy didn't really match The Haven's aesthetic.

"Maybe you should support your friend by reading more of her books, Wren. You seem rather tightly wound this morning. How long since you've indulged in proper self-care? And I'm not referring to manicures or yoga."

"On that note, I'm departing. Thank you for the tea." She kissed her aunt, then her father, breathing in the familiar scent of spices and contentment that always surrounded him. "Enjoy your breakfast."

She escaped The Haven before business could sidetrack her. Jocelyn wasn't expecting a visit, but Wren needed advice, and Jocelyn had a knack for getting right to the point on matters of the heart—sort of the way a sledgehammer reveals the inner workings of a delicate egg.

When she knocked on her friend's door, Jocelyn's voice echoed from deep inside the house, muffled by walls and creative chaos. "Go away."

"Joce, it's me."

"Me who?"

"Wren."

She waited in silence until the door opened a crack and her friend peeked at her with a messy head of hair three times its usual size, mascara smudged beneath tired eyes. "Did you bring snacks?"

As their custom demanded—sort of like a toll one had to pay to interrupt Jocelyn's writing time—Wren held up a box of donuts from The Harbor Crumb, the local bakery.

Her friend snatched the box out of her hand and left the door open.

On writing days, Jocelyn had a very specific wardrobe ritual—

silk against skin, freedom from constraints, everything designed for creative flow. She wore either kaftans or kimonos and very little underneath. She didn't like to be disturbed by bras or people, and she preferred not to break her focus for meals. She did, however, have a soft spot for coffee, booze, and sweets. It was common knowledge that any beverage in Jocelyn's hand after eleven a.m. was adequately spiked, which she claimed helped to keep her romances extra spicy.

"I thought you'd be heading into town to set up for your fundraiser tonight."

Jocelyn grunted over a sugary bite as she walked, crumbs trailing behind her like literary breadcrumbs. "I wanted to get a few words in first. Besides, that doesn't start until later. Plenty of time."

Wren gave her a skeptical look. "Did you delegate?"

"Of course, I did. You know I'm too pretty to do the heavy lifting. So, what brings you by?"

They sat on the sectional in the living room, and Wren pulled a cozy blanket onto her lap, needing the comfort of soft fabric against her skin. "I have a problem."

"You think you have problems? I've got two characters who can't stop fucking. I mean, it'll sell, but the plot's been nothing but blowjobs and buttfucking since chapter two. My agent's going to hate it. Ooh!" She grabbed for a second donut, tossing her already half-eaten one back into the box. "I love a Boston crème!"

"My problems are a little more PG than buttfucking and blowjobs."

"Pity." She sat back and closed her eyes over a bite of the cream filled donut, moaning with theatrical appreciation. "So, what's got your panties in a bunch? You can't figure out what to wear tonight to my fabulous auction of man meat?"

Wren sank a little. "You know that's not my thing—"

"Nope." She cut her off with a finger wag, powdered sugar dusting her silk sleeve. "I'm your thing. As my official BFF, your attendance is mandatory. You can show your emotional support by buying a donated book or bidding on a hot item to support my fundraising endeavors. Be a good citizen, Wren."

"I am a good citizen."

"Then be a hornier one. It might do you good to bid on a hottie for a night. Clear out some of those coochie cobwebs you're so fond of collecting."

"My coochie does not have cobwebs!"

"Really? When's the last time a guy's been in there to… *dust?*"

"I handle my own damn dusting."

"That's not the same."

Wren rolled her eyes and mumbled, "You'd be surprised."

"So, let's hear it." She took another bite into the donut and moaned with exaggerated pleasure. "Did someone piss in your lube and call it foreplay?"

"Dear God, where does your head go?"

"Right to the dick. It's a wonder we're best friends, being that you've lived the last thirty years without one."

"Seriously. But that's why I'm here."

Jocelyn sat up. "Oh?"

"Times, they are a'changin'."

Sudden interest sharpened her features. "Do tell."

Wren drew in a galvanizing breath, her pulse fluttering with nervous energy. "Logan kissed me."

Jocelyn stilled and gaped at her, pastry nearly falling out of her mouth. "Logan Hawthorne?"

"What other Logan do you know?"

"Ho-ly shit. I knew he always had a thing for you! When? How did it happen? I want all the details!"

"It was behind the corner market. We were on a date."

Jocelyn curled her lip in a look of disappointment. "Behind the corner market? Like where the dumpsters are?" She rolled her eyes, unimpressed. "He could have done a little better than that."

"It was cute. It was a scavenger hunt thing."

Her friend snicked her tongue against her teeth. "Well, you didn't mention that. That's adorable."

"I know!"

Jocelyn looked off in the distance as if picturing it, then moaned with appreciation. "If I had a shot at Logan Hawthorne I'd break him in one use." She grinned wickedly. "How was the kiss?"

"Sweet. Gentle."

"Ugh. I'm so sorry to hear that. Maybe he just needs a good spank—"

"I also kissed Soren."

"Wait! What?" She shoved the donuts away to focus, chocolate smearing her fingers. "This. Just. Got. Interesting. Spill! I want all the tea, you little hippie harlot!"

"We had a date... Last night."

"Where?"

"Salt & Ember."

She physically melted from the couch and onto the floor with dramatic flair. "Of course, he would take you there. That boy has such alpha energy. He's the sort of guy a woman can run a few rounds with. Tell me about his kiss."

"It was a *really* good kiss." Even now, Wren's toes curled remembering the way he held her close, the taste of champagne on his lips. "Slow, but deliberate. Sort of forceful, but not in a rushed way."

"Uh-huh. Uh-huh. Go on." She pulled the donuts back to her lap as if holding popcorn for a movie.

Wren bit her lip, heat climbing her neck. "I haven't even told you the biggest part yet."

"Wait, there's more? Oh, my God! Did you go to bed with him? Because if so, that calls for more than donuts."

"No." Her face burned as a nip of shame tightened her throat. She bit her lip and covered her face in embarrassment. "Greyson also kissed me."

Silence.

Wren peeked through her fingers. Jocelyn just blinked at her, mouth hanging open. "Say something, Joce."

"I don't know what to say." Then she snorted with disbelief. "Holy crap on a cracker, Wren. You've actually rendered me speechless. That's never happened before. Three Hawthornes? Three!" She climbed back onto the couch to give this conversation the respect it deserved. "I guess my first question is... how?"

Over the next hour, Wren gave Jocelyn a full rundown of everything that had been happening in her life. Of course, Jocelyn wanted every inappropriate detail, but that was what made her a bestselling author of some of the hottest Viking smut to ever hit the page.

When Wren finished, Joce looked at her watch and whistled low. "Damn, it's only ten-thirty. Ah, fuck it. Close enough. This calls for something stronger than caffeine. Oh! And I just got a new bottle of that peanut butter whiskey! Be right back."

"If you're hosting an event tonight, should you be drinking?"

"It adds to my charm," she yelled as she rummaged through the shelf of bottles in the other room, glass clinking against glass. "Besides, I have an iron liver."

When she returned with a bottle and two glasses of ice, Wren stopped her. "I have a yoga class to teach in an hour."

"One glass won't kill you. We have to celebrate. You got fingered by Greyson Hawthorne. This is mega big."

"Ugh." Wren winced. "We're too old to use words like 'fingered.'"

"Says the thirty-year-old virgin."

"Hey! You keep that information in the vault."

She waved her concerns away with amber liquid sloshing. "Who doesn't love a virgin trope?"

Sometimes Wren felt like the most inexperienced woman in the world. "Does it even count as fingering if there technically wasn't penetration?"

Jocelyn cocked her head in confusion, ice cubes clinking.

"Jesus, any slower of a burn and the fire's going out. What do you mean he didn't penetrate?"

"I don't know. It was more…rubbing."

"Like an old-school bump-and-grind?" Jocelyn cocked her head, thought about it for a second, then shrugged. "Okay, that's hot. But which billionaire bad-boy will it be? So many options! The golden retriever, the reclusive woodsman, or the alpha." Despite her objections, Jocelyn poured two glasses. "What about the bonfire incident? Are you finally over that?"

The bonfire was something they never discussed because it had been that big of a deal to Wren when it happened. Just the mere mention of it made her entire body tense, muscles coiling with remembered humiliation.

It had been years ago. She was still in high school, but Greyson was years past graduation. She'd just heard back from the business school she'd applied to. *Rejected.*

The sting still resonated, a paper cut on her pride that refused to heal. Who knew it would only get worse before the day was over?

Wren didn't know why Greyson was the first person she ran to for comfort, but he was. When she got to his house, he had some friends over. This was before he'd built his home in the woods, and he still lived with Magnus.

She'd walked up on them in the midst of a conversation about typical guy stuff—work, sports, women. One of his friends spotted her first and smiled. The other men quickly noticed her as well. Everyone seemed friendly enough, except Greyson.

"What are you doing here, Wren?" They no longer spent as much time together as they had in high school, and she wondered if that was more than circumstantial. Sometimes, it felt like a personal choice—but never hers.

"I didn't know you had company."

"Whoa, Grey, did you double-book?" one of the guys sitting around the bonfire joked, flames casting shadows across their faces. "We can take a walk."

"Shut the fuck up, Andy."

She realized then that his friends assumed she was just one of his booty calls, another girl in a rotation she never knew existed.

"This isn't a good time, Wren."

"Oh." The sting of the rejection letter burned through the back pocket of her jeans like a brand. She didn't want to go home, and she didn't want to think. She came there because she wanted to forget, to lose herself in his familiarity.

Without invitation, she pulled a beer from the cooler, condensation slick against her palm.

Greyson caught her hand before she could open it, his fingers firm and warm against her wrist. "What the hell do you think you're doing?"

"Having a beer."

He took the bottle from her, and his friends howled and whistled as if she'd just been called to the principal's office. "Not a chance."

He had a lot of nerve. He'd been drinking since freshman year and she was just around the corner from graduating. "Don't be a hypocrite."

"Looking out for you isn't hypocritical."

"Well, you're not my father." She yanked the bottle out of his hand and cracked it open, the hiss of escaping carbonation sharp in the night air.

Greyson scowled with disapproval as she chugged down several gulps, the bitter taste foreign on her tongue. The guys hollered in full support of her rebellion and pushed another chair closer to the fire, sparks dancing upward into the darkness.

Greyson, as always, got silent and pissed. Six beers later, and she was tripping over her words, laughing at jokes that probably weren't that funny, and speaking without a filter while woodsmoke clung to her hair and clothes.

When she needed to pee, she excused herself. The walk back to the house from the yard was a long one that gave her plenty of time to realize she was drunk and should probably go home. But she wasn't ready to leave—wasn't ready to face the rejection letter or the uncertain future it represented.

After using the bathroom, she came face-to-face with Grey's friend, Andy, who waited just outside of the bathroom like a predator who'd cornered his prey.

"Having fun?"

"Mm-hm. I am." Beer was amazing, and she wondered why she'd waited so long to try it, why she'd been so good for so long.

Andy stepped closer, close enough that she could smell cologne mixed with smoke and beer. "So you're a senior?"

She nodded, the movement making her head swim.

"Planning on going to college?"

She didn't want to think about college at the moment, didn't want to face the reality of closed doors and limited options. "I'm undecided."

He looked down and took her measure with eyes that seemed to catalog every inch. "You seeing anyone?"

She shook her head. Andy was one of those guys who was always in the background at Greyson's table or parties. She'd met him years ago but never really talked to him.

"How come?" He was standing right in front of her now, close enough to touch her, and when he did—fingers trailing down her arm with clear intention—she didn't pull back. "You're pretty enough. You should have guys falling all over you."

It was a little hard to date when Logan or Soren or Greyson were always chasing guys away from her and scaring them off with threats and territorial glares. When she did get the slightest attention, it reminded her how much she wanted a boyfriend and how nice it would be to have someone special in her life.

She looked up at Andy through beer-blurred vision. He seemed interested. He had a nice face and dressed okay. There wasn't anything wrong with him that she could tell.

He grinned, catching her checking him out. "Like what you

see?" he asked, holding her stare with confidence that left her unsure. He was either grossly cocky or attractively assertive.

Did he just move closer?

She had no game when it came to flirting. Her head was fuzzy with alcohol and rebellion, and she really didn't have any concrete thoughts about Andy.

"I like your hat." It wasn't a typical baseball hat. It had a smaller brim, and she liked the olive green color. It looked vintage.

"Yeah?" He lifted the hat and turned it around so the brim was facing backward, then he angled his arm onto the wall to lean over her, caging her in. "What else do you like?"

She looked up into his eyes, very aware of his proximity, of the way her back pressed against the cool wall. "I don't know."

"How about being kissed? Do you like that?"

She shrugged and nodded at the same time, her heart hammering against her ribs. Andy leaned down and—

"What the fuck do you think you're doing?" Before Andy could answer, Greyson ripped him off of her and threw him a good six feet in the opposite direction, the sound of impact echoing through the hallway.

"Greyson!"

"Shut the fuck up, Wren!" He towered over Andy, every muscle coiled with rage. "What did I tell you about going near her?"

"We were just talking, Grey."

Mortification choked her as Greyson turned into a complete Neanderthal. She shoved him with both hands. "Knock it off!"

He spun and caught her by the shoulders, his grip firm enough to bruise. "I told you to go home."

"You're not in charge of me!"

"This is my fucking house!" He pointed in the direction of the door with violent emphasis. "You're drunk and making a fool of yourself. Go find Soren and tell him to drive you home."

She glared up at him, fury and humiliation burning through her veins like poison. "You're not the boss of me."

Andy stood, brushing dust from his jeans. "I'll take her home."

Slowly, Greyson turned to face his friend and growled with lethal quiet, "Do you have a fucking death wish?"

"You're being a prick, Grey. She's graduating. She can do whatever she wants. Lighten up."

Greyson literally seethed, tension crackling off of him like electricity, as he turned back to his friend.

"Grey, it's fine." Wren caught his arm before he could advance. Violence coiled beneath his skin. He was going to kill Andy. "I'll go get Soren."

"I want you both out of my house."

Andy scoffed. "You're ridiculous. If you're gonna be that fucking territorial over some kid, maybe you should date her." With that, he grabbed his jacket and stormed off, leaving the air thick with unresolved tension.

Greyson wouldn't look at her. "Grey—"

"I don't want you around my friends anymore if this is how you're going to act." He glared at Wren, his blue eyes dark as wet denim and his mouth firm with disapproval. "What were you thinking?"

"I was just having fun. Nothing even happened."

"Your fun leads to trouble."

"He didn't even kiss me."

"He's lucky he didn't. And you're lucky I stopped him when I did."

Her confusion turned to anger, alcohol making her bolder than usual. "Lucky? Is that what you think I am? What are you even doing, Greyson? This isn't about Andy. Whenever any guy comes within two feet of me, you turn into a complete caveman. Why?"

"Andy's three years older than you."

"What does that matter when I'm an eighteen-year-old adult?"

"It matters when you've got no experience, and you're drunk and leading guys on!"

"I wasn't leading him on!"

"I know how you are when you get like this."

She staggered back as if he'd physically struck her. "When I get like what?"

"You show up here, looking for attention like a pick-me girl—"

She slapped him before she even realized she'd lifted her hand, the crack echoing between them like a gunshot. Her palm stung, but not as much as her heart.

He glared at her, a red mark blooming across his cheek. "I can't do this with you anymore."

"Do what? The only thing you're doing is making me feel like a whore when I didn't even do anything."

"You need to find your own friends."

The space around her heart seared like molten metal as she looked up at him, stunned that he would say such a thing to her. He was supposed to be her friend, her safe harbor in every storm. "What happened to you?"

"I grew up. One day you'll understand."

"No, I won't. I don't care how old we get, Greyson. We aren't meant to outgrow each other. Our bond's deeper than that." Tears burned behind her eyes. "If you hate it here so much, why did you come back?"

His mouth formed a firm line, jaw clenched with unspoken truths.

Realizing he wasn't going to explain himself to anyone, she said, "You should have stayed out at sea. At least then I'd remember you as a decent guy."

"I'm still a decent guy."

"No, you're not. The Greyson I knew would never treat me like this."

"If I wasn't decent, I would have had you six ways to Sunday by now."

She was speechless, shock coursing through her like ice water. She didn't know this side of him—this crude, territorial stranger wearing her best friend's face. "You're an asshole."

"I'm just trying to be honest. You can't keep coming here looking for something I can't give you. I don't have feelings for you, Wren. You need to get that through your head. You're like my kid sister. That's all."

The words hit her like physical blows, each one more devastating than the last. "Well, if that's all I am, you're a shitty fucking big brother. Here." She flung the rejection letter at his chest, the paper fluttering between them like a wounded bird. "I came by because I was upset and wanted to show you this. Pardon me for thinking you might care."

Thinking back to that horrible day, she suffered the same ache she had when he said those mean things to her. Greyson always swore he never saw her as anything more than a little sister, but of all the Hawthorne brothers, he was always the most territorial.

They didn't speak for almost a year after that. But he spent so much time working for the fishery, she hardly saw him anyway.

It wasn't until she started construction on The Haven, six years later, when he'd built his cabin and settled back in Hideaway, that they actually found a somewhat normal vibe again.

She rubbed her temples and groaned. "Oh, God, Jocelyn, what the hell am I doing?"

"Okay, take a breath. You're safe, and this isn't anything we can't handle."

Wren reached for the donuts and shoved half a glazed in her mouth. "I cranft neef'n figreah Greyson oub."

"Honey, when you talk with food in your mouth, no one knows what you're trying to say. Wash it down." Jocelyn pushed the rocks glass closer, and Wren took a sip.

"Wow." She swallowed and examined the glass, warmth spreading through her chest. "Why is that so good?"

"I know, right?"

She took another small swallow, then set down the glass. "I said, I can't figure Greyson out. Every time he touches me, he tells me it can't happen again."

"And then he makes you come."

"Exactly! What is that?"

"Look, obviously, he has feelings for you. We always assumed that was why he didn't want other guys sniffing around your territory."

"But at the bonfire—"

"Fuck that bonfire! That was one day, Wren—like a million years ago. Look at the big picture. His fingers were in your pants."

"Do you have to be so graphic?"

"Hey, I write 'em like I see 'em."

"Well, you're not writing about this." She frowned, confusion swirling with the whiskey. "As soon as we stopped, he told me to date whoever I wanted. He doesn't care. Even if it's his brothers, he acts like it means nothing to him."

"Oh, he cares. He's just being a little bitch about it. I bet he cares so much it's making him crazy. As a matter of fact, next time you go out with Soren, you should go somewhere right in the open where Greyson can see."

"I can't use Soren that way." She thought again about the way he'd kissed her last night, the heat and promise in his touch. "At least Soren is actually talking about a possible future."

"That's true." Jocelyn scratched her chin in thought. "I mean, he's nothing like Greyson, but maybe that's a good thing. At least he's not afraid to go after what he wants."

"But what do I want?"

Joce raised a brow as if to ask if that needed to be verbalized. "Where does Logan fall in all of this?"

Wren dropped her head into her palms and groaned. "I don't know. Logan felt too personal. I can't go there with him. He's always been different with me than the other two."

"It's because you're closer in age."

"Probably. But how will he feel if I date his brother or brothers after turning him down? *Gah!*" Wren slouched and groaned, covering her face with both hands. "I'm a terrible person! I should just tell them all no and go out with Noah."

"Hold up. Who the hell is Noah?"

"Some guy from my yoga class who asked me out."

"Damn, girl, your shit's on fire. *Four* men?"

She looked at her friend through splayed fingers. "Joce, what do I do?"

"Get comfy. You're on the Naughty List this year. Why not enjoy it?"

Wren looked at her in pure desperation. "I don't know how to enjoy this without hurting them. This is all going to blow up in my face."

"No, it's not. We just need to set some ground rules." Her posture straightened as she ticked off fingers. "First, Logan's too deep in the friend zone. You can nip that one in the bud right now. This Noah guy... What's he like?"

"Meh." Wren shrugged. "He's all right, I guess—"

"Gone. Off the list. We're not wasting time on meh." A third finger went up. "Soren's got game and he's a good kisser."

"He's also open to talking about a future."

"Right, but we don't know if he's in it for love, or just doing this for the inheritance."

Her blunt summation left Wren startled. "Do you think that's it?"

Jocelyn shrugged. "I think it's a part of this. I mean, would he have come at you so aggressively if there wasn't a time crunch with his dad's health?"

"No."

"So, it's definitely a factor. In book world, we call that the catalyst. But there are always unforeseen twists. And, hey, there are plenty of arranged, contractual marriages that end in orgasms and love."

Wren tried to envision a future with Soren, but the vision was blurry. Familiar settings but no one had a head. All the males in her fantasy were faceless and unidentifiable. "My future's headless."

"Stop. What about Greyson?" Jocelyn did that slow, wicked smile that was usually followed by a phone call requesting bail money. "Now, Greyson is a man who needs massive emotional exfoliating. He's been compressing his feelings for so long, I think he's man-stipated."

"Man-stipated?"

"Yeah, you know... Emotionally constipated, repressed, his heart's too small, like he has Grinch syndrome. He's a Great Wall of Guy. Emotionally Amish and suffering from the feelings famine. He's in a tear duct drought—"

"Okay, okay. I get it." If you didn't stop Jocelyn once she started, you ended up with a bit of a runaway train scenario.

"But you get it?"

Boy, did she ever. "Yes, I'm well aware that Greyson buried his feelings the day we buried our moms."

The appropriate silence followed at the mention of her mother. Life would have been so much easier with her here. There were times Wren could have really used some wise, feminine guidance. Of course, she had her dad and Aunt Astrid and all of her friends, but nothing ever replaced a mom.

Wren had a terrible thought. "What if he just... can't?"

"Can't what, perform? What were you dry humping the other day? I assumed he was at least hard."

"No, I mean, what if it's just not in him to open up?"

"Look, I've written thirty-five books, and conquered my fair share of emotionally repressed lumberjacks. That man needs to be climbed like a snowy mountain. He's one of those guys where you gotta break 'em down casually. Show 'em a boob or two. Get them hooked on the hookup. And then—slowly—dissolve his other barriers."

"He won't let that happen. Every time he touches me he tells me it can't happen again."

"He's like a masochist. I think he gets off on denying himself."

"Or, he's just not that into me."

"Don't make me slap you. First of all—" She went back to ticking off fingers. "All the Hawthornes are secretly in love with you. Everyone knows it and so does Greyson, which is why he's always told them you're off limits. I'll die on that mountain, and if you deny it, you're as much of a liar as he is. Second—" Another finger went up. "Greyson goes nuts whenever anyone shows any interest in you. He's the worst of all of them. And C, he's prime male lead material—strong, independent, silent, pensive... *Gah!* They're the best ones."

Wren laughed despite herself. "You think?"

"Absolutely! If I were to write him into one of my Viking novels, I'd name him something like *Gunner the Broody*. He exudes moody recluse vibes. Very hot. Women eat that shit up."

They shared a moment of silence to sit back and sip their peanut butter cocktails, picturing Greyson's handsome body under all that emotional intensity. Wren smiled, recalling how entranced she had been by the sight of him without his shirt, all muscle and scars and masculine beauty. She was so much calmer than she'd been minutes ago and realized why.

"Good call on the whisky."

"Right?" Jocelyn turned the bottle to admire the label. "Speaking of protein, are you gonna blow him?"

Wren choked as a sip went down the wrong pipe. Gasping and sputtering, she wiped her eyes with the back of her hand. "There's something wrong with you."

Jocelyn laughed. "One hundred percent. But can you imagine him staring down at you with that predatory smolder? Girl, you need to get him inside of you one way or another."

"It's not like I live a celibate life by choice."

"There's always a choice, Wren. You could have had a road-banger take your cherry years ago. I think part of you always wanted to save it for…a special Hawthorne."

She shot her an unimpressed look. They both knew there was only one Hawthorne she ever fantasized about that way. "What the hell's a road-banger?"

"You know, a rando, someone who gets the job done but never learns where you live."

"Gross. I still have standards, Joce."

She didn't need her first time to be with *The One* but she also didn't want it to be with a meaningless stranger. Truthfully, Greyson was always supposed to be her first. He's the only one she ever pictured. When that didn't happen, she figured he just needed more time. So she pushed herself a little longer, then a little longer, then... a little longer.

"What if it never happens?"

"It's happening!"

Wren sighed, not sharing her friend's optimism or confidence. "What can I do?"

"What can you *do?* Wren, honey, you're beautiful. You've got tits and a great ass. Use them."

"To do what?"

Jocelyn pinched the bridge of her nose. "For the love of orgasms, read some romance. Help yourself to anything in my library."

"This isn't fiction. It's real life, Joce."

"Real life can be hot and romantic too, Wren."

"How? How do I make it hot when he still sees me as off limits?"

"This sort of reminds me of chapter twenty-three of *Ravished by the Fjord King*."

"That doesn't help me."

"You're dealing with a slow-burn romance. The excruciating sort, since I'm pretty sure he's carried a torch for you since kindergarten."

"No, he hasn't."

Jocelyn rolled her eyes. "He absolutely has, Wren. I've watched him watching you. The man is completely enamored by you. Why do you think he's always hanging around The Haven?"

"He's our contractor."

"When's the last time he accepted money for any of the work he's done?"

"What do you mean? I pay him."

Jocelyn gave a disbelieving look. "Really? Has he cashed the checks?"

"Of course, he has."

"Are you sure?"

"Yes." It wasn't like she reviewed every statement with a fine-tooth comb, but she wrote the checks, and he took them. "I mean, wouldn't the bank notify me if he didn't?"

"The bank wouldn't know the checks even existed if he didn't deposit them."

She frowned. "That's ridiculous. Why wouldn't he cash the checks I pay him?"

"Because he's in love with you."

"He is not, Joce!"

"See if he cashed them. Where's your phone?"

"I'm not going to check—"

"Because you know there's a chance I'm right!"

"Fine." Wren pulled out her phone and logged into her bank app while grumbling, "I don't know why I'm friends with you."

Jocelyn sat back and swirled the rocks in her glass. "I keep your life spicy. I'm like a vitamin that gives you a little edge. You need me for moments like this when your sweet, little granola vibe isn't savage enough to get the job done."

Wren rolled her eyes.

Once logged into her business account, she scrolled down. "I just paid him last week for plowing the parking lots, but he probably hasn't deposited that check yet."

"I'm sure that's it," Jocelyn said dryly. "Go back a few months. When did you pay him for the studio fit-out?"

That was September. She scrolled back, reviewing each state-ment for images of checks cashed. She saw deposits from the food supplier's checks, the plumber's, the vet bills, the payroll checks for the massage therapists and estheticians, but nothing cashed for Greyson Hawthorne.

Her stomach twisted. She went back further. In June, he'd done some work on the Zen garden for her. That was a few thousand dollars. "What the hell?"

"Find anything yet?"

Not a single check had been cashed. Her fist tightened around her phone as she lowered her hand. "I'm going to kill him."

"Because I'm right?"

"You're not right... I mean, yes, he hasn't cashed any of the checks, but you're wrong about him being in love with me. It's because he doesn't need the money."

"Really? That's what you're taking from this? Chalking it up to him being a Hawthorne?" Jocelyn tsked. "How the hell are we ever going to get him inside of you if you keep making excuses?"

"I'm not making excuses!"

"Wren—" She sat up and set her whiskey aside so she could grip her shoulders and look her in the eye. "I love you, honey, but sometimes a girl has to take the Viking by the horns."

"I can't with Greyson. He'll see it as manipulation. The moment anyone tries to control him, he purposely goes in the opposite direction."

"Then that leaves you one other option."

"Which is?"

"You're gonna have to fuck the yogi."

She scrunched her nose. "How is that the solution?"

"You said you can't go there with Logan."

"True, but Noah does nothing for me. He's sweet and handsome enough, but he's just not my type."

"Then Soren."

"No." She, once again, thought of the kiss, the way he'd looked

149

at her like she was something precious and carnal. Something about Soren felt…dangerous.

Jocelyn snickered. "I see Soren's not an instant no."

But he was. She couldn't go there with him. Not unless she was really considering his offer. Maybe she was so afraid of Soren, because part of her was considering it. "No, I can't."

"I think you don't want to involve Soren because there's a chance you might actually like him."

She pressed her lips tight, and Jocelyn gasped.

"I knew it! Ooh, it's that billionaire energy. He's so cocky in all the right ways."

"I don't care about his money."

"That's not what I mean. I'm talking about his essence. Soren goes after what he wants, and he doesn't stop until he gets it. He's the total opposite of Greyson."

"That's very true." And, according to what he'd said last night, he wanted Wren, not just as a girlfriend or possibly a future wife, but he was actually attracted to her. And it felt really nice to feel wanted. "We did have some chemistry."

"Yassssss! Tell me more."

Wren couldn't shake the strange guilt that lingered whenever she tried to surmise her feelings for Soren. She couldn't stop seeing him as 'Greyson's brother,' which was crap.

"It's just nice to be pursued," she admitted. "He doesn't play games. He's into me."

"Are you into him? Not just to piss off Greyson, but is this an actual competition?"

"I... I don't know."

"Oh, shit. Okay. I didn't realize you were feeling things where he was concerned. I thought it was just about the kiss." Jocelyn picked up her whiskey and tucked her legs under her knees. "Let's talk Soren. Besides being a good kisser, what made you feel attracted to him on your date?"

"I don't know. I wasn't at first, but by the end there was a spark. We definitely have a special connection. He knows me. I know him. He's handsome. Thoughtful. And, of course, there was the kiss."

"Yup. Yup. Does Greyson know there was a kiss?"

"No."

"You should tell him."

"I can't do that!"

"I can."

"Joce, don't."

She waved away her warning. "You need to go out with Soren again and see if there's actually something there."

"I don't know if that's a good idea. We have a second date scheduled, but I still feel like I'm doing something wrong whenever we cross that line."

"That's because it's a line you've been told not to cross your entire life. That'll fade once you get to know his dick."

Wren snorted. "There you go again."

"I mean it, Wren. This might just come down to who has the nicest penis."

She ignored her. "Soren wants a traditional marriage. I like my independence too much to even consider such a thing. He also wants a lot of children. My plate's already full with The Haven."

"You can do both. Plenty of moms own their own businesses. Plus, it really pisses off the patriarchy, so it's a win-win."

"Moms are important. I'd want to be there for my kids."

"You don't have to be at home twenty-four-seven to be a good mother, Wren."

"True, but... I don't know. Long-term is a scary thing to predict. What if it doesn't work out and everything gets wrecked? I can't lose the Hawthornes. They're my boys. My family."

Jocelyn nodded, recognizing the risk. "But you're not ruling it out?"

Wren slowly winced. "No?"

"Atta girl!"

Embarrassed, she covered her face and groaned. "I can't believe I'm actually considering this!"

"I can. And, I think you should give Logan another shot."

"*What?* My life is already complicated enough."

"I'm just going to say it, Wren. You're not going to let them lose the company."

Wren did a double take. That was not at all what she'd expected her to say. "Jocelyn, I can't take responsibility for what Magnus does with his legacy."

"No, but we both know, in the end, you'll help them any way you can. You always do. They're your boys. You even have that stupid Goonies name you call yourselves—the wilderness gang or whatever it is."

She smiled. "The Wildlings."

"Whatever. My point is, if they're desperate and you can save them, you will. Even if it comes down to Logan being the one who wants it most. Maybe you have a lavender marriage, and the spice isn't off the charts, but you'd still be married to one of your best friends. That's more than most people get."

She shook her head, unable to picture such a thing.

"My advice is to get cozy with the idea of becoming a Hawthorne. One of them is getting to Level Two. Why not take them all for a test drive—"

"No."

She held up her hands. "I'm not suggesting reverse harem. But there's nothing wrong with a little heavy petting and kissing before making a commitment."

"I'm not like you, Joce. This is all brand new territory for me. And it's delicate because they're my boys. I don't want to hurt them."

"They hold some accountability in this, too, you know."

"I know. It's just…" The truth finally occurred to her. She met her friend's stare and shrugged. "I want love."

Jocelyn leaned over and squeezed her hand. "We all do, sweetie. Your problem isn't finding love. Your problem is that you already love them. And they each love you in their own weird little Wildling Hawthorne way."

CHAPTER 10

"Fill My Stocking With a Duplex and Checks"

GREYSON STEPPED OUT OF THE SHOWER, WATER STILL BEADING ON his shoulders, and froze. Someone hammered on his front door with enough force to rattle the windows. He quickly wrapped a towel around his hips and dashed out of the bathroom, frowning when the knob jiggled.

He flung open the door, ready to rip someone's head off, then stilled, mouth open and confused. "Wren?"

"Why haven't you been depositing your checks?" She stormed into the house without invitation, bringing a gust of winter air and righteous fury.

"Huh?"

"Years of checks, Greyson! You've never cashed a single one! What the hell?"

"I..." This wasn't on his bingo card for today.

"If you do jobs for me, then I get to pay you. That's how it works!"

Did she have to be so sexy when she yelled at him? Her cheeks flushed that perfect pink that made his pulse hammer against his throat.

Get your head out of the gutter, Hawthorne!

He scowled. "Why are you yelling at me?"

"Why aren't you cashing your paychecks?"

He shrugged, blurting out the first lame excuse that came to mind. "The bank's on the other side of town."

"Don't give me that crap!" She flung her hair out of her face, cheeks tinged with the same pink that colored her nipples whenever she got heated. "I reviewed all my bank statements. You've been doing this for years. *Years*, Greyson!"

He wondered how she managed to run a business if she missed such an enormous clerical error. "You should keep a better eye on your books—"

"That's not the point!"

"What do you want me to say, Wren?"

"I want you to fix it."

He gave her a stern look that said that wouldn't happen. If she didn't realize he wasn't cashing his checks, she likely spent the money elsewhere. The sum of money he'd let slide over the years would add up to a fortune by now. He couldn't bury her in that sort of debt.

"I always tell you I don't want your money."

"If you don't let me pay you, Greyson, I'm going to start hiring someone else."

His jaw locked, muscles tensing with territorial fury. Like he'd let someone else do the jobs he did for her. She'd get ripped off left and right, not because she wasn't sharp, but because most contractors overpriced their work and took advantage of anyone with limited options. It was extortion. His prices were reasonable and fair, even if he didn't take the money.

Done with this argument, he walked away from her. "That's not happening."

"Where are you going?" She followed him into his bedroom, her footsteps quick and determined. "You don't get to decide what does and doesn't happen in my business, Grey. This is my company, and I choose how it's run."

He yanked open a drawer and pulled out a pair of jeans, the denim rough against his damp hands. "And I'm running my business. I choose how I charge. Same difference." He stepped into the jeans, pulling them up as he yanked off his towel.

"*Oh!*" She covered her eyes and spun around. He hoped she got an eyeful.

"This argument is over, Wren. I worked all day, and I just ordered dinner. I'm hungry—"

"No, this discussion is just getting started. It ends when we reach a compromise."

He yanked up his zipper and closed the distance between them in two strides, close enough to feel the heat radiating from her skin. "The compromise will be you choose what to pay me, and I choose what to do with my money." His voice dropped to dangerous quiet. "The. End."

Her shoulders shook with frustration. "Are you dressed yet?"

"Yes."

She pivoted and drew back. Angling her chin up, she glared at him with fire in her eyes. "That's not fair, Greyson. You're actually losing money on supply costs—"

He took a step closer, purposely crowding her until her back nearly touched the wall. He couldn't intimidate her—she knew him too well for that—but, this time, she wasn't getting her way. "It's fair enough."

"No, it's not. The materials alone... Your labor..."

He wondered how anyone could have that much hair. Distracted by her long braid, he remembered his earlier years on fishing boats and recalled his father teaching him and his brothers all about nautical knots. Some part of him ached to braid her hair a thousand different ways, simply because he knew how.

"Are you listening to me?"

"No."

"Damn it, Greyson!"

He grabbed the braid, sliding the thick length through his hand like silk rope and tugging her closer, the texture soft against his calloused palm.

"I..." She lost her train of thought, pupils dilating as her breath caught.

Good. He liked seeing her all worked up, cheeks flushed and eyes bright with anger. "You what?"

"I..."

He followed the braid to the tapered end, just above her ribs, and let his fingers linger there, feeling the rapid rise and fall of her breathing.

Her breath hitched. "Greyson..." She looked up at him in question, confusion and desire warring in her expression. "We're having a fight."

"No, we're not."

He told himself this wouldn't happen again, but then she stormed into his home, feisty and hot-tempered, and he forgot why he made such a promise. He could throw her onto his bed and bury himself inside of her in two seconds flat.

Would she stop him?

Given the current trend, probably not.

His cock throbbed at the possibility and he swallowed hard. The temptation only an inch away. His bed a mere ten feet. He pictured the tight grip of heat and—"You shouldn't have come here."

She noticeably swallowed, her shoulders lifting with each shallow breath. "Why?"

"You know why."

Her gaze lowered to his bare chest and held, taking in every ridge of muscle and each old scar. She trembled, but he didn't think it stemmed from fear. She knew he'd never hurt her. But he wasn't sure she was safe with him anymore.

Taking a baby step forward, her chest brushed his through that negligible strip of clothing she tried to pass off as a shirt.

He took in every subtle tell. The hitch of her breath quickening. The slight parting of her lips. The way her body trembled harder than it had a moment ago.

"Do I scare you?"

"No," she whispered, her voice barely audible. "I'm only afraid you'll push me away."

A realistic fear to have. And strange how he feared this time he might not possess the strength. "You don't want that?"

"No, Grey, I don't want that. I've had that, and it hurts."

He never wanted to hurt her, but somehow always managed to. "You shouldn't look at me like that, Wren."

"Why?"

"You know why."

She chewed her lower lip, something she only did when nervous. Her lashes lowered, hiding her gaze.

"You could have called on the phone."

A slight nod. "I wanted to see you."

"Why?"

She didn't answer immediately. Her breathing turned labored as she kept her head bowed, pulse fluttering at her throat. "I don't know."

"Yes, you do."

Another beat. "I wanted…to see you."

"Then why aren't you looking at me?"

"I don't know."

Maybe it was easier not to look at each other. Easier to be honest about what they both seemed to be fighting.

"Turn around."

With a shaky breath, she slowly pivoted to face the wall, no questions asked.

"Good girl."

He glided his palms over her shoulders and down her arms. Goosebumps rose under his touch. Lifting her hands, he pressed them into the plaster, angling her body forward. Stepping closer, he closed the distance, showing her exactly how hard he was.

"Is this what you want?" His hand flicked under the hem of her shirt, teasing her bare skin that felt like silk under his calloused fingers.

"I..." She nodded, her voice barely a whisper. "I came because of the paychecks."

"Enough about the fucking checks, Wren."

She wore those high-cut, loose yoga pants again, and his hand slipped easily past the waistline into her panties. He delved right between her folds, finding her soaked and ready.

Her breath caught when his finger narrowly slid deeper, teasing without fully penetrating. Fuck his promises. He tapped her ankle with the side of his bare foot.

"Show me you want this. Don't make me question it."

Her steps widened and her head lowered in surrender.

If she kept putting herself in these situations, he'd show her exactly why it was dangerous. "Is this what you need?" His finger glided deeper, but he kept his touch light, almost reverent. "You want to feel something, Wren? You want me to get you off?"

"Yes," she breathed, and the soft confession nearly dropped him to his knees.

He barely moved. "I can do that for you."

The tight way her pussy clenched around his finger reminded him of her innocence. He both loved and hated the reminder. In one aspect, it showed just how precious she was. No other man had ever been inside of her. In a way, he felt like that made her…His.

But it also made her fragile. Breakable. He'd kill anyone who hurt her. What if he ended up being the worst of them? Maybe the best thing he could do involved protecting her from himself.

Her breath hitched, and he stilled. "Still okay?"

"Mm-hm."

"Good." He teased his finger deeper, gently brushing his palm over her swollen clit.

The thought of anyone else touching her so intimately made him insane. Part of him wanted to claim her innocence—here and now—so no one else could, but that wasn't a good enough reason.

"Does that feel good, baby?"

Every jagged breath spoke of her tense desire. "Y-yes." Her sudden shyness further confirmed her inexperience. Thirty-fucking years old and still a virgin? How did that even seem possible?

Maybe he bore the blame.

Maybe he wasn't even sorry.

God, he was a prick.

He at least owed her this much. "I'm going to make you come harder than you've ever come before." He rocked his hips forward, showing her what she did to him. The nearly imperceptible motion nudged her into a slow swaying rhythm.

"Who else touched you here, Wren?" He wanted names, so he could hunt each one down and murder them.

Her voice became a sliver of its usual strength. "Only me."

Fuck.

Picturing her alone at night, sliding her fingers into her panties... His dick pulsed.

Did she rub her tight little clit until she came or did she finger herself to release?

"Like this?" He withdrew his finger and glided it through her slit without penetrating, her swollen clit dragging slowly against his slick fingers.

"Sometimes."

"Or do you do it like this?" He rolled his fingers in tight circles over her clit and she gasped.

"Both."

He nudged inside, but kept the intrusion shallow. "How about like this?"

"Yes." She ground herself against his hand, forcing his fingers deeper. She grew braver.

"Tell me to stop, Wren. Tell me to take my hands off of you, and I will."

Silence.

Tight heat wrapped around his finger, clenching as it slowly pumped in and out. His cock pulsed in his jeans, seeping pre-come like tears, as if crying to get out of his pants and inside of her tight little hole.

He breathed out a curse. How did they get here again, when he swore the last time was the final time? She didn't make it easy to walk away, and that was exactly what he should do. Walk the fuck away. But willpower escaped him as another soft moan slipped past her lips.

"That feel good?" His mouth lowered to her shoulders as he worked his finger deeper, moving slowly and gently to get her off.

"Yes."

He took his time because he needed time to think. They needed a new set of rules.

One, his pants needed to stay on. That stretched as far as he could think.

"That's it, baby. Let me hear you."

He lived for the pitch of her voice, so stunned and curious, innocent yet carnal.

He pressed his finger all the way in, leaving her seated against his palm. "I don't want to hurt you."

"You won't."

He grinned at her cockiness, but feared there was more at stake between them than the physical. "Ride my hand." He purposely used the weight of his body to overwhelm her, showing her the way he wanted her to move. "Like this." He rocked his hips against her ass. "Like we're fucking."

She was a quick study. Her hips rolled as his finger teased inside of her tight heat. Her moans grew louder and her fingers curled against the plaster wall. His other hand rode up her front, past her neck, to frame her jaw. He turned her ear toward his mouth and whispered, "Last night, after you left, I went to bed, but I couldn't sleep. Do you know why, Wren?"

"Why?"

"Because I could smell you on my fingers all night."

She shivered, her fingers splaying on the wall as her body shook. Slick heat washed over his touch as she moaned his name. "Grey..."

That little plea was his undoing.

Holding her jaw, he took her mouth in a hard, possessive kiss. "You like the thought of driving me crazy?" He fucked his finger deeper. Drunk on the taste of her forbidden kisses, he growled. "Say my name again."

"Greyson..."

"Fuck." He withdrew his touch and lifted her into his arms, carrying her straight to his bed. Kissing her hard, he stretched his body over hers, pinning her beneath him so she couldn't escape. He couldn't stop kissing her, pawing at her like an animal. "Don't hate me, Wren."

"I could never."

"We'll see." Shoving her pants past her hips, he rubbed the bulge of his hard cock against her wet panties. If he took his dick out this would be over. "We're breaking all the rules, now."

"What rules?"

She knew the fucking rules. He scooted lower, framing her breasts but not taking off her shirt. He kissed whatever skin he found, licked over the strip of exposed flesh by her hips, bit at the tender side of her belly. She arched and pulled at his clothes, but he forced her hands to her side.

"Stay like that."

He tugged her ass to the edge of the bed and knelt on the floor. Down went the panties to her knees. Slowly, he pushed her thighs apart. Glistening, pink folds.

Wren's pussy.

He couldn't breathe.

She looked fucking perfect.

There.

Everywhere.

Too goddamn perfect.

This could only be wrong, but he couldn't stop himself.

He traced a finger between her folds, and a jagged breath escaped in a moan. Glossy. Soft. He blew over her slit, showing her how close he sat.

His mouth watered as her unique scent intensified. He licked his lips, his hunger for her doubling as he pressed a kiss to her inner thigh.

Her clothes tangled at her knees, limiting his access, but adding another layer of protection. All pants needed to stay on.

Leaning forward, he whispered, "Just a taste."

Sharp and earthy, he closed his eyes and savored the flavor of Wren. A thousand unique notes of her danced on his tongue. "Jesus. You taste better than I imagined." Sliding his tongue through her slit and closing his lips around her clit, he shut his eyes and groaned.

She tasted like Wren. Wild. Unrefined. Natural. Familiar. Forbidden. He would go straight to hell for this.

Her breath hitched when he buried his face between her legs with ruthless abandon, claiming her with savage intensity. When she squirmed, nervous and edgy, he caught her hands, devouring her like a man starved, feasting with ravenous hunger.

"Greyson!"

Attacking her with his tongue, he worshipped every secret crevice of her with brutal devotion. Whatever she assumed she knew, he proved her wrong. She didn't know this side of him. But now, she would never forget it.

"Greyson, wait!"

He paused, and kissed her stomach. "You're okay."

"It's too much."

"No, it's not."

She looked at him in a way that nearly broke him. Realizing he might have gone too far too fast, he moved up to better see her eyes. "Hey. You're fine, Wren. It's supposed to feel intense." She looked unsure, so he asked. "Did I hurt you?"

"No."

Nodding, he pulled her closer to the edge of the bed. "Just relax. Let me take care of you. Lean back. You don't have to do anything."

She reclined, her motions surprisingly stiff for someone who did yoga every day. "Sorry."

"Don't apologize."

"Sorry."

He chuckled and lifted her closer, draping her legs over his shoulders. "Let's try it like this."

She gasped when he buried his face between her lush thighs again, placing a full-on open-mouthed kiss over her slit and stabbing his tongue deep.

Her breath hitched as her warm pussy welcomed his tongue. Groaning against her heat, he flicked and swirled, scraping his fingers along her ass with contrasting roughness as he ground his cock into the mattress, seeking the slightest relief.

Her moans drove him to the edge of ecstasy, and he fought the urge to jerk off. He would eventually, but first he wanted to taste her come rushing down his throat. He tugged the front of her shirt, and reached for her tits, teasing her tight little nipples into sharp points.

His lips closed around her clit, nibbling and sucking. They were crossing a line, and there would be no uncrossing it.

Suckling her clit, he wedged his fingers inside of her clenching pussy, driving her to deeper places she'd never known. She cried out, her moans matching the pattern of his thrusting fingers. Faster. Harder. He stretched her as he sucked her clit. Constantly reminding himself that she lacked experience and forcing himself to dial back his needs. This revolved around her.

A vision of flipping her to her belly and fucking her hard from behind flashed in his head. Fuck. He wanted her body fisting his cock. He wanted to grab her hard and watch her come apart under his touch. He didn't want to be gentle, but he also didn't want to hurt her. Not really.

He pinched her nipple—slightly harder than he had before—and she cried out his name.

"Grey!"

Fucking himself into the side of the mattress, he growled against her drenched skin. "That's it, baby. Let go." He pressed another finger inside of her, stretching her, pushing her body to accept his touch. His lips tightened over her clit and she came hard on his fingers, pulsing and clenching as she screamed out his name.

He drank from her as if she were the fountain of youth. He wasn't ready to stop, despite her trembling. She jerked and gasped, the longer he sucked her clean. Every part of him wanted to wring ten more orgasms from her, just because he knew her body could deliver, but her mind might not be able to take that much so soon.

He slowed to gently teasing her, giving her body a chance to come down. She provoked this. All her little pokes and side glances. This was the consequence of her actions. And if he needed to teach her a lesson, he might as well teach her.

"I'm not done." That was the only warning she got as he went at her again, hard and relentlessly.

"Grey!"

He only growled in response, not letting up until he wrung every last drop from her.

When she shook uncontrollably, he still took more. He needed to show her just how greedy he could be. Not to punish her, but to show her why he'd tried to stay away.

Shame on him. No matter how much he took, he still wasn't satisfied.

She shivered, her breathing erratic and her body too weak to do more than surrender at this point.

"Shh, just lay there. Let me finish." This had to be the last time.

Her words were no longer coherent, her moans a mixture of pleasure and weak sighs.

He licked over her swollen folds softly, no longer fingering her, just enjoying her addictive taste. She twitched and gasped through random aftershocks, but never pulled away. Could she if she wanted to?

He wasn't sure he could. He tried to give her space, but kept easing in for another soft lick.

"You're gorgeous." He stared at her swollen, pink folds, sure they felt tender from the scrape of his beard. He liked knowing he marked her. Loved knowing she'd feel him there tomorrow.

Quietly, he pulled down the zipper of his jeans and gripped his cock. His fist tightened. He broke his own rules, but it didn't take long. Thick and throbbing, swollen to a point of pain, he came in two hard tugs.

"Fuck." Pressing his cheek to her thigh, he clutched her hips as his muscles jerked and come spilled over his clenched fist. His body went slack as he gasped, and he shut his eyes. It was probably the most intense orgasm of his life, and they hadn't even had sex.

"Greyson?" Her voice sounded raspy and unsure.

"Yeah."

"Did you just..."

Embarrassed by his own actions, he shoved his cock back into his pants and wiped his hands on his jeans. "Needed to." He pressed a kiss to her thigh, stood, and stilled.

She was a fucking vision, lying on his bed half naked and spent. It took everything in him not to go back to the bed and fuck her raw. He wasn't sure how long he'd be able to hold off with her lying there like a partially wrapped present. "You should get dressed."

She slowly sat up, face flushed, breasts rosy, and hair falling out of her once tidy braid. She was a fucking goddess.

A crease formed between her brows. "Can we talk about what just happened?"

He braced his arms on the dresser, keeping his back toward her but watching her in the reflection as she awkwardly adjusted her shirt. "What's there to talk about?" Dropping his gaze, his hands curled into fists. Those fingers had been inside of her. Inside of Wren.

"Can you look at me?"

He could barely look at himself. Lifting his head, he met her stare in the mirror. This wasn't the Wren he'd watched clumsily stumble through the third grade or the gawky girl he used to play manhunt with in the woods. This Wren was dangerous. And he could still taste her.

"Are you mad at me?"

"No." He could feel his control slipping.

"I'm fine with what just happened, Grey."

"Good." Chances were, now that they'd crossed that line, it would happen again. No matter what he fucking wanted.

Apparently, he'd lost all willpower where she was concerned.

"It would be easier if you faced me."

He turned, leaning his hip against the dresser and crossing his arms over his chest.

"You're acting weird."

"I'm acting like myself."

"You won't even look at me."

He met her stare. Couldn't she figure out why this was difficult? He'd just come and was ready to bust another nut from simply looking at her. Only, next time, it wouldn't be in his hand. "Do you have questions?"

She blushed and dropped her gaze. "N-no. But... I can't act like you didn't just..."

"Eat your pussy."

She flinched. "Do you have to be so crude?"

"It's not crude. It's what I did. It's what made you come. Again and again. You said you wanted to talk about it. How can we talk about it if you can't even hear the words?"

"You're purposely trying to shock me."

Maybe he was. He wasn't thinking clearly at the moment.

Despite blowing his load in the shower and again in his hand, all he wanted to do was wrap that braid around his fist, and fuck her hard. Every part of her. Her pussy. Her mouth. Her virgin asshole. Jesus. "You should probably go."

Her stare jumped to his and she blinked rapidly, pink glistening in the whites of her eyes. "What?" Her jaw quivered.

He died a thousand deaths under that sad stare. But that was for the best. This was the most he could offer. "I can't give you…" How the fuck did he make this clear without crushing her. "I tried to warn you, Wren."

She looked ready to throw something at him. "You know, you can really be a complete bastard sometimes." She slid off the bed, her steps unsteady.

"I know." He warned her. But she didn't listen.

She dressed quickly and it took everything in him not to go to her. "Where's the kitten?"

"He's in the spare room."

"Have you checked on him lately?"

"He's handled."

She looked over her shoulder, skepticism narrowing her eyes. "I'll check on him before I go." Shoving her feet into her little boots, she left the room.

He exhaled hard and rubbed his chest. The ache returned. Drawing in a few deep breaths, he looked up at the rafters and counted silently to ten, then went after her.

Wren sat on the floor of the spare room, cross-legged, holding Rat against her face as she scratched his little head and made kissy sounds in his ear. "When did he last eat?"

Did she think he neglected his duties? "Little over an hour ago. He's not due to eat again until ten."

"You can't just leave him in here, Greyson—"

"First of all, he only stayed in here so I could shower. He's been with me all day."

The little rodent fit perfectly in his pocket, and no one seemed to mind when he brought him into town this afternoon to run a few errands.

She gave him a doubtful look. "He needs companionship, especially at this age."

"Rat's fine. I don't need a lecture."

"Ugh, please stop calling him that. His name is Tinsel." She kissed his head and set him back on the blankets Greyson had laid out. "You should probably put a space heater in here so he doesn't get cold."

He scooped Rat up and cradled him in his arm. There was no reason for a heater. The cat was alone for no more than a few minutes—tonight was an exception, but he hadn't been expecting company. The damn thing even slept with him.

"I know what he needs."

She met his stare with silence.

Why was this so hard? He didn't want her to hate him, but he hated how out of control she made him feel. This was a dangerous game they played and she was lucky he only fucked his hand today.

She stood and brushed off her clothes. "I'm writing you another check. Cash it this time."

"We'll see."

"Damn it, Grey—" He shut her up with a kiss, all the tension in her body instantly softening.

Holding his lips to hers, he growled, "Enough about the fucking checks, Wren."

She pushed him away. "It's compensation for your work—" Her phone rang, cutting off her words. She rummaged inside her tote bag, but didn't give up. "You're making a big deal out of a totally normal practice."

"You gonna get your phone?"

"I'm trying," she snapped. The ringing stopped just as she withdrew the phone. She glanced at the screen and frowned.

"Who called?"

"No one."

"You're not gonna tell me?"

She scowled at him. "It's none of your business."

"Why so secretive?"

"Why so nosy?"

The phone started ringing again, and she silenced it. She tried to drop it back into her bag, but Greyson snatched it out of her hand and held it above her head.

"Greyson!"

"No more talk about checks."

"Give me my phone."

"Say you'll drop the issue with the checks and I'll give you the phone."

"This is so stupid."

"Agree to drop it."

"Fine," she snapped. "I'll drop it for now, but next time you work for me, I'm paying you in cash."

He'd see about that. He lowered his arm and stilled—grip tightening around the phone as the screen showed two missed calls from his brother. It lit up again, vibrating with another call. "Why is Soren calling you?"

She yanked her phone out of his hand and sent the call to voicemail. "People call me all the time."

Not Soren. If they wanted to talk to Wren, it was a general habit that they just stopped by. Which reminded him... "How did the date go?"

She pursed her lips. "Really?"

He shrugged. "Why not?" They could talk about this. It probably seemed good that they did. Keep things real. "Did you have fun?"

"We're not doing this."

She put on her coat. Her phone vibrated in her bag. "Sounds like Soren left you a few voicemails."

She ignored him and buttoned a jacket he didn't recognize. What happened to the flannel he gave her?

"Are you going to check your messages?"

"Later."

More vibrating. What could his brother possibly have to talk to her about that required another phone call?

Sorry it didn't work out. Let's still be friends.

She'd gone out with Logan, too, but for some reason, that didn't bother him as much as the idea of her on a date with Soren.

"You're playing all the angles, aren't you?"

She stilled, her hand an inch from the door. "What's that supposed to mean?"

He shrugged. "It's not a bad position. Pick the right brother, and you're set. It's not the life of a fisherman's wife everyone imagines, that's for sure. I'm not sure Soren even remembers how to cast a line, but you two will find other hobbies."

When she turned, her eyes glistened again. "Why are you acting like this?"

"Like what?" He leaned casually against the wall, stroking Rat's head. The cat climbed onto his shoulder. "I'm always supportive of your business endeavors."

"Fuck you, Greyson." The words tripped out on a laugh but there was no humor in her eyes.

"Why fuck me?"

"Stop implying I'm some sort of gold digger."

"Are you saying you would've agreed to go out with Soren under normal conditions?"

"As a matter of fact, yes."

His body stiffened, but he played it off.

"Your brother and I actually had a nice time on our date." She hesitated the way she sometimes did whenever she stretched the truth. "We barely talked about your father or the fishery or his money." She lifted her chin, petulant and pissed. "For your information, we have plenty of other stuff in common."

"Good."

"It is good. And I'm going out with him again this weekend."

His jaw locked and nostrils flared, but he still refused to admit that he was bothered by the thought of her and Soren. "Great," he said through clenched teeth.

Her hands balled into fists at her side. "Maybe he's the right kind of guy for me. Unlike some people, Soren's not afraid to talk about his intentions or feelings."

"Good for him."

She vibrated with tension, but she gave it right back. "Not just good for him. It's good for me. As a matter of fact, it's sexy and refreshing."

He didn't want to play this game anymore. "Then you better call him back."

Now, only anger glittered in her eyes. "You're a child."

"That's me."

She shook her head and walked out the door, but not before muttering, "Grow up, Greyson." The door slammed behind her and he growled.

Fucking Soren.

CHAPTER 11

"Santa Claus Wants Some Lovin'"

WREN SERIOUSLY NEEDED A BREAK FROM HAWTHORNE MEN. THE moment her phone stopped buzzing, it instantly started again.

As soon as she reached the safety of her soundproofed car, she snatched the phone out of her bag and snapped, *"What?"*

"Wren, thank God. I need you!" Soren said in a panic, his voice cracking with desperation.

Her frustration immediately transformed into concern. "What's wrong?"

"I'm going to fucking kill Logan! He signed me up for some bachelor auction with a bunch of feral romance readers! I was getting lunch at Vine & Barrel this afternoon when your horny author friend accosted me."

"Jocelyn?"

"Yeah. She raved about me finally doing my civic duty. I didn't have a clue what she was talking about until she showed me the

175

signup sheet for her event tonight. Logan put my name on that damn list. I know it was him."

Wren exhaled her concern with an eye roll. Why was this her problem? "If you don't want to do it, Soren, just tell her you had a change of heart."

"Have you met Jocelyn? She's a lunatic. I tried getting out of it, but she threatened to tell everyone we slept together and that she broke it off because I wasn't ergonomically satisfying in the pants department—that's total bullshit, by the way. I'm above average and surprisingly impressive. Once, I even made a woman speak in tongues."

"I don't need to hear that."

"I'm just trying to protect my reputation. I can't have some Viking porn author making up stories about me and my man parts."

She laughed. "Just play along with the auction, Soren. It's for charity."

"No. I can't. The chick with the blue hair from the sex toy shop turned up too. Those two should never be able to team up. She said she'd back Jocelyn's made-up story if I didn't show up."

"Then you better go."

"I'm seriously going to murder Logan the next time I see him."

"What's the big deal, Soren? You could actually meet someone—"

"Uh-uh. No way. You have to help me."

Someone hollered in the background, and Wren frowned. "Where are you now?"

"I'm at Vine & Barrel. The auction starts in thirty minutes. And Wren... these aren't regular women. They're all boozed up and catcalling like this is some sort of construction site. I've never felt so objectified. They're looking at me like a prime cut of beef. I'm scared." His voice cracked.

Wren could hear the volume of the bar in the background. It sounded way too wild for the typically swanky vibe of the restaurant. "It's for a good cause, Soren. Jocelyn's trying to build a new wing on the library. You like books."

"Not the sort these women like. The last thing Hideaway Bay needs is more women like Jocelyn. They're feral! One tried to take my shirt off and lube me up with some strawberry-scented shit."

Wren laughed. "Come on, Soren, be a good sport."

"They won't let me leave! I've tried several times. Apparently, I'm prime pickings. You have to come save me."

"How am I supposed to do that? There's no reasoning with Jocelyn once her mind's made up."

"Then you have to come bid on me. I can't go home with these women. I'm already feeling objectified. I'm a piece of meat here!"

She rolled her eyes. "I don't know. That doesn't seem like a sensible investment. The holidays are coming, and I've been saving up for some new yoga equipment—"

"Wren!" he snapped, voice back to shrill. "Do not let me get sold off to these jackals. They'll rip me apart like the last big ticket item at a Black Friday sale. I'm not charming enough to survive this."

"Yes, you are."

"No, I'm really not. Please, come rescue me."

She sighed. "Fine. I'll be there soon."

"Hurry!"

She ended the call and laughed. He was definitely going to kill Logan.

Vine & Barrel was one of Hideaway Bay's most upscale bars, where leather and mahogany usually whispered sophistication under dark wood beams and candlelit tables. But that hushed, romantic atmosphere was not what Wren walked into.

The deep emerald velvet booths overflowed with well-hydrated women whose laughter bubbled like champagne. The air fizzed with anticipation, and they hooted and cheered whenever a bachelor walked by. It was as rowdy as the New York City trading floor five minutes before closing.

"What the..."

The anchors and vintage fishing gear adorning the walls were draped in flashing red lights, giving the usually tasteful establishment a more sinful, red-light district appearance. A runway stage made from a glossy wooden dock platform, complete with string lights and garland, protruded into the main lounge. Jocelyn's books were displayed throughout, along with naughty toys from Lola's adult store, Knotty & Nice.

She grinned, thinking of how great it would be if they forced Soren to strut his stuff down that catwalk. He was going to beat the crap out of Logan for setting him up like this.

Red velvet curtains tied back with gold rope created a lush backdrop that shimmered under stage lights like liquid sin. A large, hand-painted sign read, *"Raiders of the Lost Heart Fundraiser: A Holiday Hero Auction Benefitting the Hideaway Bay Public Library!"*

"Oh, this is too good." Rather than find Soren, Wren sat down at the bar. The place was packed, so there weren't many options for seats close to the stage.

Her eyes widened when she realized the ornaments on the Christmas tree by the bar displayed anatomically correct molds of genitals—clitorises to be exact. There also hung crab claws, wine corks, and bottles, and such, but once one saw a set of dangling Christmas balls—not the Hobby Lobby sort—it became a bit difficult to notice anything else.

"What can I get you?" the bartender asked, having to shout over the boisterous crowd.

Wren glanced at the signature cocktail menu for the night. "I'll take a spiced cider."

"Rum or whiskey?"

"Um, rum, please."

"Coming right up."

Cranberries, pine sprigs, and floating tea lights added some tasteful holiday charm to the lounge, but nothing could distract from the potent essence of female hormones in the air.

"You came!" Jocelyn tackled her with a clumsy hug that reeked of rum and victory and nearly knocked Wren off her stool.

"Phew." She fanned a hand in front of her face. "Good God, Joce. You smell flammable." Wren did quick math. " I left you more than eight hours ago. Have you had any water or food?"

She waved away her concern. "I'm the host. I had to sample a little of everything."

"Why would you do that when you know you have to emcee?

She shrugged. "My Vikings weren't cooperating. And you know my motto: when life gives you writer's block, make martinis."

"Does that actually help?"

"No, but I don't care about the writer's block anymore." She reached for a program on the bar. "Can you believe this crowd? I never expected this great of a turnout."

Wren scanned the women. She only recognized a few from Hideaway Bay. These ladies weren't town locals. "Where did they come from?"

"They're Viking lovers like me! Some are fellow authors, others are readers, and a few are just single women looking for a good time." She grinned and hooted when the handsome, young barback walked by with a case of beer on his shoulder.

Several women catcalled and whistled.

"These are my people!" Jocelyn reached for a program that shamelessly advertised her newest release, *The Viking's Heart*. "Have you seen this lineup?"

"That's sort of why I'm here. Soren called me in a panic."

Jocelyn laughed. "How very territorial of you to come to his rescue. Careful, Wren, do anything public and by tomorrow, the town will think you're in love."

Wren's face went slack, and Jocelyn, despite her intoxication, read her like a book.

"Oh, my God." Jocelyn grabbed her by the arms and shook her like a rag doll. "There have been new developments. Tell me!"

Wren disentangled from her grip. "Shh!"

"You saw Grey." Her eyes grew wild with curiosity. "What happened?"

Where did she even begin? "That's a story for sober Jocelyn."

"Oh, come on. She's the lamest of all my personalities. Just give me the CliffsNotes. Did you fuck him?"

"Joce, shh!" Wren winced and quickly looked around for anyone eavesdropping. "And no."

"Blow him?"

Realizing she wouldn't stop, Wren blushed and whispered, "It went the other way around."

Her eyes went wide and she leaned in. "Really?" She grinned, her gaze drifting upward.

"Stop trying to imagine it!"

"What? That's what I do!" She laughed. "If you had a nooner with Grey, why the hell are you here?"

"To support my friend."

"No, Wren. If you were making progress with one, why would you come to rescue the other?"

"We're just friends, Joce. I'm only here because Soren begged me."

"Sounds like a setup if you ask me."

"Logan signed him up as a prank."

"I know." She laughed. "I was there. But if you ask me, it's not much of a prank if Soren gets to go home with you."

"No one's going home with me. It's only for a date, anyway, right?" Leave it to Jocelyn to start a prostitution ring in their wholesome little town.

She held up her palms. "Hey, where people put their no-nos on said date remains totally up to them."

"You're a master of prose."

"Don't judge me. I've had enough rum to sedate Santa himself."

Jocelyn sipped from the tiny swizzle straw of her red cocktail and snorted. "Logan's his own worst cockblocker. What did he think would happen?"

"Speaking of Santa..." Wren lifted the paddle she received when she bought her ticket at the door. It featured a sexy, shirtless Saint Nick glued to a tongue depressor stick. "Is this your doing?"

"Good swag remains the name of the game, my friend." A number appeared printed boldly on the back of each paddle. "And you're gonna need that to bid on your boyfriend's brother."

"Jocelyn! He's not my boyfriend."

She smirked. "Exactly why you have every right to take someone else home tonight. I can't wait until Grey finds out."

"Why do you hate me?"

"Honey, I love you. That's why I want this for you. Sometimes, us women need to light a fire under a man's ass." She flicked the sexy Santa paddle. "This will get Greyson Hawthorne's temper burning red hot. May the horned god of Yule be with you. The competition's fierce, and Soren's stirring a lot of interest."

"Ugh, I sort of hoped this could be a discreet transaction."

If Wren publicly bid on Soren, the town would assume something was going on between them. Which it sort of was. But not really. It was a delicate balance, and they didn't need meddlers to add pressure to the situation. "I'm so fucked."

"You don't have to save him, Wren. Soren's a big boy. He'll figure it out."

She debated, unsure if she would rescue him from a mystery date or let him take the fall. She decided to play it by ear. "Honestly, I'm not sure I have the stamina to face off with these women."

Jocelyn grinned proudly. "They're a voracious bunch, but that's why I love them." She looked at her smartwatch. "Oh, shit, that's Lola. It's time to start the show. I gotta go."

"Good luck!"

Jocelyn raced to the stage, grabbing a glitter-covered, horned Viking helmet from Lola on the way. Wren laughed and rolled her eyes when she noticed more naughty ornaments hanging from each horn. With her thigh-high boots and ruby red corset, she looked like a bedazzled concubine from the Middle Ages waiting for a possessive Norse god to take her away.

She took the stage and yelled into the microphone. "Are we ready to have some fun, ladies?"

The women cheered and hollered. One even whistled like a conductor.

"That's what I like to hear! Loosen those corsets and lower your inhibitions. It's time to raise some funds for a great cause!"

More wild cheers.

"My fellow lovers of questionable decisions and throbbing plotlines," Jocelyn said, expression sobering and tone shifting into satirical deadpan as if announcing a humanitarian disaster. "We gathered tonight, not just for a good time, though let's be honest, several of you are already halfway there, but because there exists a crisis in Hideaway Bay. A quiet, devastating, deeply unsexy crisis. Our local library's romance section is growing, and all those glistening, shirtless men on the shelves need a bigger home. We must find them shelter by adding additional shelves in the new wing your charity supports tonight."

The women gasped as if clutching their invisible pearls, then booed.

"I know. I know. Don't even get me started on the surge of homeless Vikings," Jocelyn continued. "How are we, as a community, supposed to raise empowered, well-read, emotionally intelligent, and sexually satisfied women if they can't access the books guaranteed to get them off? They deserve more than fade-to-black-off-the-page romance, and to make that happen we need more shelves!"

"Save the shirtless cover models!" one woman yelled.

"New bookshelves! New bookshelves!" a rowdy horde at the back table chanted.

"Give us more man chest!"

"And more Viking kidnappings!"

Jocelyn nodded with great aplomb. "The youth deserve better. We deserve better."

"I wanna be tied up by a pirate!" someone screamed, and Lola made a slashing gesture across her neck, signaling to the bartender that the woman was flagged.

"So tonight, my darling romance readers, I ask you to bid as high as your standards, drink deeply, and give generously. Now, let's support those book stacks and admire some six-packs." She raised her drink and shouted, "Send out the men!"

The crowd went wild as festive music blasted from the speakers. A parade of holiday-themed men strutted onto the stage, but she didn't see Soren.

Wren reviewed the program. He was number twelve on the list. The last bachelor on the block. And he was probably trying to wiggle his ass out of a bathroom window at the moment.

The first few bachelors brought their holiday spirit. One wore a glittery red bowtie, and another wore a black tux. One even came out topless with a red nose and reindeer antlers. The audience went nuts, jumping to their feet and shouting wildly whenever they got a muscle flex or little dance from the men.

As an MC, Jocelyn was perfect. Her unfiltered, inappropriate humor kept the crowd engaged and anxious to start the bidding.

"You can trim my Christmas tree!"

"Let's see those Yule logs!"

Wren never saw anything like it. She wondered how much alcohol the bartenders put in the drinks.

"I got your *ho, ho, ho* right here!"

The whole thing was a sexual harassment case waiting to happen. It was probably good that Hideaway Bay didn't have an HR department that Wren knew of.

When she finally spotted Soren, he looked terrified, like cornered prey. Rather than strut onto the stage like the rest of them, he reluctantly shuffled onto the platform, his hands buried in his pockets and his shoulders rounded protectively.

Wren snorted into her spiced cider. He wasn't dressed like the others. There was nothing festive about his dark jeans and black corded designer sweater.

"Meet Soren Hawthorne," Jocelyn announced, waving him onto the catwalk. "He's broody and moody, but he knows how to use a rope—both nautically and recreationally."

He looked absolutely terrified. The women acted like they'd never seen men before.

Soren scanned the audience, squinting through the blinding stage lights. When he finally spotted Wren at the bar, he dropped his head back and visibly sighed in relief.

"All right, men, line up along the back, and let's start the bidding. And remember, ladies, when you bid, you get one of these exclusive bookmarks to take home." She held up the swag and squinted at the design. "They say, *'I came. I saw. I bid. And I hope to come again.'*"

The music shifted to a much sexier rhythm as holiday music started to play.

"First up, we have bachelor number one, Shaun Eriksen. Shaun's a thirty-two-year-old CrossFit enthusiast who rides a motorcycle and works in real estate."

As Jocelyn gave the bachelor's stats, he strutted down the catwalk, turning for all the ladies and getting the crowd even more excited than they already seemed. "The bidding starts at twenty dollars."

Naughty Santa paddles went flying into the air.

"I see twenty. Do I see thirty? I see thirty. Do I have a forty?"

Bachelor Number One's confidence immediately bolstered. That's when the real showing off started.

"Honestly, ladies, who needs books when you have biceps like that? Wowzers!" Jocelyn pointed into the crowd. "One hundred and twenty dollars! Do I hear another bid? Last call for Mr. Tall... One hundred and twenty dollars going once, going twice, sold—to the lucky woman in the red hat and blinking clitoris earrings!"

The bachelor carried a red rose off the stage and presented it to the winner.

"Next up..."

Turning back to the bar, Wren sipped her spiced cider. She didn't know where her friend found the stamina. Or where she found such insatiable readers. These women seemed horny, hungry, and well-financed. What if she couldn't outbid them?

She checked her wallet and winced. Twenty-six dollars. Did they take debit? Soren was going to pay her back every cent for this.

"Who knew there were this many dirty Christmas songs?" a woman passing the bar said to her friend.

As naughty holiday music continued to play, Bachelors Two and Three had their turn on the catwalk, both selling for a generous two hundred dollars.

The closer it came to Soren's turn, the more he fidgeted on stage. Wren laughed when he flagged over a waitress and ordered two shots, slamming both down as Bachelor Number Eight went off to old Mrs. Pierce for the hefty sum of three hundred and eighty dollars.

By the time the bidding started for Bachelor Number Eleven, Soren's face glistened with sweat. He tugged anxiously at his collar, eyes wide, like a reindeer caught in the headlights.

"Sold—for four hundred-forty-five dollars! Thank you, Bridget." The music shifted to another sultry holiday tune. "Our last and final bachelor of the evening tried to sneak out through the chimney, but you've gotta get up earlier than that to fool Jocelyn Collins. They don't call me the queen of plot twists and Viking steam for nothing!" Jocelyn laughed, and Wren wondered who kept bringing her friend fresh drinks. "He's a little shy, but I promise you, ladies, he's worth the wait. Let's start the bidding on Soren Hawthorne—"

Everyone cheered and jumped to their feet. The bidding moved so fast that they passed two hundred dollars before Wren even got her paddle in the air.

"Shit." She panicked and called out, "Four hundred!"

But three other women outbid her.

"This is getting ridiculous." Wren waved her paddle higher in the air, now kneeling on her barstool. "Four-ninety!"

"Wren's back in the game! Do I hear five hundred?"

The battle continued. The younger of her two opponents dropped out, but the middle-aged woman in the blinking elf hat meant business.

"Five-thirty!" Wren yelled. How high did they expect her to go?

When Little Miss Elf Ears passed six hundred dollars, Wren hesitated.

"Six-hundred going once," Jocelyn called. "Six hundred going twice."

Soren's eyes bulged as he gave her a signal to bid again. This had to end. Wren plunged her paddle into the air. "Seven hundred dollars!" Soren better have cash on him.

"Seven hundred-fifty!" the relentless woman in the front shouted.

Was she kidding?

Soren waved her on, his eyes anxious as he fidgeted on the stage. The excitement made it hard to breathe.

"Who's going to end this?" Jocelyn asked, her eyes teasing as she smirked at Wren with that cocky I-told-you-so grin.

The aggressive bidder in the front flashed a confident grin as if already tasting victory. Wren had a feeling she wouldn't back down until she tasted Soren as well.

Her competitive nature couldn't let that happen. Shooting her paddle overhead, Wren yelled, "Two thousand dollars!"

A collective gasp rippled across the bar. Her antlered opponent tossed her paddle onto the table in defeat.

"Sold, to Ms. Wren Wilde!" Applause erupted, and Soren loped off the stage, not stopping until he scooped Wren off her stool and into his arms. Holiday music exploded from the speakers and the room spun as he twirled her around.

"Kiss her!" Women yelled from various corners of the lounge.

Soren handed Wren his red rose and purred in her ear, "My hero."

Wren sniffed the rose and blew out a breath. "That was intense! I almost failed you."

"I never lost faith."

Wren's relief turned to panic as the chanting around the bar grew louder.

"Kiss! Kiss! Kiss! Kiss!"

The blood alcohol levels reached through the roof, and the women were out of control. They weren't ready for the entertainment to end.

Wren took Soren's hand and tugged him toward the door. "We need to get out of here."

"Wait." Soren pulled her back. She expected him to say something about cashing out, but instead, he snatched the mistletoe off the nearest pendant light and slammed his lips to hers.

The roars blurred into white noise as Soren held nothing back—dipping her passionately so that she had no choice but to cling to him. His mouth tasted of whiskey and desperation, his body heat cutting through the cool winter air that seeped through the door.

"Merry Christmas, Wren." He released her with a promising glint in his dark eyes, and she wobbled to her feet, her mind spinning.

Soren grinned, and launched their interlocked hands victoriously overhead—a proud crowd pleaser if there ever was one.

Wren's face scorched as a hot flush rushed to her cheeks. "Soren, let go." Tugging her hand free, she grabbed her bag and threw a few dollars on the bar, racing for the exit.

The cold air hit her burning face like ice as the door slammed behind her.

A second later, it opened and slammed again. "Wren, wait! Where are you going?"

She spun on him. "Why did you kiss me like that?"

He drew back, shocked by her temper. "I was just having fun."

She shook her head. "Everyone's going to talk about us."

"So? Let them."

She closed her eyes and pinched the bridge of her nose. "I hate being the center of town gossip, Soren."

"You're overthinking it. We were just having fun. It's for charity." He shot his fingers in the air like pistols. "Go books."

That reminded her. "I need two grand."

"I don't carry that kind of cash on me. Besides, if I pay the tab, they'll know it was fixed. Pay with your card and I'll write you a check tomorrow."

Check? "Actually, you know what? I have a better idea." She went to her car and retrieved her checkbook from her glove compartment. Soren glanced over her shoulder as she filled out the payee information.

"Whoa, what are you doing? Why are you making it out to my brother?"

"Because Greyson loves playing the humanitarian, and he refuses to take my money. Now, he's Jocelyn's problem." She tore off the check, and Soren followed her back inside.

Jocelyn spotted them immediately. "Oh, there you two lovebirds are!" Her words slurred as she hung on Soren's shoulder. "Where'd you go? Quickie in the parking lot?"

"Wouldn't you like to know?" Soren snickered, and Wren shot him a warning look.

"I had to get my checkbook. Here." Wren handed her the check. "Put that somewhere safe. Tomorrow, get Greyson to endorse it."

"Greyson?"

"Yeah."

Jocelyn's smile grew slow and beyond pleased. She clicked her tongue. "Aww, look at you giving me drama for Christmas! That's exactly what I wanted."

Part of her knew this was a mistake, but Grey left her with little choice. If he wasn't going to accept her money, she'd make sure he put it to good use. "Just make sure he signs it. Don't take no for an answer."

"Aye-aye." Jocelyn did a sloppy salute and knocked her glittered Viking helmet over her eyes.

"Perfect." Wren now felt vindicated and smiled at Soren. "Let's go."

He dragged his feet when they hit the parking lot. "I'm confused. Why would Grey pay to bid on me in a bachelor auction?"

"It's not about that." She walked toward her car.

"Then what's it about?"

"It's a long story. But your brother refuses to take my money, so I'm taking away his choice."

The two thousand didn't dent the balance she still owed Greyson, but it seemed enough to make her point. She wasn't a charity case. If he wanted to play the philanthropist, he could donate his paychecks to whatever fundraiser he chose—Hideaway certainly had enough of them.

"That's gonna be a fight, Wren."

"Why? He knows we went out. And he told me himself that he doesn't care who I date." She thought about how dismissive he acted toward her this evening, after he did things to her no man had ever done. "He's getting exactly what he deserves."

"Wren," Soren scoffed. "We both know he cares."

Fed up, she flung her hands out to the side. "Then where is he, Soren? Everyone's always so certain Greyson's hiding feelings for me. What if he's not? What if he's just a guy who grew up close to a girl, and that's where the story ends?"

He seemed to want to argue. "Somehow, I know I'm gonna get punched for this."

"If Grey punches you, you tell me. I'll take care of him."

Again, he scoffed. "Great, I have a bohemian lightweight for a bodyguard. I've never felt more masculine." He sighed. "You want to go back to my place and have a drink? I could use one after that."

"I can't."

She might be fed up with Greyson and his mind games, but it felt wrong to follow another Greyson encounter with a Soren date—or whatever the hell this was. There had to be some unspoken rule about playing the field with brothers within the same twenty-four-hour span.

"Besides, we have our date this weekend," she reminded.

"Fine. But that's not the one you paid for. You've gotta get your money's worth, and I plan on pulling out all the stops."

"I didn't actually pay for a date."

"Doesn't matter. You won the auction, and as official Bachelor Number Twelve, I'm obligated to deliver you a good time. It's my civic duty."

"Well, you'll have to take a raincheck. I promised Bodhi I'd hang out with him for the parade and fireworks."

"That's fine. Gives me time to plan something really special. But we're still on for tomorrow night." He brushed a kiss on her cheek. "Pick you up around seven."

"Okay. I'll see you then."

On the ride home, her mind dwelt on the echo of screams as Soren kissed her. The gossips in this town lived for drama like that. Such a juicy public display of affection could haunt her for life.

"Crap." This would never pass without Greyson finding out about the kiss.

CHAPTER 12

"Oh, How They Pound, Raising the Sound"

"Coming!" Wren rushed to the front door as someone's pounding fist shook the snow off the awning of her house.

She flung open the door and Greyson stood there, fist suspended in midair. His narrowed glare snapped to her face as he thrust the check forward. "What the hell is this?"

She rolled her eyes, leaving the door open behind her. "You Hawthornes sure know how to make an entrance. Did you ever hear of a phone?"

"Cut the crap, Wren. I went to grab a coffee in town this morning, and several busybodies told me you put on quite the show last night at Jocelyn's event. Mind filling me in?"

She picked up her mug, hiding behind it like a shield. "I don't know what you're talking about."

"Oh, you don't? Well, let me clue you in. Apparently, you and a horny elf got into a bidding war for my brother last night at Vine & Barrel. You put on quite the spectacle and ended up mopping the

191

floor with her." He leaned close and growled, "You severely over-paid, by the way."

"Actually, I didn't pay. You did."

"Yeah, about that. It's not fucking happening. Soren can buy his own sorry ass."

"I'm afraid there's no way out of it now. I told Jocelyn you'd endorse the check, and you know how she is. She takes her town fundraising very seriously."

"I'm not using my paycheck to buy my brother so you can date him."

"Technically, it came from an unclaimed paycheck. You said you didn't want it, so why do you care what the money goes toward?"

He took a menacing step forward, then stilled as if catching himself. "You're not baiting me today." Tossing the check on the counter, he said, "Tear it up."

"Can't."

"Wren."

"Greyson, just because you growl at me doesn't mean you get your way."

They held each other's stare for an excruciating few seconds as the threat in his eyes darkened. "You know the rumors aren't gonna stop. This is just the beginning. You ready for that?"

Her stomach twisted. As much as she hated being the center of Hideaway Bay gossip, there was no avoiding it now. Not only did Soren come with a ridiculous price tag, but he kissed her like he was claiming territory. Greyson got his brother's message loud and clear.

She shrugged. If he planned to act unaffected, she could also pretend. She played it off as if the attention didn't bother her. "Soren does what Soren wants."

"Oh!" he laughed. "Is that what you think they're talking about? That's not how I heard it. No one's talking about Soren."

Her shoulders fell. "What do you mean?"

"They're talking about you, how aggressively you bid on him, how you wouldn't let the other women have a shot, how your bid was, by far, the highest of the night." He cocked his head. "You made a public claim, Wren, and that's how they saw it."

She looked up at him in panic. "No. On some level, they all knew it was a joke—"

"Maybe they would have, but not after..." His words faded away as he searched her face. "Did you do it? Did you kiss him?"

An avalanche of shame swept over her as hurt flashed in his eyes. "Soren—"

"Did you fucking kiss him, Wren?" he snapped, wanting only the truth. "You either shoved him away or..." His jaw ticked as the air crackled with tension, as if he couldn't bear to even finish the question. "Did it mean something to you?"

"It was a joke, Grey. We're just friends."

"That's not what you said yesterday."

"That's because you pushed me away, and I wanted to push back."

"I told you I don't play games."

"Then be direct with me! What do you want?"

The air sparked with a mixture of tension and aggression. He appeared upset but also angry.

"Answer me, Greyson. Everything you've ever asked of me, I've given you, yet you can't even give me an explanation about what we're doing. What is this?"

He closed the distance, quickly rounding the counter. She took a step back and looked up at him. Shaking under his hard, punishing stare.

"I deserve the truth, Grey."

His nostrils flared, and his mouth formed a flat line. "Fine. I can't be your friend anymore."

His words cleaved through her heart like a blade, knocking her off balance as her vision blurred with unshed tears. "Get out."

He caught her arm. "No. I warned you. Once crossed, some lines can't be uncrossed."

She did this. She ruined everything. Looking down, she nodded. He needed to leave before she completely fell apart. "Please, just go."

His laugh turned cold. "You think you're getting rid of me now? You made me your problem."

Her stare jumped to his, confused. "I thought—"

He sealed his mouth to hers, demanding and possessive, tasting of coffee and desperation, his stubble rough against her skin as if trying to erase the memory of all other kisses that came before. Tears sprang to her eyes, but now for different reasons.

Was this really happening? Had Jocelyn's advice actually worked?

She pulled back in shock, afraid she was reading him wrong. "Are you sure?"

"No," he admitted. "But I don't have a choice."

She frowned, confused by his answer.

Tinsel peeked out of his coat collar and meowed. "Not now, Rat." He stuffed the kitten back into the shelter of his jacket.

"You're still calling him that?"

"It's his name."

She untangled herself from his hold. "I think we should talk."

"I don't want to talk."

"Well, I do."

He yanked her close again. "I'm through talking."

"Greyson, stop. You can't keep distracting me with kisses whenever I ask for a real explanation of your feelings."

He released her to pace the tiny kitchen. "I'm not Soren. I don't perform."

"I'm not asking you to perform. I'm asking you to be honest about your feelings for once and have a real conversation with me."

Tinsel climbed out of his coat, using his body as a jungle gym.

Wren wasn't going to be distracted. She'd waited him out for fifteen years. After everything that happened, he owed her an explanation. Soren was willing to open up. The least Greyson could do was admit he cared on some level.

Several minutes passed in unmoving silence as she waited for him to talk.

"Say something!" she finally snapped.

"Are you into him?" he barked, his anger startling her. "Honesty, Wren. I want the truth."

"So do I."

The hard glint in his eye told her he wouldn't confess anything unless she talked first. But what if she confessed her feelings and he rejected her all over again. She wouldn't be able to bear it.

"You know I like you, Grey—"

"Do. You. Like. Soren?"

She swallowed around the lump in her throat. "I don't know."

For once, Greyson didn't look unaffected. "I see." He only took a small step back but it felt like an uncrossable abyss forming between them.

Tears rushed to her eyes. "You're the one who told me to date whoever I wanted."

"I did." He scooped Tinsel off his shoulder and subdued him with a scratch between his ears. "Soren's a good guy."

"Don't do that!" she snapped. "If you don't want me to date him or kiss him, then make me a better offer. You know you have an advantage."

"Yeah, right."

She scoffed. "You say you want the truth, but you're too afraid to give it back. You know there's a difference, Greyson. Everybody knows. And if you're really going to stand here and deny it, then you're the one lying."

"You have no experience with these things—"

"Why?" she snapped. "Because I'm a virgin? This isn't about fucking, Greyson! This is about honesty. It's about communication." The word love rested on the tip of her tongue, but she couldn't bring herself to say it. "I'm literally right here, waiting for you to admit how you feel, but you won't. I've waited a lifetime for you to confess you care about me, but you just keep pushing me away."

"Because you're you!" he yelled. "I've been protecting you from assholes all my life."

"You're not an asshole!"

"I am! If you knew what lived in my head—"

"Oh, please, Greyson. I know you better than anyone. You're not a bad guy."

"I'm not a good guy either. What you want, Wren, what you deserve, I won't be able to give it to you."

"You don't know the first thing about what I want."

"I know you as well as you know me."

"Well, you don't know the future. You're so afraid of disappointing me, you won't even try."

"Because I know enough."

"So, what? You want to fuck me but not be with me?"

"No. That's the exact opposite of what I want."

"You do want to be with me? But not have sex?"

He raked a hand through his hair. "No one's having sex."

"Well, I'd like to."

He glared at her, and she scoffed.

"I'm sorry if that's upsetting for you to hear, Grey, but I'm tired of being alone. I want someone to come home to, someone to ask me about my day. I want to be kissed and touched and treated like a woman deserves to be treated. You have this delicate image of me that just doesn't exist anymore."

She crossed the kitchen, needing to touch him. "Your dad got it wrong, Greyson. Loving someone or showing emotion does not make you weak."

"This isn't about that."

"Yes, it is. Magnus is sick. All those feelings you had when you lost your mom, they're starting to repeat." She squeezed his arms. "Salting the roads won't save him, Grey."

His brow creased as he looked away.

Their mothers would still be alive if the salt trucks had shown up that night. Since then, Greyson made it his job to keep everyone in Hideaway Bay safe. But no amount of salt could save his dad, and there wasn't time to fix the parts of their relationship that were broken.

"You always took care of me, Grey, even at the height of my grief. I let you in. I let you see the ugliest sides of me, and you didn't run. Do you think I would abandon you? All I've ever wanted was for you to let me in. Let me help you with everything you're feeling."

His tense, pensive stare averted hers, but by the way his shoulders moved with every breath, she knew he absorbed every word.

"Let me in, Greyson. Let me be there for you so you don't have to go through this alone." She gently rubbed his back as the kitten played on his shoulder. "I want to comfort you, to be everything you need, but first you have to be honest about the things you're feeling."

As always, silence followed.

"Please, Grey. Just talk to me."

He looked ready to shatter, every muscle coiled with the effort of holding himself together, and then something shifted. That ever-present mask of composure slid back into place. "I have nothing to say."

He broke her heart. "Go home, Greyson. You don't get to be jealous and still shut me out."

She stepped back, and he caught her hand. "Wait." Something desperate flashed in his eyes. "I'm trying, Wren. But I honestly don't know what you want me to say." His hand tightened around hers.

"What do you feel for me, Greyson?"

His breath turned labored as he tried to find the right words. "Everything! Too much." He pressed a fist to his chest. "You touch me, and I forget how to breathe."

It was the first time he ever honestly gave her any sort of confirmation. Relief left her shaken, her knees threatening to buckle under the weight of fifteen years of hoping. "It's the same for me."

Waiting for Greyson to think through his feelings felt like waiting for the glaciers to shift from one side of the ocean to the other, but when he finally found the right words, they hit a million times harder than all the painful silences.

He shook his head, still unsatisfied with his words. "I forget how to stop myself."

"Then don't."

"You deserve better—"

"I don't want better."

"One day you'll need it though, and I'll let you down."

"You don't know that."

"I do." He looked at her then, his eyes desperate to get through to her, but his mouth unable to speak the words he wanted to say. "You're perfect, Wren."

"I'm not—"

"But you are. To me, you are."

She looked down and untied the sash of her robe, letting it drop like a whisper to the floor.

"What are you doing?"

Standing in only a linen nightgown, she looked up at him. "I'm giving myself to you." She pushed the straps of her nightgown off her shoulders, and down it went.

"Wren..." He made no move to touch her.

She took the kitten, gently placing him in a laundry basket with towels that needed to be folded. "Now, it's your turn to tell me to stop." She cautiously removed his coat. When she reached for his belt, he caught her wrist in an unbreakable grip.

"No."

She hadn't expected him to actually stop her.

"I mean, leave it." He pulled her hand to his chest. "That can wait."

"I've waited—"

"Trust me."

She nodded, backing off, and his grip loosened.

She ran her palms over his chest, wrapping her arms around his shoulders, pressing her naked body into him. Slowly, she rose on her toes and brushed her lips to the corner of his mouth, breathing in his familiar scent of cedar and winter air. "You can't scare me away, Greyson. I've seen you at your worst. And I know, at the core, you're a good man."

"You haven't seen all of me."

"Then show me."

He backed her into the wall, cupping his hand around her throat where her pulse beat wildly. His hand slid high enough to show her he wasn't messing around. "You're already shaking."

"You're holding my throat."

"Are you scared?"

"No."

"You should be."

"Then you're going to have to do better than that." She relaxed into the wall, letting all the resistance melt out of her muscles.

His mouth slammed against hers, hard and punishing. His tongue swept into her mouth with dark promise, commanding control, as she surrendered to his lead. When he grabbed her breast, he wasn't gentle. He tried to shock her, but he couldn't.

His clothed body pushed against her naked one, grinding into her, showing her how much she affected him.

He dragged her hand to the bulge in his pants. "This is what you do to me."

He bit her lip, as if to punish her. She gasped and covered her mouth. *"Ouch."*

His hand tightened in her hair as he kissed away the pain. "This is my mouth, Wren. Do you understand? No more Soren, or anyone else. No one kisses you but me."

"Okay."

"Promise me."

"I promise."

"Good." He released her and shivers chased over her skin.

"Why did you stop?"

"I've dealt with you. Now, I have to deal with my brother."

"Grey—"

"Don't. This is between me and Soren." He picked her robe up off the floor and handed it to her, then adjusted the bulge in his pants. "Come to my place tonight."

"When?"

"Seven. We'll finish this then." He scooped Tinsel out of the basket.

When he grabbed his coat, she quickly slipped back into her robe and followed him to the front door. "Grey, you can't fight with Soren over this. You've won."

"That doesn't erase what he did."

She caught his arm. "Greyson, please! Don't turn this into a scandal."

"It's only a scandal if no one backs off. He'll back off. You'll see."

CHAPTER 13

"Ding, Dong, Ding, Dong, Ding"

GREYSON BLEW INTO SOREN'S HOUSE LIKE AN UNWELCOME blizzard, his presence crackling with barely restrained fury. *"Soren!"* he bellowed, shaking the rafters. "Get your fucking ass out here!"

His brother appeared at the top of the landing, strategically keeping a flight of stairs between them like a shield. "I'm not doing this, Greyson."

"The fuck you aren't."

"Look, the check was her idea."

"It's over." His words sliced through the air with deadly finality.

"No. I'm not going through this with you again. She's thirty fucking years old, Grey. You don't get to control us like kids anymore."

"She's done with you."

"Bull. Shit. We have something—"

"You have nothing."

"Says who? You?"

"Says Wren. It's over between you two."

Soren's spine stiffened as suspicion crawled up his rigid back. "What did you do?" He pulled his phone out of his pocket and shot Wren a text.

Greyson crossed his arms over his chest and waited, every muscle in his body coiled like a predator ready to strike.

The awkward silence stretched taut between them as they waited for her to respond.

"She'll get back to me in a second."

"I'm sure." Greyson's words dripped with skepticism.

"She will."

"Maybe if you stare at the screen a little harder, text bubbles will appear."

Tension radiated from his brother as he forked his fingers through his dark hair, sweat beading at his temples despite the cool air, the strands falling in disheveled waves. "She typically answers right away. Maybe it's a bad signal."

Bullshit. Wren was surgically attached to her phone, her lifeline to the world. She paid extra for her plan to ensure she had the best service, while everyone else barely got by with two bars.

She was probably panicking as much as Soren right now, her pulse hammering against her throat as she bit that sexy lip of hers. Greyson wouldn't let things get any further between them until they cleared this up. Best his brother learned the truth sooner rather than later.

"She's obviously ignoring you."

"Give it a sec!"

Greyson paced toward the wall where Soren had a pretentious assortment of unopened champagne bottles displayed like trophies. It made quite a collection, yet he never saw his brother drink a single glass of champagne in his life.

"What are you saving these for?"

Soren shrugged, his shoulders heavy with something unspoken. "A special occasion."

There were at least fifty bottles, some worth well over a thousand dollars, their labels gleaming like promises. "That'll be some occasion."

"Yeah. I guess I've been preserving them so long they seem a little too special to crack open."

He understood that sentiment all too well, the ache of it settling deep in his chest. He'd been protecting Wren for more than a decade, keeping her at arm's length like his most precious possession. Opening this particular Pandora's Box felt wrong on every level. Dangerous and reckless. It also felt like the reward of a lifetime, the sweetest sin he'd ever consider committing.

"Did you hear that?" Soren frowned, his head tilting.

"What?"

"I heard a squeak. Did that come from your stomach?"

Greyson unzipped his coat, the metallic rasp cutting through the silence. "It's Rat."

"You brought a fucking rat into my house?"

"No." He lifted the kitten like a toast, and the tiny creature squawked again.

"What the fuck is that?"

"I found it under my porch. He's too small to live with the other rescues yet."

"So you're just carrying him around like a Momma Kangaroo?" His brother laughed, the sound rich and incredulous. "Living in the woods is making you weird, bro."

Greyson stroked Rat between the ears as his little sticky claws tried to catch his calloused fingers. "He's feral. The mom abandoned him, so he needs to be socialized for a few weeks."

"So, you're just sittin' at home playing with yarn and bottle feeding that runt? Charming."

"Wren's got a lot on her plate right now."

"There it is. I knew you didn't volunteer to play nursemaid to a cat on your own."

His brother cut straight to the bone. Nothing in him wanted to take care of an underweight kitten, but Wren had assumed he would, and he didn't have the heart to tell her no. Besides, Rat actually seemed kind of cool, growing on him like moss on a tree.

"Nothing charming about this little hell spawn. He might look like a dust bunny, but he's packin' murder mittens. He has no regard for personal space or the laws of physics, and I'm pretty sure he's training for a prison break. I'm not adopting him. I'm just trying to keep him alive until he's big enough to move in with the others at the sanctuary."

"Keep pretending it's an inconvenience. Nicely played."

"What the hell's that supposed to mean?"

"Come on, Grey. That little rodent keeps her coming by, doesn't it? Pretend all you want that you don't know what you're doing. I'm not that stupid."

Sharp truth cut him open like a blade. As long as Rat lived with him, Wren would stop by to check on him, her presence filling all the empty spaces in his life.

He'd been running out of excuses to visit The Haven now that construction on the yoga studio had concluded. And, God help him, he really liked when she came to his house. He liked the way her scent clung to the furniture, and how she unconsciously arranged the crap by his sink whenever she used the bathroom, making his space more homey.

Feeling exposed and desperate to flee, he snapped, "She get back to you yet?"

Soren tapped his phone and frowned, the expression darkening his features. "No."

Greyson shifted and glanced out the front window, letting Rat tour the sill with curious whiskers twitching.

"Dad tried talking to me about his funeral yesterday."

Greyson looked back at him on the landing where he now sat on the top step, waiting for his phone to ping like a lovesick teenager. "And?"

Soren shrugged. "He wants his ashes scattered off the back of one of his ships."

"How on brand."

"At least he didn't request we fly Bette Midler out to sing *'Wind Beneath My Wings'* or some shit like that."

"Small mercies."

They fell silent again, the air thick with tension no matter how much Soren tried to dissipate it with small talk. He wasn't letting him off the hook that easily. His brother would either admit defeat, and promise to back off of Wren, or he'd get a size twelve boot up his ass.

"Dad also told me—"

"I'm not here to talk about Dad."

Greyson wasn't in the mood to grapple with his guilt, grief, or regret. Not that he had much guilt regarding his father, but it was hard not to have regrets when dysfunction reached its endgame with no resolution in sight. Some part of him always hoped they would eventually get over the loss of their mom and be a family again, whole and unbroken. That never happened.

"Did you hear that Logan's trying to be a hand model?"

Greyson frowned and glanced up at Soren, confusion creasing his brow. "Didn't he lose a nail in a pickleball game last week?"

"Yeah. That's a real crusher in his industry."

They both chuckled, the sound breaking some of the tension. Greyson lowered into one of the high-backed leather chairs in the foyer, his body sinking into the expensive material as he checked his watch.

Soren's home was completely different from his rustic cabin. Everything smelled like expensive leather and furniture polish, the scent of money that never knew a hard day's work. There wasn't a speck of dust anywhere. Maybe such privilege was a testament to his manhood, but Greyson never felt the need to flex their wealth in such a suffocating way.

Soren stood from the steps, paced the landing like a caged animal, checked his phone, then paced again. "How do you just sit there like this isn't weird?"

"It's not weird. We all knew you and Wren weren't going to pan out."

"Fuck you, Grey. No one knew that."

He lifted a brow, his expression maddeningly calm. "Sure."

"You've got some balls. All our lives, we listened to you and backed off. Any one of us could have gone after her the minute she became an adult."

"But you didn't."

"But we could have."

"But you didn't."

"But. We. Could. Have."

"But. You. Didn't."

"Yeah, well, neither did you. Why the sudden interest? Is this even about her or do you just need to fuck me over to feel like a big man?"

"Watch it."

"Or what? There's only one of us feeling threatened right now, Grey, and it's not me."

He sent him a silencing glare. "I'll let Wren explain it to you."

Soren shook his head and scoffed. "Is it so fucking hard to stomach that she might be into me?"

His scowl drilled into him like a physical force. "She's not."

Soren laughed without humor, the sound bitter and sharp. "You weren't there. We had an awesome date the other night. And last night—"

"The whole town's talking about last night. I don't need the recap." The words tasted like poison on his tongue.

"She kisses me back, Grey. It's not pity or Dad's will or anything else you want to blame. There's something between us, and if you honestly cared about Wren, you'd back off for once and let us figure it out."

"I won't let you hurt her like that." The accusation ricocheted between them like a bullet.

"Get the fuck out of my house."

"I'm not leaving until you admit it's over."

"Fuck you, Greyson. You think I'd ever hurt her? You're the one who won't let her live her damn life. Look at you, man. You can't stand the fact that some things are simply out of your control. Go back to your tree fort in the woods and let the grown-ups do their thing."

He stood and took a threatening step toward the stairs. "Come down here and say that to my face."

Soren rolled his eyes from the safety of the landing and tapped his phone again. One huff of frustration and Greyson knew she hadn't responded. "Did you threaten her?"

The tin taste of uncertainty made him swallow. Why wasn't she getting back to him?

He could easily explain that Wren took her clothes off that morning, that she basically threw herself at him and said things that still had him reeling. But Soren was his brother, and as much as he needed him to admit defeat, he didn't need to totally destroy him in the process.

Trying to make him see reason, Greyson calmly said, "You don't love her, Soren. Not like that."

"And you do?"

The unspoken truth rested silently between them. If he couldn't say it, did he even deserve her?

Soren scoffed. "I can love her better than you, Greyson. For fuck sake, at least I can say it out loud."

He suddenly couldn't breathe. "I need coffee."

Soren followed him into the kitchen at a distance. Tall, midnight blue cabinets and state-of-the-art appliances filled the space like a magazine spread. He scowled at the fancy machine on the counter. "What the fuck is this?"

"Move. You'll end up breaking it."

Greyson stepped back as Soren turned dials and twisted valves. "She get back to you yet?"

"No."

"Could you find a more complicated coffee machine?"

"I have sophisticated taste. Once you get to this level, there's no going back."

Greyson rolled his eyes, exasperation bleeding through his impatience. No matter how similar their upbringing, the three of them were miles apart in differences.

As he watched his brother make a single cup of coffee with the meticulousness of a brain surgeon, he wondered if Soren's attention to detail and over-preparedness might ground Wren.

Maybe she needed someone to contrast her free spirit, someone to remind her there was more to life than frolicking in the woods or fermenting kombucha in mason jars. What if she needed someone more like Soren?

Unease crawled through him like spiders under his flesh, making his skin feel a size too small. Why was she taking so long to respond?

He flexed his hands to release some of the nervous energy tingling up his arm. She had to have seen Soren's text by now. Maybe he should try texting her. What if something went wrong and she changed her mind?

"What did you say in your text?"

"None of your business."

Greyson pulled out his phone, the device warm in his palm.

"Now, you're texting her?"

"It's weird she's not answering."

"She's probably in the shower or something. Don't text her."

Did Soren fear she'd answer Greyson first?

The coffee machine steamed and whistled like a countertop

locomotive, filling the kitchen with rich, dark aromas that made his mouth water. He handed a fancy cup to Greyson. "Drink your coffee and chill the fuck out."

He had to admit, it was better than the bitter swill they served at the hardware shop in town. "Wow."

"Yup. Welcome to the *bougie* side."

Yeah right. Greyson could never be as high maintenance as Soren, but goddamn. "Why is it so good?"

"It's a more nuanced coffee. The brewing process is cleaner with a crisper extraction."

Greyson laughed, the sound rough but genuine. "Could you be anymore pretentious?"

"I could try." Soren sipped from his mug and sighed like a man tasting heaven. "Nothing like that brown piss you drink."

He was finished with the small talk and his dainty coffee. Setting the glass mug in the sink with a sharp clink, he leveled with his brother. "Look, she's gonna get back to you eventually. And you know how this is going to play out. Can we cut the crap?"

"We don't know anything. You're not the expert you think you are on Wren anymore."

Maybe he was right, but Greyson didn't want this to go any further than it had to. Every cell in his body rebelled against the thought that Soren or anyone else might touch what he now considered his.

"This is different, Soren. I'm not backing down."

"Yeah, well, until I hear otherwise from Wren, neither am I."

"You'll lose."

His younger brother laughed. "It would be so easy if you could convince me of that, Grey. But you and I both know I have a chance here. That's why you're panicking."

His hands balled into fists. "You don't have a chance. I'm trying to save you from—"

"I don't need a fucking savior." His scowl darkened. "What's the endgame for you, Grey? Are you really prepared to love her? Because I actually could. I'm willing to. With everything I've got."

"She's not a means to an end."

"Of course she's not. But with everything going on with Dad and the will, I'd be doing all of us a favor. There's no burden in winning a girl like Wren. She's the cherry on top."

His knuckles popped like gunshots. She was *his* fucking cherry. "She's not your prize."

"That's where you're wrong. She'll always be a prize. We were all fools to wait this long. I'm not waiting anymore."

His jaw locked tight, tension coiling around his neck like a vise. The air in his lungs turned heavy and thick, as his mind flashed with vivid images of their future—not his and Wren's, but Soren's and Wren's—and damn it, it made sense in a way that made him sick.

"I'm calling her." Greyson pulled out his phone, his patience finally snapping.

Soren scoffed and paced away from the counter. "Unbelievable. You just can't leave it to chance."

"Fuck chance." He hit send with more force than necessary.

"This is Wren. I'm unavailable. Leave a message."

His jaw clenched so hard his teeth ached. He checked the time with growing dread. She wasn't in her yoga class. There was no reason for her to be unavailable, no excuse that would satisfy the growing panic in his chest.

Soren chuckled, the sound cold and knowing. "Looks like you're getting the brush-off too."

What was she doing? They had an understanding.

"Looks like you've got nothing, big brother."

Greyson's shoulders stiffened, then he pocketed his phone with deliberate calm. Time to come clean. "I was with her an hour ago, Soren."

They locked eyes, the air crackling between them. "You lie."

He shook his head. "Kissing her. Touching her. Do you want me to go on?"

"Manipulating her." Soren glared at him through dark, narrow eyes that burned with betrayal.

"More like fighting her off and trying to do the right thing."

"You're so full of shit."

"Am I?" Distrust flowed in the chasm between them like poison. They'd always been loyal—brothers for life—but things started to feel less stable, the foundation cracking beneath their feet. "It's a courtesy—me warning you to stay away from her. Next time I won't be so calm."

Soren crossed his arms over his chest, his stance defiant. "Any man who tries to control a woman's friends has no real control over anything."

"I never told her you two couldn't be friends. But I'm telling you, if you kiss her again, I'll break your face."

He laughed without humor. "And what about afterwards?"

Grey frowned. "What do you mean?"

"I mean, after it gets too real for you, Grey. Dad's dying. I know how you get. You take off whenever things get too intense. How will that translate to a life with her? You gonna run every time things get real? Marriage? Babies? Things can get pretty heavy when you're talking about the forever."

His chest tightened like a vise, each breath becoming harder to draw.

"That's you, Greyson. That's what you've been protecting her from your entire life. She needs more than you're willing to offer. You know it. I know it. And Wren fucking knows it. All you're doing is leading her down a path that will eventually end with her tears."

He took a step forward, then stilled, his hands fisted at his sides and ready to swing, violence humming through his veins.

Soren glanced at his clenched fingers and scoffed, unafraid. "You can't hit me, because you know I'm right."

He could have laid him out with one swing, could have felt the satisfying crack of bone against bone. He should have. But Rat was in his pocket, and Wren would hear about it, would be disappointed in him again, and that would cut deeper than any blade. How many times had he already made her cry?

Soren's words echoed in his skull like a gong. "I should kick your ass for saying that."

"Some things are worth getting your ass kicked for. It needed to be said."

He couldn't listen to anymore, couldn't bear the images Soren's words painted. He also couldn't make promises he wasn't sure he could keep. "I gotta go."

"That's it. Run away like you always do when things get too real," Soren called after him, his voice cutting through the air like a whip.

The ringing in his ears turned deafening. By the time he reached his truck, hands shaking as he gripped the steering wheel, the engine roaring to life, he could hardly breathe. Did he make a mistake? He couldn't get the image of her crying out of his head.

What if Soren was right and he was the wrong guy for Wren?

CHAPTER 14

"Busy Sidewalks"

Small towns were charming, until they weren't.

Soren called her several times after Greyson left, but she couldn't bring herself to respond. Her stomach churned and knotted every time another notification came through—each buzz like a tiny electric shock to her already frayed nerves—even when it came from Greyson calling. This represented what she'd dreaded from the start. She never wanted to hurt any of them.

She had no clue what Greyson had told Soren. Embarrassed and confused, she feared Greyson might still have a change of heart, the weight of fifteen years of disappointment pressing against her chest.

A lifetime of experience warned her not to trust his mercurial moods, but her heart sang a different tune. Was it a mistake to trust him?

He'd done stuff like this before. Interfered in her love life, then disappeared like smoke on the wind. What if this was just another way to keep her like a bird in a cage?

Wren bounced between doubt and desperate hope. By the time she dressed, she figured nothing out, but felt motion sick with uncertainty.

Skipping over Soren's thirteen texts that demanded she call him, she went right to the messages from her employees.

Freya ran out of valerian root, and Bodhi had a meltdown without his usual blend of calming tea for his daily cat summit. River texted because the new shipment of eucalyptus oil smelled 'off' and he wasn't comfortable using it, but he had a massage client scheduled for that afternoon who specifically requested the eucalyptus aromatherapy scalp massage.

Wren grabbed her keys and coat, needing to collect the supplies and return to The Haven before his client arrived.

But the requests didn't stop there, piling on like autumn leaves, she could barely sift through the demands. When she parked in town, she had three more texts. Two from Soren and one from Lilly.

The printer at The Haven ran out of toner. That meant she also had to make a trip to Paper Moon, the stationery store in town. Hopefully, they had their brand in stock, because a delivery wouldn't get there until next week.

As soon as her feet hit the pavement of Main Street, someone called her name like a siren's song.

"Wren!"

Her shoulders hunched inward as the overwhelming scent of baby powder and flowers wafted on the breeze like a perfumed assault that made her want to hold her breath. Bracing for the gossip storm about to unleash on her, she pasted on a smile and turned. "Birdie, how are you?"

The old woman panted in her pastel joggers as she met Wren on the sidewalk, her chest heaving under the gold cross she somehow believed shielded her from sin. "Oh, well, you know... This weather and my arthritis."

For someone as arthritic as Birdie Quinnley claimed to be, she sure jaywalked quickly.

"Where's your coat?"

She waved a hand of half-painted fingernails like a dismissive queen. "I came from the salon when I saw you."

Uh-oh.

Birdie clutched her cross with dramatic flair. "Everyone's talking, dear, about you and that Hawthorne boy—the dark-haired one. Is there something going on?"

Wren panicked, her pulse stuttering as she quickly sewed together a lie. "Not that I know of."

"Oh…" Birdie frowned, pursing her lips like a disappointed fish. The woman gossiped so much her signature frosty pink lipstick never stayed put on her mouth. "That's not what Eileen said when I got my coffee this morning. You know, it's getting to the point that I can't trust her sources anymore." Birdie tipped her head to look over the rims of her bedazzled glasses, her stare sharp and calculating. "Did you hear about the ruckus they caused at Nonna's Kitchen last night? These bachelor auctions are cropping up all over the place. At this rate, we'll be erecting a whorehouse in Hideaway Bay by New Year's." More cross-clutching. "I swear, you kids don't know how to woo each other the way my generation used to."

Wren smiled, the expression feeling brittle as glass. "You know me, Birdie. I mostly mind my own business."

She arched a silver brow. "Well, it's not gossip if it's true, dear."

"That's one way to look at it," Wren responded with little inflection as she walked.

"Have you heard about what Brody King did?"

"No."

"Well, let me tell you…" Birdie went on and on. Every few words, Wren took another step, but the town gossip kept pace. If there was a way to harness the energy from Birdie Quinnley's mouth, they could probably light the whole town for Christmas without the usual outages.

"I really would love to keep chatting, Birdie, but I have to be back at The Haven in less than an hour."

She tsked like a disapproving mother. "How's your father?"

"Bodhi's great."

She tipped her head and bobbed as if she'd said the opposite. "Poor thing. He never did recover after losing your mother."

Wren frowned. "He's okay. The cats keep him company."

"Cats are not the same as human companionship, dear." She covered her smeared lips. "Oh, what am I saying, you two are one and the same."

"I…I have friends."

"What you need," she whispered behind her hand, "is a lover. Are you sure there's nothing going on with you and that Hawthorne boy?"

Wren laughed nervously, the sound sharp and brittle. "I'm not sure what you heard, Birdie, but—"

"I heard quite a bit. That author friend of yours—what's her name?"

"Jocelyn."

"Yes, Jacqueline. She's up to no good. Parading all those women into town with their phallic jewelry and selling sex toys and pornography."

"Um, I wouldn't know anything about that."

"I know what's in her books, dear. And now she's trying to take over the public library so she can brainwash our youth."

Wren hitched a thumb over her shoulder at the Wilde Kettle. "I really have to go, Birdie. Aunt Astrid's expecting me."

Birdie's pruned face pursed as if she sucked on a particularly sour lemon. She and Astrid used to be bridge partners and the best of friends, until something happened a few years back. Now, they couldn't stand in the same room without drawing blood.

"Oh. Well. I should get back to my appointment. They'll probably have to repaint this finger."

"Then you better go. It was nice seeing you."

"You be careful out there, dear. And try to spend a little less time with those cats. Find a man."

Wren's fake smile started to feel like a plastic mask. "Bye."

Rusted wind chimes clattered like old bones as she pulled open the door to the Wilde Kettle. The trail of baby powder and flowers vanished, overwhelmed by the potent scent of patchouli and herbs that wrapped around her like a comforting embrace.

"You look like you're running from something, Wren," Aunt Astrid greeted as she ground herbs into the old stone mortar on the counter with practiced precision.

"I just got accosted by Birdie Quinnley."

"What does that old witch want?"

The warm aroma of dried lavender, cloves, and something vaguely medicinal wafted from under the pestle as she crushed the leaves and seeds into a fine powder. "Does anyone ever know?"

"Good point." Aunt Astrid sniffed the concoction with a connoisseur's appreciation and pulled an oil off the shelf to add a few drops. "So, are you just looking for sanctuary or did you come in for a reason? Perhaps some chamomile and ginger to soothe those inner muscles?"

She frowned, heat creeping up her neck. "Why would my inner muscles need soothing?"

"Oh, you know, in case you had a long night."

Dust motes floated lazily in the golden sunbeams slanting through narrow windows, shifting as Wren blew out a frustrated breath. "What did you hear?"

Her aunt shrugged and nosed through the glass jars filled with loose tea leaves, curled roots, and brittle flower petals. "Me? Oh, sweetie, you know I'm not one for gossip."

"Right."

"But I will say this. If you're going to start having a social life with the son of a man as formidable as Magnus Hawthorne, you should probably take something stronger than herbal tea. Don't want a litter of little ones running around before you're ready."

She drew in a deep breath, her nose tingling with the hint of a sneeze from the dust dancing in the air. Did everyone feel entitled to the details of her sex life? If only they realized how non-existent it was.

Wren changed the subject. "Do you have any eucalyptus oil? The stuff we ordered for the spa smells off. I can't use it on our clients."

Astrid pulled down a jar with her faded handwriting on the label and dumped whatever herbs she'd been crushing inside. The wooden floor creaked like old joints. "You know better than to order off the internet, Wren. From now on, just come here."

"We go through our supplies too fast."

"You think I can't keep up with your demands? All I've got is time on my hands." She moved to the hutch on the back wall and pushed a sleeping cat off the shelf to open the cabinets. "I just made some the other day. Let me find it." Glass bottles clinked like wind chimes. "Ah, here it is."

"Thanks. What do I owe you?"

"It's on the house." She jotted down a note to make more. "Come by in a week and I'll have a bigger order ready—one that isn't rancid."

"Okay." Wren dropped the oil into a paper bag and stuffed it into her tote. "I also need more valerian root for Bodhi."

Her aunt filled a bag and handed it to her. "Anything else?"

"That's it." Except it wasn't. Curiosity ate at her like acid. "What are they really saying about me?"

Her aunt brushed a few crushed herbs onto the floor, which looked like it hadn't been swept in a year. "Just that Magnus's middle son kissed you hard enough to knock you up."

Wren winced.

"But the big gossip's about how much you paid to let him stick his tongue down your throat. Why would you pay him?"

"I didn't."

"That's not what I heard. People are whispering something to the tune of five thousand dollars."

She scoffed. "Yeah, right. More like two."

Astrid raised a brow like a disapproving teacher. "Not something to brag about, dear."

"You're right. But I didn't pay it. I mean, I paid, but it wasn't my money. It came from Greyson's account. It's a long story."

"Tell me you're not involved with both of them like some 1970s key party."

If only it seemed that simple. "Don't believe everything you hear." She clenched the paper bag in her fist. "I gotta go. Thanks for the oil."

Stepping back onto the cold sidewalk was like coming up for air. Wren drew in a deep breath. It was getting late and she needed to hustle.

On her walk to Paper Moon, the town stationary store, Wren passed several townspeople who stared at her as they whispered behind their hands like conspirators. The more looks she got, the more self-conscious she grew, her skin crawling with unwanted attention until she regretted ever going to that damn auction in the first place.

Next time Logan played a prank on Soren, they could figure it out themselves.

By the time Wren made it back to The Haven, Bodhi seemed a mess, his energy scattered like leaves in a windstorm. He didn't like his routine disrupted, and without his morning tea to level him out, he'd entered a manic mood and completely fell out of alignment with his usual chill frequency.

"Freya, can you…?"

"On it," the chef said, taking the bag of herbs from Wren. "The kettle should still be warm."

Wren only had a few minutes before her yoga students arrived. And she needed to check on her dad. "Where's River?"

"He's with a client," Lilly said, a smitten smile spreading across her face. "Heard you had quite the night last night."

Despite Lilly's innocent big eyes and pixie-like haircut, she had a wickedness about her that sparkled like mischief. Most of the time, she acted so laid back people assumed she used drugs, but when good gossip came around, she perked up like a flower in sunlight.

"My night was boring."

Lilly snorted. "Please. I can tell when you're lying. Besides, everyone's talking about it."

Wren massaged the back of her neck where a kink had formed, tension coiling around her like a snake. Not giving the comment any oxygen, she set the toner on the front desk. "Have you seen Bodhi?"

"Check outside."

Wren turned and spotted two locals walking from the parking lot with yoga mats under their arms. Her phone buzzed and she distractedly glanced at the screen.

Soren again.

He sure was persistent.

Especially compared to Greyson, who only called once. She sent the call to voicemail.

"Tell the students to start with a meditation. I'll meet them in the studio in ten minutes." Wren rushed out the side door to find her dad. As expected, Bodhi wandered the Zen garden.

"Dad?"

He paced in circles around the gravel paths with his coat half-buttoned, a single glove dangling from one hand like a forgotten memory. He didn't seem to notice the chill in the air.

"Dad?" Wren approached slowly.

He mumbled something about the cats' shelters. "The eastern winds knocked more cedar shingles loose." He paused to adjust a small, empty bird feeder like it operated a pressure valve on a steam engine. "I told myself last spring, didn't I? Told myself we'd replace the shingles. But look at that. Look at that one, Wrennie. It's leaning like an old man in a storm."

Wren stepped onto the path with slow, careful steps, knowing Bodhi didn't like to feel rushed when he got like this. Her heart ached for him.

"We can fix the roofs, Dad."

"We'll have to. More snow's coming. The elders must be protected."

"I know. We'll make sure all the cats are fine." She dusted a few pine needles off the stone bench, shivering as she wrapped her arms around herself. "You're not wearing your hat."

He didn't answer, but felt his head. "Missing my own shingles," he joked, and Wren smiled.

"What do you say we go back inside before you catch a chill?"

He crouched beside one of the cat shelters and ran his hands along the edge of the little roof, his fingers trembling slightly from cold or anxiety. The sun hadn't reached this part of the garden yet, so the cats hid elsewhere. Probably curled up in the kitchen sunroom, waiting for him like devoted subjects.

"I went into town and picked up more of your tea." She kneeled beside him on the cold gravel. "It's steeping on the counter with honey, just the way you like it."

He blinked at her, still somewhat confused. "We're out of valerian. I checked twice. Maybe three times. I could've sworn I had more in the green tin."

"I got some today." She reached out, adjusting the open flap of his coat with gentle fingers. "Let's go inside where it's warm and you can have some."

He pulled back in quiet defiance. "Not until we fix the leak in the corner cat house."

"Dad, your hands are freezing. Greyson will come by and fix it later."

"Greyson's busy."

"Not too busy for you."

He frowned, then nodded, his breath forming small clouds in the cold air.

"You're shivering, Dad. Come inside. We'll look at the shelters after you've had your tea."

Still, he hesitated. Rolling a loose pebble between his finger and thumb, squinting toward the treetops as if trying to remember something lost among the bare branches.

And then, in a soft voice, he said, "You're so much like her."

Wren swallowed hard, her throat burning. She didn't ask who. She didn't need to.

"She could hear people, even when they didn't say a word."

Her throat burned. "Mom would want you to go inside, Dad."

"I'm not ready yet." He shook his head. "She should have been here, with us."

Wren never complained about the care her father needed, but sometimes, when his episodes came during busy days, it was hard to prioritize his needs over hers. She'd been doing it since she was fifteen, and learned long ago there was no rushing him when he got like this.

She picked up the glove he'd dropped. "Come inside with me, Dad. We can have tea together, and you can tell me everything that needs fixing. We'll make a list, like we used to."

He nodded. Not really agreeing, but yielding to the possibility. "A lot needs fixing around here."

That hurt to hear, being that The Haven was less than five years old and she'd spent every spare minute she had fixing it up. "We'll take care of everything. We'll make it perfect—for Mom."

He finally gave in and they walked toward the doors together.

Most days, Bodhi did as he pleased, taking care of the grounds, seeing to the cats, and drinking tea with Aunt Astrid when she visited. But every once in a while, he had an episode.

Maybe it stemmed from the drugs he did in his youth. Maybe his manic moods had to do with depression. Or maybe this represented just the broken pieces left over after a broken heart that never quite healed.

When he got confused like this, the best thing to do was get him back on track and make sure he got a decent night's sleep. Wren didn't pity her father or herself. This was what was left of their family, and she was grateful she still had one parent in her life.

It didn't matter what others in the town said or thought about them. As long as they had each other, they were all right.

She set her father up in the sun room with his tea and asked Lilly to teach her class. The cats greeted Bodhi—their god—with purrs and loving headbutts.

"How's the tea, Dad?"

"Perfect."

There was less risk in taking care of him now than when she was younger. She didn't have to worry that someone might see him or judge him as an unfit parent. She didn't have to worry someone might take him, or her, away.

Sometimes, his episodes lasted days. She used to miss school and truant officers would show up at her house. Then came the social services. If not for Greyson stepping in and helping her with Bodhi, she might have been forced into foster care.

Settling beside her father with a notepad, she clicked her pen. "Are you ready to make our list?"

Appearing startled by her company, he grinned. "No class today?"

She didn't bother rehashing the last thirty minutes. There was no point. "I wanted to spend some time with you."

His hand trembled as he set down his tea. "Well, that's a treat. What kind of list did you want to make?"

"Whatever kind of list you want." She set her pen to the paper and waited.

He sat back, cradling his mug in the sunlight that streamed through the windows. "Did I ever tell you about my time in Bali?"

"Yes, but tell me again." She set down the notepad.

They never did make a list, but that was never the point. The point was making sure he felt safe and knew his world wouldn't crumble without warning again.

By the end of the day, she was utterly drained, her emotional reserves empty as a dry well.

Several "new" students came in for the yoga class, and Wren

was glad she ended up skipping. Most of them were town rumor-mongers, likely showing up for the gossip rather than the downward dog.

She had a quiet dinner with Bodhi that night, and helped him settle in. She stared at the clock, wondering what would happen at seven. After such a trying day, the thought of having a deep, emotional conversation with Greyson—no matter how long she waited for that moment to come—was the last thing she wanted to do.

She was obviously procrastinating and still hadn't responded to Soren, whose texts had gone from sweet to anxious to concerned to irritated, then back to sweet, then frustrated again. It was a roller coaster of emotions in digital form.

She deserved all of it, but wanted to deal with none of it.

On top of everything else, she'd forgotten they had a date scheduled. In his last message, he told her she acted like a coward. He was right.

With a sigh, she texted him back.

I KNOW I owe you an explanation for breaking our plans, and I promise one is coming. I just need some time. I'm sorry. I'll explain everything next time we talk in person. No matter what, I love you. Please don't be mad at me.

"SEND." She waited for a response, but his silence stretched like an accusation.

When she pulled up at Greyson's, she hung in the car for a few minutes, wondering if this represented a mistake. Even if she was unsure about the conversation to come, she wanted to be held, and his arms were the ones she craved like an addiction she couldn't shake.

Maybe the heavy stuff could wait until tomorrow.

God knew they waited long enough to get there. Whatever they had to say to each other should keep another twelve hours.

She pulled the keys out of the ignition and navigated the icy path, surprised Greyson hadn't salted it. When she knocked, she had the strange sense that something wasn't right. The house was dark, and she couldn't smell wood burning.

"Greyson?" She knocked again and jiggled the handle. *Locked.*

Stepping off the porch, she walked backwards to look at the chimney. *No smoke.* Navigating the icy walk, she went to the garage and pulled the sliding barn door open. *Empty.*

Her insides shook like a water balloon as realization settled in, rupturing all the lies she told herself that day. The truth rained over her like shattered glass.

"Mother fucker." Lips firmed, jaw tight, she breathed deeply to calm her fury, and failed spectacularly.

He did it to her again.

CHAPTER 15

"Right Down Santa Claus Lane"

THE SCENT OF ROASTED CHESTNUTS AND KETTLE CORN WAFTED ON the crisp December air as Wren tucked her gloved hands deeper into her coat pockets, her breath curling in soft clouds while the drum beats echoed down Main Street. Hideaway Bay's annual Holiday Parade blazed in full swing—loud, cheerful, bedazzled, and unapologetically festive, despite her conflicting mood.

Children in crooked paper crowns and glitter-drenched elf hats skipped along the sidewalks, their laughter rising above the jingle of sleigh bells and the slightly off-key hum of the high school brass band. Bodhi stood beside her, his expression peaceful as he clapped politely for the passing float—an old Hawthorne fishing boat decked out in twinkle lights and towing a giant inflatable lobster wearing a Santa hat that bobbed merrily in the winter wind.

The sight should have made her smile, but the Hawthorne name only twisted the knife deeper. However, no Hawthornes attended.

The operator of the float was someone Wren had never met or seen before.

Greyson avoided large crowds and, after standing her up last night, he probably assumed she'd be present and wanted to avoid crossing her path.

She didn't want to see him either.

Soren typically loved being in the spotlight, but this year he wasn't waving from the Hawthorne Fishery float, his charming smile melting hearts along the parade route, as he'd been doing since the age of eighteen.

Even Logan, who usually came with her and Bodhi because he enjoyed the show and sweet treats wasn't present. She'd done exactly what she wanted to avoid doing and ruined everything.

Forcing a smile, Wren watched as dancers pranced by and waved, but her chest ached with unspoken disappointment. She would not shed one more tear, especially not here, surrounded by peppermint-scented joy and delusions of picture-perfect happiness that outsiders assumed existed only in America's small towns.

Okay, maybe she was a little bitter…

Across the street, Captain Claws, the town mascot, waved his oversized claw from the back of a vintage convertible wrapped in garland and velvet bows. He blew exaggerated kisses toward the crowd as if he ruled Hideaway Bay. Rufus, the town's communal dog, nibbled treats from children's hands while they stared transfixed at the show.

"Watch out!" someone called, and Wren pulled Bodhi aside just in time as a group of dachshunds dressed as reindeer pranced by, their owners struggling to keep them in line as they sniffed out spilled popcorn on the pavement like furry vacuum cleaners.

"Sorry!" the handler yelled, wrestling with the mess of leashes that looked like Christmas ribbon gone wild.

Bodhi erupted in a hardy belly laugh that made Wren smile—really smile—for the first time since last night, the sound warming her more than any hot cocoa could.

She could do this. She could pick herself up and put herself back together because she'd mastered this art since childhood. She had years of experience in surviving rejection and remarkable resilience.

But it hurt. Christ, did it hurt. Like a fresh wound that wouldn't stop bleeding, she wondered if she'd ever fully heal from so much rejection.

The moment she realized she was thinking about him again, she chased the thought away. No more Greyson fantasies. Or thoughts of Soren. Or Logan thoughts for that matter. At least for a little while. She needed a Hawthorne break before the heartache suffocated her completely.

Wren spotted Jocelyn near the bookstore, balanced precariously on a folding chair, snapping proof-of-life photos for her social media while wearing a shirt that read *"Naughty List Survivor."* She shouted for someone to bring her a candy cane martini from the Vine & Barrel float—a makeshift sleigh complete with bartenders mixing up cocktails in elf costumes that jingled with every shake.

The music shifted in waves as floats passed by. Wren blinked against another swirl of confetti drifting through the air like artificial snow. The colors blurred together in a kaleidoscope of holiday cheer. Red. Green. White. Gold. A thousand tiny reminders of what Christmas was meant to be. What she almost had within her grasp.

Families corralled little ones closer to the barricades, handing off clouds of cotton candy, and cheering for the magical festivities. Couples cuddled to keep warm, their bodies pressed together like puzzle pieces that fit perfectly.

Eyes drifting shut, she pictured Greyson there with her, his strong arms wrapped around her from behind, but the momentary warmth morphed quickly into sharp betrayal. That fantasy had dissolved now, like sugar in rain.

They were done.

Had to be.

She refused to chase men who ran from her like she carried some contagious disease.

Keeping her gaze forward, she watched a troupe of local dancers kick and twirl in candy cane-striped leggings, their cheeks flushed with cold and joy.

"Will you look at that." Bodhi nudged her elbow and pointed at one of the dancers doing flips with athletic grace. She forced another smile.

He looked better today. Clearer eyes. His face much less ghostly and confused.

The brass band now blared a jazzy version of *Jingle Bells,* and the town collectively flinched every time the trumpets hit the wrong key. Wren was present in body but absent in spirit. Swallowing hard, she focused on the glittering wreaths sparkling from the lampposts like jeweled crowns.

"I see Astrid," Bodhi pointed to his sister, perched front and center on a camping chair in front of The Wilde Kettle. "How am I going to get over there?"

"You have to walk around, Dad."

He searched for a shortcut and Wren watched tensely as he slid past a barricade and shuffled between the dancers, who pinged him around like a vintage pinball. An officer appeared and tried to escort Bodhi off the road, but Bodhi assumed she wanted to dance, twirling the officer and then pirouetting to the other side of the street with a theatrical bow. Astrid clapped, thoroughly amused by her brother's impromptu performance.

Adjusting the knit hat over her ears, Wren retreated to the back of the crowd so little ones could see. The dancers had moved on, replaced by a fleet of festively decorated trucks honking holiday jingles, one blasting *All I Want for Christmas Is You* from speakers bolted to its roof.

She smiled reflexively, clapping her gloved hands along with the rest of the onlookers. Alone in a sea of togetherness.

Again.

Hell no. You're not going there.

Every time she had a negative thought or suffered even a nip of self-pity, she shoved it back down like swallowing bitter medicine. She thrived. She owned a successful business she built from the ground up to honor her mother's memory. She was complete. A lack of a partner should not determine her self-value.

And hey, there was still Noah.

Her gaze returned to Bodhi across the street, laughing with his sister as if nothing was wrong in the world. And maybe, for him, in this moment, nothing was. That made her happy. That sufficed.

The crowd around her thickened, bodies pressing closer as anticipation hung in the air like morning mist before the storm.

"You think you can just text me *'I'm sorry'*?"

Wren went rigid at the accusing voice and turned, coming face to face with frigid fury. "Soren. Hey."

"What the hell, Wren? I thought we understood each other." Breath clouded in the bitter air as he cornered her against the storefront window, looming with poorly contained fury.

"Soren, I told you there was an explanation."

"Yeah, Greyson. I got the memo. You also told me you'd explain it to me next time we were face-to-face. Well, here I am. Start explaining." But he didn't give her a chance to respond, his words tumbling out like an avalanche. "You explain to me how a man who offers you absolutely nothing in terms of a future, possesses the emotional communication skills of a tree stump, and would rather surround himself with chipmunks and deer than actual people somehow appeals to you more than real fucking stability."

She stepped back, crossing her arms defensively. "That's not fair."

"No, it's not. None of this is fair. But that's exactly what you chose."

People began to look at them and whisper behind gloved hands. "Can we discuss this later?"

"No. You said we would discuss it next time we saw each other. You had all day yesterday to come up with excuses."

"Yesterday was a bad day."

"You think you're the only one with bad days?"

"I didn't say that. Of course not."

When people actually turned to gawk at them like they were part of the entertainment, he shook his head. "Fuck this. Enjoy your miserable life chasing him down in the woods, because you and I both know he's never going to change. I thought you were smarter than that, Wren. I honestly did."

The high school marching band clanged their cymbals, and she flinched, the jarring sound loosening the tears in her eyes. "Wow, Soren." She blinked, his words hitting like physical blows. "Thanks a lot."

"No, you don't get to cry. Not when this was your choice."

Never before had he spoken to her in such a way. She stood speechless.

"I'm not a consolation prize, Wren. I'm not your backup or your insurance plan or whatever you thought."

"Soren, I never thought that!"

"Yeah, you did. At least be honest with yourself. I was always the second choice." He scoffed, the sound bitter and cutting. "I used to think you deserved so much better than Greyson, but you know what? I'm the one who deserves better than you."

His words sliced through her like shards of glass. She didn't know what to say. She just knew she needed to get out of there—now.

She shook her head, blinking furiously against the sting of tears. "You're right," she said, voice steady despite the earthquake in her chest. "You deserve better. But so do I, which is why I'm done with all of you."

He froze, his anger faltering. "Wait—what?"

"I'm done, Soren." Her voice cracked. "Done pretending any of this is romantic or hopeful or even remotely close to a healthy relationship. I'm not someone you get to use to shore up your future. I'm not even sure why I let the three of you decide so many things about my past." She shook her head, disgusted with all of them. "I'm just…done."

"Wren, wait, what happened?"

"It doesn't matter. For all your charm, you're equally complicated, and frankly? Exhausting. I'm finished with all of you. Enjoy the parade."

Before he could stop her, she slipped into the oncoming shuffle of Girl Scouts and crossed the street.

"Wren, wait!" he called, but she kept her head down and kept moving.

She needed to reach somewhere private before tears streamed down her wind-chapped cheeks. Weaving through the crowd, praying others didn't notice her, she sprinted against the current of dancers and pedestrians until disappearing through a narrow alley beside the Wilde Kettle.

The muffled thrum of the parade echoed in the distance as she caught her breath and wiped her eyes. Wren pressed her back against the cool brick wall and sank to the ground, wrapping her arms around her knees as she tried to hold it together. The cold seeped through her coat, the rough brick catching strands of her hair, but she barely noticed through the flood of emotion.

Silent. Shaky. Crying in an alley like some tragic heroine, she tried to ground herself. But Soren's cruel words overwhelmed her, each accusation a dagger to her already wounded heart.

She waited in the alley until the sounds of the parade faded then went to her aunt's store to find her dad. Bodhi announced he wanted chowder for supper. Knowing the chowder house served as one of Greyson's regular spots, Wren opted to sit that one out.

"You and Aunt Astrid go. I'm not hungry."

She minded the store for Astrid until six, then locked up. People were already gathering around Town Square for the fireworks display. Wren didn't have the strength to sit in a sea of cuddling couples hunkered together under blankets while sharing hot cocoa, so she decided to go home.

She reached her car when the first boom crackled into sparkles above. The *oohs* and *ahhs* of onlookers echoed from all corners of Hideaway Bay. Wren seemed the only one not enchanted by the show, perhaps because she had no one to share it with.

Another burst exploded above like war drums dressed in red and gold glitter. She caught the reflection in her windshield but didn't look back. The rich aroma of cinnamon and smoke hung heavily in the frigid night air as she rummaged in her tote for her car key.

"Wren."

Her whole body seized at the sound of Greyson's voice, her blood freezing. The thought of another Hawthorne confrontation threatened to shatter her completely.

"I don't want to talk, Greyson." Her survival instincts broke her out of paralysis, and she pulled the car door shut.

He caught it before it closed. "Just give me two minutes. Please."

"Leave me alone!" She frantically fished through her bag for her key.

"Wren, please!"

She glared at him. It was a mistake. The fireworks reflected across his face as he searched her eyes. She refused to feel bad for him.

His five o'clock shadow stretched more than twenty-four hours old, proof he hadn't slept at home. Dark circles shadowed his eyes, and his hair stuck up at odd angles like he'd been running his hands through it all night. The evidence of his rough evening should have satisfied her, but instead it only made her sick.

"Whatever you're going to say, I don't want to hear it!"

"Wren, I didn't mean to stand you up last night."

She covered her ears. "I said I don't want to hear it."

He yanked her hand away. "Tough. You have to."

"No. I don't have to do anything. You had your chance. You had a hundred chances. I'm done, Greyson! Done with all of you."

He recoiled. "You don't get to throw us away like that."

"There is no us."

"You don't understand."

When he stepped closer, she shoved him back. "No, *you* don't understand. Do you think last night was the first time your disappearing act made me cry? You've been doing this to me my whole life."

"That's not fair. I wanted to be there—"

"Then why weren't you?" He was one of the most capable men she knew. "If you truly wanted this, you would have been there."

"I do want this!"

"It's my fault." She batted away a tear. "I pushed you for more than you wanted to offer. You weren't ready—"

"I'm not fucking scared, Wren. I want to talk about things. I want to talk about us. I'm ready."

She offered him a sad smile. "No, you're not. You spent fifteen years filling my head with empty promises, knowing deep down you were never going to truly be there for me."

He released her car and staggered back. "That's below the belt."

"No, it's dead-on." She yanked the door shut.

"Wren, please. I know I messed up."

The urge to hear him out pulled at her like gravity. She'd done it before—forgiven him for ghosting on her, excused him because she knew he struggled to communicate his emotions. But not this time. He was a grown man, and the time had come for him to understand his actions had consequences.

"I'm all out of second chances, Greyson." She kept her eyes forward as she pulled away.

In her rearview mirror, she caught a glimpse of him standing alone under the streetlight, his hands clenched into fists at his sides as another burst of fireworks painted the sky in shades of gold. For a moment, his expression looked almost desperate—but she forced herself to look away.

This time, she wouldn't turn back.

CHAPTER 16

"It Came Upon a Midnight Clear"

Sleep eluded Wren.

She flipped the pillow again, and kicked off the blanket like a frustrated child. Pulling back the sheet, she rolled left, rolled right, then tried lying face down like a corpse preparing for burial.

"Fuuuuuccccckkkkk..." she groaned into the mattress, her voice muffled by cotton and desperation.

Nothing worked. Her thoughts roared. Clanging-pot-in-a-small-kitchen loud, banging against her skull with the relentless persistence of a sledgehammer swinging from a metronome.

She growled and flopped onto her back, staring at the ceiling where twinkle lights reflected like fallen stars. Cozy, soft, warm. Useless.

The tangled sheets wrapped around her legs like restraints, and she kicked them away with growing frustration. Even the pillow she'd hurled across the room in a moment of desperation mocked her from its place on the floor.

"What was his excuse?" she whispered into the dark like someone who had lived alone so long they now had full-blown conversations with themselves.

Curiosity caffeinated her brain as she sifted through endless possibilities, wondering what excuse Greyson could possibly have for standing her up.

Alien abduction—no.

Boat trouble—too cold and too ten years ago.

Lost in the woods—unlikely.

Cold feet—bingo.

He was a man-shaped cliché.

But… why then, would he say he wanted to be there? He even said he wasn't scared when she called him out on his bullshit.

She frowned, thinking about how devastated he looked when she refused to hear him out. Not stubborn, not mad, not even like he knew what was best for them. He just looked…terrified, like a wounded animal hiding in the shadows.

That look in his eyes haunted her—raw, desperate, as if her rejection had physically wounded him. Recalling how his shoulders sagged in defeat, she replayed his words.

He said he had a good excuse. Swore she'd understand if she'd just listened.

And that was the problem.

When Greyson talked to her, he could get her to believe anything. She was powerless to resist him when he tried to get his way.

It was time to break the cycle.

Time for sleep.

Checking her phone—12:31—she huffed and concentrated on thinking about anything else.

She would get the staff customized bags for Christmas and fill them each with personal items. A vintage T-shirt for River, thread and sewing supplies for Lilly, a nice kitchen accessory for Freya, and new socks for Bodhi. Her dad would also get a personal gift from her, but that covered the company presents. Greyson was, technically, part of the team, but she wasn't thinking about him right now.

Hell no. Not thinking.

No Greyson.

Greyson who?

Never heard of him.

She was definitely losing her mind.

Did sleep deprivation do this to a person? How long could a human being survive without sleep? There had to be a Russian study on that.

She turned again, flopping around for the next hour or so, only growing more restless, until she couldn't take it anymore. With a growl, she reached for her phone.

"Two-fifty?"

She gave up. Kicking off the covers, she flopped to her back and dramatically sighed like a heroine in a tragic opera.

"No, Wren. No. We are not doing this. We're not that girl anymore. We don't show up at people's houses in the middle of the night like some needy doormat. No."

She stared at the shadows, waiting for the urge to fade. She could make more chamomile tea, but she had already downed two cups.

Maybe just a little drive-by. Just to see if his lights were on. Not like a stalker. Like a curious citizen. Like Nancy Drew with slightly worse boundaries.

The fresh air and gentle purr of the car might tire her out like a baby in a car seat.

"You're thinking crazy." Saying the warning out loud didn't deter her rebellious impulses.

Before she could talk herself out of it, she stuffed her pajama pants into her wool-lined boots. Completely judging herself and doing it anyway.

The frigid air slapped her face the moment she stepped outside, making her gasp. Each footstep crunched on the frozen ground, the sound unnaturally loud in the stillness of the night.

The car started ten times louder than usual, and Wren ducked as if someone might be watching from behind the winter-bare trees.

"You're pathetic," she berated her reflection in the mirror, rolling her eyes and backing out of her parking spot.

Two minutes later, she pulled up to Greyson's. The house was dark, but she smelled wood burning like incense in the frigid night air. Was he home?

She tiptoed over the frozen ground to his garage, wincing when the latch of the hanging barn door squeaked obnoxiously like a skyscraper imploding in the silence. A bright light flashed on, and she froze like a striped bandit caught in a mask and beret.

"Shit."

"Wren?"

She winced, but didn't turn around. "Yeah?"

"What are you doing?"

"Would you believe me if I said I was checking your coolant?"

"Only if you can tell me where coolant goes."

"Damn it." With a sigh, she turned. "I couldn't sleep."

"So you decided to break into my barn?"

"I wanted to check if you were home."

"You could have called or knocked."

"True." But that would have been too normal for her current state of mind. She exhaled a cloud of vapor that dissipated like her common sense. "Well, now that I see you're home, I guess I can go."

"Wait." He rushed off the porch, the beam of the flashlight jiggling. The approaching crunch of his booted steps hiked up her nerves as he closed the distance and she stepped back. "I'm glad you're here."

She held up a hand. "This doesn't mean I forgive you."

He caught her hand and brought it to his lips, pressing a kiss through her gloved fingers. "You're shivering. Come inside."

She dug in her heels. "I can't."

"Why? You have somewhere else to be at three in the morning?"

She pulled her hand out of his grip. "I'm still mad at you."

"If you come inside, I'll rub your feet, and you can tell me all the things I do wrong."

She chewed her lip, torn between desire and self-preservation.

"Fire's warm, Wren." He excelled at wearing her down, chipping away at her defenses like water on stone. "Please," he whispered, closing the distance between them.

Despite her efforts to resist him, she melted. "I didn't come for foot rubs."

"Is that a yes?"

A war raged inside her chest, desire winning over self-respect, despite her best efforts. Women everywhere would be disappointed in her lack of backbone.

"Just because I'm going inside does not mean I forgive you."

"Uh-huh." He took her arm and towed her toward the house. Once inside, he took her coat, gloves, and hat. Then stilled when a small squawk of despair screeched from the bedroom.

"Shit. I left Rat in bed." He darted to the back of the house.

"You're letting him sleep with you?"

A moment later, Greyson reappeared, nuzzling the kitten's tiny face with his chin. "Of course. Where else would he sleep?"

Stunned, she shrugged. "In a box."

"That's not how we treat family, Wren. Besides, the little rodent's growing on me. He goes everywhere I go."

She watched him nuzzle the kitten with a mixture of pride and envy.

Greyson warmed some formula as the kitten scaled his shoulder like Spidey-cat. Never once did he complain or appear bothered by the demanding fluffball.

"He's getting attached to you."

"We have a symbiotic relationship. I feed him and show him the town. He protects me from pickpockets and other threats."

The way he cradled the little kitten undid something inside her, triggering an unexpected maternal longing, a deep ache she hadn't realized existed. Her anger softened around the edges, melting like snow under warm sunlight.

"There you go," he said softly, nudging the tiny bottle into the kitten's mouth with his seemingly giant hands.

The little guy seemed ravenous for its late-night feeding. "Maybe he's ready for solids."

"Probably. He burns a lot of calories hunting when we're not on the road." Greyson's usually deep voice shifted into a gruff coo. "Just like your daddy does." He looked back at Wren and smiled. "Today he caught a string, massacred a fleet of dust bunnies, and spent a good ten minutes stalking his tail. He hasn't realized it's attached yet."

She couldn't watch anymore. The sight of him all gentle and nurturing was too damn irresistible. She shouldn't have come here.

"Don't go," he said, sensing her urge to bolt. "Please."

She sighed, noting the creases of exhaustion surrounding his eyes like worry lines etched in stone. "I don't want to fight."

He frowned. "Who's fighting?"

Wren shrugged. "I guess no one."

"Let me get Rat situated and then I'll make some tea. I have the kind you like."

Uncertain, she nodded and made herself cozy under a blanket on the couch. Greyson filled a tea kettle and set up a mug with a teabag and honey, all while holding the kitten in one arm and propping the formula bottle against his chest. When the cat fell asleep, he set it in the basket of blankets on the floor.

Turning his attention to the stove, he casually confessed, "My dad's in the hospital."

Wren immediately sat up, her heart clenching. "Oh my gosh, is he okay?"

"He will be. For now."

Magnus had been sick for some time, and the doctors weren't

optimistic. They told the boys he only had a few months left, but their relationship with their father was so strained, none of them seemed to be taking his prognosis seriously. At least not outwardly.

She wondered if this served as the wake-up call they needed. "What happened?"

He sighed and turned to face her, the strain of his concern evident in his tired posture. "He wasn't feeling well. Monica, his maid, tried to get him to call the doctor, but he refused. It took three of us to force him into the car. Once they got some fluids into him at the hospital and ran some labs, they figured out the issue."

"What was it?"

"Pneumonia. They're treating him with antibiotics and keeping him for a few days."

The kettle whistled, and he removed it from the burner, pouring water into the mug to steep. He carried it to the coffee table and tossed another log on the fire. Rather than turn on the lights, he lit the candles on the mantle, then sat beside her.

The flames cast shadows across his features, softening the harsh lines of exhaustion and painting everything in an intimate golden glow. He settled beside her, the amber light making his eyes appear almost molten.

"That's why I wasn't there last night. I know I should have called, but I wasn't thinking."

She sighed, guilt washing over her. "I don't know what to say." He had a valid excuse. Why had she not considered an emergency with his father? "I'm sorry, Grey. I can't imagine how hard that was for you."

He took her hand. "What do you say we stop apologizing to each other and start over?"

That sounded like a fair plan. "Okay." When he leaned in to kiss her, she drew back. "That doesn't mean I want to be more than friends."

His brow creased, but he didn't argue. Instead, he pulled her feet to his lap. "I promised a foot rub."

She didn't stop him, because no one gave a foot rub better than Greyson Hawthorne. "My dad had an episode yesterday, too."

His fingers already worked their magic, but momentarily stilled. "How bad?"

"We've had worse episodes. It took a while for me to get him inside. I had to skip my yoga class."

"I'm sorry."

"I thought we weren't apologizing anymore."

"Right. I wish you didn't have to deal with that."

She lifted a shoulder. "It's Bodhi. I'm used to it."

"Is he back to normal now?"

"Pretty much. He went on and on about the loose shingles on some of the cat shelters—"

"I'll come by tomorrow," he said, before she even had a chance to ask.

"Thanks."

He tugged her toes gently. "No one warns you about how hard it gets… watching our parents struggle."

Stunned to hear him sharing his feelings, she didn't speak. Her breath caught at this rare glimpse of vulnerability—Greyson Hawthorne was opening up to her.

"Seeing someone as indomitable as Magnus taken down by a cough…" He swallowed hard. "It's insane to me."

Bodhi was the complete opposite of Magnus Hawthorne. Her father was passive, gentle, and soft-spoken. Magnus Hawthorne terrified people. "Your dad's still stronger than most."

"I guess it's a good thing he's always been a defiant prick. If anything, he won't go until he's damn well ready."

She smiled, hoping he spoke the truth.

He stripped off her socks so he could better work his knuckles into the tight tendons of her feet. "You have the tiniest toes."

"They're horrible little sausages."

"I love sausage." He lifted her foot to take a bite, and she squeaked, pulling her leg to her chest. He laughed and continued massaging.

For several minutes, they said nothing, but soon enough, her curiosity got to her. "What did you tell Soren?"

He wouldn't meet her stare. "I told him it was over between you two."

"He yelled at me."

Greyson stilled, the flames from the fire reflecting in his eyes when he looked at her. "What?"

"At the parade. In front of everyone."

"I'll kill him—"

"Greyson, don't. He was upset because of the way we handled everything. It was wrong."

"That doesn't give him the right to yell at you."

"He's hurt."

His eyes rolled with little sympathy. "That's not an excuse. Soren needs to accept reality."

She lowered her gaze. "He's not the only one."

He tugged her leg. "Hey, what does that mean? I told you I was ready. I'm all in, Wren."

She reluctantly met his stare. "I meant me. I think you were right. It's safer if we're just friends."

"I don't want to be your friend anymore. I told you that."

"I know, but—"

"But nothing." He tugged her leg, pulling her until she lay flat on her back, then he pinned her down. "I'm ready to talk."

Her brain ached from overthinking. "I don't feel like talking anymore, Grey." She softly touched his cheek, and he studied her.

"Acting like our feelings don't exist isn't going to make them go away. Trust me."

"Is that what you did, pretended your feelings for me didn't exist?"

"Longer than I care to admit. And all it did was make them grow stronger."

She smiled. "Yesterday, when I felt like everything was falling apart, do you know what I wanted?"

"What?"

"One of your hugs."

His arms tightened around her like a protective cocoon. "You can always come to me, Wren."

That wasn't true. She couldn't go to him when her issues centered on him. "You were right. The whole town's gossiping about me."

"I get no satisfaction out of hearing that."

He trailed his fingers from her neck to her cheekbone, making it difficult to think clearly. The roughness of his fingertips against her skin sent tingles racing along every nerve ending. When he brushed his lips over hers, she didn't have the strength to resist him.

Slow, languid kisses had her arching beneath him. Without asking, he unbuttoned her flannel pajama top, exposing her bare breasts. Her nipples tightened in the cool air, and she shivered.

"Look how beautiful you are."

For once, he wasn't fighting her off. He cupped her breast and dragged his thumb over the sharp tip, and she moaned. Pulling her closer, he took her nipple into his mouth and sucked slowly.

Sensation rolled through her, awakening her body and heating her blood like liquid fire. She locked her arms around his neck, the bulge in his pants pressing against her.

When she tried to shimmy out of her pants, she accidentally kneed him. "Sorry."

He grunted and laughed. "Don't apologize."

Every time he called her out for over-apologizing, she blushed. "Sorry." She winced, having done exactly what he told her not to do.

He released her nipple with a pop and chuckled. "We're going to have to think of a way to get you to stop using that word."

"It's only because I'm nervous."

"You don't have to be nervous with me."

How could he maintain a conversation while doing such things to her?

He held her stare and slowly licked around her nipple. "Something wrong?"

"No, just…you touching my boobs."

He laughed. "Something you should probably get used to."

She pushed her luck. "Does that mean we're finally going to sleep together?"

He smirked. "I think you can feel how badly I want to get inside you."

"Will you—"

He kissed her, cutting off her questions and distracting her with the slow rocking of his hips. Her fingers forked through his hair as liquid heat swirled in her belly. "Greyson…"

"Shh…" His hand slipped into her pants, his fingers sliding into her with ease. "I want you to come all over my fingers."

She moaned. For a man who used his words sparingly, he sure knew how to talk dirty.

Nudging his fingers inside of her with slow, shallow dips, he whispered, "Can you do that for me?"

"Yes."

The tension crested as her body wept over his exploring touch. His fingers glided in and out of her.

"That's it, baby. So sexy. So wet. Just like that."

She lost herself, riding his fingers and grinding her clit against his touch until she trembled through her release.

He withdrew his hand and kissed her softly. "Let's take these off."

Stripping her naked, he pulled her nipple into his mouth, nibbling and sucking the tip. The pleasure felt so acute it teetered on pain, but she loved the way he played with her. Leaving one nipple hard and wet, he moved to suck the other. His fingers pinched her sensitive flesh, tugging deliciously.

As the sensations built, traveling down her body into her throbbing clit, she moaned louder and faster. He trailed his hands over her curves, between her thighs, and pressed his fingers inside her until she trembled again.

"So responsive." He rolled to his back, pulling her on top of him. "Come up here."

"W-what?" She didn't know what position he intended, and it seemed unfair that he was still fully clothed.

He scooted down and pulled her to his chest. "I want to eat your pussy."

"Like this?"

"Yes. Get your sexy ass up here." He tugged her forward.

"Greyson, I can't!" Her face burned. "I'll suffocate you and— *ahhh!*"

He yanked her to his mouth, latching onto her clit before she could utter another excuse. With a jerk of her hips, he forced her to sit on him, his tongue stabbing into her with deep, hungry licks.

"So fucking delicious." He dug his fingers into her ass, and she caught her weight on the arm of the couch.

"I don't think—"

"Stop thinking." His words vibrated hot and muffled against her sex. "I want you coming down my throat."

Wide-eyed, she gaped at the empty room. Who was this man?

"Oh, my gosh." Pressure built inside her with nowhere to escape. Greedy growls vibrated against her folds as he gripped her hips and held her to him.

"Oh my God!" She teetered. A little further and…She jerked when he dragged a finger over her asshole. *"Greyson!"*

He chuckled, but kept devouring her.

When he reached up to hold her chest, she realized just how coordinated he was. She didn't know if she should feel humiliated, petrified, or if she should thank the gods that he finally shared this part of himself with her.

"Ah!" A wave of pleasure built inside of her, zinging through every nerve along her spine. Her toes curled and she started to move without guidance. Then she screamed his name.

His fingers dug into her hips, holding her as close as possible as her pussy pulsed around his tongue. He groaned with dark, masculine satisfaction, drinking down every drop of her release.

She fell back, gasping for air. His smile radiated full-on arrogance as he wiped his mouth on the back of his hand. She gaped at him, wondering how anyone could be so secretly filthy and unhinged. "Could you look more impressed with yourself?"

"I could try." He flashed a wolfish grin.

"Who are you?"

"A hungry man. I could eat you for breakfast every day."

She glanced at the bulge in his pants. "Is it my turn now?"

"I'm pretty sure you just had your turn."

"No, I mean, is it my turn to do that to you?"

He stilled. "Not tonight."

"Why not?"

"Because I said so."

She reached for him anyway, and he caught her arm and she frowned, confused. "Are we back to this?"

"My cock comes out, Wren, and I don't know if I'll have the strength to stop."

"Who says you need to?"

He was silent for a moment, then he folded his hands behind his head, giving her full permission to roam about his body. She reached for the waistband of his lounge pants then hesitated.

"Having second thoughts?"

"No." She flushed. "Just a reminder…I've never done this before."

He caught her chin, lifting her face so he could look into her eyes. "Just trust your instincts."

She bit her lip. "I'd prefer a little direction."

He studied her a moment longer before nodding. "Pull it out."

She stared at the cotton stretched over the thick form of him and hooked her fingers beneath the elastic band. When he lifted his hips, she lowered his pants. There it was—Greyson's cock, thick and long, smooth and dark at the tip. Slightly damp like a flower wearing a drop of dew.

Her breath caught at the sight of him, so male and intimidating yet beautiful in its own way. Heat flooded her cheeks as she took in every detail, committing this moment to memory.

"Wrap your hands around it."

The gravity of this moment sank into her soul. "Like this?"

"Perfect." His eyes drifted shut. "Now, stroke it, nice and slow, with a little pressure."

He released a deep sigh when she did as he instructed, appearing completely content. She leaned forward and licked the tiny pearl of arousal from the tip, and his eyes flashed open.

Seconds stretched like years as he silently watched her. "Keep going."

She smiled and placed a chaste kiss on the tip. He flexed his hips, nudging the swollen head against her lips. She liked the way the smooth tip felt against her skin.

"Are you purposely trying to tease me?"

She blinked innocently, playing dumb. "Is this not how it's done?"

He smirked. "You know it's not."

Maybe she teased him a little. At thirty, there wasn't much mystery left—thanks to the internet.

Sitting up, she glanced around the room.

"Something wrong?"

"Nope." She dropped a pillow onto the floor. "I think I want to try it this way." She slid off the couch to kneel on the pillow.

All humor left his face as he stared at her.

She fidgeted. "Is this okay?"

"Yes," he rasped, shifting to stand before her, his cock in his hand. "Are you sure?"

She looked up at him with trust in her eyes and nodded. "Very."

"Give me your hand." He wrapped her fingers around his engorged flesh, grip tight, showing her how hard he liked to be stroked. "You're good at that." He traced a hand down her cheek. "You ready for the next part?"

Lifting her weight off her heels, she rose to press her lips to him. He flexed and groaned, his fingers sliding into her hair.

"That's it, baby. Now, open your mouth."

She licked down his length, and he groaned.

"A little more." His hand tightened in her hair, angling her head back.

She looked up at him in question.

"Let me see your tongue."

She parted her lips, and he guided his thick length into her mouth until her eyes widened.

"Good girl." He applied pressure to the back of her head, pushing her all the way down, until he nudged the back of her throat.

"Hold it there. Get used to it. Now, fist it." He dropped his head back and groaned as she did exactly as he instructed. "Fuck. Use your hand and your mouth."

He kept his hand tangled in her hair, guiding her rhythm and sometimes surprising her with a bite of pressure when he wanted her to stay. He liked filling her mouth, but he was a big man and she coughed whenever he bumped the back of her throat.

"Sorry." She sputtered.

"Don't apologize."

She tried again, but her eyes watered the moment she gagged. Frustrated that she wasn't able to do it like the women she'd watched online, she grew annoyed. What if other women had done this better for him? Performance anxiety gnawed at her.

"Do you want to keep going?"

She wasn't giving up that easily. "I want to finish you."

He blew out a breath. "Keep saying stuff like that and you will."

Smiling, she wondered if her words affected him as much as his affected her. "I like when you hold my hair."

"Good, because I'm fucking obsessed with your hair."

She laughed. "Really?"

"Yeah. It's a problem."

She had no idea. "Oh, well, that's good, I guess."

He wrapped the length of her waves around his fist and gave a gentle yank, tipping her head back. "Try it this way." He stepped forward. "Don't lean in. Just open your mouth. That's it. Now, let me see that tongue again."

Did he mean it? She stuck out her tongue and he rimmed her lips with the swollen tip of his cock.

"Keep it open." He angled his hips and slid inside. Her lips stretched, and her eyes widened. Before she could gag, he withdrew, only to slide back in again. "That's it." He kept his strokes fast and light as his hips flexed. Sometimes he stood still and simply guided her by her hair.

She loved hearing him grunt and moan. Adored the idea that she caused him to make such sounds.

"Jesus. Do you have any idea how long I've wanted to fuck that beautiful mouth of yours?" His pace increased as did his sounds of satisfaction.

Then he withdrew from her mouth. He pumped his hips as he rapidly stroked his flesh, gripping his cock, tugging hard. She flinched when his hot release shot past his pumping fist onto her breast. More followed as his strokes tightened and slowed, and then he panted.

"Shit. Let me get something to clean you up." He returned a second later with a warm wash cloth. "I'm sorry. I didn't want to assume you'd…"

She frowned as he awkwardly wiped her breasts clean. "What didn't you want to assume?"

"You know."

She looked at him expectantly. "Greyson, if you couldn't tell, I know nothing."

He hesitated, then said, "Swallowing."

"Oh." Of course, that's what he meant. She knew women did that. Did it make it better? "Next time?"

He smiled. "Maybe."

Why maybe? "If there's something you want, I'll do it, Greyson."

"That's not how this works, Wren."

She frowned. "How does it work?"

"It's about your pleasure as much as mine."

"That's sweet. But next time I want you to finish in my mouth."

He stilled and laughed.

"Why are you laughing?"

He helped her up from the floor. "There's just some things that are going to take a minute to get used to. You're Wren."

"So?"

"So, I'm still reeling at the fact that my cock was just in your mouth. It's going to take a bit for me to wrap my brain around coming down your throat."

She smiled. "But you want to?"

He kissed her, hard. "Yes, I want to. I want to do every possible thing with you. Over and over again."

She wanted the same. "Me too."

He looked in her eyes, then kissed her slowly. "I don't think you realize how surreal this is for me. What we just did… I don't have the words to tell you how incredible you are." He dragged his thumb over her lower lip and grinned.

She bit his thumb and laughed.

He scooped her into his arms and carried her to bed. Exhausted, she fell asleep the moment he tugged her safely into the shelter of his body.

CHAPTER 17

"Up on the Housetop"

Wren awoke, warm and well-rested, only to remember she wasn't in her own bed. But this *Goldilocks and the Woodsman* situation wasn't one she'd ever experienced before. Slowly, she turned to Greyson.

Yep, he was asleep and *still* naked.

She looked up at the rafters, unsure what the protocol entailed in situations like this. Did she just lie there and wait, sort of like when a waiter brings one person's dinner out before everyone else's arrives? Or did she get up and start her day?

She should at least brush her teeth, right? But she didn't bring toiletries. Maybe this explained the concept of a walk of shame.

But no shame existed here.

Her smile rested like a precious secret on her lips. Now she possessed secrets. Big secrets. Huge secrets that made her feel like she glowed from the inside out.

The warmth of his skin still lingered where their bodies had touched, and the unfamiliar masculine scent of his sheets surrounded her like an intimate cocoon. Her mind played over visions of last night and she shivered with delicious memory.

Had they really done those things? Her heart quickened at just the thought, heat pooling low in her belly.

A thousand jittery sparks danced in her stomach when she looked back at Greyson. The little kitten curled like a furry black snail shell at his neck. She could stare at him forever. Greyson, not the kitten. Although the kitten looked damn cute, too.

She silently giggled. Holy crap. She was in bed—naked—with Greyson Hawthorne.

It was a rare opportunity to be able to stare at him this closely. In sleep, his features softened, making him look younger, and more vulnerable.

Sandy brown hair swooped over his brow, reminding her of high school Greyson. Soft golden lashes crested like feathers, casting delicate shadows on his tanned cheeks. Through the scruff of his stubble, she could see the scar from where Mrs. Kolb's dog bit him. That dog ended up falling in love with Greyson like everyone else who got to know him. It followed him around all summer long.

The intimacy of studying him like this felt profound, almost sacred. This quiet moment was hers and hers alone—no misinterpreted looks, no shared glances across crowded rooms, no stolen touches when no one was looking. Just her, memorizing every detail of the man who'd finally let her in.

Last night, she met a brand new side of Greyson. And he met a brand new side of her. Did he like seeing her that way? She certainly enjoyed seeing herself that way—liberated, all her inhibitions gone, and feeling wild.

"How does anyone wake up that beautiful?"

Her gaze jumped from his mouth to his eyes. "Your eyes aren't even open."

"I peeked. Still pretty."

Something soft and light fluttered in her stomach. "I was just thinking how hideous you are."

"Brat." He pinched her hip and she squeaked.

The kitten roused and moved right into pounce mode. Greyson wiggled a finger to scratch his head, which then turned into a teasing game of get-the-finger-snake.

When he got tired of the game, he set the kitten on the floor where it pounced on a crumpled receipt abandoned in the corner.

Wren watched enchanted as Grey stretched and groaned. There had never been someone more comfortable in their own skin.

His stare met hers again and his smile was subtle but full of secrets. "Hungry?"

How did he do that? How did he act so casual as if waking up with someone naked in his bed happened regularly?

Then she had a terrible thought. Did this happen regularly? How many other women had awakened right in this spot?

Her stomach tightened with unexpected jealousy, and she clenched her jaw against the unwelcome images that flooded her mind. Soft prancing sounds echoed across the floor as the kitten discovered the laces of Greyson's boots.

"Not really." She decided to keep her sudden girlfriend psychosis to herself. Did that make her his girlfriend? Her brain raced way too fast for seven-thirty in the morning. "Are *you* hungry?"

"I could eat." His hand slipped between her legs, startling her.

"Oh."

"This okay?"

"Um…Sure?"

His other hand slipped under the covers, pulling her close. His palm splayed flat on her belly as he curled possessively around her. She hadn't expected to jump right into— *"Hello."*

He chuckled, his stiff cock nudging at her back.

There was no effort to pull back. Fingers teased. Soft kisses peppered her shoulder. Shivers raced up her spine. He was really going for it. Her toes curled as he pulled her legs open, sliding his hand lower—then her phone rang.

"Shit."

"Do you have to get that?"

She gave him an apologetic look and nervously scooted out of bed, holding a pillow to her front. "It's probably Bodhi wondering where I am."

Greyson rolled to his back and folded his arms behind his head, the blankets tenting over the enormous erection standing like a maypole between them.

The sight of him displayed like that made her breath catch. Part of her wanted to ignore the phone completely and return to bed, to lose herself in him again. But responsibility called, even if her body protested.

She snatched her phone off the nightstand. "Hey, Dad."

"I'm at your door."

"Oh…I'm not there."

"Where'd you run off to this early in the morning? The Elders aren't even up yet."

"I, uh, had to drop something off at Greyson's. What did you need?"

He rambled off a list of things that he needed from the store and stuff that he wanted to do that day. If she didn't cut him off, he'd go on forever.

"Okay, Dad. I'll be there soon. Why don't you go have your tea and commune with the cats? I'll meet you in the sunroom in an hour."

"Sounds good. And tell Greyson we're going to get some weather this week. I feel it in my knees."

"Will do." She ended the call and turned to face Greyson. "Bodhi said to expect snow this week."

He frowned. "There's nothing in the forecast." He grabbed his phone and waited for the signal to catch so the page could load. "Son of a bitch. How does he do that?"

"Is he right?"

"Yes. Two big storms. I swear that wasn't on the Doppler yesterday."

"Does that mean you're going to be busy today?"

"According to this, it's not starting until tomorrow night, but yes, I'm very busy today."

"Oh." Disappointment hit differently now that they were tearing down walls. "Will I see you?"

"I'd say yes, since I'll be fixing the roofs on the cat shelters and whatever else Bodhi has on his list."

Her heart swelled. "You don't have to—"

"Stop. I know I don't have to. I'm doing it because I want to."

Afraid she might say something too intense, she simply smiled and mouthed, "Thank you."

"We should probably get moving." Classic Greyson. He never wanted recognition for anything.

She glanced at his lap. "What about that?"

"I have a feeling that will remain an ongoing problem. At least for a while."

They dressed with an easy intimacy that felt both natural and thrilling. She borrowed one of his flannel shirts, rolling up the sleeves, while he watched her with an intensity that made her skin tingle. Every mundane morning ritual felt charged with new meaning.

Wren had grown used to Greyson working at The Haven, but never in such an open, here-I-am-world manner. He had set up for work before she even drank her coffee, making himself right at home.

He arranged sawhorses into a makeshift work table on the sunny side of the parking lot. Used the outlets hidden behind furniture in the lobby to charge his tools. He even stashed his travel coffee thermos by the pot in the employee kitchen. Wren loved seeing him assume his territory in such an authoritative way. He even recruited Bodhi as his right hand, arming him with a set of work gloves, a carpenter pencil, and a notepad to make a list.

When Greyson sauntered into the lobby in his tool belt, Wren lost her train of thought. The weight of the tools made him move with a confident swagger that screamed competence and raw masculinity. The leather hung low on his hips, accentuating the lean strength of his build and drawing her eyes to places they shouldn't wander during business hours.

"Um…" Lilly waited for her to finish her statement about the reservations, but she completely lost track of what she had been saying. "Hello?" Lilly tapped a finger on the counter. "Earth to Wren."

"Huh?" She pulled her attention away from Greyson as he inspected a crack in the molding. "Sorry. I got distracted."

"I'd say. What's up with you today?"

Her cheeks heated like summer pavement. "Nothing. I just have a lot on my mind. This all looks great. You seem to have everything handled." She rounded the desk to follow Greyson outside where he now rummaged in the back of his truck.

"But we didn't go over the guest arrivals."

"I'm sure everything will run smoothly." Wren stepped outside in the frigid air, forgetting her coat. "Hey."

He immediately stopped and turned. "Hey."

They closed the distance like magnets, drawn to one another, but careful not to touch. If they did, nothing would pull them apart. An unspoken rule dictated that they would keep their personal life private for now.

She scuffed her foot over the pebbled landscape. "What are you working on?"

"The caulk in the lobby needs touching up. You've got some cracks."

"Oh. Thanks."

He nodded. "Of course." His eyes dropped to her chest and she shivered. "Where's the coat I gave you?" He pulled off his canvas jacket and draped it over her shoulders.

She pressed her nose to the collar, breathing in his familiar scent. The smell enveloped her—sawdust and wood smoke, mixed with something clean and entirely him. It was becoming her favorite scent in the world.

"It's hard not to touch you," she admitted.

He held her stare. "It's very…hard."

She hid a smile. "Well… I should let you get back to…fixing my crack."

He raised a brow. "I can do that as soon as I'm done working my caulk."

She glanced at the caulk gun sitting on the tailgate. "It's thick."

He nodded, sucking his lower lip between his teeth. "Makes a tight squeeze."

He excelled at innuendos and she smiled nervously.

"Don't worry, Wren." The corner of his mouth curved upward. "One way or another, I'll make it fit."

She laughed and had to look away, her cheeks on fire. "You're trouble." She handed him back his coat. "I'm taking my cracks back inside where it's warm."

When she looked over her shoulder, he unapologetically watched her walk away. Heat trailed down her spine as his gaze followed her movements, making her hyperaware of every sway of her hips. Maybe she should work a cold plunge into her day. She needed to cool off.

By that evening, Greyson had fixed every possible thing that needed repairing and then some. He caulked all the cracks in the molding, patched the greenhouse roof, replaced the wooden steps to the sauna that had rotted, oiled the squeaky doors, pumped up the wheelbarrow tire, tightened the window latch on the third guest cabin so the cats stopped getting in, fixed the drip in the faucet, leveled the drying rack for the herbs that had been sagging, tidied up the woodpile, drilled new hooks into new posts for the hammocks, picked up a pallet of fuel for the lanterns and stocked it on the shelves in the shed where he'd also built a new wall rack for Bodhi to hang all his rakes and shovels.

But that wasn't all!

He walked the grounds with Bodhi, giving her father the time and space to voice his concerns for the cats. Greyson listened to every point he made and kept a meticulous list. Then he carefully checked off every needed repair. The cats would be dry and warm for the snow this week, because Greyson ensured it.

Wren felt blown away. Greyson always worked hard, but never before had he attacked a punch list with such focused intensity. Was he trying to prove something? Show his commitment to her and The Haven? Did blowjobs possess this kind of power? Or was this something more?

The intensity felt almost desperate, as if he needed to demonstrate his value through sheer productivity. Whatever drove him, she found herself both impressed and slightly concerned about his motivation.

A box of new trail markers arrived, and she needed to replace the old ones. She bundled up for a long walk in the woods and told her staff she'd be back in an hour.

On her way back to the property, she felt surprised to see Greyson's truck still there and all his tools still out. He typically cleaned up around four-thirty and left by five on the days he worked.

Her flashlight cast a dome of light over the ground as she walked briskly toward The Haven, her mind focused on a hot cup of ashwagandha and lemon balm, when she came across Greyson, hunched over and rubbing his back as he worked on some sort of gutter protruding from the foundation.

"Did you hurt yourself?"

He stood up and winced. "I'm fine. Where were you?"

"The new trail markers arrived." She held out the box of old faded markers. "And you're not fine. What happened?"

"It's nothing. I must have wrenched my back moving logs." He tried to play it off, but when he twisted to unplug his drill charger from the wall, she saw him flinch again.

"You're in pain."

"I'm fine, Wren."

"Nothing's wrong with admitting you're hurt, Greyson." She set down the box of trail markers and approached him. She rubbed a hand along his back. "Where's the boo-boo?"

"I'm telling you, I'm—" He hissed in a breath. "It's just tight."

"You're ridiculous." She stepped behind him, trailing her hands slowly over his broad shoulders and down his spine. "Here?"

He grunted. "Yeah."

"That's your QL."

"My what?"

"Quadratus lumborum. It's a deep stabilizer that runs from your iliac crest to your lowest ribs." She traced her fingers along his ribs for a visual. "It's a common strain for people who do a lot of lifting and rotating, especially if your glutes aren't firing properly." She pressed two fingers gently above his hip and he flinched. "Exactly as I suspected."

He stepped away as if to maintain professional boundaries, but this wasn't sexual. This time, his reluctance centered more on masculine pride. When he straightened his shoulders despite the obvious pain, his jaw set in stubborn determination.

She rolled her eyes. "You know, I can fix it for you."

He cleared his throat. "A hot shower should do the trick."

"It won't, but if you want to try that and suffer for the next few days in pain, go for it. Just know that when the inflammation gets worse and you start overusing your thoracolumbar fascia, the opposite side's going to tighten and the pain will likely spiral because you're overcompensating with other muscles."

He just stared at her. "How do you know all that?"

She laughed. "I'm more than a pretty face, Grey." She nudged him toward the building. "Come inside and lie down so I can work it out for you. You've been fixing my stuff all day—let me fix this for you."

"Are you sure you know what you're doing?"

"You've got hypertonicity in the QL and a little compensatory tension in the multifidus."

"Right."

"We can try to fix it in one session, but it depends on how long you've had the injury. My guess is you've been trying to treat it for a while without much long-term relief."

"Pretty much."

She clicked her tongue. "Greyson, why wouldn't you come to me?"

"I don't know. Massages aren't my thing."

"Fifty percent of our clients are men."

His expression hardened. "You mean River's clients?"

"Relax." She laughed. "I'm very professional with all the men who get naked on my table."

He growled as she took the drill out of his hand and pulled him gently toward the spa. "Come on, big, strong man. I promise I'll be gentle."

CHAPTER 18

"Incriminatin' Claus Marks on Her Back"

"Where is everyone?" Greyson eyed the dim blue halls of The Haven, not used to seeing them so quiet or empty.

"It's Sunday, so most of our guests check out by eleven, and the new round of residents don't typically check in until mid-week. Aside from spa appointments, yoga, and morning tea, we don't have a lot going on at this time."

For years, he kept his visits public, only allowing himself to see her in broad daylight to keep himself in check. "I guess I'm usually gone by now."

She looked back at him and smiled. She'd been doing that a lot. And when she wasn't near him, she was on his mind. He hadn't stopped thinking about her all day.

One crack in the dam had brought all of his barriers crumbling down. The carefully constructed walls he'd built over the years lay in ruins around his feet, and he found himself both terrified and exhilarated by the exposure.

265

His gaze drifted back to the doors. "You should lock up if no one else is expected for the day."

"I like to leave the studio available for meditation. We still have a few guests who prefer to retreat in private. And you never know when someone might stop by."

Exactly, he thought. "I don't like the idea of you being alone here at night—"

"I'm not alone. I have you here to protect me." Another enchanting smile nearly distracted him from his concern, but he didn't like overlooking possible security risks, especially where Wren was involved.

He'd order some cameras to install next week. Hideaway Bay might have one of the lowest crime rates in the Northeast, but he wasn't taking any risks.

She turned to face him, taking his hands as she walked backward toward the massage room, towing him along. "Relax, Grey. It's just a little backrub."

Her laughter teased his senses, putting him at ease, but he dragged his feet anyway, if only for the chance to look at her a little longer. Christ, she looked too pretty like this—playful and in her element. He loved the way The Haven added to her confidence. She knew what she wanted and she had brought all her dreams into reality. Watching her succeed filled him with a pride so fierce it sometimes took his breath away. He'd been there to witness her whole dream unfold, and knowing he'd played even a small part in its creation made something warm settle in his chest.

"Don't be shy." She pulled him through the door at the end of the hall.

He followed her into the massage room like a man walking to his own execution. She knew full well that he wasn't getting naked on her table. He didn't need a massage. A hot shower and some ice would do the trick. But he'd play along for a bit, let her feel around, then they'd head back to his place and—

"Hand him over." She held out a hand.

"Huh?"

"Tinsel."

He laughed at her stubborn refusal to let him name the cat. "You mean Rat?" He dug the kitten out of his hood, and it hissed with irritation. The little creature had been sound asleep.

She rolled her eyes as the little warrior caught her thumb with his tiny murder mittens. Unconcerned with the kitten's fury, Wren carried him out of the room.

Greyson frowned with the concern of a helicopter parent. "What did you do with him?"

"He's safe."

His stare lingered on the door as she gently shut it.

"You can take off your coat and start undressing."

"What's that now?" His brows shot up.

"Are you really going to challenge me every step of the way?" She pressed her front to his and rose on her toes to brush a teasing kiss across his lips.

All reluctance shifted into complete agreeability the moment her mouth touched his. Her arms wound around his neck, and the tension in his body melted like ice in sunshine.

"Mmm," she moaned. "I've been wanting to do that all day."

His cock had been maintaining a semi since dawn, but now it stood as a solid slab of granite. He kissed her again, a little more possessively and with a lot more hunger. When he pushed her back to the door, she giggled and turned her cheek, gently prying him off of her.

"Massage first. We don't want that back injury disrupting any of your...extracurricular plans, Mr. Hawthorne."

She had a point. He had planned numerous extracurricular activities for the near future. And he wanted his performance unhindered.

She patted his chest and slipped out of his hold. "Clothes off."

Warm light glowed from a salt lamp in the corner. Something lavender-scented hung in the air like a gentle caress. The massage table looked harmless enough—until he thought about lying face-down on it naked—with a massive hardon.

The room felt smaller now, more intimate with the door closed and the soft lighting creating pools of shadow in the corners. Heat seemed to radiate from the table itself, and he could hear the gentle hum of whatever system kept the space warm and inviting.

While she busied herself at the counter, he stripped off his coat and adjusted his stubborn cock.

He took in the room and knew the layout well, since he built the damn thing, but the last time he stood in here it wasn't painted and didn't have all the plants and equipment set up.

Wren softly hummed and swayed her hips as she organized whatever she prepared over at the little sink. Did she have to be so damn sexy? His cock grew harder by the second.

He tried to think of everything that turned him off, but his mind blanked and his dick throbbed when her raspy voice teased through the silence like an erotic caress.

"Is it warm enough in here for you?"

He grunted as he cautiously watched her. She moved with quiet authority about the space, completely in her element.

When she dimmed the lights another notch and lit a candle, he knew he was fucked. Then she hit a switch on the wall, and tranquil music started to play over the sound of trickling water and thunder in the distance.

"You're still dressed." She rolled a fresh white towel into a bolster.

"I, uh, guess I'm a little nervous." Was seducing a massage therapist legal if you already had seen them naked and brought them to orgasm? The professional boundaries blurred.

"There's no need to be nervous. I'm a professional." Her voice was gentle but clinical. "You're going to lie face down with your head in the cradle, completely covered with a sheet."

Did she honestly think nudity made him nervous? He was more

worried about keeping control of his impulses and not throwing her over that table and fucking her hard into next week.

She's still a virgin. She's still a virgin. She's still a virgin...

The reminder grounded him, but also reinforced how badly he wanted to get inside her. She wouldn't be a virgin for long. And then he would forever own that part of her.

His.

His cock stiffened another inch as his throat tightened. "Wren—"

She silenced him with a kiss. "No more excuses, Grey. In here, I'm in charge."

Christ, he would break his dick on that damn table. She tugged at his shirt and he caught her wrist. "I've got it." If they proceeded, she couldn't touch him.

How will that work, genius? Her hands will be all over you...

He stiffly pulled off his shirt and removed his belt. He hesitated at the button of his constricting jeans. "Is it cool if I keep my pants on?"

She smiled and executed a sexy little eye roll. "If that helps you, fine. But you'll get more out of it if you're naked." She pulled back the crisp white sheet draped over the table and turned around to give him privacy. "Once you're ready, get under the sheet and we'll begin."

He was so royally fucked.

He shoved down his jeans, and his erection angled toward her like a stiff German hunting pointer. Thankfully, the table had enough padding that he could make it work. He shoved his cock down and gently lowered to his stomach, unsure where to put his arms.

Pulling the sheet over his ass, he dropped his face in the hole. "Ready."

"Good." She adjusted the sheet. "Lift your feet. I'm going to put the bolster under them to make it a little more comfortable for you."

The rolled towel helped distribute his weight more evenly. He closed his eyes and tried to breathe a little slower.

"I'll start with some light effleurage to warm the tissue. Let me know if anything feels too intense."

Effleurage? What the hell was effleurage? It sounded like something that should be illegal in at least three states.

He cleared his throat. "Got it."

"Just a warning, I'll need access to your lower back and glutes. Are there any areas you want me to avoid?"

He literally wanted her hands everywhere. "Nope."

The first caress sent a shockwave of pleasure straight to his groin.

"You're tense. Try to relax, Grey. I've got you."

I've got you...

Why did those words hit like a punch to the chest? No one had ever said that to him before—not in a way that felt true. He'd spent his entire life being the one who took care of others, who solved problems and fixed things. The idea that someone could take care of him, that he could let go and trust someone else to hold him together, was both foreign and desperately needed.

Swallowing hard, he prayed to every deity that his enthusiasm remained hidden.

Think of hunting. Think of fishing. Think of her dad. No, wait— don't think of her dad. Shit.

The massage started light, her palms gliding over his back in long, fluid strokes like silk against skin. She pressed down, slow and even, tracing along his spine, then out to his lats. Restraining a moan was difficult.

Did other people moan in these sorts of situations? Was this always so...sexual? He didn't liked the idea of her doing this to other men.

"Your paraspinals are working overtime," she murmured, breath teasing softly down his spine. "I can feel the tension along your erector spinae, especially the left side."

Wait 'til she discovered the tension in the front side erector...

"I'll start loosening up the surrounding fascia." Wren discussing anatomy should not be this sexy. Every word out of her mouth unlocked a new kink.

As she kneaded into his lower back, her thumbs pressing into that deep tissue, a groan slipped out.

"Painful?"

He tried to say something but a strangled, "*Mmf*," escaped. Between the pinched nerve and his crushed dick, he was dying.

"That's your QL. It's definitely angry. You've probably been lifting with your back instead of your legs. I'm going to hold sustained pressure for a minute and let the muscle release on its own."

She used her forearm now, leaning into him with the weight of her whole body, her tits pressing like soft pillows along his bare skin.

He curled his hands around the edge of the table, digging his fingers into the padding, white-knuckled. She pressed into the ache and held—for a solid thirty seconds he couldn't breathe—then the pressure gave way and a subtle release occurred. He exhaled, shocked by how quickly she had located and eased the pain.

"Good." Her hands slid higher, thumbs working through the tight cords of muscle near his spine. She paused at the base of his neck.

"You've got some tension buildup here. I'm going to try some cross-fiber friction to loosen it up. You'll feel it more sharply, but it'll help break the cycle."

Cross-fiber what?

She applied pressure in short, deliberate strokes against the grain of his muscles and he hissed in a breath. The sensation brought a good pain, the kind that made him want to flip over and kiss her senseless.

"Does that feel good?" she whispered, mouth close to his ear.

"Yes," he rasped, his body a knot of tension, the kind that needed other care to cure.

"Good. Now, breathe with me."

He matched her rhythm without thinking. *Inhale. Exhale. Inhale. Exhale.*

The room heated. Everything smelled like soothing herbs and Wren. Her hands kept moving, firm and skilled. In some ways, she knew his body better than he did. The realization that she could read him so completely, that her hands could find and heal places he hadn't even known were broken, left him feeling exposed in ways that had nothing to do with his nudity.

"I'm going to do some pin-and-stretch on the glute medius now."

Glute what now?

She lowered the sheet and his asshole clenched. If she saw, she made no comment. Her fingers anchored deep into the side of his hip, and his spine tightened. No one had ever held him in such a vulnerable position.

"Try to relax." She moved over his tight muscles with controlled precision. The sensation burned, but in a tolerable way. The combination of everything she performed started to unravel him from the inside out.

His body slowly loosened as she hit some pressure points that literally knocked the breath out of him, making space where pain had resided for longer than he could remember.

"You should keep a standing appointment, Greyson. For a man who works with his body as much as you do, I should be seeing you in here at least once a week."

"'Kay." His body existed in ecstasy, making it difficult to utter more than a simple syllable.

"Are you okay with a little heat?"

"Bring it." His body already blazed. What did he have to lose?

She used hot stones on his sore muscles and wrapped his legs in warm towels. No one had ever touched his feet, and whatever she did to his toes, pulling and pinching, the sensation reached all the way to his tingling scalp.

"Time to turn over." Cool air hit his ass as she lifted the sheet and his eyes widened.

"Uh…"

"I'm not looking. Just roll to your back and tell me when you're ready."

He quickly rolled over. "Ready."

The sheet dropped like a blanket of air over him and tented at his groin. He deliberately looked as far away from her as possible, but felt her staring directly at his dick.

"Sorry."

She pressed a calming hand on his shoulder and rounded the table to stand behind him. "No apologies for stuff like that between us, remember?" She bent and pressed an upside-down kiss to his lips. "And now, I can kiss you."

Her soft breasts nudged his head as her scent enveloped him. The angle felt awkward, and his fingers itched to knot in her hair and pull her on top of him, but he resisted, keeping his death grip on the table.

"That better not be something you do with your other clients."

"My other clients don't get hard when I touch them."

He doubted that.

As she worked her hands over his shoulders, he stared at her. Then she caught him watching her and smirked with those full lips. He was a dead man.

Closing his eyes only enhanced his other senses. Every touch carried the weight of a thousand caresses. His mind dwelt on her mouth, remembering the way she used it on him last night.

Don't think about that!

No woman had ever made him feel like such a king. And never before had he been so comfortable communicating his desires.

Christ, his hard-on was never going down.

He focused on the ceiling, which wasn't remotely helpful

because the scent in the room shifted—richer now. Warmer. Something earthy and sharp that he recognized as her arousal, the intimate musk that meant she was getting as turned on as he was.

"Do you mind if I switch to a CBD-infused oil?" she asked in a soft whisper. "It'll help with inflammation, but more than that, it's good for nervous system regulation. You've been carrying a lot of stress."

Baby, if you only knew….

"Whatever you think." He trusted her to know best.

"Look at this as a full-body reset. No more overthinking. Clear your mind."

Too late. His mind filled with a thousand versions of Wren. Naked Wren. Wren on her knees, shimmering eyes looking up at him as she devotedly swallowed his cock. Wren on all fours. Wren laughing. Wren with her hair mussed and her lips swollen from his kisses. Wren spread eagle, with all her glistening pink folds inviting him in.

His cock pulsed and he grimaced, sure a wet spot had formed on the sheet where pre-come leaked.

As she smoothed the oil across his chest and shoulders with featherlight strokes, he found it difficult yet somehow easier to breathe. Her hands felt warm and right on him, as if they were built to touch him. He couldn't help the disappointment he felt when she switched back to the hot stones—though they did feel incredible.

"Let me know if the heat's too intense."

The smooth stones glided across his pecs and up toward his collarbone, leaving delicious heat in their wake. She alternated pressure, sometimes using the stones, sometimes her palms, sometimes just her thumbs tracing the edge of his traps. Every stroke teased his sanity a little looser.

She leaned in to reach the far side of his chest, her breath just barely grazing his neck, and he turned. He couldn't help himself. He reached for her hair, tugging her close as he captured her mouth.

She didn't object to the kiss. As a matter of fact, she moaned into his mouth as if she wanted more, but somehow found the will to pull away.

"We're not done yet."

He wanted to be done. He wanted to take her home and—

"Deep breath for me," she said, pressing her palm flat to the center of his chest.

His eyes flew open as she pushed, and something cracked within his ribs. Tension he'd been carrying for God knew how long disappeared, and he exhaled roughly.

"What was that?"

"Just a little trick to release your pecs so your shoulders can move back into alignment. That should also help with the strain on the rhomboids and traps. That kind of tension builds in the thoracic spine until something gives. Releasing the chest wall can help decompress that entire chain."

"You're fucking hot when you talk like that."

She laughed. "I don't know if that's a good thing."

For him, it was a great thing. However, it did make him want to hunt down all her past male clients and skin them alive.

"I'm going to do a rosemary mint scalp massage next," she said, moving behind him again. "It's cooling, invigorating—really good for clearing mental fog. You okay with that?"

She owned him now and he was basically her greased up bitch. "Yup."

She worked her palms through his hair, massaging his temples, scalp, and the nape of his neck. Her thumbs made slow, lazy circles just behind his ears and down into the hollow where tension pooled at the base of his skull.

He groaned in ecstasy as she introduced him to new kinks he'd never considered before. Who knew pressure points were the g-spots of the spine?

"That good?" she murmured, still working his ears.

"Too good."

She chuckled, the sound light and nonchalant. Of course, she felt unfazed. She was in her zone. Meanwhile, he was distracted by how close her tits currently were to his face.

He would literally die of ecstasy and blue balls if this didn't stop soon.

She placed a warm towel over his chest, tucked it around his shoulders, then moved to his side. "There's one more strain I want to check."

Cool air ghosted over his abs as she pulled down the sheet. He jackknifed forward. "What are you doing?"

She gently pushed him back to the table. "Just relax."

"Wren—"

"It's fine, Greyson." She moved to the door and flipped the lock.

That soft click changed everything. All professional pretense vanished, replaced by something electric and inevitable. The air thickened with possibility as she turned back to him, her eyes holding a heat that had nothing to do with therapeutic massage.

His alert gaze followed her back to the table where she looked down at his swollen cock, her fingers trailing slowly up his thick thigh until she casually gripped his engorged flesh. "You're very tense here."

He should have been riddled with shame, but he wanted her to do whatever she had planned. How had this become his sweet little Wren? She stroked him like a woman with years of experience under her belt, and so help him God, he was about to blow his load and embarrass himself like a teenage boy.

She rounded the table, never taking her hand off of him. Something buzzed, and the table lowered. Lifting a knee to the padded surface, she pulled herself up.

"Is this okay?"

"Yes," he croaked, voice dry, unsure how far she was willing to go. The wait, though only a few seconds, felt excruciating. He sucked in a sharp breath as she knelt between his legs and held him in both hands.

"Is the pressure okay?"

Christ. He couldn't talk, let alone think.

"Grey, tell me if you want more pressure. I like when you guide me."

His dick already pulsed and leaked. The mere whisper of her breath had him ready to explode. "You can go a little harder."

"Like this?"

"Exactly." His legs fell open and he moaned as she worked his cock with long, firm strokes. His breath turned heavy at the exquisite pressure. Scented oil coated his flesh and perfumed the air.

"I was thinking about what you said last night."

He couldn't even remember his name at the moment. "Remind me…"

"About…finishing in my mouth."

Christ… "And?"

"I think we should try that."

"Jesus," he breathed. Looking at her was a mistake. The way she leaned over him, jerking his cock, he could see right down her shirt.

She blushed, smiled, then lowered her head to take him in her mouth.

He drew in a full breath as the suctioning heat engulfed him. His hands sank into her hair, guiding her, as she stroked her hand beneath her sliding lips.

"Fuck." Nothing should feel that good.

She moaned, and the sound vibrated through him. He drew his knees up and tightened his fingers in her hair. He'd been hard for hours. No chance in hell existed of him making it through this without coming down her throat.

"Wren," he groaned, letting the surrealness of her mouth on him settle in. That was all it took. His ass cheeks tightening as his dick started to pulse. "Baby—"

He grunted as she pumped his cock faster, sucking even harder.

She finished him without letting up, and his muscles spasmed as he surrendered his control.

The softest sound of distress escaped her throat when that first shot jetted into her mouth. Her shoulders tensed, but then she went down. His head fell back as she sucked him tighter before slowly pulling back.

She smiled proudly, licking her lips. All traces of his release gone. "Is that what you had in mind?"

He threw the towels onto the floor and pulled her into a hard kiss. "You're fucking amazing." Despite finishing, he remained hard. He wanted to rip off her clothes and claim her.

She buried her face in his throat and shyly laughed. "So it was good?"

"Beyond." He kissed her again, this time softer. "Not just the blowjob either. The massage was incredible. My back feels amazing. What can't you do?"

She laughed again. "I kill orchids."

"I don't know what an orchid is, so that means nothing."

"They're really pretty flowers, but I can never keep them alive."

He would buy her a hundred orchids. She could murder every single one. She was still fucking perfect in his eyes.

CHAPTER 19

"SNOW, SNOW, SNOW, SNOW, SNOW ..."

"HOW DID YOU GET HIM TO DO ALL OF THIS?"

Wren looked up at Lilly from where she fussed with the printer on the shelf. "What do you mean?"

"Greyson," Lilly said, "He fixed everything." A wicked smile curved along her pert lips. "Are you two sleeping together?"

Wren gawked as a choked sound escaped her throat. "No."

"Are you sure?"

"I'm one hundred percent sure that Greyson and I did not have sex." On a political level, that rang true. However, she hoped that would become a lie very soon. "There. Paper jam's fixed." Wren stood and tossed the crumpled culprit that had caused the jam into the trash bin. "We need to clean the therapy rooms before our afternoon massage clients arrive."

Lilly arched a brow. "Oh yeah? Why? Is the energy off?"

Wren gave her a silencing look. "Just run through them with some sage and get all the corners."

"Right," she said dryly. "Well, speak of the devil." Lilly balanced her chin on her knuckles, elbow on the reception desk, and grinned widely as the lobby doors opened. "Hello, Greyson."

"Lilly." He nodded then turned his attention to her, face placid, but his eyes holding a thousand secrets. "Wren."

Wren's stomach swooped as his hungry gaze whispered over her. She could still feel his phantom touch from this morning. Who knew a man could do things that made a woman make sounds like that? He had her so hot she'd hit opera-level high notes. One more orgasm and her cries could have shattered glass.

Heat crept up her neck as awareness flooded her body. Every nerve ending seemed to remember exactly how he'd touched her, how he made her feel. Her skin tingled with the memory of his hands, his mouth, the way he'd worshipped her body with such reverent intensity.

"Greyson," she greeted, her voice a complete contrast to the orgy of pornographic memories playing in her head.

Lilly snorted. "Okay, what's going on? Something's definitely up between you two."

Greyson's stare snapped to Lilly. "Nothing's up. I came by to go over snow prep with Bodhi."

Lilly rolled her eyes. "Sure." Grabbing her teacup, she left the reception area. "He's in the back. I'll get him. Wren, can you watch the desk for a sec? We have guests coming in this morning."

"Of course."

The moment they were alone, Wren rounded the desk and glanced back at the empty hall. Satisfied they had privacy, she pressed herself to his front and leaned up for a kiss. "Hi."

His hands dropped to her ass, squeezing and pulling her closer. "How was your ride in?"

She breathed in his familiar scent, smiling at the trace of coffee and frigid air that clung to his clothes. He must have stopped at the café. "I can't stop thinking about this morning."

He grinned. "I can't stop thinking about you."

She squirmed to get closer, but they wore too many clothes and were in a public place. "I wish we didn't have to work today."

Voices traveled from the hall and he released her. Greyson cleared his throat. "They're expecting quite a bit of snow tonight. You should probably stay at your place, in case you need to get back for anything. I'll be out plowing most of the night."

Disappointment doused her euphoric mood. "Oh." She twisted her lips. "Okay."

He looked like he wanted to touch her again, but the sound of Lilly and Bodhi approaching kept them at a distance. "You can catch up on rest."

True, she'd been a little sleep deprived since things started up with him, but she had no complaints. "Sure."

"And, if you want, I can come by when I'm done."

She smiled, relieved she'd still get to see him. The thought of him creeping into her bed did things to her...delicious things. "People might see your truck."

"I'll walk."

They hid their relationship only to protect it. Things still felt delicate, and they didn't need outside pressure. They also didn't want to hurt anyone.

Soren had yet to return her calls and refused to talk to Greyson. Logan was also laying low. Then came the town gossips... She and Greyson both decided to keep things quiet until they felt fully ready to come out as a couple, because once they did, going back would be impossible, every interaction scrutinized, every gesture analyzed. The town would have opinions, and some of those opinions would hurt.

Keeping this secret felt like holding her breath—sustainable for a while, but not forever.

"Are you sure you want to walk?" What about the snow?" They expected several inches.

"As long as there's a fire on and you're willing to warm me up when I get there, I'll be fine."

She bit her lip, trying to hide her smile and failing miserably. "I can do that."

"Greyson," Bodhi appeared with Lilly wearing a big smile. "It's gonna be a big one."

"Did your elbow tell you that?" Greyson teased.

Her dad frowned. "No. I feel this one in my knees."

"Right." While Greyson preferred a much more scientific approach to forecasting the weather, he learned not to completely write off Bodhi's arthritic predictions. "The weather channel's saying five inches tonight and another four or so tomorrow. Visibility's going to be low, so we need to handle the guests' cars early."

"We only have a few guests staying in the cabins tonight," Wren said. "We're waiting for the one more to arrive."

"That makes things easier." He turned to Bodhi. "Grab a coat and we'll take a walk outside."

"Oh, that reminds me," Wren said as her father pulled a patchwork poncho off the coat tree. "I got something for you when I went to town this morning."

Greyson looked at her questioningly, as if he wanted to do more than stare at her. "What is it?"

"It's outside." She bundled up and followed them out front.

Heavy clouds blanketed the pewter sky. The promise of a storm hung loud and clear in the air for anyone accustomed to living this far north.

Something happened to Greyson when snow threatened. He became more animated and purposeful. He loved taking care of others, and inclement weather gave him the chance to do just that. Winter brought out his deepest protective instincts—the same ones that had been forged in tragedy when he'd lost his mother to an icy road one December night. Ever since then, he'd made it his mission to ensure no one else would suffer from winter's cruelty if he could prevent it.

Wren had no doubt he had spent the entire morning calling on every senior citizen of Hideaway Bay to make sure their fuel tanks were full and their logs were stacked somewhere dry and accessible. Later, he'd have each one of their walkways gleaming with salt.

She smiled as he moved across the lot, sturdy as ever, his boots hitting the pavement with the purposeful sound of a man on a mission.

Greyson Hawthorne didn't do whimsical. He specialized in checklists. "First thing I want to do is get some salt down by the guest cabins."

Bodhi, on the other hand, sniffed the air and held up a licked finger.

The cats disappeared, likely sensing the incoming weather and making the most of the back room where the eastern sun hit. That space was the only indoor part of The Haven they could visit, other than their heated cat huts, of course. But when Greyson opened his tailgate, something he often used as a makeshift desk to go over plans with Bodhi, Figgy came wandering out for the meeting.

The blue-grey short hair hopped onto the truck bed and sauntered over to Bodhi. All the cats shared a special bond with the man who fed and took tea with them, and they liked to make sure he stayed chaperoned.

But just as Figgy curled his long tail around her dad, he turned and went straight to Greyson, sniffing him with the pushiness of an investigative reporter.

"That's strange. He's got a real interest in you, today."

Figgy pawed Greyson's coat with no regard for personal space, then hissed.

"Now, now," Greyson said, lowering the zipper of his coat. "None of that." He pulled the kitten out of his jacket. "Figgy, meet Rat."

"His name is Tinsel," Wren teased and Bodhi gaped at the new furry resident.

"Where did this little guy come from?"

"Found him under my porch." Greyson handed him off to Bodhi, who protectively welcomed him into his arms. Her father swore cats were nothing more than reincarnated ancestors sent to protect humans. Sometimes she wondered if he spoke the truth.

He looked into the squirming kitten's face as if able to read his future, and Figgy, absolutely betrayed, hissed.

"Be nice, Figgy." The jealous short-haired grey abided Bodhi's orders, his growls turning into cries for attention.

"His name's Rat," Greyson informed Bodhi. "Because he's so scrawny."

"Well, he won't be scrawny for long." Bodhi continued to inspect the kitten. "See these tufts by his ears and how his muzzle's slightly square?"

Greyson looked at Rat, studying his little jaw. "Yeah."

"Those are signs of a Maine coon."

"A what?"

"Maine coon. The gentle giants of the north." Bodhi handed the kitten back to Greyson. "He's going to grow."

Greyson frowned. "How big?"

"Oh, I'd say to about twenty pounds. They can get up to forty inches long."

"*Forty inches?* That's more than a yard!"

Bodhi nodded. "You're lucky he chose you. Maine coons bring positive energy."

Greyson turned the cat and lifted him to eye level. "Are you my lucky charm?" His gaze shifted to Wren and he winked. "I'd say you're already working."

The wink sent heat spiraling through her chest, a warmth that had nothing to do with her winter coat. Even the simplest gesture from him could make her feel like she was melting from the inside out. She ducked her head to hide her blush, but not before catching the knowing smile that tugged at his lips.

He sat Rat—she still could not believe that name stuck—on the bed of the truck near Figgy. The two cats inspected each other. Rat seemed more intrigued with Figgy's tail than anything else.

Greyson pulled out a little notebook. "Okay, let's go over a game plan."

Bodhi raised one finger. Not in a just-a-minute way—more in a let's-all-honor-the-sacred-pause-of-life way.

Wren almost laughed. "Dad, Greyson has other places to be."

"That's the problem with your generation. You're so focused on the next stop that you forget to take a moment to pause in the present. Look at this beautiful winter day. It hurts nothing to show a bit of gratitude, especially when a new elder has joined us."

"I've got ten more stops today," Greyson said. "We need to map out a plan—especially the paths."

"Plan," Bodhi echoed, as if he had tasted the word and found it bitter. "Such a man-made concept. Mother Nature's in charge and if you try too hard to intercept, she'll unleash on you all the more."

"Dad," Wren warned.

"Right. Paths."

Greyson pulled out a rough hand-drawn map of the grounds. "The Zen garden's already covered. I placed solar lanterns along the perimeter and draped the top of the pagoda with plastic sheeting."

"Not good for the environment."

"You want a snow-covered garden or shelter?"

"I want both, and it's possible to do so with raw materials that won't take centuries to biodegrade."

"Dad. Try to stay focused on what we can accomplish today."

"Right. Sorry." Bodhi twisted an invisible key over his lips and tossed it away.

Greyson exhaled. "It's going to be in the single digits. Chances are, no one will use the Zen garden in a blizzard."

"The elders will."

"Humans won't."

"I beg to differ. Solitude. Stillness. The crunch of snow underfoot. It's a poem waiting to be lived."

Greyson ran a hand over his jaw and met Wren's gaze.

She appreciated his patience with her father. The look they

shared crackled with unspoken heat despite the frigid air around them.

His eyes held hers just a moment too long, long enough for her to remember exactly how those hands felt on her skin, how his mouth could make her forget her own name. More secrets passed between them as they hid smiles. Maybe even a few promises for later. She had to look away before she did something stupid like kiss him in front of her father.

"Moving on," Greyson said, clearing his throat and breaking their stare. "What about the guest cabins?"

"The ones in the west grove are vacant. I left handwoven scarves for the two occupants on the north side."

"Scarves," Greyson repeated slowly.

"Yes," Bodhi said, as if this constituted a completely normal precaution. "Snow can be overwhelming to those born in the south. I infused the yarn with lavender essential oils to help ground the guests during the storm."

Greyson pinched the bridge of his nose.

Wren bit her lip. "That's very sweet of you, Dad."

Greyson kept any comments about her father's habits to himself. "The lot needs clearing, and the main trail to the yoga studio and lobby. We also have to keep access to the emergency vehicle route."

"The snow blower scares the cats."

"Dad, we can move the cats into the sunroom while Greyson plows."

"They won't like that if I'm out there helping."

At this point, Wren wasn't sure Greyson wanted his help.

"I'll use the plow for the main routes," Greyson said, already mentally mapping the turns. "You just need to mark the cat shelters so I don't bury them. And keep the air vents and openings shoveled."

"I've placed Tibetan prayer flags at each one." Bodhi grinned proudly. "The cats love the flapping. It's a soothing frequency."

Greyson muttered something under his breath. "Paths to the

main building, yoga studio, atrium, cabins—priority. Then the sauna trail if I have time."

"Not the tea garden?" Bodhi asked, aghast. "What if someone wants to enjoy their oolong in nature's silence?"

Greyson stared at him. "They can. From inside."

"You know, Greyson, you're very yang today. Maybe have a salad with some leafy greens."

Wren hid a laugh as his notebook snapped shut. He carried Rat to the passenger seat of his truck where he had a makeshift kitty-cab buckled in place so the kitten could ride safely by his side. "I'll be back in a few hours to salt everything. Stay out of the east woods and don't move the cones this time."

"I only moved them because they looked decorative."

"They're not."

"Dad, why don't you take Figgy back to the sunroom with the others. They're probably wondering where you are."

Bodhi scooped the cat off the truck and carried him inside. Greyson exhaled.

Wren stepped closer, brushing a hand down the sleeve of his coat. "Sorry about that. He just thinks differently."

"I know. I don't mind."

"I'll make sure he's not in your way."

He cocked his head. "He's never in my way, Wren. He's your dad."

She smiled, loving how tolerant he always was when it came to her father's eccentric and sometimes draining tendencies. "Thank you."

He reached for her, but caught himself. They stood in clear view of those occupying the front desk. "You said you had something for me?"

"Oh! Right." She rushed to the bench under the awning and lifted a green wreath with a red bow. "They were selling them in town. I thought you might want it for your truck."

He took the wreath in both hands and looked down at it as if it held a map to the Holy Grail. "You got me a wreath?"

His voice carried such genuine surprise, as if no one had ever bought him something just because they thought he'd like it. The wonder in his expression made her chest tight with emotion. For all his strength and capability, sometimes he seemed genuinely shocked when someone took care of him.

"I won't be offended if you don't hang it—"

"No, I love it." He dug through his tools and pulled out some wire and pliers. "I'm gonna hang it right now."

She followed him to the front of the truck, where the big red plow hung elevated, and watched as he wired it to the grill.

"Straight?"

She nodded. "Now, it's really a Christmas truck."

He grinned at the wreath then turned to her. "Thank you."

"You're welcome."

Just then, a BMW came whipping into the parking lot. Greyson grabbed Wren's sleeve to tug her out of the way. "Who the hell is this?"

"I'm guessing that's our new guest."

The muffled sound of music pounding from inside the BMW cut off, and the door popped open with an audible air-tight seal. A male foot in a polished leather shoe crunched onto the pavement, then a long, naturally fit man with salt and pepper hair unfolded from the petite sports car.

Everything about him screamed expensive—from his perfectly tailored cashmere coat to his Italian leather shoes that probably cost more than most people's monthly rent. He scanned the wilderness, his expression suggesting he'd rather be anywhere else.

Stunned and a little concerned, Wren approached him. "Hi, are you checking in?"

The man's sharp gaze latched onto her intensely, as if just noticing she existed. "Unfortunately." He scrunched his nose at the view that most guests gushed over. "You work here?"

"Yes, I'm actually—"

"Great." He reached into the car and pulled out a sleek, leather weekender bag, then shoved it into her arms. "I have to make a call before checking in. See that this gets to my cabin. Name's Greg Drummond." He pulled out his phone and turned away.

Greyson yanked the bag out of her hand. "Let me take care of that."

Mr. Drummond turned away from them as he tried to get a cell signal.

Greyson walked the bag to the automatic double doors that led to the lobby and unceremoniously launched it inside.

Lilly jumped from behind the desk, startled that people were throwing luggage toward her. "What the hell, Greyson?" she snapped as the automatic doors closed.

Greyson returned to Wren and mumbled under his breath, "Hope there wasn't anything expensive in there."

"There better not have been," she hissed. As much as she appreciated him jumping to her defense in the face of rude men, she scowled. Mr. Drummond was a guest.

"Great," Mr. Drummond snapped. "I'm in the middle of nowhere with no fucking signal."

"There's a phone at the front desk—" Wren's words cut off when the man gave her a cold look that said that wasn't the solution he wanted.

She sensed tension radiating off of Greyson in waves. He despised big city men like Mr. Drummond and had no patience for their lack of manners. He crossed the lot and shook the man's hand with stiff dislike. "Greyson Hawthorne." There was an unmistakable, deliberate firmness in his grip.

"And that means…?"

"Just an introduction. Here in Hideaway, we all watch out for each other."

"Cute." Drummond pulled back his hand and flexed his fingers as if they hurt. He sighed. "My therapist recommended this. I need to find a new shrink."

They hosted all kinds of guests at The Haven. Some celebrities, some earthy types, others just looking for a chance to disconnect and recharge, and, unfortunately, the CEO sort.

The CEOs were the hardest to please because their stays were usually booked by an angry spouse on the verge of divorce or a desperate assistant, following directions after some sort of mental breakdown. By the tension in Drummond's body language, Wren assumed he fell into the latter category.

No wedding ring. Either the divorce already happened or no one had married this gem of a man in the first place.

He adjusted the collar of his cashmere dress coat and mumbled, "Fuck my life." He slammed the car door and popped the trunk, walking toward the lobby entrance. "Espresso machine's in the trunk. See that it gets to my room, Paul Bunyan."

Wren caught Greyson by the back of the coat. "Don't."

His jaw clenched, his eyes narrowing on Drummond as he disappeared through the automatic doors into the lobby. "I can't stand men like that."

"Well, he's a guest." She reached into the trunk and awkwardly lifted the small but heavy espresso machine out. "Can you shut the trunk?"

"Give me that." He took the machine out of her arms.

"Don't throw it like you did the bag."

Greyson grumbled and carried it inside.

Settling Mr. Drummond took three times as long as usual check-ins. Greyson left to do his rounds and Wren spent most of the afternoon making sure all of Mr. Drummond's requests were met.

The high-maintenance guests had the power to devastate her retreat with one negative review, which they were more likely to leave—or pay an employee to leave. It didn't matter if she impressed them. These type-A tight-asses loved to complain and barely praised anyone but themselves. They came to places like The

Haven to find a sort of reset that didn't exist for ninety percent of them.

She could tell right away that Drummond would be a difficult, impossible-to-please sort of CEO guest. Very rarely did a pinstripe suit change its stripes.

"See if Drift & Dwell carries the kind of sheets he wants, Lilly."

Lilly rolled her eyes and picked up the phone to call the store.

Drift & Dwell was the only home goods store in town. It offered limited linens, handmade quilts, ceramic dishware, and vintage-inspired table settings. Chances were, they wouldn't carry the Egyptian cotton sheets Drummond requested—at least not at the specific thread count he wanted.

Wren always over-extended herself for the difficult guests because it honored her mother's belief that nitpicky people only needed repositioning to find their Zen. She used to say, "Unhappy people are just souls with tangled roots—repot them, water them, give them light and space, and they'll bloom."

Her mother possessed a gift for bringing grumpy people out of their bad moods and Wren tried to honor her memory every day by becoming the same kind of caring person. It was this philosophy that drove her patience with even the most demanding guests, the belief that underneath all that anger and frustration was simply a person who needed tending.

Her mother had never met a soul she couldn't soften, and Wren refused to give up on that legacy, even when faced with the Greg Drummonds of the world.

But by the day's end, Wren's nerves and patience had been put through the wringer. When she got home, salt covered her walkway and extra logs sat stacked neatly by the door. She smiled, knowing Greyson had visited.

Several cats followed her home, sensing the incoming storm and hoping to find a warm lap for the night. "No, no," she told Spruce, the fat tabby who never gave up trying to be an indoor cat. "You have a home. Go there."

The sanctuary cats lived incredible lives. They stayed safe from traffic, well fed, loved, spoiled by Bodhi and the rest of the staff at The Haven, and their kitty condos offered state-of-the-art solar heating and custom cat furniture Greyson built.

"You're being a drama queen." She waved Spruce away. "Go home before the snow starts."

She hadn't realized how exhausted she felt after two nights of very little sleep until she settled into the tub and almost drowned by accidentally dozing off. After her bath, she cuddled up by the fire with a book, but fell asleep before turning the first page. She didn't wake until Greyson lifted her off the sofa.

Not needing to open her eyes to recognize him, she smiled into his chest. "You smell like snow."

The scent of winter clung to him—crisp, clean cold air mixed with the warmth that was uniquely his. Underneath the outdoor chill, she could detect traces of his soap, the faint tang of motor oil from his truck, and something indefinably masculine that made her want to burrow deeper into his arms.

He carried her quietly through the dark house, and she nestled into the safe sanctuary of his arms. When he lowered her into bed, he pulled the covers over her and kissed her temple. "Go back to sleep. I'm going to stoke the fire and take a quick shower."

"What time is it?"

"A little past four."

"Mmm." She cuddled closer to the pillow and fell right back to sleep. She didn't wake again until morning. But by that time, Greyson slept soundly.

"Poor guy," she whispered after kissing his cheek. He didn't even twitch. He'd stayed up for almost twenty-four hours, most of which he had spent working, and not even working for a paycheck. Greyson took care of the roads and the seniors around town out of the goodness of his own heart.

Settling in front of the fire with a cup of hot tea, she remembered how, back in the day before he had a car, he'd walk around with a shovel whenever it snowed. Sometimes, he even got yelled at by the older residents for coming into their yards without an invitation. They worried his kindness was some sort of a scam, the sort where work gets done and then they're left with an unwanted bill. But Greyson never charged for snow removal. He did it all out of the goodness of his heart.

Snow always made Wren think of their mothers. Sable Hawthorne had been her mother's best friend, like an aunt to Wren, just as Haven had been like an aunt to Greyson, Soren, and Logan. Losing both women at the same time devastated the four of them in more ways than they could count.

The tragedy had shaped Greyson in ways that still showed themselves every winter. His compulsive need to clear every walkway, to check on every elderly neighbor, to ensure everyone had enough fuel and food—it all stemmed from that terrible night when the roads were too icy and help came too late. Winter would always be the season when he fought against helplessness, when his protective instincts went into overdrive.

Wren still avoided driving in the snow when visibility dropped low and the roads turned icy. Thankfully, almost everything in Hideaway Bay sat within walking distance. Almost.

She looked outside at the blanket of white, loving how the pines bowed under the weight of snow and ice. Greyson had cleared off her car and plowed the lot, but she didn't know the condition of the main roads.

She would probably be fine taking a short drive. The snow had stopped falling, and everything looked so peaceful, as if the world were made of frost and glass.

The scratchy cry of Rat broke the silence as the little guy came wandering out from the bedroom. He grew braver, which meant he had entered the stage of escape artist.

"You're going to get me in trouble with the others," she said, scratching Rat's little chest. "I hope you appreciate how privileged you are to sleep inside." Wren played with him for a bit, then barricaded him in the bedroom with Greyson and a makeshift litter pan.

Wren was a softie, but too many stray cats existed to bend the rules for just one. But Rat didn't feel like hers, so he was the exception to the rule. She had the sneaking suspicion he would become a daddy's boy. A big, forty-inch daddy's boy.

Greyson softly snored from the bed. Pressing a kiss on both his and the kitten's head, she quietly left the room. If she wanted to be back before he woke, she'd better get moving. She had another grumpy CEO to check on.

CHAPTER 20

"You Better Not Pout"

THE WIPERS SCREECHED AGAINST THE WINDSHIELD IN A TENSE rhythm, flinging slush and salt grime from one side to the other the two blades waged an endless grudge. Wren's hands clutched the steering wheel in a white-knuckled grip as she navigated the treacherous roads without blinking.

Massive snowbanks rose on the shoulders, making the streets of Hideaway Bay narrower. More snow threatened this afternoon into the evening, which meant Greyson would likely sleep all day and disappear around dinner time for another round of plowing.

She wanted to make it safely back to The Haven before the next temperature shift. Right now, the sun blazed and the drifts melted, but as soon as the temperature dropped again, all that slush would turn to ice.

Her palms grew slick with sweat despite the cold, and her heart hammered against her ribs with each slight slide of the tires. Every turn brought flashes of that terrible December night when her

295

mother never made it home, when winter claimed two lives in a single, senseless moment.

"I hate this," she whispered to herself, swallowing as the car slid ever so slightly on a turn. She tapped the brake, slow and steady like Greyson had taught her years ago.

She'd avoided driving until she turned eighteen. Greyson told her she needed to face her fears. He forced her behind the wheel of his truck and taught her how to drive, despite her constant complaining and worries.

That happened right around the time he started building his cabin in the woods—feeding his own demons. But by the time she passed her driver's test, he had disappeared again for another year-long expedition at sea with the fishery.

She now realized he'd disappeared like that to avoid what he couldn't control. Whenever they got close, he pulled away. Part of her still feared his old habits might resurface, which explained why she felt perfectly fine with taking things slow.

When another car rushed by, startling her, she winced, wondering again why she had chosen to do this.

"You're doing this for Greyson," she reminded herself.

Over the years, he'd shown patience with Bodhi. He always stepped in whenever they needed something she couldn't manage on her own. Now, her turn had come to do the same. But the truth was, she owed Magnus Hawthorne nothing.

After years of disparaging remarks and resentment towards his sons, the boys held little expectation that their father would change in the short time he had left. Magnus had trained his sons to hide their emotions, and now, as he reached the end of his life, he reaped what he sowed. Three sons and not a glimpse of concern or emotion over his peril.

The truth was, she was doing this as much for herself as for Greyson. Her mother's voice echoed in her memory, *"Even the thorniest roses need love and water, sweetheart."*

Magnus Hawthorne might be dying alone by his own design, but that didn't mean she couldn't ease his suffering. As Haven's daughter, she felt compelled to put even the most difficult men at ease, but she also felt she owed this visit to Sable.

Relief flooded her when she made it to the hospital in one piece. Wren pried her fingers from the wheel and took a few minutes to simply regulate her breathing.

The hospital smelled like lemon disinfectant until she reached the wing where Magnus stayed. The subdued scent of a luxury furniture store overtook the air. The floor gleamed like a gallery, and the art on the walls wasn't mass-printed. Instead, it showcased collection pieces from local artists, featuring coastal oil paintings displayed in brass frames.

The Hawthornes had built the wing before Sable died. But she never had the chance to use it. The irony wasn't lost on her—Sable had helped plan this beautiful space meant to heal the wealthy and powerful, but died before she could benefit from her own generosity. Instead, her bitter husband would likely be its most prominent patient.

Wren hated hospitals, so she tried to pretend she simply walked through an ordinary hall in an ordinary building, and all those beeps and bells sounded like creaks and birds chirping.

She adjusted the woven basket on her arm and covered the collection of self-care items she brought. They weren't anything special, just a few things she had around the spa, but she had chosen each item to bring Magnus a little peace. Handmade peppermint balm, beeswax salve for the rough spots of his heels, elbows, and hands, a lavender eye pillow, some infused oils to help with inflammation, an old hardcover biography of *Reagan*, and a knit throw Bodhi insisted she bring.

At the end of the hall, a polished brass plate read, *Private Suite: M. Hawthorne.*

She hesitated, drawing in a deep breath. Magnus had earned a reputation for cutting his sons off mid-sentence and he took no issue verbally eviscerating them in Wren's presence—most likely because he never took much notice when she entered a room.

She steadied her hand and knocked lightly—then entered before she could lose her nerve. "Knock, knock."

The room looked more like a hotel than a hospital. A sitting area occupied the corner, complete with tufted chairs, heavy navy drapes framing a wall of windows, and a side table with a crystal water pitcher and cut-glass tumblers no nurse had ever touched.

Magnus lay sunken into a reclined hospital bed positioned toward the windows. If he spoke, she couldn't hear him over the murmur of the television. As she rounded the bed, she met his ice-blue eyes over the oxygen mask and smiled nervously.

The sight of him shocked her more than she'd expected. This was Magnus Hawthorne—the man who'd intimidated her since childhood, who commanded rooms with his presence and could silence his grown sons with a look. Now he appeared diminished, almost fragile, his powerful frame reduced to sharp angles beneath the hospital blankets.

"Hi, Mr. Hawthorne." While Sable had always just been Sable, Wren had never received an invitation to call Magnus by his first name. She only referred to him as such in the presence of the boys, who also called him Magnus. She set down the basket with a shaky hand. "I brought you some presents."

His brow furrowed with confusion as she lowered the basket gently, not wanting to rattle the glass of water.

"Is it okay that I'm here?"

He didn't respond with a yes or a no.

"If you're too tired for visitors, I can come back."

His rheumatoid finger pointed to the chair, slow and unsteady, then lowered with a commanding gesture. She obediently dropped into the seat.

Months had passed since she last saw him, and the changes in his build startled her. The bare arms peeking from the gown revealed crepe skin that sagged where muscles had once shaped his limbs. Pale skin collapsed beneath his cheekbones where the fabric strap of the oxygen mask pressed. Most startling was the unexpected sight of him unshaven with his hair tousled from sleep. Seeing a man who had always been so put together in a state of coming apart felt wrong.

A blanket covered his chest, but his weight loss was obvious. Beneath the translucent creases of his eyes, his glare was sharp and observant. He looked at the basket then back to her.

"I brought you a few things to make your stay more…" Her words faded, and she cleared her throat, trying again. "Just some creature comforts and things that help me when I'm not feeling well."

She struggled with long silences—they made her nervous.

She pulled the folded throw off the basket and said, "Whenever I'm sick, I always like to have a cozy blanket." She draped the soft material over his legs.

Still no response.

Maybe this visit had been a mistake. "Anyway… I won't stay long. Just wanted to check in."

Magnus lifted a trembling hand to the mask and pulled it aside, wheezing as if that slight exertion had cost him.

She jumped up. "Do you need something?"

"Sit."

She dropped back into the chair. "Yes, sir."

He studied her for a long, hard minute. "I thought you were one of Logan's… *pursuits*."

She blushed and shook her head. "No, sir."

"Hmm." He took a long breath from the mask then moved it aside. "So you brought me—what—herbs and knitted things?"

His tone dripped with condescension, each word designed to make her feel foolish. Wren's cheeks burned with embarrassment, but she forced herself to remain calm.

"I actually forgot the tea, but…" Realizing that he was mocking her gift, she wilted. "I can just go." She stood again, this time collecting her basket.

"Sit."

"Yes, sir. Sorry." She dropped to the chair again, now protectively holding the basket on her lap. "I'm nervous." Why had she told him that? "Sorry." And she wasn't supposed to apologize.

He frowned. "Let's see what else you brought."

Her gift seemed foolish now, so she reached for the most conservative item inside. "I, um, brought you a book. It's a biography." She flashed the cover. "I remembered you saying, once, that Ronald Reagan carried himself like a big tent showman."

"Smiled too much," he agreed. "Too busy performing for those he should have shut down."

Her hand shook as she set the book on the bedside table. "I thought maybe you'd like something to read."

"Books are a female hobby." His lips pulled tight. "That was Sable's job. Reading. Nurturing. Men follow current affairs and are better off sticking to newspapers."

He spoke his deceased wife's name with bitter venom, revealing more than she'd ever understood about their marriage. Wren stayed very still, unsure how to respond.

Magnus eyed her critically. "You're a carbon copy of your mother."

"I like to think so."

He looked away, turning his attention to the window. "Unexpected visitors tell me things look worse than I feel."

"How do you feel?"

"Like I'm dying."

Bodhi would have said something like *we're all dying*, but she didn't think Magnus would appreciate that kind of enlightened observation.

A wet cough shook his frame, the sound jarring and painful to hear. He took a few deep breaths from the oxygen mask. Wren used the pause in conversation to lay out the contents of the basket. As a defense mechanism, she shifted into professional mode, handing him a glass of water. After he sipped and his breathing calmed, he leaned back and eyed her with suspicion.

"Why are you really here?"

Wren paused. She couldn't very well explain that his roots had tangled and he needed light, so she said, "This is what I do."

"Visit hospitals?"

"Help people relax."

"I'm on a gurney. Do I look particularly stressed to you?" His stare didn't waver.

"I think you've led a life with higher stress than most."

"You're correct there."

Wealthy men struggled to empathize with the hardships of the less fortunate. They also failed to accept a reality outside of the one they chose.

Men like Magnus believed they were masters of the universe, until the universe proved they were not. Disease offered a powerless position that powerful men rarely enjoyed. It exposed vulnerabilities they didn't want to acknowledge. Watching him now, reduced to oxygen masks and hospital gowns, she saw how terrifying it must be for someone who'd controlled everything to lose control of his own body.

"Have they been taking good care of you?"

"If you consider good care three lukewarm meals a day, thin blankets, and a draft."

"Well, you're lucky I brought you an extra blanket then, aren't you? And, I'm yours for the next hour."

"Oh?" He perked up.

"Not..." *Oh dear.* "Not in that way." She uncapped the salve, and worked the waxy ointment between her fingers, warming it. "Have you ever had a hand massage before?"

"Can't say I have."

"Then you're in for a treat. I brought a special oil infused with rosemary and peppermint to help with the swelling in your hands."

"Is that what I smell?"

Rather than acknowledge his snide tone and unappreciative comment, she asked, "Do your joints hurt?"

"Only for the last thirty years."

"This will help." She stood, holding out a lavender eye mask. "Just relax." She slid his oxygen mask back into place and then covered his eyes. Knowing he couldn't watch her made it easier to concentrate.

She pulled the chair closer to his bed and cued up her meditation playlist. "I'm going to start with some light reflexology."

At first touch, he felt stiff and tense, but once she started hitting the pressure points along his palm, he moaned and sighed like the rest of her clients. Slowly, his hands relaxed and he surrendered to her care.

She worked methodically, finding the tender spots where tension had gathered for decades. His hands told the story of a life spent gripping too tightly—to control, to power, to the belief that everything could be managed through sheer force of will. She pressed into the web between his thumb and forefinger, targeting the liver meridian point that helped release anger and frustration. When she found the heart point on his palm, he released a sound that was almost vulnerable.

"You're carrying a lot of tension here," she murmured, working her thumbs in small circles. "This point connects to emotional stress. I'm going to apply steady pressure and let your body release what it's ready to let go of."

His breathing deepened under the oxygen mask, becoming less labored as she continued. She moved to his wrists, gently manipulating the joints, then up to his forearms where decades of physical labor had left the muscles knotted and tight.

By the end of the hour, Magnus looked refreshed, his dry skin now moisturized, as he snored like an elderly baby. Her selfless act for the day was complete.

She felt proud and courageous for having faced a man who

always intimidated her, glad she was able to share this small moment with him.

As she gathered her things, his eyes fluttered open. For just a moment, without his usual armor of disdain, he looked almost grateful.

Wren left the basket with its contents and quietly backed out of the room. She might not have untangled him from his contracted, stiff ways, but she felt pretty sure she had loosened him up. Men as root-bound as Magnus Hawthorne would require a few more therapeutic shakes.

But maybe, just maybe, she'd planted a seed.

CHAPTER 21

"Baby, It's Cold Outside"

Blankets. Heat. A faint citrus-and-clove smell that didn't belong to him…

Greyson groaned groggily, confused but too comfortable to spring into action.

His stiff body stretched, and he stilled, realizing he lay on his couch, not in bed. He sensed someone watching him.

He rubbed one eye open, momentarily blinded by the afternoon light spilling through the window. Then he recognized her silhouette, angelically perched across from him on the edge of the coffee table.

Wren.

She clutched a steaming mug in her hands. He smiled, but as his vision cleared and he focused on her beautiful face, he realized she frowned with concern. Or perhaps exasperation?

"Am I in trouble?" he croaked, his voice grating like sandpaper.

He cleared his throat and winced as fire scorched his chest. *What the hell?*

"You've slept the day away, Rip Van Plowman. I was starting to worry."

He grunted, trying to sit up, but immediately regretted it. His head throbbed as if packed with snow, and his throat burned like he'd swallowed a fistful of glowing briquettes. Every muscle in his body ached, and a bone-deep exhaustion weighed him down like lead blankets.

"What time is it?" he painfully rasped.

"It's almost five. You've been out for—what? Twelve hours? Thirteen?" Her hands should have felt warm from the mug, but when she brushed them across his forehead, they felt like ice. "You look like hell, Greyson."

He sank into the cushion and groaned. "I feel like I got run over by all nine of Santa's reindeer."

"Nine? Isn't it eight, after Odin's eight-legged horse?"

"Rudolph," he mumbled into the pillow. He was burning up yet somehow chilled to the bone and damp with sweat. His teeth chattered. "Do we need wood for the fire?"

"It's warm in here, and the fire's fine, Grey. I think you have a cold. A mean one." Her cool fingers brushed over his brow like a divine blessing. He shut his eyes and sighed at her sweet touch. She smoothed out his blankets and adjusted some of the throw pillows. "I'll make some lemon ginger tea with honey. That'll help with your scratchy throat."

"You don't have to do that," he grumbled weakly but she had already moved toward the kitchen.

Pots clanked as cabinets opened and closed. Water ran, followed by the faint sound of chopping. What was she doing in there? It sounded like a lot for tea. He felt too tired to think about it.

Rat scaled the couch, and Greyson coughed, the sound wicked and dry, ripping through him like fire. The kitten padded over to him, concerned and wearing an expression of pure feline judgment.

He reached for the little puff ball, then hesitated. "Can cats catch human colds?"

Wren carried a steaming mug of tea out to the living room and set it on the table. "I don't think so."

His body ached everywhere but he forced himself to sit up. Rat climbed up his chest and nestled into his neck, using his shoulder as a balcony.

"You look terrible. Maybe we should call the clinic and see if you can get in to see the doctor."

"I'm fine." He winced, head throbbing and throat burning. He definitely felt anything but fine.

"Sure you are, tough guy." She handed him the tea. "It's a tincture, so it's already steeped."

He tried not to whimper as he reached for the mug.

"Smells good," he croaked, breathing in the fresh scent of ginger as the mug warmed in his hands. Staying awake required great focus. He almost spilled the mug when he shivered. "I'm freezing."

"Keep the blankets on." She bundled him up like a Jedi master, brushing her cool fingers over his forehead again. God, he loved when she did that.

Such vulnerability felt foreign to him and he didn't like being this dependent on someone else's care. His father would say he was being weak.

Greyson spent most of his adult life being the one who took care of others, who solved problems and fixed things. Being on the receiving end of such gentle attention should have made him uncomfortable, but with Wren, it felt right.

"I think you have a fever. The soup should be done soon."

His brows lifted. "Soup?"

"It's Freya's recipe." Freya was the new chef at The Haven, but he'd yet to try any of her food.

Wren pulled a pillow onto her lap and watched him with concern. She took Rat from his shoulder so he could drink the tea.

The fuzzy little bastard didn't realize how lucky he was to have her hands on him, stroking and caressing. Greyson couldn't help but envy the little rodent.

"You didn't have to trouble yourself with soup—"

"I know I didn't, but I wanted to. Your body needs medicine, and Mother Nature's comes in the form of soup."

His muscles ached as he reached for her hand. "You've been here all day?"

"I left to pick up some items at the market and then stopped back at The Haven to teach my yoga class, but that turned into a bust."

"Wh-*uh-uh*—" His chest spasmed with a vicious cough, and he quickly set down his tea. Each breath a hard punch in the lungs.

As soon as he managed to draw a full breath, Wren handed him the mug. "Take a sip."

He did as she instructed, and the hot honey soothed his burning throat. "Why was your class a bust?" Every word was gravel scraping over smashed glass.

"Only two people showed up. One of them included Drummond."

So the CEO was still in town. "When's the douchebag checking out?"

She rolled her eyes. "He's booked for the week, but he's not getting anything out of his stay. I never say this, but I wish he would cut his visit short."

That made two of them.

Greyson didn't like that guy from the moment he set his designer, leather-soled shoes on Wren's property. He probably loved watching her bend around in her sexy yoga pants and those criss-cross belly shirts she wore for class. His grip tightened on his mug. Maybe he could talk her into wearing one of those monk habits that covered the body from hood to ankle.

"I can't imagine him doing yoga."

She rolled her eyes. "He left his cell on and interrupted savasana to take a call. Then he proceeded to walk around the studio searching for the lost signal."

Despite the pain, Greyson laughed. Once snow hit the towers, cell phones became useless in Hideaway Bay.

"Hopefully, your other guest understands some things are outside of your control."

"The other student was Noah, so he understands."

Another stray he had to watch. It was an infestation.

She gestured toward his mug. "How's the tea helping?"

"It's good. Thanks for making it." It wasn't healing his throat, but it certainly soothed the burn. "You don't have to stay here, you know."

"Someone has to take care of you." She stood and adjusted the pillows in a pretty way he never thought to set them up. *How did women know to do shit like that?*

"I don't want you to catch whatever this is, Wren."

She ignored his concern and continued rearranging his living room, straightening his books and arranging the clutter he had dumped from his pockets last night. God, he loved seeing her hands on his stuff.

"I'll be careful. Besides, I don't feel like being home right now."

He frowned. "Because of the CEO?"

She shrugged. "Maybe."

Greyson scowled. Her place sat slightly removed and on the outskirts of the commercial lot. That entitled prick better respect the property lines. "Did he trespass on your property?"

She looked away and he sat up.

"Was he at your fucking house?"

She bit her lip. "He was looking for a cell signal."

"I'll—" His protective outrage stirred a cough that turned into a full-blown hacking fit.

"Easy." She patted his back. "I took care of it."

He took a big gulp of tea, his face hotter than it had been a minute ago. "That prick better stay away from you."

"I handled it, Grey. He's not a prick. He's just annoying. His cologne's probably the most obnoxious thing about him. He's harmless."

If he were harmless, she wouldn't be stressed out. "Trust your gut. You've always been perceptive when it comes to reading people. And tell him his cologne's disturbing the other guests."

"There are only a few other guests right now, but they're here until Christmas and I barely see them. Our next one doesn't check in until Thursday."

Night shift plowing always blurred the days together. "Is that tomorrow?"

She nodded.

He jerked back as his lungs sputtered with another coughing spell. "Sorry." He gasped. "We probably shouldn't get too close."

"I'll get you some water." She disappeared into the kitchen but continued to talk. "I have another session with him tonight."

He sputtered to speak as the coughing continued. "Session…" Cough. "…for…" Hack. "…what?"

"A Swedish massage."

Greyson stiffened, alarm bells going off in his congested, pounding head. "Where's River?"

"He specifically requested a female masseuse." She returned with a glass of water. "I squeezed a little lemon in it. The vitamin C's good for you."

He guzzled the water and reminded himself that massage therapy was a part of her job, but his filthy mind dwelt on the ending of their one-on-one session a few days ago. The thought of that entitled asshole laying on her table made his blood pressure spike.

"Isn't there someone else who can do it?"

She laughed. "You sound jealous."

"It's called territorial, which we already established I am. Consider yourself marked." He tried to go all alpha, but he was too weak. Instead, he reached out a hand, then wilted as if shot.

"You're adorable when you're congested." She came to him and kissed his forehead.

He smiled innocently while imagining plowing that douchebag's BMW into a snowbank. "You're so warm."

"And you're burning up."

"I'm—" Another hard cough rattled his chest.

"All right, no more talking." She easily took control and pushed him to lie back down. "You're officially benched." She tucked a blanket around his legs and set a box of tissues within reach.

He would have objected, but he was too weak and feeble. The more he fought, the more he embarrassed himself. So he just groaned.

"Such a big, tough man," she mocked.

"I mildly overexerted myself. This is just lag from snow removal."

"Sure."

"I am sure. A baby aspirin and a hot shower, and I'll be good as new." He coughed again, this time curling to his side with a groan.

"The universe is telling you to stop talking and rest. I only want you opening your mouth to drink water. You need to stay hydrated." She disappeared into the kitchen, humming softly. Stirring. Clinking things.

The sounds were... nice. Especially considering how shitty he felt. Years had passed since anyone had nurtured him and he'd forgotten what a comfort that could be. The last time someone had taken care of him like this was when his mother tucked him in with chicken pox, bringing him soup and cool washcloths for his fever.

"Whatever you're making in there smells incredible."

"I said no talking. Your vocal cords need a rest or the inflammation won't go down. The soup will be ready in a few minutes."

As he sank into the couch cushions, his mind drifted to his childhood. He recalled the old daytime sitcoms he used to watch whenever he got sick as a child, and how his mother waited on him.

One time, he had the chicken pox and was stuck on the couch for a week.

He hadn't thought of that memory in years, but he couldn't stop thinking of it now. He remembered the scent of his mom's shirts—a cross between flowers and fabric softener. He missed that smell. He hadn't smelled it since she died.

Wren returned with a bowl of steaming soup. "This has to cool." She pulled the table close and set him up with a little placemat and more tea. Then she refilled his water.

"Thank you."

She smiled. "It's nothing. I like taking care of you."

And he liked being taken care of, especially by her. Very few people could get this close to him. He wasn't used to being vulnerable in front of others, but for some reason it didn't bother him with Wren.

She settled next to him on the couch and reached for the remote. "I always like *Gilmore Girls* when I'm sick."

"I don't have cable."

"I can sign into my account. We can stream something."

Greyson rarely watched television. He mainly relied on books for entertainment, so he wasn't even aware that sharing accounts was possible, but he liked the idea of Wren further mingling her life with his.

Once she logged into Netflix and played a preview for the chick show she wanted to watch, he frowned, dizzy from just a preview of such small-town chaos.

"What do you think?"

"Absolutely not."

She clicked her tongue. "It's a perfect show for binge-watching."

"They talk too fast, and I already have a headache." No way could he put up with hours of that. "Find something with a little less estrogen."

She rolled her eyes. "You mean something more manly?"

"Yes." He sniffled, and shivered under the blanket, cradling his soup as he waited for it to cool.

"Of course, my fragile little cupcake."

She scrolled for a while as he slurped and hummed over the delicious comfort food. Who knew so many shows existed? The overwhelming amount of choices exhausted him.

"What about vampires? Is that manly enough?"

He'd probably fall asleep as soon as she put something on. "Sure." He swallowed down the last drop of broth. "Is there more soup?"

She cued up a movie and took his bowl to get a refill.

He watched what seemed a dreary opening to a thriller. "I think this is the longest I've watched my TV since I bought it."

"I can tell."

A moss covered forest filled the screen as a young deer nibbled at a fern and some chick talked about dying. The deer bolted as something chased it then a teenager appeared holding a cactus. "What is this?"

"*Twilight*."

He frowned. "Isn't this a show for little girls?"

"No. It's a saga for all ages. Shh, you have to listen."

Fantastic, he was locked into a five-movie marathon about high school vampires. "I should have picked the small-town fast talkers."

"Give it a chance."

Too weak to steal the remote, and unsure how to even use the damn thing, he settled in with his second bowl of soup. He must have had quite the fever, because the movie actually held his interest. By the time Bella fell in love with Edward, Greyson was thoroughly invested.

"Isn't he a hundred years older than her?"

"It's an age-gap romance."

"I'd say."

By the second movie, he was locked in and pissed at Edward for disappearing on Bella. It made him think of all the times he'd done that to Wren. Glancing over at her, his stomach bottomed out at the sound of her delicate sniffle.

"Are you crying?"

"Don't judge me." She wiped her eyes. "It's sad."

He stared back at the television where Bella sobbed in abandonment and guilt choked him. Was that what it had been like for Wren?

He never imagined her missing him that much, but whenever he came back from his long trips at sea, she always welcomed him with cold fury. The realization hit him like a physical blow. He was as bad as Edward, disappearing without explanation, leaving her to wonder if he'd ever come back.

He took her hand and squeezed. "I'm sorry."

She frowned. "For what?"

He shook his head, unsure if she even thought of those times anymore. "Not telling you what was in my head."

Her smile looked sad. "You're getting better at sharing your feelings."

"I'm trying."

The plot on the screen thickened. Edward needed to get back to Forks and do something about Wolf-Boy. "He better handle that dog sniffing around his territory."

"I like Jacob. Edward abandoned her."

He scowled, shocked to find them on opposing sides. "Wren, we like Edward. She's supposed to wait for him."

Wren laughed. "Well, I guess we know what team you're on."

Greyson pulled Rat to his chest as Wren cleared the dishes. He was totally comfortable until she reappeared in her coat and hat.

He sat up. "Where are you going?"

"I told you, I have that massage."

He paused the movie, wishing for a way to prevent her from rubbing oil all over some big city jerk. "How long will you be?"

"A little over an hour."

He wobbled to his feet. "I'll get my keys."

"Sit your butt down." She pushed him back and he collapsed like a sack of rocks. "You're not leaving that couch."

Defeated and annoyed with his weakness, he coughed. "I should drive you. The roads are getting icy."

"It's a two-minute ride, Grey. I'll be fine. Besides," she pointed to the television. "You're so into this."

"Am not."

"Whatever you say." She bundled up in her scarf and gloves and then kissed his head. "We'll see if you're still team Edward when I get back."

"Who else's team would I be on?"

She gave him a knowing look, then chuckled and opened the door.

"Text me when you get there so I don't worry."

"I will." She shut the door and left.

Greyson looked down at Rat. "As soon as I'm over this cold, you and I are going douchebag hunting." He hit play.

A few minutes later, his phone pinged with a text from Wren. He smiled whenever her contact picture popped up. It showed her from when she was about ten years old, hair curly and wild as she laughed, her smile slightly hidden by a melting ice cream cone.

As soon as he knew she was safe, he tried not to think about what she was doing. That city slicker better behave himself on her table.

He focused on Edward and Bella to avoid getting worked up, but it turned out that Edward was a gaslighting jerk who didn't keep his word.

A while later, the door opened. "You're still awake?"

"*Shh...*" He waved, but kept his eyes fixed on the screen. "Edward's going to the Volturi. Bella and Alice are trying to stop him."

She took off her coat and laughed. "Oh, you're deep in it now."

"They're not gonna make it." He sat up, body tense and eyes unblinking.

"I really thought you'd be Team Jacob."

"I'm Team Get-It-Together, Bella. She jumped off a cliff, Wren. A cliff." He paused the movie. "And Edward's a jerk for leaving her. You didn't prepare me for that."

"I told you it was angsty." She came to sit beside him on the sofa, smelling like the spa.

"Alice and Carlisle are the only sane ones. Charlie's not bad either. I can't believe Bella lied to him."

She laughed, and he hit play, fully aware that she was laughing at him, not with him.

He didn't care. "Don't judge me. I am what you made me."

Thankfully, things worked out. *New Moon* left him so drained that he passed out at the start of Eclipse, just as the camera panned over the snowy trees.

He awoke in the middle of the night, mind fuzzy, and the house silent. Wren lay curled up beside him on the couch, television off, the glowing embers in the woodstove the only source of light. How she hadn't fallen off the edge was a mystery.

The fire needed another log, but he felt too tangled up in her sleeping body to move without waking her. And he didn't want her to fall. He'd better keep holding her, so he stayed put.

God, she looked pretty. And fucking perfect in his arms.

This close, he could see every freckle on her nose and count each individual eyelash. She'd showered between movies last night and put on one of his flannels. The sight of her in his clothes, curled up in his space, made something primitive and possessive unfurl in his chest. She belonged here, with him, wearing his shirts and falling asleep in his arms.

He hadn't expected her to stay, but was glad she did.

Honestly, he never wanted her to leave. She fit perfectly into his space, as if the house had been built to fit her into the design. And maybe it had, on some subconscious level. He certainly thought about her when he stocked it. Why else would he own a tea kettle when he only ever made black coffee?

She nestled closer to him and he pressed his lips to her hair, breathing in her unique scent.

She moaned softly against his chest and rasped, "What time is it?"

"I don't know," he whispered, glad his throat no longer burned. "It's still dark outside."

"Do you need anything?" She was so damn nurturing, she even checked on him in her sleep.

"I've got everything I need right here." He kissed her head again.

"Mmm," she responded, the soft moan fading into a feminine snore.

"Thanks for taking care of me," he whispered, keeping his voice low as he gently played with her hair, happy to hold her as she slept in his arms. "I remember how my mom used to take care of us."

He stared into the dim glow of the fire, aware he was mostly talking to himself, but it felt good to share those personal memories, even if she was sleeping through his confessions.

"She used to mother us the most when we were sick. Popsicles and soup, warm baths, and our favorite snacks. Whenever one of us got sick, the others always got jealous."

Nothing beat a mother's love, he thought, but Wren's care came pretty close today. He felt so much better than he had last night, and could only attribute his miraculous healing to her care.

"I don't even remember her voice anymore," he admitted shamefully. "Isn't that awful?"

"It's human," she whispered, and he realized she was actually listening.

"I should remember everything about her. She was my mom."

"When something hurts that much, Grey, our mind hides the details to protect our heart."

Maybe that was it. Maybe his forgetfulness was a coping mechanism. He did what he had to do to get past the pain. But the guilt remained, and his throat tightened every time he felt that shame resurfacing.

"We weren't allowed to wallow."

"Talking about her isn't wallowing."

"It was to my dad."

There was never space for their grief. Magnus forbade them from crying and sent them away anytime they moped about the house. All the forgiving softness of childhood disappeared with their mother. After her passing, their home became just a cold dwelling where their father loomed.

Greyson was the first to move out. He spent years working out at sea with the fishery, hoping the experience might clear his head, but when he returned home, all his abandoned emotions remained. He returned to the North Sea again and again, waiting for his feelings to wash away, but they always came crashing back whenever he returned to Hideaway Bay.

When he realized he couldn't drown his grief at sea, he tried to bury it in the woods. That didn't work either. Because the longer he tried not to feel, the more he felt.

"I miss her," he confessed quietly.

"I miss my mom, too."

The fact that they shared the pain made it easier to bear. Maybe that's why he always returned to her—she understood.

Greyson hadn't been raised with strong faith. The little he had came from the spiritual things Wren said to him on occasion. He liked her insights and found himself pondering her perspective on life more than he was willing to admit.

She soothed him. And now, more than ever, he realized how much he craved her nearness.

He could have settled anywhere. He'd visited every coastal town up and down the Atlantic and crossed international waters. But she always pulled him back to Hideaway Bay. Every journey away from her had been an exercise in futility, a desperate attempt to outrun feelings that only grew stronger with distance.

Wren was his North Star, the magnetic pull that called him home. And, over the years, he slowly gave in to that pull, setting down roots and making excuses to see her. She never left his mind, even when he ordered himself to stay away.

There was no denying the truth anymore. Not when he finally admitted this was what he wanted. Pressing his lips to the top of her head, breathing her in, he closed his eyes. She felt right in his arms, like he'd been built to hold her. He never wanted to let her go.

He needed to finally set himself free and stop holding back the feelings his father claimed made a man weak. "I love you, Wren."

She drew back and blinked up at him, a stunned expression on her face. "What?"

"I love you. I've always loved you. In case you didn't know…"

She tightened her arms around his ribs and pressed a kiss to his lips. "You know I love you too, right?"

Of course, she did. But this was different. He wasn't talking about a platonic love or the kind of love that develops over time. This was a love that determined his life, the kind that dictated a man's future. Soon enough, she'd understand just how serious he was about her. Now that he had her, he was never letting her go.

"Get some sleep." He pulled the covers higher to tuck her in tight against his chest.

By morning, he felt fully recovered. Wren, however, had caught his cold.

"I feel terrible."

"You should." She coughed. "You did this to me."

He should have insisted she leave and protect herself.

His eyes widened when she blew her nose, the sound more like a dying elephant. "Good God, woman, did you eat a French horn?"

"Shut up," she said with a nasally speech impediment as she created an environmental crisis with the amount of tissues she blew through in one minute.

"How can someone so small make that much noise?"

She looked up at him, nose as red as Rudolph's, then toppled to her side and whined. "You gave me your cooties."

"I'm a boy. We're well-known cooty carriers. I warned you to stay away."

"Ugh," she groaned, plucking more tissues from the box as she sneezed three times in a row.

"You sneeze like a kitten in a teacup but blow your nose like a foghorn kicking off a moose hunt."

She sniffled and moaned, hiding her face in the blankets. "Look away. I'm hideous."

"You're adorable."

"No. You shouldn't see me like this. We're supposed to be in the new, seductive stage, not the drippy, gross phase. I want you to think I wake up beautiful, not icky."

"Believe it or not, you're still adorable—even with a red nose and glassy eyes."

"We'll never sleep together if you keep looking at me like this."

Was she nuts? "Nope. Still want to fuck you thirty ways to Sunday." He tucked the blankets around her like a tightly wrapped burrito. "I'm running to The Chowder House to get you some soup. What else can I pick up while I'm out? Cough drops? Something for tea?"

"Maybe ask Aunt Astrid for something that cures death."

"On it."

She groaned. "I have my class—"

"Lilly can teach your class. I'll swing by and tell her, then I'll check on Bodhi."

She coughed. "People will get suspicious if you start relaying messages for me."

"Let them. I've got nothing to hide."

She blew her nose and moaned in defeat. "Fine. Thank you."

He kissed her head then kissed Rat. "I'll be back soon. Call me over the radio if you need anything."

"Take your phone!"

"I will, but it's windy today. Use the radio if it's important."

She groaned and tossed a crumpled tissue beside the waste basket by the couch.

A LOUD BANG WOKE WREN, the ache drilling behind her eyes still jackhammering away.

"Grey?" she croaked, startled by her voice. When she coughed, it hurt so much she fell back asleep out of sheer defeat. The pounding continued and then someone bellowed for Greyson and her skull shriveled.

Wren's eyes popped open and she groaned as the door opened, letting a cold draft in.

"You've got some nerve, man!" Whoever was yelling was about to catch her wrath.

They yanked the covers off of her. "Hey!"

Logan blinked, confused. "*Wren?*"

She weakly pulled herself up, snatched back the covers, and collapsed. The air outside the blankets was freezing.

"What are you doing here?"

"I'm sick," she rasped. Anything over a whisper burned like a scream.

He took a step back and pulled the collar of his shirt over his mouth and nose. "What do you have? You look like death."

"Thanks," she croaked, tugging the blanket over her shoulders.

Logan looked around, confused. "Where's Grey?"

"He had errands." No need to explain more than she had to. Her throat couldn't take it.

"Are you... sick-sick? Or like... dramatically hungover?"

She hacked into a tissue. "Sick."

"Damn," he muttered. "Soren told me..." He scratched the back of his head, rethinking his purpose. "I didn't realize you were sick."

Should she tell him? Weakness made it difficult, but he deserved the truth. "Grey got sick first. I caught his cold."

"This is a cold?"

She blew her nose and hacked. "Yes. I should feel better tomorrow."

"So it's true? You two are…"

She nodded and closed her eyes, too tired to face his censure. "If you came here to yell, please do it in a whisper."

He exhaled and dropped into the armchair across from her. "It's hard to yell at someone who looks like roadkill in August. You want tea or something?"

She knew Greyson was full of crap when he said she looked adorable. Peeking at Logan through one eye, she asked, "You're not mad at me?"

"Come on, Wren. You know I can't stay mad at you."

"But you're mad at Greyson?"

"He's different."

"How?" She reached for another tissue and blew her nose.

"Dear God, I think you just called a few ships into harbor."

"Shut up." She sniffled, resting her head on the pillow. "He didn't do this to hurt you."

"I know. But that doesn't mean it doesn't hurt."

Her heart pinched. "Logan…"

"Don't. I don't need anyone's pity, and it would kill me to be on the receiving end of yours, Wren."

"Sympathy isn't pity."

"Well, it's damn close."

Her head pounded, but she cared more about him than herself in that moment. "We can talk about it if you want."

He shrugged. "What's there to say? Greyson always gets what Greyson wants. Now, he'll have everything."

She frowned. "What does that mean?"

"Come on, Wren. He's got you, and now he'll get the company. What else is there?"

She stilled. "That's not what this is, Logan."

"No?" He looked around. "You're in his shirt, in his house, on his couch. Try and tell me that's not winning."

"He doesn't want to marry me and this has nothing to do with the fishery."

"He told you that?"

He hadn't told her, but she knew Greyson. He wasn't doing this for an inheritance, and they hadn't even slept together yet, so marriage was light years ahead. "This thing between us has nothing to do with your father."

"That's what you think."

"That's what I know, Logan. It's taken us thirty years to get here. We're not rushing."

"He had his entire life to go after you, and he didn't. Now, he's suddenly changing his mind? Seems a little fast and coincidental to me."

She was too tired for this conversation. "You're wrong."

"We'll see." He stood. "I guess congratulations are in order. Let's just hope he sticks around and doesn't pull a Greyson."

She wanted to tell him that wouldn't happen, but she honestly shared the same fears. "He's not like that anymore."

He paused and spared her a pitying glance. "For your sake, I hope you're right. Feel better, Wren. Tell him I stopped by."

The door shut, and she slumped weakly into the cushions. Boys could be so much drama. She coughed, moaned, and rolled onto her side, drifting back to sleep.

A while later, she awoke to Greyson speaking softly to someone in the kitchen, his voice low and indulgent.

"You like that, huh?" he murmured, a soft chuckle following. "That's it. Take a little more."

Wren frowned, recognizing the voice as the same one he used for dirty talk?

"Easy," he said, tone coaxing in a familiar way. "That's it. Nice and slow."

Wren blinked and struggled to sit up.

"Don't choke." Greyson's teasing laughter curled around his words, affection coloring every syllable. "Look at that dirty mouth."

Her jaw dropped. What. The. Hell?

"You're a filthy little thing."

Having heard enough, she bundled herself up in the blanket, and shuffled into the kitchen like a walking burrito.

"Hey, you're awake." Greyson set the kitten down and pressed a hand to her head. "Your fever's down."

She squinted at the cat. "You gave him solid food?"

"He loves it." He lifted an old, battered thermos out of a bag. "I had them put the soup in here to keep it warm. Good thing, because you've been asleep for a while. Hungry?"

She looked out the window, surprised it was dark. "Do you mind if I shower before I eat?"

"Towels are on the shelf."

"Thanks." She smiled weakly and turned. "Oh, by the way, Logan stopped by." She sensed him stiffen but didn't stick around to see his reaction.

The shower helped clear her head. Unfortunately, that opened the door for more thoughts, and the only thing she could think about was what Logan had said about Greyson getting the company now.

She put on a fresh shirt from Greyson's drawer and returned to the couch. Greyson had Eclipse cued up where they left off, and a bowl and spoon waited next to the thermos.

He smiled and lifted the blanket for her to return to her now tidied spot. "Did the shower help?"

She nodded and pulled the blanket over her, not having much of an appetite, or a filter. "Are you planning on taking over the fishery?"

Greyson stilled, startled by her question. Setting down the thermos, he looked straight ahead and frowned. "Where did that come from? Oh, wait, let me guess. My brother."

"This isn't about Logan."

"Yes, it is. He's putting stuff in your head."

"It would have crossed my mind eventually."

He sighed. "He just couldn't resist throwing that out there."

"Well, do you?"

He stood. "I forgot napkins."

"Greyson."

He stilled. "For all we know, my dad's got another ten years in him."

But he didn't. "Grey, you know what the reality is. The doctors said—"

"They don't know my dad."

So much vulnerability flashed in his eyes, she didn't push the subject. "Okay." She glanced at the bowl. "What kind of soup did you—"

"That clause has nothing to do with my feelings for you, Wren."

Was he trying to convince her or himself? "Are you sure?"

He met her stare and a cold silence drifted through the room. Finally, he turned away and said, "Fire needs wood. I'll be back."

The door slammed behind him. It wasn't total abandonment, but it also wasn't what she'd call an affirmation. For the next hour, she listened to him chop wood by the shed, despite the piles of already cut wood stacked neatly on the porch.

His frustration didn't scare her. What terrified her was his impulse to run away the moment she brought up something emotionally challenging. Magnus was going to die. His demise would undoubtedly stir up a lot painful feelings for his three sons, whether they were willing to face them or not.

Greyson might be willing to discuss his love for her, but how would he handle the excruciating love he harbored for his difficult dad?

CHAPTER 22

"Baby, Let's Just Light the Fire"

WREN AND GREYSON CIRCLED EACH OTHER LIKE WARY PREDATORS, choosing to avoid eye contact or conversation at all costs. After an evening of aggressive wood chopping and restless home repairs, Wren spent the evening dozing on and off on Greyson's couch. She awoke at three a.m. with a full bladder and found him snoring softly in his bed. Alone.

He'd put another blanket on her, refreshed her water, and checked the fire while she slept, but he wasn't sleeping with her anymore. Now, it could have been due to the endless sneezing, obnoxious coughing, and stuffiness that made her snore like a lumberjack. But more likely—according to her inner critic—he was mad about the reference to his dad's will. And when Greyson got upset, it took him years to confront his feelings and get over it.

In other words, she fucked up.

She pushed for too much from him too fast, and her desire to help him confront his father's health might have truly crossed a line. But what if the clause in Magnus's will was actually the catalyst to Greyson's sudden interest in her?

This thought, and many other worries, kept her up until four a.m. That was when she decided to drive home—just before dawn.

She questioned if skipping out on him was the mature response to an argument, all the while knowing in the back of her mind it was the cowardly thing to do. But by that afternoon, when Greyson hadn't stopped by or even texted to ask why she left, she spiraled into a whirlwind of doubts and realized—where relationships were concerned—she knew nothing at all.

She hated when her inner critic was right. But not as much as she hated that she questioned his motives. Why had she done that?

She'd been under the weather and exhausted. Logan got in her head. She should have never listened to him.

Glancing at her phone again, she suffered another wave of anxiety.

What if she'd ruined everything?

What if Greyson took such offense to her question that he no longer wanted her?

What if this went beyond that and she damaged more than just their current relationship?

She went against her silent promise to give him space and texted an *I'm sorry*. Twenty minutes later her stomach hurt and she still had no response.

"Damn it."

"What's wrong with you?" Lilly asked, as she stepped into the employee kitchenette.

"Huh?" Wren looked up from her phone. "Oh. Nothing."

"Doesn't sound like nothing, the way you're huffing and fidgeting over there. You're biting your nails down to nubs. Eat something else. Here." She tossed a cookie tin onto the table. "Birdie stopped by to drop these off."

"I'm not hungry," Wren said as she cracked open the container. Foil-wrapped chocolate kisses dotted with powdered sugar littered the mix of chocolate chip, peanut butter, and thumb-pressed jam cookies. She pulled out a peanut butter one and bit into it, then frowned. "Why do I taste mint?"

"Because Birdie made them. She's a hot mess. I doubt she even owns measuring cups. She only brought them here in search of gossip."

"Then why did you give them to me?" Wren spat the cookie back into the tin and shut the lid.

"Because you've been pouting all day. It's the Christmas season. Don't you know the rules about that?"

"What rules?"

Lilly bopped her head from side to side. *"You better not pout, you better not cry..."* She looked at her expectantly. "No?"

"I know the song, I just..." She didn't have an excuse, not one she'd share with her staff. "Sorry. I'll cheer up." Wren tossed the tin of cookies into the trash and glanced at the schedule on the wall, searching for a distraction.

It might have only been December ninth, but Christmas ruled the calendar. Bodhi and Astrid were hosting a sound bath in the studio that evening. She stopped by to check on them, happy to see so many guests making use of the cozy chairs and the inviting fireplace in The Haven's lounge on the way. Pine garland draped the mantels, and the scent of cinnamon candles mixed with woodsmoke created the perfect holiday atmosphere.

From the hall, she could hear the rattle of gongs and the hum of sound bowls, followed by her aunt's voice. "It sounds better over here, Bodhi. The acoustics are just better when we aren't up against the glass. Plus, I don't fancy freezing my ass off. There's a draft."

"There's no breeze, Astrid."

"Then why do I have wind up my back?"

"It's probably coming from your own keister."

"How's it going in here?" Wren asked as she stepped into the studio.

Bodhi rolled his eyes as he relocated the gong away from the window.

"Your father thinks I have gas. I know my own damn smells, Bodhi. There's a draft!"

Wren inspected the window. No obvious leaks caught her attention, but the temperature had dropped enough that a draft appeared to be present. "Maybe she's right, Dad, and the wall would be a better backdrop. Especially for an evening session, when the sun's down. I can also turn up the heat."

"Speaking of turning up the heat," Aunt Astrid said as she rummaged through her carpet bag. "Have you read the latest copy of *The Beacon*?"

Wren reluctantly took the town newspaper. "Why?"

"Page six."

"Oh, no." Wren turned to the opinion section, where Lady Lovewatch's latest column dominated the page. Lady Lovewatch—if she even existed as a lady—was Hideaway Bay's most informed and mysterious gossip.

Wren skimmed the column, her stomach sinking each time she spotted her name printed in black ink. There was a write-up about the auction, and then the debacle about the check. Lady Lovewatch questioned why one brother would pay for the other. Then came the spectacle at the parade, reported in hearsay meant to pique the interest of those who still weren't sold on the newest small-town secret romance. The more she read, the more she wanted to hide under a rock until the New Year.

"So, which is it?"

"Huh?" she looked up at her aunt from the paper.

"Which Hawthorne's been buttering your biscuit?"

Wren crumpled the paper. "It's just a gossip column, Aunt Astrid. There's no real truth to this stuff."

"Oh, I don't know about that." Her aunt laughed. "The truth's written plain across your face, dear, in a blush darker than whatever ink the printer's using." She cocked her head inquisitively. "There's no shame in taking care of your needs, sweetheart. Girl's gotta eat."

"Astrid, are you going to help move this stuff, or what?" Bodhi dropped the xylophone windchime with a clatter.

"What did I tell you about being delicate with my instruments? You're like a bull in a china shop!"

Wren backed out of the studio, her fist cinched tight around the newspaper, when she bumped into something firm. She turned and immediately stepped back with a wince. "Mr. Drummond."

"I put a request in at the front desk for more soap an hour ago."

"I'm sorry. I can get that for you." She led him down the hall to the supply closet where Lilly currently exited, an armful of toiletries in her grip. The moment the receptionist spotted their challenging guest, she scowled.

"Mr. Drummond needs more—"

"Soap for his room. I know," Lilly said dryly. "I told him I'd deliver it."

The CEO glanced at the haul of branded Haven products overflowing from her arms. "Is that conditioner? I need more of that as well."

Lilly protectively turned away to shelter the supplies from his view.

Wren stole a bar of soap and a mini bottle of conditioner. "Here you go."

"Is that an eye mask?"

"No," Lilly said.

Wren plucked the mask from her arms. "Of course. There you are."

He narrowed his eyes at Lilly, then winced when a sound bowl hit a particularly sharp frequency that howled long enough for everyone in The Haven to notice. "What is that ungodly noise?"

"That's just our team getting ready for tonight's sound therapy session. Have you signed up?"

"No, and I don't plan to. Do you have any earplugs? How loud does it get?"

Lilly rolled her eyes. "You probably won't hear it back in New York."

"Lilly," Wren snapped, then placed a hand on Mr. Drummond's shoulder to walk him away from her feral receptionist. "I'm sure you won't be disturbed by the sounds once you're back in your cabin. And the sound baths usually only last an hour."

"*That* for an hour? People pay for that?"

"It can be very centering."

"So can a migraine."

"Sound therapy can actually lower stress, help with sleep, and even reduce muscle tension and pain, Mr. Drummond."

"Right," he said, tone full of doubt.

"You might benefit from such an experience." She gently squeezed his arm. "You're still carrying a lot of tension in your shoulders."

His oppositional mood softened until he glanced over her head and scowled. "Something you need?"

Wren turned and immediately let go of Mr. Drummond's arm. "Greyson."

"Wren, honey!" Aunt Astrid rushed out of the studio. "Your father got a splinter from your cactus plant. Do you have tweezers?" Her aunt paused and took in the crowded hall where Greyson and the CEO faced off. "Goodness, there's enough testosterone in this hallway to fuel a small army." Her smile curved as her gaze bounced between the two men. "Mr. Hawthorne."

"Astrid." Greyson nodded in greeting, never taking his eyes off Drummond.

Wren's heart fluttered, but not in a good way. She kept her eyes on Grey's scowling face, not daring to leave to find the tweezers. "Lilly, see if there's a pin or something in the drawer at the front desk."

"I need to speak to you," Greyson growled.

"Correct me if I'm wrong," Drummond interrupted. "But you both work here and I'm the guest, right? We were in the middle of something."

Greyson turned his head, his attention slowly returning to Drummond as if he were a glob of shit on his new shoes. Before he could say anything, Wren pushed him into the stock room closet. "Pardon us. We'll just be a minute." She shut the door and turned on him. "Grey, you cannot growl at my guests."

The cramped space reeked of industrial cleaning supplies and fresh linens, but underneath it all, Greyson's familiar masculine scent of cedar and something uniquely him, made her pulse quicken. Shelves of toilet paper and towels boxed them in, creating an intimate prison where every breath seemed to echo.

"Fuck that guy." Thankfully, his voice muffled behind the shelves stocked with paper products. But she still worried the guests might overhear.

"Keep your voice down."

"Why were you touching him?"

"I wasn't—"

"Wren."

"Fine. I did. But only in a professional sense. I simply pointed out that he carried some tension in his shoulders so he would get off my back about the sound therapy starting in an hour."

"I don't want you touching him."

The possessive rasp in his voice sent heat spiraling through her belly. "Well…I don't want you ignoring me to chop wood all night. Why are you even here?"

He drew back. "I told you I'd come to take you home."

She frowned. "No, you didn't."

"I texted you."

She pulled out her cell and flashed the screen. "No, you didn't. I'm the one who texted you." She showed him her thread of unanswered texts, and he growled.

"This is why I tell you to use a radio. These things are completely unreliable."

In the cramped space of linens and supplies, tension seemed to ricochet off the walls as quickly as it radiated from his broad shoulders. There wasn't enough oxygen to think straight, especially when he was sucking it out of the room with one threatening look after another.

The rough metal shelving pressed against her back while his imposing frame blocked any escape. "Look, I'm sorry if I missed your text, but that's not my fault."

"Well, it's not mine either. I've been texting you since I woke up alone this morning. Where did you go?"

"Home. And you woke up alone, because you went to bed alone."

"Only because you were sick and I didn't want to disturb you."

"Are you sure about that?" She held his stare.

"Yes, Wren," he said through gritted teeth. "You were coughing all night. You needed rest."

"Well, I'm better now."

"Good," he snapped. "Glad to hear it."

"Me too," she snipped back, unsure why she was using her illness as the means for this argument. But her feelings were hurt and her head was a mess all day, and she needed some damn answers. If he wanted out, she wanted to know, sooner rather than later, so she gave him an open invitation to exit. "We can pretend it never happened, Grey."

His eyes narrowed. "Oh, it happened."

She shrugged. "It could have all been a dream."

He took a step, crowding her against the racks of toilet paper in the already cramped pantry. The heat from his body enveloped her, and she could feel the steady thrum of his pulse where his chest nearly touched hers. "It wasn't a dream. It happened."

"Did it?"

"You know it did."

She lost her courage and lowered her gaze, fearful that he might have regrets. Maybe she pushed him further than he wanted to go. Maybe she used her body to seduce him into a situation he otherwise wouldn't have chosen.

Shame softened her voice to a rasp. "It doesn't have to stay this way, you know? We could just…go back to the way things used to be."

Another step. He gently lifted her chin, forcing her to meet his eyes. The rough pad of his thumb traced along her jawline, sending shivers down her spine.

There was too much reality in his stare. Too much feeling.

That's how it always was with Greyson. He gave her the most intense looks but never validated his emotions with words.

Claiming he loved her didn't excuse him from answering for other things. She was tired of guessing how he felt, and it wasn't fair of him to walk out on a conversation when she had questions.

"Is that what you want?" he whispered, his chest heaving slowly as he commanded nothing short of honesty.

Her chin trembled, and her vision wavered. "No."

"Me neither, Wren." He took another step, pressing his front to hers. The solid wall of his chest trapped her against the shelving, and every nerve ending sparked to life. "I told you how I felt. One little argument isn't going to undo those feelings."

"You walked out."

"I'm sorry." He brushed a kiss to her mouth.

She softened and closed her eyes. The tension that had been building inside her all day slowly subsided to a gentle hum.

Tracing the backs of his fingers over her cheek, he rasped, "You asked me a question I didn't know how to answer."

Her heart dropped and unease returned. If it was that difficult for him to answer, did that mean his actions actually *did* revolve around his dad on some level? "Oh."

"Before you get ahead of yourself, let me make myself crystal clear. This—us—it's happening because we want it to. No one else has anything to do with it."

She looked up at him, needing to read the truth in his eyes. "Are you sure?"

"Very."

"Then why did you get so defensive?"

"I wasn't angry, Wren. I needed time to think. I went to get soup, and the next thing I know, I'm being questioned about my future career plans and how my dad's death might play into that. It's a lot."

"You're right. I'm sorry."

"Don't apologize."

"Well, what the hell am I supposed to say, Greyson? I am sorry. I never meant to upset you."

His mouth formed a flat line. "We're both coming off of whatever bug we had, and neither of us was thinking clearly. My fucking brothers aren't helping matters either."

As much as it might seem like Logan said those things to spite Greyson, Wren understood his warnings were more out of concern for her. "I don't like fighting with you."

"We're not fighting." He stepped back, giving her space to breathe. "I came by to tell you something."

She looked up at his intense blue eyes. "What?"

"I'm going home with you. Tonight."

"Because…?"

"I don't wanna talk anymore, Wren. I'm done with talking and I'm done with waiting."

Her belly swooped. "You mean…"

"Yes. It's happening. Tonight."

She looked up at him, once again finding it difficult to breathe. She was suddenly aware of every hidden crevice on her body as strange sensations fluttered at every nerve ending.

Her voice trembled, "O-okay."

"I'll pick you up at five." He pinched her chin and brushed

another kiss across her lips, and whispered, "We're crossing lines that can't be uncrossed, and that will be the end of it. No more mixed signals. Understand?"

Her entire body had a pulse as he released her, and she clung to the inventory racks so her knees didn't give out. She nodded her consent as he opened the door.

In a daze, she watched as he exited the stock room. Astrid, Lilly, Bodhi, and Drummond still gathered in the hall.

Greyson stepped out and looked directly at Drummond and growled, "Watch it."

The four turned to stare as Greyson exited The Haven.

"Wait until Lady Lovewatch hears about this." Astrid fanned her flushed cheeks.

Bodhi looked at Wren in confusion. "Did I miss something?"

Drummond frowned. "So, what's the verdict on earplugs?"

Lilly turned on him. "Seriously, dude?"

Wren snapped out of her daze. "Lilly, find Mr. Drummond whatever he needs. Dad, you and Aunt Astrid need to make sure the studio door is closed for tonight's session. I need my keys."

"Where are you going?" Bodhi followed her out of the supply closet and down the hall.

"I have errands to run."

"Now? We have a class tonight."

"I can't make it."

He stopped, and she paused, realizing the sudden change of plans might trigger an episode. Calmly, she clasped his shoulders. "Dad, you and Aunt Astrid are going to have an amazing class. You've got this."

He smiled as something shifted in his eyes. "You sound like your mother."

She grinned, never disappointed to hear that. "The towers are out, so if you need anything, use the radios."

He drew back his shoulders and lifted his chin. "I won't need anything. You go run your errands."

"Thanks, Dad."

As soon as she found her car keys, she drove to Jocelyn's. Her friend didn't like having her writing time interrupted, and as Wren pounded on her door, she vaguely heard grumbles from the other side—something about the vicious fate of those who rudely interrupted a Viking's orgasm.

"This is exactly why the Vikings died out." The door whipped open mid-threat. "Don't you people—Wren?" Her scowl flipped to a blasé greeting. "Come in."

Wren didn't move from the threshold as Jocelyn drifted through the house.

"We really need a secret knock," her friend continued from somewhere in the kitchen. "I almost castrated you for interrupting my sex scene. Ragnar the Fierce was just about to blow his load."

"I'm losing my virginity. Tonight."

Jocelyn's head popped back around the corner. "About-fucking-time. Let me see what I have in terms of champagne. Give me a sec."

She disappeared again as bottles clanked from the bar. "So, who is it?"

Wren shut the front door. "What do you mean, who is it? It's Greyson, of course."

Jocelyn reappeared with a bottle of prosecco. "This is the best I can do for bubbles and stems." She snickered, twisting off the cork. "Sounds like an idiom for tits and dicks."

Wren followed her into the newly renovated kitchen, numb from face to chest. "I thought you'd be a little more shocked."

"Shocked? Wren, honey, you're thirty. The shock lies in the fact that you made it this far. It's about fucking time you got that cherry smashed."

She blew out a shaky breath, her body processing the strange anticipation in a thousand strange ways.

"My god, look at you. Relax! Fucking is fun." The cork popped, and she filled two tall glasses.

Wren pulled out a leatherback stool and sat before her legs gave out.

Jocelyn lived too eccentrically to actually cook for herself, but when she got her last six-figure deal, she used a portion of it to design a state-of-the-art kitchen, which mostly functioned as Hideaway Bay's largest liquor cabinet.

"I knew you'd eventually break him."

Wren frowned. "I didn't break him."

"Well, not you, *per se*. Lady Lovewatch has the whole town curious. Which brother will it be? Did you read what she wrote about my event?"

"I did."

Jocelyn slid her a glass and lifted her own. "To your hymen."

Wren rolled her eyes and sipped. "It's a little jarring how much detail Lady Lovewatch was able to gather."

"Hmm. Yeah. Weird." Jocelyn took a long swallow and grinned. "But we all knew Greyson Hawthorne was a jealous man, and now look where you are."

Wren needed to plan for the future, not dwell in the past. "I don't have much time. I need your best advice, and I need it quick." She guzzled the prosecco, hoping it might calm her nerves.

"My advice?" Jocelyn's silk kimono sleeves gathered at her elbows as she dramatically fanned her face and flattered herself. "Well, I am an award-winning author of Norse cock. And the Hawthornes do have old Scandinavian roots."

"Jocelyn, focus!"

"Right. Well, the first thing I can tell you to do is hydrate. A good battle always starts with a full flask."

"Okay." Wren nodded, drinking down her sparkling wine. "Got it, what else?"

She tapped her chin. "Make sure he gets you nice and wet. Otherwise, things can tear."

"*Tear?*"

She waved away her concern. "I'm sure you'll be fine.

Greyson's a real guy. I'm used to writing fictional men with baby arms between their legs."

"Baby arms?" Wren wasn't sure her friend's visuals were helping to calm her nerves.

"Yeah, my readers like 'em big and veiny."

Wren's eyes widened. "Greyson's pretty big. Do you think it's going to hurt?"

"Even if it doesn't, act like it does. Men like to think they're giants. I'd definitely throw out some *oohs* and *ahhs* to play it up right."

"Joce, I don't want it to hurt!"

"Then you shouldn't have waited this long, toots. Your shit's probably atrophied."

She planted her face in her hands and groaned. "Why did I come here?"

"Relax. You came here because I'm the most unfiltered friend you have, and you know I'm going to give it to you straight."

"I think you mean unhinged."

"Unfiltered, unhinged. Tomato, tow-mah-tow. The point is, once he's in there, you're going to ride that man like he's the last warhorse out of Valhalla."

Wren choked on her prosecco.

"I'm serious. You summon your inner shieldmaiden, and you plunder that man's soul. Leave him so dazed he forgets his name but remembers yours for the rest of his life."

"Jocelyn!"

"Don't you dare go in there shy, Wren. Be the Viking princess I know you are."

"My family's from Boston."

"Well, Bostonians are a little nuts. Channel your inner Viking and don't ask for permission—just conquer. Storm the fjord. A true heroine doesn't tiptoe into a love scene—she raids it."

Wren blinked. "What does that even mean?"

"Flip him. Mount him. Ravish him like it's Midsummer and there's a fertility festival on the line. Make your ancestors proud."

"I'm pretty sure my ancestors included English Puritans."

"Then make his proud. Moan like a war horn. Scratch his back like you're climbing a glacier to save your life. And for the love of Freyja, move your hips like the fertility goddess you are. A true Viking wench never lies still."

"Okay, okay! I get it."

"No, you don't. But you will." Jocelyn tipped the bottle to refill her glass.

Wren put a hand over the rim. "I have to drive."

"Oh. Right. You want the bottle? It might help."

"No, that's okay. I probably shouldn't drink."

"Why?" Jocelyn scrunched up her nose.

"I want to be fully aware."

"Oh. Smart. Especially if it hurts."

On second thought, Wren grabbed the bottle by the neck. "Maybe I'll use it to ice my crotch afterwards."

"Atta girl! Now, you're thinking. And one more thing…"

"Yeah?"

"Trust your body. It knows what it wants, even if your brain's overthinking everything. Let instinct take over."

"Thanks for the advice." She slid off the barstool.

"Any time."

Bottle in hand, Wren exited the kitchen with a slightly haunted expression. "Sorry, I disrupted your sex scene."

"It's okay. This actually helped." She followed her to the door and yelled, "Go forth, my Valkyrie! And remember, if he's not limping by morning, you probably will be."

Wren drove home through the darkening harbor streets, Jocelyn's outrageous advice echoing in her mind as anticipation and nerves warred in her belly.

When she pulled into her driveway, Greyson's truck already waited in the shadows, headlights cutting through the evening like predatory eyes. Her pulse hammered against her throat as she spotted his silhouette in the driver's seat, broad shoulders unmistakable even in the dim light.

The engine shut off.

Her hands trembled as she gripped the steering wheel, watching him emerge from the truck with that confident, purposeful stride that had always made her stomach flutter. Tonight, that flutter had transformed into something deeper, more primal.

Tonight, everything would change.

CHAPTER 23

"From Your Lips, She Drew the Hallelujah"

Short-lived flurries danced around Greyson as he stepped out of his truck and waited. He tracked her every movement, his predatory attention to detail making her hesitate. Finally, she shut off the car and opened the door.

He crossed his arms over his chest, as if giving her a chance to change her mind. "Having second thoughts?"

She laughed nervously. "No."

"You sure?" His gaze dropped to the half-empty bottle of prosecco clutched in her white knuckles. "Tough afternoon?"

"I stopped by Jocelyn's."

"Ah." He drew in a slow breath, never taking his gaze off of her. The scent of cedar and winter air clung to his jacket, mixing with something uniquely masculine that made her pulse quicken. "Do me a favor. Whatever advice she gave you, leave it alone."

Wren laughed, thinking of some of the more colorful tactics Jocelyn had explained to her over the years. "Are you sure?"

"Very."

"Okay." She stepped over Figgy to walk up the steps. "But she told me to ride you like the last warhorse out of Valhalla." She glanced back at Greyson and laughed at his blank expression.

He climbed the steps and mumbled, "What the hell did you tell her?"

Wren unlocked the door, her hands trembling slightly as the key turned. "That's sacred information kept strictly between me and my best friend. Do you want some wine?"

"No thanks."

"Do you mind if I have some?"

"Not at all."

"Good." When she pulled a glass down from the cabinet, she confessed, "I'm a little nervous."

"It's just me, Wren."

"That's why I'm nervous." Her smile turned shy. "It's you."

He took off his coat and hung it next to hers on the wall, the simple domestic gesture somehow intimate in its familiarity. Then he crossed the small den into the kitchen, his boots heavy on the hardwood floor. "You have nothing to worry about."

He placed his hands on her shoulders and gently massaged, his calloused palms rough against her skin through the thin fabric of her sweater. Shivers raced up her spine as he pushed her hair aside to kiss the nape of her neck. Her breath hitched as her nipples tightened under her shirt. Was it already starting?

"Grey…"

"It had to happen this way, Wren, with the two of us." His voice rumbled against her neck, vibrating every nerve.

Her heart skipped a beat as his mouth moved slowly toward her racing pulse. She licked her suddenly dry lips.

"*Wait, wait, wait.*" Slipping out of his grip, she backed out of the kitchen. "I need…to freshen up." She reached for her glass and the bottle. "Can you give me a few minutes? Meet me in the bedroom?"

"There's no rush, Wren. We can grab dinner—"

"No." The thought of doing this on a full stomach didn't sound wise. "I have my dinner." She lifted her glass. "You can help yourself to anything in the fridge."

"Are you okay?"

"I'm fine," she said in a high-pitched voice that sounded nothing like her own. "I'll be two seconds." She rushed into the bathroom and locked the door with shaking fingers. "Shit."

Dropping to the toilet, she rocked forward, her heart hammering so hard she could feel it in her throat. She pressed her slick palms against her cheeks, trying to cool the fever burning through her, and guzzled her glass of wine, hoping the alcohol would calm the butterflies rioting in her stomach.

"Breathe." She forced air into her lungs. "Breathe." She practiced her breathwork, but it only made her lightheaded. "You've got this. Nice and deep…" Hearing her own words she stilled. That was exactly how it would be. Nice, and probably very fucking deep.

Why did Jocelyn say that thing about tearing?

The breathing exercises weren't working, so she tried to massage her vagus nerve while doing various face contortions. Her hands trembled as she pressed her fingers to her neck, searching for some magical pressure point that would transform her from terrified virgin to confident seductress. Nothing worked.

"Fuck." She drank directly from the bottle, and quickly emptied it. Her head was spinning, yet she was still somehow way too sober. "Shower."

She pulled her hair into a messy bun and stripped while the water warmed, her fingers fumbling with buttons and zippers. Hopefully, the heat would calm her anxiety. She could also try a cold plunge.

There isn't time for that.

Two seconds turned into ten minutes. By the time she left the bathroom, she was more worked up than she'd been when she ran away.

Wrapped in a towel, Wren awkwardly sauntered out of the steam, prepared for embarrassment but shockingly soothed by the sight that greeted her.

He knelt by the fireplace, coaxing flames to life, the golden light dancing across his broad shoulders, casting shadows that accentuated every ridge of muscle. Her nervous energy quelled the moment her brain remembered this was Greyson, not some stranger.

He was right. This was always the way it was supposed to be—the two of them.

She smiled. "The scent of burning firewood always reminds me of you."

He glanced back from the hearth and stilled, his eyes drinking in the sight of her. Slowly, he stood from where he crouched and crossed the room, each step deliberate and predatory.

A burst of butterflies took flight in her stomach, and her hand tightened on the towel wrapped around her chest as he closed the distance. The firelight played across his angular features, highlighting the intensity in his blue eyes.

Of course, Greyson missed nothing. "If you're not ready, we can wait."

"I'm ready. I'm very, *very* ready."

"You're sure?"

She looked up at him, the gravity of this moment weighing her down like lead. "I've waited years for this, Greyson. Don't tease me with something only to take it away."

He glanced down at her chest and stepped closer, tucking a damp curl behind her ear. His fingertips lingered against her temple, tracing the shell of her ear with devastating gentleness. "I'm not taking it away. You're mine, Wren. You've always been mine." His voice lowered as he stared into her eyes with hungry promise. "Haven't you?"

She nodded, wanting nothing more than for him to claim her in that moment.

"No more waiting." He bent to kiss her, and she wreathed her arms around his neck.

She tried for graceful and failed miserably. It seemed neither of them had any patience left. Hauling her off her feet, he gripped her ass and backed her into the wall. She locked her legs around his hips as his body ground against hers, hard denim against soft flesh, the rough texture of his jeans creating delicious friction against her bare thighs.

Her fingers raked through his hair as he pinned her to the plaster, devouring her mouth with enough pent-up passion to get her quivering before he even put his hands on her. The towel started to slip, but she didn't care. All that mattered was the heat of his mouth, the possessive grip of his hands, the way he consumed her like a man starved.

"Bedroom," she rasped between kisses.

He carried her into the back room and followed her down to the bed, his mouth savagely staking its claim over her chest as he yanked away the towel. The soft cotton sheets cooled her heated skin, a stark contrast to the furnace of his body above her.

"You're so fucking beautiful."

She arched into him, pulling at his clothes. "I want all of you, Grey. Take this off."

He sat up, fumbling with the buttons of his flannel as his boots hit the floor in two hard thumps. Thick ropes of sinew bunched at his arms as his shirt pulled off, revealing the landscape of scars and muscle she'd glimpsed but never fully explored. His abdomen flexed in tight rows of muscle as he reached for his belt buckle, and she couldn't help but stare at the trail of golden hair that disappeared beneath his jeans.

She grinned and sat up to see the big reveal.

"Something wrong?"

She grinned and shook her head. "I...don't want to miss anything."

He chuckled, the sound vibrating through his chest. "Believe me, baby, you aren't gonna miss it." He flicked the button of his jeans loose, showing her just how constrained he was.

Her eyes widened as he lowered the zipper and gripped his engorged flesh. Meeting his gaze, she hid a smile and teased, "You could make a Viking jealous."

He pushed her down to the bed and kissed her, his weight settling over her like a claim. "I guess I'll take that as a compliment."

"You should." Her humor turned to nervousness as he pushed off the last of his clothes. Nothing between them but a lifetime of unspoken sexual tension and her own shallow breaths. The fading light painted his skin in shadow, every muscle defined, every scar telling a story she wanted to learn by touch.

He calmed her with slow, hungry kisses, his hands framing her face with reverent touches. "Look at me, Wren."

She lifted her gaze to his familiar stare, and the last of her nervousness shifted into something manageable. This was Greyson. Her Greyson. The man who'd protected her, comforted her, loved her in silence for years.

He caressed her cheek, his thumb tracing the line of her jaw. "We have our entire lives to get it perfect. Don't overthink the first time."

She bit her lip. "I waited too long."

"You were waiting for me." The certainty in his voice made her heart skip.

When he said it like that, all her regret disappeared. "You're worth the wait."

He kissed her in a way that put love before urgency. He grounded them in the moment, slowing time, laying their emotions bare, until they were both shivering as they edged closer to the precipice of this next chapter together.

"Just relax. Let me take care of you." He bent to capture her nipple, pulling tenderly at the tip.

The longer he touched and kissed her, putting her at ease but also working her up, the more her body responded. His hands mapped every curve, every sensitive spot, as if memorizing her for all time. Soon enough, she was arching into him and panting toward her first climax.

"That's it, baby. I can feel your body clenching around my fingers." He teased his hands between her thighs, driving her closer and closer to that edge of ecstasy. "So wet for me already."

"Ah," she cried, rocking her hips as he sank his fingers deeper. His mouth closed over her nipple, and her fingers knotted in his hair. "Greyson…"

He sucked and teased her into a state of erotic delirium. Every touch awakened another part of her. Dragging her nails over his shoulders, she clung to him as heat and desire coiled tighter and tighter at her core. The scent of his skin, soap and something uniquely masculine, drenched her senses.

When he kissed a trail down her stomach, she tried to slow him. It overwhelmed her. But he forced her legs open and showed her how much more she could take.

"There's no hiding from me now, baby." His warm breath teased her drenched folds as he crouched lower, pressing her thighs open with firm hands. "I told you." He licked in warning. "You're mine."

Again, she cried out his name, too drunk on lust to choose her words carefully. He devoured her in long, languid licks, sucking her clit, fingering her to an ongoing state of ecstasy. Driving her higher and higher until she was rambling gibberish and clinging to him with a sort of desperation she hadn't known she could feel.

He was an addiction she couldn't satisfy. The more he gave, the more she wanted. "Please, Greyson… I need…"

"I know what you need." This time, when he kissed her again, his tongue rich with her taste and his body hard and ready, all the words fell away.

Her breath caught as the smooth head of his cock pressed against her sex and their eyes met. The moment held and she nodded, then he pressed forward and the world aligned on its axis, everything coming into balance the way it only did during moments of divinity and the purest truth.

The pressure overwhelmed her as he sank into her, inch by devastating inch. His weight grounded her when she might have tried to otherwise pull away, his forehead pressed to hers as he gave her body time to adjust.

"I've got you, baby. You're okay." His voice was strained, every muscle taut with the effort of holding back.

She met his stare, her mind spiraling at the sense of unity. They were one. Connected. Inseparable for the briefest moment of time.

Awareness washed over her as tears sprang to her eyes. She clung to him, afraid to move, never wanting to let him go. *This* was what it meant to belong to someone completely.

"I love you, Greyson."

He pressed his brow to hers, absorbing every breath, every syllable, every twitch like a stroke along his buried cock. "I love you, too. So much it scares me."

Her breath hitched, and he pulled back. She watched him with a tearful smile.

"Jesus, Wren." He took her mouth in a slow kiss that ended in a whisper that struck more like a prayer. "I'll never hurt you, Wren. I'll always take care of you." He sealed his vow with a slow, devastating kiss. "You're never getting rid of me now."

She drew in a jagged breath, twin tears spilling past her lashes. He kissed the corners of her eyes, slowly rocking into her. She'd never experienced anything so intimate before, and somehow she knew that had more to do with Greyson than it had to do with this being her first time.

"My Wren." He tipped his head back as if overcome by emotion. "I don't…" His breathing turned ragged. "I don't understand what I'm feeling." A storm of emotion played in his eyes as he stared down at her in awe. Intensity washed over them in waves.

She ran her fingers through his hair, lifting to press her lips to his. "It's okay. I feel it too."

"You do?"

She nodded. "I've always felt it around you. It's love, Grey. That heaviness that makes it hard to breathe, it's why they call it a crush."

"Fuck." He pressed his face into her neck, and she realized how much effort he exerted to hold himself back, his muscles trembling with restraint.

"You can let go, Greyson. You won't hurt me." She cupped his jaw and turned his face back to hers. Slowly, she kissed him. "It's us. We can be real together. It was always going to be this intense."

His breath rushed out in shaky realization as her words resonated with everything they were feeling. "You'd think this was my first time."

"Maybe it is. Maybe this is the first time it truly mattered."

"Fuck." He kissed her, deep and desperate, like a lost man racing to find his way home. "How do you always know what I'm trying to say?"

She framed his face. "Because I know you, probably better than anyone else in this world."

"You're fucking perfect." He rolled his hips, and her communication skills disintegrated with a moan.

She gasped when he flexed, his cock pulsing inside of her as her body gripped him tightly. The moment she found her rhythm he cursed. "Wren, wait."

"What's wrong?"

"We forgot a condom. In my jeans—"

"It's okay."

He frowned. "Are you on the pill?"

"No." She bit her lip. "Do you care?"

Shock flashed in his eyes when he understood what she was asking. Then he smiled with absolute male satisfaction as he possessively pressed deeper. "Hell no, I don't care." He took her mouth in a demanding kiss, primal need consuming him as he thrust into her, hard. "The thought of you having my baby…" He kissed her again, this time locking his fingers with hers and pressing her arm over her head. "I fucking love you, Wren."

He claimed her in every way she wanted to be claimed. Her nails scraped down his back as he pounded deeper, burying himself to the root. Her body contracted tightly around his pumping cock, his muscles pulsing under her touch as her entire body throbbed.

His hips flexed and jutted forward. Faster. Harder. Until they were both wild, going to a place so unrefined and raw she couldn't imagine ever sharing this side of herself with anyone else.

"Come with me." He reached between them, finding her swollen clit and rubbing her rapidly to climax.

The moment she came, her back arching off the bed as pleasure exploded through every nerve ending, his head jerked back and a sound of pure masculine ecstasy escaped him. His release pulsed deep, as he held himself buried inside of her, a gravelly roar escaping his throat. Not a whisper of light could slip between them.

The world silenced with dizzying speed. She shivered but wasn't cold. Breath shaky, she met his stare and laughed, her body humming with aftershocks.

"I'm not sure laughter's the reaction I envisioned."

"Sorry." She laughed harder, and he drew back his hips with a hiss.

"What's so funny?"

"I think we both might be limping tomorrow."

He chuckled and pressed a tender kiss to her temple. "Worth every ache." His voice turned soft, vulnerable. "Are you okay? Really okay?"

She smiled up at him, her heart so full it might burst. "I'm perfect. We're perfect."

He gathered her close, rolling to his side and pulling her against his chest. The moonlight stretched across the walls. His strength cocooned her in warmth as the intimacy of his hold healed something lonesome and longing inside of her. His fingers traced lazy patterns on her bare shoulder as their breathing slowly returned to normal.

"No regrets?" he whispered against her hair.

"Only that we waited so long." She pressed a kiss to his chest, tasting salt and satisfaction. "This was worth every year of wondering what if."

"Every day of wanting you and thinking I couldn't have you." His arms tightened around her possessively. "You're mine now, Wren. Completely mine."

"I always was," she whispered.

CHAPTER 24

"Everyone Knows The Christmas Lobster"

"Here, see if these fit." Greyson handed Wren a pair of ski pants that buckled at the chest. "They belonged to Logan."

Pulling the water-resistant material to her nose, she breathed in the scent of cedar and old fabric softener. "How old are they?"

"Probably twenty years. You might want to shake them out to make sure there aren't any mice living in the legs."

She dropped the pants immediately and jumped back. "Greyson!"

He laughed and kissed her head, his lips lingering against her hair. After last night, everything had changed. Even the smallest touches now carried new meaning.

"Just kidding. If anything, there would be spiders."

Snatching the snow pants, she marched down the hall and threw them in the dryer. "There. The high heat will kill any stowaways."

Greyson gasped dramatically. "What would Bodhi say?"

She playfully gave him the finger and disappeared into the bedroom to finish dressing.

Today brought the official lobster trap tree lighting ceremony, one that the Hawthornes had participated in for decades. This would be Wren's first time seeing it from his perspective on the water, and the first time he'd have someone who mattered beside him.

He recalled all the times he'd pulled that old boat into harbor with his dad, each time his eyes searching the wharf for any sign of her. Now, she'd be right by his side.

"Will Mayor Quimby be there?" She hopped awkwardly out of his room into a pair of his hunting socks, the thick wool bunching around her ankles.

"Of course. He's Santa."

She stood and chewed her lip the way she often did when nervous. "He'll wonder why I'm with you."

"Let him."

He saw no point in pussy footing around the truth now. But Wren had been conditioned to keep her private life private in order to protect herself and Bodhi.

"Maybe I should stay back with everyone else at the wharf."

Disappointment crashed through his good mood like a rogue wave. "Why?"

Fidgeting, she avoided his eyes. "I don't know. People will talk. They'll wonder why I'm on the boat with you."

"You're not a kid anymore, Wren. We aren't doing anything wrong."

"I know. I just can't escape this feeling like something bad might happen if I let too many outsiders in."

That fear came from years of protecting her father. For too long, she'd been forced to be the adult, shielding him from scrutiny to keep their family intact and avoid the foster care system that threatened to tear them apart.

Greyson closed the distance and hugged her tight, his arms wrapping around her like a fortress. "Hey." He pressed a kiss to her head. "What did I tell you? I'll always protect you. Nothing bad is going to happen."

She sighed against his chest. "Even from Lady Lovewatch? Do you know she wrote about me last week? I despise being the center of town gossip."

"I don't know why you read that drivel. Lady Lovewatch is a lonely spinster with nothing better to do."

"If she even is a lady. I always thought that pseudonym served as a cover. She's probably some big burly dude hiding in a shed, eating cheese puffs and extracting his revenge for all the parties he didn't get invited to."

"Whoever it is, they're no concern of ours. Besides, we've got nothing to hide."

Going to check on the snow pants, she pulled them out of the dryer, the fabric warm and charged with crackling static electricity. He didn't understand her sudden tension.

"Why are you afraid of what people might think?"

She shook out the pants and shrugged. "I just don't want anything to ruin what we have."

He took her arm and pulled her close, the warmth from the dryer still clinging to her skin as he brushed a soft kiss on her lips. "As long as we're open and honest with each other, nothing can break us. Understand?"

Nodding, she softened under his touch. "Yes."

"Good. Now, kiss me like you mean it." She dropped the ski pants, and looped her arms around his neck as he lifted her to sit on the dryer. The warm metal buzzed beneath her as the residual heat from the cycle seeped through her jeans.

The kiss went from slow and drugging to ravenous in two seconds flat.

Hungry gasps and greedy hands undid all the layers they spent the last twenty minutes putting on. The scent of fabric softener and detergent surrounded them as she playfully licked at his mouth for more.

He unbuckled his belt with practiced efficiency. "Such a tease." Scooting her closer to the edge, he wedged her panties aside and aligned himself. The moment he pulled her onto him, penetrating her deeply, she gasped. "Feel that?" he whispered against her ear, his breath hot against her neck.

"Mm-hmm."

He rotated his hips, the movement sending sparks up his spine. He wanted to show her all the amazing things her body could experience. Gently, he traced his fingertips up her thigh. "Still sore?"

"A little, but it's okay." Her muscles had yet to recover from last night, and he'd had her more times than he could count.

"We'll take it slow." Gripping her ass, he pulled her down on his hard length with each languid thrust.

She bit his ear. "What if I want it hard and fast?"

His cock pulsed inside of her and he growled. "Ask and you shall receive." Drawing back, he thrust deep.

The dryer banged into the wall, and the washer shook as spare change and laundry cups fell to the floor with metallic clatters. The machine's vibration amplified every thrust, creating a rhythm that matched their desperate need. Angling back against a folded pile of towels, she braced her hands against the shelves and walls as he fucked her into the laundry closet. Fast and dirty, exactly as she requested.

Her nails scratched down his arms and his breath quickened. Every muscle in his body twitched and flexed in euphoric bliss. The small space trapped their sounds—her gasps, his groans, the rhythmic banging of the machines against the wall. Their eyes met the moment he lost control, a thousand treasured secrets passing between them as they voraciously licked and bit at each other, needing to get as close as possible.

His release rushed out of him and he pumped his hips hard as he grasped her breasts. He couldn't get enough of her mouth. Starved for every inch of her, he panted, dragging his hand down to her ass as he squeezed hard enough to leave a mark. She was an incredibly quick learner and he was a very happy teacher.

He grunted with one more flex of his hips then slowly pulled away, breaking the kiss as they both panted. Her hair was a mess, and her cheeks were flushed. A quarter stuck to her arm, and the laundry detergent had spilled across the floor in a blue puddle.

"Shit."

"I'll get a mop."

Greyson helped her down, and she swayed, a little off balance. She giggled as she wobbled down the hall, completely naked aside from her thick wool socks, her skin still flushed from their encounter.

"Careful."

She returned a moment later with the mop, still gloriously bare. "Give me that."

Rat peeked out of the bedroom to see if the noisy part was over and Wren scooped him up, her breasts pressing against his soft fur. There really was nothing sexier than seeing a naked Wren nuzzle his kitten.

When he cleaned up the mess, he closed the laundry closet. "I hate to rush you, but we've gotta get moving."

Once dressed again, they secured Rat in the spare room with his litter box and some toys, then finished bundling up against the December cold.

"Do you have sunglasses? The wind off the coast will make your eyes tear."

The thirty-minute entrance into the harbor on the vintage boat was something Greyson's family orchestrated every year. He wanted a flawless trip since it was Wren's first big voyage with him as the acting captain.

She slipped on a pair of aviators. "Think I'll be warm enough?"

Even bundled up like an arctic explorer, she was freaking adorable. "You'll easily be the hottest woman in Hideaway."

She laughed and tossed him his keys. "Let's go."

Cruising through several stop signs and yellow traffic lights, Greyson made it to the fishery on time. Wren bounced nervously on the front seat of his truck where the makeshift cat bed for Rat usually sat. He didn't understand why she was nervous, but he figured it just had to play itself out for her to see there was nothing to worry about.

The moment they got to the docks, her worry was distracted by the blustery winds rushing off the waves. It was too damn cold to think, let alone stress about anything other than delivering Captain Claws to the harbor and getting the hell back on land—preferably some place warm.

The bitter wind cut across the bay in sharp slices, gnawing at their exposed skin and rattling the frost-covered rigging like bones in a barrel. A boat in December waters might be unusual, but the Hawthorne fleet was not for pleasure cruises. These ships were industrial machines, meant for the toughest seas on earth.

"Wait." He tugged Wren's jacket tighter, inspecting that she was fully covered, his hands lingering possessively on the zipper. "Ready?"

He was excited to show her this side of his world, the maritime heritage that ran in his blood like saltwater. "Show me how it's done, my rugged mountain fisherman."

He kissed her but forced himself to cut it short. The temptation to take her again was real but he had a commitment to meet. "Your ass is mine the second we get home."

"Silly man, I'm always yours."

He growled like a caveman and took her gloved hand in his, tugging her toward the docks. His heavy footfalls clunked against the planks as he led the way to the antique ship, Sable Rose.

The ship was named for his mother. Unlike their other state-of-the-art vessels, this one held a special place in the heart of Hideaway Bay. His father had donated it to the Hideaway Bay Trust & Reserve after its last operational voyage nearly two decades ago. The town liked to bring it out for special events.

They kept a plaque at The Reserve where the boat usually stood on display to honor their family's history and keep their mother's memory alive. Every word of that plaque was burned into his memory from countless visits during his youth.

'Named for Sable Hawthorne—fierce, graceful, and the heart of the Hawthorne family—this vessel carried three generations of fishermen before retiring into local legend. Now restored and preserved by Hideaway Bay Trust & Reserve, The Sable Rose only sails for ceremonial journeys. In her lifetime, Sable never set foot on a boat, but this one still carries her name.'

Boats didn't remind him of his mother, but they became his escape after she disappeared from his life. His world had shifted so dramatically after her passing that home didn't carry the same warmth anymore. He traveled to the opposite ends of the earth in search of any place that did. It took him years to realize the love he was searching for was always waiting for him at home.

Glancing at Wren just as her scarf flapped from her collar and whipped in the wind, she smiled, and the wake inside of him settled to a peaceful calm. She was his home, his North Star, his guiding light through any storm.

His breath came out in clouds as he yelled, "Warm enough?"

Nodding, she tried to project confidence, but it would get much colder once they left the dock.

He secured the rigging and readied the ship for her and the others to board. "Almost ready."

The sea churned out the kind of cold that bit through denim and flannel, and clawed into muscle. The kind of cold that reminded a man he lived and breathed, but also had a way of making him wish he didn't.

Preferring these little vanity excursions over the long trips he used to take with the fishery, Greyson reflected on those icy winters, long gone and hardly missed, but it was nice to stretch his sea legs every once in a while.

The Sable Rose rocked in its slip, tethered like a patient ghost to her berth. Scrubbed down, polished, and adorned with strands of pine garland and red buoys for her ceremonial voyage. Which reminded him…

Shading his eyes from the setting sun, Greyson scanned the vacant marina. "Where the fuck is Simon?"

There was no sign of the flaming redhead anywhere along the docks.

Hauling himself back onto the decking with practiced ease, he hugged Wren to offer some shelter from the wind. "Soon as they get here, we can go."

"I'm fine, Grey. I've lived in this weather all my life. Go do what you need to do."

He kissed her nose, tasting the salt spray already misting her skin, and climbed back on the ship. Every move came as second nature. His hands traveled on instinct, checking lines, flipping levers, testing the throttle. Salt and diesel lived in his blood. He could handle a fishing boat in a blizzard with his eyes shut. But today, he had a co-captain, so he took extra care to make sure nothing went wrong.

"Greyson," Mayor Quimby yelled, his stuffed belly bouncing as he jogged down the dock plank in his red velvet suit. Staggering to a stop when he reached their slip, he shaded his eyes to identify the additional passenger. "Wren? Well, this is a surprise."

Wren's rosy cheeks darkened as she waved. "Hi, Mayor Quimby."

Climbing the plank to board, the mayor grinned. "It's not often we get a female to join us. My wife wouldn't dare go out in this weather."

Smiling, she followed the mayor aboard. "I'm honored."

"Take my hand." Greyson guided her onto the ship with possessive care. "It's warmest in the sun."

The mayor pulled at his snow-white beard to keep it from whipping into his face and held out a large thermos. "Erica sent me with some mulled cider to keep us warm. Have some."

"I thought you were more of a milk and cookies sort of guy," Wren teased, eyeing his Santa suit.

"Cookies are fine, but I prefer my thermos with a bit of rum—especially for a cold day at sea." Looking around the marina, he frowned. "Where the hell is Simon? If he's not here in the next ten, Captain Claws is going to be hauling himself into Hideaway Bay on a dinghy. I have a reputation to uphold," the mayor said, adjusting his wide, black leather belt. "Santa's always on time."

Wren eyed his protruding belly. "That pillow must be warm."

"It definitely helps."

Checking a few more dials, Greyson continued to search the marina for their red-headed lobster. Leave it to Simon to miss his one big commitment this holiday. "Come on, Simon," he muttered under his breath.

Pointing to the parking lot, Wren announced, "I see him."

Simon struggled through another day of his small-town life, teetering like a drunken sailor as he jumped into the lobster suit and stumbled between the parked cars. When he situated the top-heavy headpiece, he nearly fell off the edge of the dock.

"Should someone help him?" Concern scrunched Wren's nose.

"Put the mask on after you get on the boat," Mayor Quimby yelled, but his words got swallowed by the wind.

"What a dumbass," Greyson mumbled, deciding it was better not to watch.

Waddling down to the slip, Simon nearly bit it on the last plank. His massive lobster costume dragged with every awkward step. The oversized claws—cheap foam wrapped in painted duct tape—hung limp at his sides as he struggled to carry the gigantic headpiece. One antenna had collapsed from the skirmish on the shore.

"Sorry, I'm late. My mom needed help finding her big winter coat." Common knowledge held that Simon lived with his mother, and likely always would.

"About time." Greyson brought the radio crackling to life, more than ready to get this show on the road. He didn't wait for a response as he clicked the receiver on. "Silver Spoon, this is Anchor One, are you there?"

Wren grinned and came to stand by his side where the action was. "Silver Spoon?"

"Soren."

"Ah. And Logan is…?"

"Tadpole."

She snorted and shook her head. "Cute. He must love that."

"Baby of the family doesn't get to choose."

"What's your dad's code name?"

"Big Fish."

"And your mom?"

"My mom hated boats."

"Of course, she did."

The radio crackled. "This is Silver Spoon to Anchor One. Wharf is filling up. I'll alert you when the harbor's full."

"We're leaving the docks now." Greyson set the receiver aside to man the wheel.

The motor reverberated with age as the scent of diesel fumes overpowered the briny sea air. Moving quickly, he unhitched the last of the ship's ties.

"Can someone give me a tail tuck?" Simon barked, spinning in circles, then tripping over the thermos bag.

"Watch the rum!" Santa yelled, grabbing the thermos before thinking to save Simon.

"Careful," Greyson warned. "Or Captain Claw's going to remember what it's like at the bottom of the sea. Everybody good to go?"

"As good as a *lobstah* can be—to the harbor!" Simon called, pointing his claw into the air. It immediately drooped and clunked him on the head.

"Captain Claws *is* having a hard time keeping it up," Wren murmured close to Greyson's ear.

He chuckled. "I don't have that problem."

"No, you definitely don't."

Already counting down the hours until he could have her again, Greyson steered them toward open waters.

It was a proud day for New Englanders, one where harbor accents came out in full force. Hideaway's heritage was a blend of Nordic and colonial settlers. Somehow, that added up to Santa Claus sailing into the harbor with a giant red-headed crustacean to light a tower of lobster traps designed to resemble a Christmas tree. Weird, but one of many weird traditions Hideaway Bay loved and honored, and one of the few that the Hawthornes actually participated in.

First, his father had captained the Sable Rose. Now, it was Greyson's turn. One day, he'd pass the torch to Soren, and then Logan would have it last. The thought suddenly occurred to Greyson that that might not happen if the company got divested. But that wasn't his problem, so he pushed the thought away. Except this time it came back with boomerang force.

Maybe it was his problem.

He glanced at Wren. Maybe, even if it wasn't, he might have a solution.

No, he wasn't going to pollute a good thing with his father's toxic thinking.

Once out of the marina and turned around, his gaze drifted back to Wren. Standing near the stern, bundled in coat and ski overalls, her mirrored sunglasses reflected the sun as she smiled and laughed with the mayor over something he said. Her cheeks flushed pink from the cold, and her hair whipped like golden kite tails from the knitted hat she wore. Holding the beanie in place by the fur pompom on top, she looked sexy as sin all bundled up at sea.

The mayor pushed the thermos on her again, and this time Wren took a sip. "*Whoo!*" she hollered, coughing into her gloved fist. No doubt the mayor spiked the mulled cider with a heavy hand of rum to keep himself warm.

Mayor Quimby laughed. "That'll put a little hair on your chest."

"I hope not." Sputtering and laughing, Wren shook her head.

"You better be careful with that. Too much, and Santa could wind up run over by a reindeer like Grandma."

Clapping a gloved hand to his head, the mayor perked up. "That reminds me. Simon, did you bring the music?"

"I've got it on my phone." Reaching into the red lobster costume, he fumbled with the claws. As soon as the phone came into view, it went hurling through the air. Lunging forward, Wren caught it in the nick of time.

"Thanks, Wren."

"No problem." Holding onto it, she took pity on Simon and offered, "Do you want me to set it up for you?"

"Yeah, if you don't mind. I can't get these darn claws to cooperate." As soon as he lifted a hand, the oversized claw sagged dramatically, whacking him in the head.

"The town really should invest in a newer costume."

"That's up to the treasury," Mayor Quimby said, refilling the thermos cup with more steaming cider.

Simon frowned from under the enormous headpiece. "Yet, somehow Santa got some new duds this year."

When they all looked over at Mayor Quimby's spiffy new boots, he blustered, "Well, let's face it, Santa's the main event. You have to know where you rank, Simon."

"Captain Claws is a beloved mascot of time-honored traditions! He's just as popular as Saint Nick. Tell him, guys."

Greyson shook his head and Wren shrugged. "Sorry, Simon. Nothing beats Santa."

"Whatever." Waving a floppy claw, he instructed, "Track one. It's a nonstop loop of holiday music. Volume ten."

As Wren connected the playlist to the Bluetooth speaker, Greyson steered them toward open waters with deft confidence. The twin diesel engines purred like old cougars beneath the deck, and sea spray hit cold against his face as the boat nosed into the bay. Wind screamed from the northeast, belting the garland against the ship rails as Simon's lobster claws twitched violently.

Closing his gloved hand around the throttle, Greyson shifted forward, easing the Sable Rose into deeper waters. The salt-stained memories of the merciless sea felt familiar and nostalgic in a way he couldn't express into words.

"Give me your hand," he called to Wren.

She stepped closer, and he moved her in front of his body, blocking her from the spray. He curled her fingers around the throttle and pulled back, giving the ship a bit more speed. She smiled as the ship's impressive power moved under her command.

"Feel that?" He pressed her other hand to the wheel. "Give it a pull. You're in control."

When she did, and the ship moved with her guidance, she squeaked with excitement. "Oh, my God! I'm steering a ship!"

He pressed his lips close to her ear, his breath warming her skin despite the frigid air. "Don't tell the Coast Guard."

As she let her weight sag into him, he once again had the urge to take her. Maybe they could steal a few seconds below deck once they dropped off the other passengers.

The radio crackled. "Anchor One, this is Silver Spoon. What's your location?" Soren's voice came clipped across the speakers as the music blasted from the stereo. "Parents are gettin' antsy and the kids are chanting. They want the big guy."

Simon perked up but instantly deflated when Greyson shook his head. "He means Santa."

"I'm sure they're just as excited to see The Captain," Wren said, taking pity on Simon.

His face lit with enthusiasm. "Thanks, Wren."

Great. Another admirer. What the hell did it say about him when a woman could make him jealous of Simon Moseley?

"Copy that," Greyson answered, then clicked off the radio as he turned the ship into harbor. They rounded the coast slowly, his gaze shifting between Wren's excited expression and the docks ahead.

Beyond the wharf, hundreds of townsfolk lined the shore. Children bounced in place, their scarves flapping, as little hands gripped the wooden rails. Adults sipped steaming beverages from to-go mugs, shoulders hunched against the whipping winds.

The music selection blared over the choppy waves, echoing off the walls of the cove. Sleigh bells clattered from Santa's gloved fist, the one not holding the thermos of spiced rum.

Leaning in, cheeks rosy and smile bright, Wren joked, "Can you believe some towns actually have serious traditions?"

"Not ours." Greyson laughed. "We were never the Plymouth Rock sort."

"Nope, nothing but unhinged settlers on our rickety version of the Mayflower."

As they rounded the jetty, the wharf came into full view under the setting sun. Pine wreaths dotted every light post that illuminated the harbor.

A giant pile of lobster traps formed a pyramid resembling a Christmas tree in the center of the crowd, waiting for Santa to do the honors and hit the lights. At the very top perched a fiberglass cutout of Captain Claws.

"Look at the top of the tree! *Ha!* Who's the star now?" Simon yelled.

"Should we tell him Santa beats angel?" Greyson mumbled.

Wren swatted him in the arm. "Let him dream."

The crowd erupted the moment they spotted the ship. "Simon, put your head on! You're gonna traumatize the kids."

"Trying." Staggering back, Simon accepted help from the mayor, who shoved the lobster head into place and secured it with a solid thump to ensure it didn't twist out of place.

"Now, wave!"

Waving a floppy claw in the air, Simon reeled from side to side with the ship. Kids craned their necks and rushed to the railings to wave and scream.

One day, his brother would be steering this ship, and he and Wren would be watching from the wharf, a little one on his shoulders and maybe another bundled up in the stroller. Maybe even one in her belly. That day might come sooner than planned at the rate they were going.

Reaching for Wren, he hooked an arm around her hip and held her to his side. Flattening his hand over her stomach possessively. She looked up at him in question.

"I want to have a family with you," he said, his voice barely carrying over the wind.

"What?" she yelled over the music and crowd noise.

"I want to have kids! With you!" he shouted, but his words got lost in the chaos.

"I didn't bring any," she yelled back, completely missing what he said.

A gust of wind shoved the boat sideways, and Greyson adjusted the rudder smoothly, shifting his weight without thought, without letting Wren go. The Sable Rose sliced through the harbor like she'd been born for ceremony.

The music blared the same holiday tune for the fifth time. Simon waved his limp claw while Santa performed with more pomp than all the English royalty and the Pope combined.

"Ho-ho-ho!" Mayor Quimby chanted with theatrical glee.

"No fair, lobsters don't talk," Simon complained.

"You just work on keeping those claws up," Wren yelled, then squeaked as her hat flew off like a gull sailing over the water. "Oh, no!" Her hair flapped and tangled wildly in the breeze, coming completely undone.

Greyson's laughter faded as he noticed the adults in the crowd pointing at something. But they weren't looking at Captain Claws or Santa.

Wren shrank into his side, slipping behind him as if to use his body as a shield. They were all pointing at her, the woman by his side. It was small-town theater, and Wren was the unwilling star. A fierce protectiveness surged through him as he blocked her from view, creating a barrier between her and the gawking crowd.

In this town, a whispered rumor could spread faster than the current. He should strangle Soren. This was his damn fault. If not for his damn brother making a scene at the auction last week, people might have overlooked Wren's presence at his side.

Speak of the devil. Soren's voice clipped over the radio. "Are you kidding me, Grey? Is that Wren with you?"

Ignoring his brother's question, he turned to Wren. "You ready for the finale?"

"I thought Captain Claws and Santa were the finale."

"Not this year." Slowing the boat as it approached the wharf, Greyson sounded its horn in a long, festive *braaahmp* that echoed across the water.

If they wanted a show, he'd give them one. He pulled the ship into harbor and docked with practiced precision. But when Wren tried to step off with the others he caught her wrist, pulling her back against his chest.

"What are you doing?"

He smiled. "If they're going to gossip about us, let's give them something worth talking about. Wave."

With wide eyes, she followed his lead and waved at the people. They cheered and yelled, but he couldn't make out a single word as that stupid lobster song played for the tenth time.

"You remember when I said you were mine?" His voice dropped to that possessive rumble she'd come to recognize.

"What?" she screamed over the music, unable to hear him.

That was fine. He'd much rather show her. Grinning, he dipped her back without warning, planting his lips on her with unmistakable entitlement for all of Hideaway Bay to see.

It wasn't a gentle kiss or a private one. He intentionally gave the town a show-stopping, hat-snatching, sunglass-tossing, spine-arching, breathless spectacle that couldn't possibly be misinterpreted by his brothers or anyone else. It was a public declaration that would leave no room for doubt about who Wren belonged to.

The crowd roared, and Wren laughed against his mouth, then smacked his chest. "You're insane."

"I'm staking my claim," he said, eyes glinting with fierce intention. "There will be no more confusion about which Hawthorne you're with from this point on."

Rolling her eyes, her cheeks a deep ruby rose, she shook her head. "You're a caveman."

He yanked her to his side and proudly grinned with absolute male arrogance. "A caveman who's finally got his perfect cave woman."

She batted the hair out of her face and shook her head. "Suddenly, you're an exhibitionist?"

"I spent almost two decades hiding my feelings. Time to switch things up."

"I'm so glad I could assist you with that."

Beyond the wharf, Simon tripped and fell on his claws. Mayor Quimby missed a step and nearly pitched over the lobster's tail. The crowd cheered when Santa caught his balance in a dramatic leap that landed him right in front of the lobster trap tree.

"Ho-ho-ho!" the mayor called out, lifting the plug to light the tree. "Merry Christmas, Hideaway Bay!"

The crowd cheered as the traps illuminated under the bright twinkling lights. Staggering forward and waving, Captain Claws shoved Santa aside. The two spent the next few minutes trying to outperform each other, but Greyson had other plans.

"Have you ever seen the cabin of a fishing boat?"

Looking up at him knowingly, Wren smiled. "I can't say I have."

"Come with me." His voice turned rough with promise. "I'll show you the catch of the day."

CHAPTER 25

"Brandy and Eggnog, There's Plenty of Cheer"

"You dirty slut!"

Everyone in the Chowder House turned as Jocelyn barreled through the mob of patrons like a Viking queen on the front lines.

"Oh, shit." Despite bracing for the collision, Wren was pummeled against the bar when her best friend plowed into her—full force—with a tackle hug.

"I saw you kissing on the ship, you naughty girl!"

Heat blazed across Wren's cheeks. "Shhh."

"Oh, please." Jocelyn waved away her prudent words. "Everyone saw." Punching Greyson in the arm, she grinned admirably. "Grey, you put that little brother of yours to shame! Nicely done." Turning back to Wren, Jocelyn smiled around the swizzle straw of her half-drunk cocktail. "Soooo…how's the cherry? Popped, I imagine."

"Oh, my God." Hiding her burning face in her hands, Wren

373

peeked through her fingers at Greyson. "Maybe I will take that whiskey after all."

"Two whiskeys," Greyson yelled to the bartender.

Straightening her cockeyed Viking helmet, still adorned with the dangling clitoris ornaments hanging from each horn, Jocelyn frowned. "Two?"

Greyson shook his head. "You look plenty hydrated."

"You're no fun." She stuck out her tongue and turned to Wren. "Tell your boy toy to loosen up."

"I claim no control over any Hawthorne."

"Yeah, right." Jocelyn looped her arm around Wren's shoulders. "Come on, let's find a table."

They grabbed an empty high-top as Jocelyn shoved dirty cups into a pile. "Girl, there's no confusion now. Greyson marked you in front of the whole town!"

Wren's face hadn't stopped burning. "Was it bad?"

"Bad? Hell no. It was awesome! Boy doesn't show his face unless it snows for nearly twenty years, and suddenly he's ramming his tongue down your throat like a sailor on leave."

Looking anxiously toward the bar, Wren waited for her drink.

"So," Jocelyn said, leaning across the table. "How did it go?"

Shifting nervously, Wren hesitated. "It was…emotional."

Her friend scrunched her nose. "Ew, really?"

"What's wrong with emotional? We've been friends a really long time."

"Do you mean emotional, like, orgasmic?"

"That, and…" She shrugged. "Earthshattering. Confirming. Beautiful."

"Are you sure you did it right?"

"Yes, Jocelyn. Besides, that was just the first time."

"Oh, thank Odin. Skip to the good stuff." She waved her on. "I want details!"

Appearing with their drinks, Greyson handed one to Wren. She eagerly took a long sip then regretted it immediately, sputtering at the straight whiskey.

The bar was packed elbow-to-elbow with holiday cheer, mismatched string lights blinking overhead as off-key patrons sang along to *Rockin' Around the Christmas Tree*.

Greyson bracketed his arms around her as if he didn't plan on letting her out of his sight until spring thawed. He'd barely taken his hands off her since they docked.

"It's so weird seeing you two like this," Jocelyn said, gawking at them. "I can't believe you actually did it."

The front door banged open, and snow flurried in with new arrivals—Soren leading the herd.

"Here we go." Greyson waved his brother over.

Soren approached, brushing snowflakes from his shoulders. "Wren. Grey."

"Hi, Soren." Wren smiled nervously, remembering the last time they spoke.

He gave a tight grin. "Quite a show you put on today."

"What can I say? I'm not one to be outdone," Greyson smirked.

"Well, well, well. Look what the nor'easter blew in." Jocelyn latched onto Soren's shoulder.

"Still got the charming voice of a sea hag, huh Joce?"

Unimpressed, Soren turned back to Wren. "Did you like the boat ride?"

"It was really cool seeing everything from the other side."

"That's probably the last one."

Her smile faltered. "Why?"

Looking at Grey, Soren shrugged. "I guess you guys haven't discussed all the details yet."

"Not now, Soren," Greyson warned.

"Better watch it, Soren," Jocelyn teased. "Your big brother staked a claim in front of the whole town. No way you're getting close enough to make her cry this time."

"This time?" Scowling, Greyson demanded, "There was a *first* time?"

"She didn't cry," Soren said, matter-of-factly, and Jocelyn scoffed.

"Like you would know. A real man would at least stick around to clean up his mess."

Soren's expression shifted to panic, but before he could clarify, Greyson took a menacing step forward. "Did you make her fucking cry?"

"Grey, it's fine." Wren caught his sleeve. "I told you we had an argument. It's over now. It's Christmas. Let's not fight."

Continuing to glare at his brother, Greyson tensed, but Soren only looked disturbed by the news. "Wren, can I talk to you for a minute—outside?"

Tightening his arm, Greyson refused, "She's staying here."

"What are you, her fucking keeper now?"

Jocelyn's gaze brightened with anticipation. "*Oooh,* them's fightin' words."

"Jocelyn, knock it off." Wrenching Greyson's arm off her hip, Wren excused herself. "We'll be right back." She didn't stop moving until they made it to the sidewalk, then she turned on him. "What, Soren?"

"I'm sorry if I made you cry."

"What about the things you said. Are you sorry for that?"

His mouth firmed. "I got pissed. I don't remember what I said."

"You basically wished me a miserable life and said I deserved to chase Greyson forever because he's never going to change."

"I got angry, and, obviously, I was wrong."

"You were wrong, Soren. And you hurt me."

Sighing, he looked down. "I'm sorry, Wren. I got jealous."

Her defenses came down. "I never wanted to hurt you."

"I know. I have feelings too, you know?"

"It's not like I planned any of this."

"But you wanted it."

"Yes," she admitted. "I wanted this for a very long time, Soren. I'm sorry if that's difficult to hear, but it's the truth."

A cloud formed as he blew out a deep breath. "Well, if that's the case, I hope he's everything you dreamed."

"Thank you."

"We're okay?"

She smiled and nodded. "Yeah, we're okay."

"Let's go back inside. It's fucking freezing and I need a drink."

Back at the table, Logan had arrived, his curls bouncing above the sea of hats. "Hey." Kissing Wren's cheek, he smiled. "You look better. Got your color back."

Looking slightly harassed after being left alone with Jocelyn, Greyson immediately moved to Wren's side. "You okay?"

"I'm fine. It was a good talk."

"So I don't need to kick anyone's ass?"

"Not tonight."

"So, this is awkward," Logan said, sipping a beer. "Grey and Wren. Wren and Grey."

"Maybe say it a few more times," Soren grumbled.

"Someone sounds jealous," Jocelyn sang into her slushy red cocktail.

"Hardly."

Greyson grinned, proudly sliding a possessive arm around Wren's shoulders. "You wish."

"Can we all just make a unified adjustment and get over the awkwardness?" Wren said, taking a deep breath. "Yes, Greyson and I are now a couple. But I'm still Wren and he's still Grey."

"Except you're banging."

All eyes turned to Jocelyn. Wren stilled. "Thanks, Joce. Helpful as always."

Logan, shoving right past the awkwardness, lifted his beer. "To the new couple."

"Thank you, Logan." Looking up at Grey, Wren prompted, "Say thank you."

"Thanks."

Soren rolled his eyes. "Oh, yeah, this feels totally natural. Like a root canal with an ice skate. I'm not at all uncomfortable."

"Someone sounds jealous," Jocelyn sang.

Soren glared at her. "Do you ever shut up?"

"Hey, my words are money. Be grateful you get them for free."

As the evening wore on, things only got messier. Even the mayor was drunk, standing on chairs with Simon organizing some kind of holiday football pool.

The boys ordered another round, but every sip only made Wren count down the minutes until they were alone again. Finally, warm lips pressed against her temple. "You ready to go after this?"

Smiling up at Greyson, she gave a subtle nod. As fun as this was, she'd rather be back in his bed.

When Jocelyn nearly fell off her chair, Soren jumped into action. "I've got her." He hooked an arm under Jocelyn's as she became as slippery as a Jell-O shot.

"You sure?" Wren asked.

"Yeah. My car's right out front."

"We're heading out, too," Greyson announced, tossing cash on the table.

Outside, the temperature had dropped another ten degrees. "How are we getting home?"

"It's taken care of." Greyson pointed to a horse-drawn sleigh waiting at the end of the street.

She gaped at him. "Are you serious?"

"Come on." He led her to the sleigh and greeted the driver. "How's it going, Gus?"

Mr. Pemberley grinned. "You did a fine job pulling that ship into harbor, Greyson. Your dad would have been proud."

Settling onto the red velvet seat, Wren pulled the emerald throw over her lap while Greyson poured steaming cocoa.

"Don't forget the lids. Trails can get bumpy," Gus warned.

Sleigh bells jingled as they literally dashed through the snow. Cuddling into Greyson's side, Wren asked, "What about the boat?"

"My brothers and I will get it in the morning."

Pulling the reins, Mr. Pemberley turned the heavy sleigh away from the breeze and headed deeper into the woods, following a dark trail that led directly to Greyson's house. The jingle of sleigh bells created the melody as they sipped cocoa and cuddled close to escape the cold.

The sleigh shifted slightly over a rut in the trail, and her hand instinctively shot out, grabbing Greyson's thigh for balance. Tensing beneath her fingers, his muscles responded, and she meant to pull away, to laugh it off—but he covered her hand with his, keeping it there, anchoring her to him.

Their eyes met and the silence between them crackled with unspoken desires. Brushing his finger along the inside of her wrist, slow and deliberate, Greyson moved his thumb with intent. Her pulse leapt to meet his touch, and a small, involuntary gasp escaped her lips. His hand closed around her wrist and squeezed.

He leaned close, his cold nose brushing her cheek. "You're trembling."

Giving him a knowing look, she said nothing. Her wanting was perfectly clear.

He silently chuckled and sat back, a confident grin curving his lips. Promises hung between them amongst the anxious need to get back home.

Sweet, unbearable anticipation stretched and tightened inside of her the longer they drove. Agonizingly delicious, in ways she'd never imagined wanting could be, she closed her eyes and got off on the sensation.

"Tired?" he whispered.

"No."

His knowing stare held hers. "I'm going to strip you naked as soon as you walk through the door." His hand slid dangerously higher under the blanket that covered their laps. "And then I'm going to lick every sexy inch of you."

She shivered as the cabin lights glowed through the trees in the distance. The closer they came to their final destination, the more Wren became fully aware of every pulsing part of her body.

"Do you think I have time for a quick shower? I can't feel my toes."

"You have until I get the fire going again."

Smoke curled from the chimney into the night sky as Greyson's home came into view. Of course, he stocked the woodstove with enough wood to keep it warm. That gave her less than two minutes. She'd be lucky to get out of her clothes.

Her heart thundered in her chest as the sleigh jostled to a stop.

"Here we are, kids."

Greyson hopped onto the snow and reached for her, lifting her out of the carriage as if she weighed nothing at all and purposely sliding her body down his front. "I'll meet you inside."

Her heart pounded with anticipation. She barely had her boots off when the front door swung shut with a promising click, and the deadbolt latched. Pivoting, Wren froze as Greyson's intense stare darkened on her.

He glanced down. "You have until I get these two logs in the fire."

She playfully staggered backwards. "What about the one in your pants?"

"That one's going inside you."

She spun and darted into the bedroom, stripping clumsily out of her clothes. She was down to long johns and her bra when he loomed in the bedroom door. The promising look in his blue eyes told her time was up.

She ran for the bathroom and turned the water on high. But as her fingers hooked into her bottoms, he caught her arms and corralled her under the water.

"Greyson! Your clothes!"

His mouth crashed to hers in a clash of hunger and need. Fumbling with the buttons of his coat, laughing breathlessly, she pulled at his drenched layers. Greyson tried to shrug out of his jacket but the water made everything ten times heavier.

"Let me help." Tugging hard, she hung from his arm and laughed.

"It's like peeling a damn onion." He finally got the coat off and tossed it onto the floor in a wet heap.

Wriggling out of her long johns and panties, she threw them on top of his sopping wet coat. Her hands went back to his shirt as water sprayed into her eyes. "You're wearing half the North Pole."

Greyson's gravelly laugh curled into her. "Take this off."

Her arms lifted as he peeled off her wet bra. It landed with a splat and everything stilled. The spray of water pouring over them as he smiled down at her, soaking wet and still in his jeans.

"Is this a dream?" He dragged his palms over her skin, lifting her arms above her head. He kissed her then dropped to his knees.

Heat carved into her the moment his mouth closed over her sex. Ripples of pleasure quickly transformed into waves, and before she knew it her cries were ricocheting off the tile walls as she came on his tongue.

Breathing hard, he stood to face her, anticipation mounting as heat crackled between them. One heartbeat. Two. Then, he crushed his mouth to hers in a hard, unstoppable kiss.

His heavy jeans hit the floor as he lifted her to his hips. "I want your tight pussy wrapped around my dick," he rasped, voice rough as sandpaper, eyes burning with molten need.

Heart hammering, she reached between them and gripped his massive cock. She angled her body, leaning into the wall, and he thrust. They both sighed. Then his eyes opened with a flash of dark promise.

"Hold on tight." He snapped his hips back and shoved forward, as she cried out.

The floor. The wall. The shower. The foyer. The location never mattered. He was a god. A master of pleasure. A king.

He pounded into her, greedy and hard, but no matter how close he came to consuming her whole, they both seemed to always want more.

"I want you from behind." He set her down and spun her to face the wall, planting her hands on the wet tile. "Spread your legs."

She widened her stance and the blunt head of his cock pushed between her slick folds, stretching her as his deft fingers worked her clit. Rising to her toes, she met his every stroke. He grabbed her hips and yanked her back, penetrating her fully.

Shocked by how deeply he filled her from this angle, she gasped. Banding his arm across her shoulders, he drew her back against his chest and dragged his mouth close to her ear.

"This is Home."

She turned her mouth to meet his as he snapped his hips, fast and hard. Tongues licking, teeth gnashing, they took whatever wildness the other allowed. Greedy and ravenous, he closed his mouth over the bare skin of her shoulder and thrust into her. All the patience he'd shown throughout the years scorched to ash.

Clutching his hair, pulling him closer with desperate, fumbling hands, Wren arched against him, drunk on his intensity. Growling and moaning against her flesh as he ground his hips into her, as his hands slid over her body with unmistakable, possessive claim, he drove into her.

"Grey!" she cried out as her body pulsed around his pistoning cock.

Nibbling kisses along her neck, he worshipped her flesh and bathed her in praise. "Give me everything you've got, baby. I want your come dripping off my dick."

Ecstasy shattered over her like rain. Pulsing, throbbing, sizzling, buzzing, she became a living emotion, controlled by this man.

"Fuck me, Greyson! Harder!"

Burying himself inside of her, hard and deep, he gripped her body as if afraid to let go. Sounds came from him that she'd never heard a man make before, and then he was kissing her again.

He took her hard and unapologetically demanded she accept every filthy desire between them. There was no more hiding. Pandora's Box was beyond opened. It was shattered.

By the time he finished, her legs were numb. He lifted her to his chest and carried her out of the shower. She wrapped her body around his and shivered as he draped her with a towel.

"I'm not through with you yet."

With a needy whimper, she looked up at him as he gently placed her on the bed. He crawled over her, grinding his still swollen cock over her tender sex, kissing her slowly. She moaned against his mouth as he tweaked her nipples in that delicious way that brought her back to life.

"Don't quit on me yet, Wren."

She moaned, too tired to speak or open her eyes.

"I want back inside of you." Carefully, he adjusted her legs and filled her once again.

She breathed with him, rocking into the soft covers as he thrust slowly. His mouth kissed down her throat to her chest, where he suckled her nipples.

He touched her with primal, predatory need. Pinning her arms in whatever position he wanted and driving his cock into her as if seeking her soul.

It was greedy and unapologetic, but she loved every second of it. When she looked into his blue eyes, she swore the devil stared back. He was made to sin, but never once stopped worshipping her.

The sound of slapping flesh became the only crescendo she knew. He yanked her closer whenever she neared the end of the bed, and kissed her softly to balance out the times he got rough. But he was never too aggressive. He was never more than she could handle. He was Greyson. This was him. And she wanted all of him.

Tonight, she finally got her wish.

He warned her. He told her he'd mark every inch of her, and by the time he was through, not a single spot of her flesh was untouched.

"Look at you. I wish you could see what I see." His fingers trailed down her sticky stomach, and her breath hitched when he grazed her swollen folds. "I'm sorry if I was too rough."

A weak laugh muffled past her lips. "No, you're not."

"You're right. I'm not." He dropped to the mattress and pulled her against him. "Do you hate me for it?"

"No," she murmured into his arm. "I love you for showing me this side of yourself. I love all of you, Greyson."

He was silent for a long moment. "I love you, too, baby. I love you, too."

CHAPTER 26

Wren pranced into The Haven Monday morning, her heels clicking a triumphant rhythm against the polished floors. Energy crackled through her veins like champagne bubbles.

"Good morning," she sang, her voice carrying the honeyed warmth of a woman thoroughly fucked for the first time in thirty years. "How was everyone's weekend?"

"Not nearly as good as yours, apparently." Lilly sipped a macchiato from a signature juice glass.

"I did have a great weekend." Rich, dark caffeine perfumed the air. "Did Freya add something new to the menu?"

"Oh, this? No, the CEO dude made it for me."

"Mr. Drummond?" Wren's brow furrowed. "Have all of his charges been calculated?"

"Not yet. He's decided to extend his stay."

"What?" Wren's smile plummeted. "Why?"

"He said he'd finally started to understand the charm and wants to grasp the immersive experience more fully. A guy like that could really help us, Wren. He invests in companies all over the world."

"We don't need any help."

"I mean, not right now. But all those expansion plans you discussed? That stuff's expensive. Getting involved with a venture capitalist like Greg might not be bad."

"Greg?" Feeling like this was rehearsed, Wren stiffened. "Lilly, what we discuss in meetings is private. Mr. Drummond doesn't understand the first thing about disconnecting from screens and reconnecting with nature."

"That's why he wants to stay. He wants to understand."

"Well, he's welcome to shop the service menu, but we're not looking for investors."

"You can tell him yourself. Here he comes."

Wren spun as the doors swept open and Drummond breezed in, completely transformed. Gone were the tailored suits. He now looked like a cover model for a luxury winter retreat, his cashmere jogger set hugging his frame with bespoke precision.

"Wren, just the woman I was looking for."

"Mr. Drummond," Wren greeted with unshakable professionalism. "Lilly informed me you extended your stay."

"Please, call me Greg. I've had a change of heart." He smiled with an edge that promised trouble. "I was hoping to convince you to have lunch."

"I'm afraid I can't. I have yoga class—"

"After."

"I'm scheduled for a shift—"

"Your schedule's empty."

Wren shot Lilly a glare.

"Just sayin'." Lilly held up her hands.

"So you have time?" Greg's smile widened.

"Only for client services."

He plucked a brochure off the rack and flipped to the service menu. "One-on-one yoga sounds perfect. Two o'clock?" He stuffed the brochure back in the rack and tapped the counter as if holding an invisible gavel—decision made.

He didn't wait for confirmation and as soon as he left, Wren deflated. "Why won't he go away?"

"I can't believe you're complaining. He's paying tons to stay here and booking private services. When did you become allergic to money?"

"You're right." She didn't know why he irritated her so much. She was used to pushy men. "I'm going to take a walk and reboot."

After her afternoon class, Noah lingered as usual.

"Have you thought about my dinner offer?"

She finally had a legitimate excuse that wouldn't damage their teacher-client relationship. " I'm flattered, Noah, but I have to confess, I'm involved with someone."

He didn't appear surprised. "The guy on the boat, right?"

Heat flushed her cheeks. "You saw?"

"Kind of hard to miss a display like that."

"I'm sorry. I should have told you sooner, but this is very new. I wouldn't want anything to make coming here awkward."

"Fair enough." She appreciated how easily he accepted her decision.

To make things less awkward, she said, "You're almost getting the sirsasana pose down."

"I've been practicing."

She smiled. "That's great. Soon enough, you'll be able to lead the classes."

"Nah. No one has your special touch. I'm just here for the experience." His words filled her with great satisfaction.

After Noah left, Wren refilled her water when a hand suddenly swooped around her waist, scaring the hell out of her.

"How come every time I visit, there's a stray sniffing around you?" Greyson's voice rumbled possessively against her ear.

She melted against his strength. "What can I say? I'm charming."

He bit at her throat. "Mmm, and salty."

"I just taught a class." She shoved out of his arms. "I'm sweaty."

"I don't mind." He backed her into the shadows, eyes burning with intensity.

"Grey, I have another appointment in less than an hour."

"Cancel."

"I can't. It's a one-on-one with Drummond."

His expression darkened. "Hasn't it been a week yet?"

"He extended his stay. Apparently, he's had some enlightenment." Skepticism colored her voice.

"I'm not buying it."

"Me neither. He mentioned to Lilly something about being a venture capitalist." She rolled her eyes.

Greyson's scowl narrowed. "Watch your back with him, Wren. Guys like that always have ulterior motives."

"I know."

Greyson left just before Drummond swaggered into the studio, wrapped in thousand-dollar ath-leisure wear.

"You can leave your shoes at the door, Mr. Drummond." A loud buzz erupted outside, and she flinched. The unmistakable roar of a chainsaw cut through the air.

Greyson.

Drummond scowled. "What is that?"

"Sorry, we're having some... maintenance." Ignoring the disruption, she lowered to her mat. "Let's start with gentle seated twists." She directed him through poses as the saw obnoxiously roared against the glass. "Good. Loosen your shoulders and relax," she said, louder than usual.

"Am I doing this right? I think I need more hands-on help."

Suppressing a sigh, Wren moved closer to adjust his position.

The windows shook with a BANG and she jumped. Greyson's

form towered on the other side of the glass. He dropped a stack of planks onto the ground and glared at Drummond.

"Must be some big project."

"I apologize. I'll speak to the contractor."

He chuckled. "Your *contractor* seems territorial."

Wren's lips compressed. "Focus, Mr. Drummond."

"Greg."

"Focus, Greg."

A metallic clang ruptured the silence. It was clear Greyson was going to do whatever he could to disrupt their session.

"Ignore everything else and feel the stretch," she said, trying to recenter herself.

"You're incredibly flexible."

"And you're incredibly chatty. Yoga's about quieting the mind."

He chuckled with complete disregard. "I'll work on that."

When poses became challenging, he stood. "You know, Wren, I've been thinking."

"We still have poses left."

Ignoring her, he paced to the window. "There's a real opportunity here. You have something special, but you're bottlenecked by budget. Cash infusion could fast-track The Haven to full potential."

Wren stayed in Warrior Two. "The Haven's progressing at a comfortable pace."

He laughed. "You can't tell me you're satisfied with only a few guests a week. You shouldn't limit yourself. You could have a Haven in every major city."

"I don't think you understand my vision."

"Spa retreats in Aspen. Bali. Global recognition."

"With respect, I'm not interested. I'm interested in finishing this session." She moved into tree pose. "Try to balance."

"I'll try to balance if you consider what I'm suggesting."

She dropped her arms. "Greg, have you heard the parable about the fisherman and businessman?"

"Sounds like a joke. Is this the one with the pope and the life raft?"

"No. A businessman visits a fisherman. He sees the fisherman catching just enough fish for his family and asks why he doesn't sell the extra fish he catches instead of tossing them back."

"Fair question."

A horrible screech of metal on metal erupted from outside, like fingernails on a chalkboard.

Wren ignored it. "The fisherman explains that he only needs enough for himself and his wife, but the businessman, refusing to listen, offers to buy the fisherman a bigger boat so he can give his wife a better life."

"Smart."

"The fisherman turns him down, claiming he's already living his best life."

"Some people just lack ambition."

"The businessman couldn't understand how the fisherman could be so content with so little. He didn't realize that the fisherman was already living his best life, fishing by day, making love under the stars with his wife at night. You see, Mr. Drummond, I don't need to build an empire to live a life of riches. I'm happy exactly where I am, here in my little studio tucked away in the woods of Hideaway Bay."

His forehead wrinkled with genuine confusion. "But you're leaving so much money on the table."

"It's only money. Not everyone values the same riches."

"Well, smart people do."

She silently grinned, certain it was a fool who needed the last word. "I think our session's finished."

"We still have ten minutes."

She shook her head. "That's not enough time for you to change my mind. So unless you're prepared to really take these poses seriously, I suggest moving on."

His eyes narrowed. Greg Drummond was used to getting his

way, but, when it came to difficult men, Wren had a lifetime of experience. She knew what she wanted and he wasn't going to change her mind.

Grabbing his shoes, he left in a huff. She used the remaining hour to stretch out her tension.

Minutes later, the studio door creaked open and she looked up at Greyson, toolbelt slung low like a gunslinger's holster. "Are you done thumping your big tools?"

His mouth quirked. "Just cleaning things up."

"If by that you mean act like a territorial Neanderthal, you nailed it. Why not just pee a circle around me, Greyson?"

"That guy's a creep. No way am I letting you near him again."

"*Letting* me?" She scoffed. "I'm going to stop you right there, Mister. You aren't *letting* me do anything. This is *my* business."

"He was scoping out your ass the entire time you were bent over!"

"Because he was trying to mirror the pose!"

"Bullshit. We both know this had nothing to do with yoga."

"And we both know you weren't actually working on anything constructive out there, making all that noise just for the sake of being disruptive."

"The path needed clearing!"

"And what, you couldn't find a wrecking ball to clear it?" She shoved him. "This isn't high school, Greyson. This is my career. You can't dismantle my life because you think I can't take care of myself."

He drew back. "Are you serious?"

She scoffed. "Very."

"You want me to stand by while some creep tries to take advantage of you? No fucking way, Wren."

"You must really think I'm helpless."

"What are you talking about?"

She flung out her arms. "You're still treating me like a child, Grey!"

"How? By protecting you?"

She scoffed. "You can't keep using that as an excuse. It wasn't always about protecting me. You were afraid of losing me. That's why you never let any other guys within ten feet of me."

He went perfectly still. "I was protecting you."

"Well, I don't need your protection. I only want your love."

The room fell into suffocating silence.

"Say something!"

His glare sharpened. "I warned you. You know what kind of man I am. Maybe I was protecting you for myself all those years. At least I can admit that. What about you, Wren?"

"What about me?"

He laughed without humor. "The least you could do is admit— on some level—you liked it. You liked having my claim on you, knowing I'd go ape-shit if anyone so much as looked at you wrong. You can't hate me for the same reasons you're attracted to me."

"That was high school. Things are different now."

He scoffed. "No, they're not. I'll never stop protecting what's rightfully mine."

She looked up at the rafters of the studio. "Well, this place belongs to me. Until you can respect everything that means, I don't think you should come here anymore."

"You're kicking me out?"

"You spent the last hour disrupting a one-on-one session with a high paying client—"

"Fuck this. Fine. I'm out of here."

She thought she could get through to him. She thought she might get him to address his emotions like an emotionally mature man. But, in typical Greyson fashion, he ran away.

CHAPTER 27

"Merry Christmas, All I want is Forgiveness"

Greyson slammed his truck door hard enough to rattle the windows. Breathing heavily, he glared out the windshield and cursed under his breath, then punched the steering wheel. *"Fuck!"*

He needed space. Away from Wren. He knew his intensity would suffocate what they'd built together.

Jamming his keys in the ignition, he hesitated, his gaze narrowing on the shoveled path to the guest cabins. He knew which was Drummond's.

"This is exactly the shit you have to stop," he grumbled, fighting the urge to further mark his territory, and starting the truck.

"Grey, you there?" His brother's voice crackled from the radio.

Great. He was in no mood. Snatching up the radio, he snapped, "What's up?"

"We're heading to the hospital," Logan said in a rush. "It's Dad."

His hand tightened on the receiver. "What happened?"

"I'm not sure. They had to resuscitate him."

"What?"

"Grey..." The radio crackled, cutting out. "...doesn't sound good. You should ..."

"Fuck!" He punched the radio. "Logan?"

There was a long silence and then the static cut out as his brother said, "Don't bail on this one."

Grief weighed like a boot on his chest. He gripped the wheel, his vision blurring down to a keyhole as he tried to breath. Hospital. He needed to get to the hospital.

"Greyson!"

Lost in unwanted thoughts, he barely noticed the truck door fling open.

"Soren called. You need to get to the hospital right away!" She grabbed his arm. "Grey?"

He recognized the look of terror on her face from years before. She needed him to be better, but right now, he needed her. For this.

"Grey, did you hear me? You have to leave. Now."

He nodded but didn't move. "Wren." His mouth filled with the bitter taste of loss. The fear of losing her choked the words right out of him.

"Greyson, you have to drive!"

He looked at her. Realizing he might lose her and his father in the same day. "I can't go through this again."

Understanding dawned, and she lunged across the seat, hugging him tightly. "It's okay."

He grabbed onto her, refusing to let her go. "I'm sorry. For everything." He'd never be less, but he could try to say more. He'd say anything if it made her stay. "Please, don't leave me, Wren."

"I'm not going anywhere. But you have to drive. Your brothers are waiting."

His throat constricted. He couldn't move.

She understood and shoved the truck into park. "Switch." Climbing over the console, she shoved him out the door. He rushed to the passenger side as she threw it into drive before he was even seated.

"I never meant to ruin anything for you."

"You didn't. None of that matters now."

He looked down, confused how he ended up in the passenger seat. "I love you, Wren. You're it for me. I can't do this without you."

She glanced at him, face tense and tears glistening in her eyes. "I know, Grey. I know. I love you, too."

Not the way he loved her. She didn't realize how many times he'd wanted to give up and disappear. She gave him a reason to keep coming back, to keep breathing. She gave him something to hope for. He just kept thinking, if he did better, made something of himself...Maybe she could love him.

The truck whipped into the hospital parking lot before he was ready to face the next step. "We're here."

"I don't know the room number—"

"Four-twenty-six." He frowned and she shrugged. "What? I visited."

She'd visited? When?

They rushed inside. The elevator was cramped and muffled in a way that made his brain itch. His clothes turned heavy and tight. He tugged at his collar, having a hard time swallowing.

Wren's hand curled around his, and warmth spread up his arm. He looked down at her, his grip tightening around her dainty fingers.

The elevator pinged and the door opened. Soren was there, pacing the halls like a caged animal. "It's about fucking time."

A second set of elevators opened and Logan rushed out. They must have just missed him in the lobby. "Where is he?"

"They took him for scans."

Wren released Greyson's hand and he went momentarily deaf. His brothers wore matching expressions from when their mom died.

Panic welled inside him as he drifted outside reality. She hugged Soren and Logan, then her hand was back in his.

Safe.

"What happened?"

Soren detailed events using words like pressure and erratic. They all knew this was coming. According to doctors, it was inevitable.

Greyson watched Wren nod, her responses genuine and unguarded. When her hand tightened around his, so did his concern. He pulled her close. Comforting her somehow eased his own fear.

They moved to a waiting room filled with blue chairs. Wren sat between him and Logan, holding both their hands. Soren paced by the door.

When more than an hour had passed, she quietly stood. He didn't want to let her go, but couldn't find words to call her back.

She approached Soren and pressed a gentle hand on his back, whispering something private into his brother's ear. Mesmerized, Greyson watched as Soren fell apart, turning to Wren and hugging her tightly. Then he wiped his tears and immediately apologized. Even in crisis, Hawthorne men weren't supposed to show emotion.

But Wren gripped his face and pressed her forehead to his. "You're allowed to cry, Soren. He's your father."

His brother's breath audibly shook. That's what she did. She made others feel right, even when everything felt wrong.

Beside him, Logan sniffed and panic surged through Greyson.

He should bolt. He should get on the elevator, get the hell out of this hospital, and head straight for the harbor. He could get on a ship and disappear. Wren could go with him.

But she wouldn't. She wouldn't leave Bodhi, or The Haven, or even his brothers. She always toughed out the difficult stuff, no matter how hard things got.

"Grey?" Wren stood in front of him, hands wringing at her waist, eyes full of concern.

He blinked. Where did Logan and Soren go?

"Do you want to see him?"

He nodded but didn't move.

"The doctor said only two at a time. We can go as soon as your brothers get back."

The doctor? How had he missed the doctor? "Will you go with me?"

Her hand curled around his. "I'm not leaving your side."

He planned to hold her to that promise.

She lowered to the seat beside him. "We can wait here until Soren and Logan are done."

Greyson sat stiffly, elbows on his knees, fingers laced so tight they ached. He stared blankly at the linoleum.

Wren waited, quiet and calm, like gravity holding the room together. She rubbed his back in soothing strokes.

When the double doors opened, Greyson instinctively stood. A female doctor in a white lab coat approached. Mid-fifties. Salt at the temples. Steady eyes. Her badge read Dr. Kim – Neurology.

"Mr. Hawthorne?"

Greyson nodded.

"I'm Dr. Kim. I've been overseeing your father's care since the stroke occurred this afternoon."

Wren retrieved Logan and Soren from his father's room. Her hand curled tightly around his as soon as she returned.

The doctor stiffly smiled in a way that brought little comfort. "I'll start with the good news. Because your father was already admitted for pneumonia, we acted immediately and got his blood pressure down."

Greyson only comprehended every other word as she explained what happened.

"So it was a stroke?" Soren asked.

"Yes. A mild ischemic stroke. There was a small clot in the right parietal region..."

Tightness cranked around his chest, making every breath harder.

"His heart isn't pumping efficiently, and we're seeing signs of progressive organ stress."

Wren spoke for the first time. "Is there anything more you can do?"

"We can manage symptoms, continue monitoring. But I think it's time we talk about the broader picture."

Their words faded as Greyson stepped away.

Standing in the doorway of his father's room, he listened as machines softly chirped. The silence between each beep hit like thunder.

"I recommend bringing in a palliative care team..."

How was this happening?

This was Magnus, their unshakable father. He was supposed to be eternal. Not weak and alone in some hospital bed.

"I'll need a signature to move forward. Which one of you is Greyson Hawthorne?"

"Greyson?"

"Grey?"

He turned to his brothers. They looked at him as if he had answers. "What?"

Wren pulled him back into the fold. "Your father has you listed as his proxy. The doctor needs you to sign papers."

"Why me?"

Soren walked away. Logan returned to their father's room.

A pen and clipboard appeared in his hands. He stared blankly at the words, trusting Wren when she urged him to sign.

Logan's voice drifted into the hall. Wren followed his stare to the elevators. "I can wait here for Logan if you want to talk to Soren."

In that moment, he didn't have the words to talk to anyone, but he needed to get the hell out of there. "Thanks."

He found Soren outside pacing beside an ambulance. "Hey."

Soren turned and twisted a red lollipop out of his mouth. "This is totally fucked up."

Greyson nodded. "Where'd you get a lollipop?"

"Turns out, hospitals don't offer bourbon."

Greyson shoved his hands in his pockets. "This is so..." He laughed without humor. "Fucked."

"Tell me about it. I knew we'd eventually get to this stage, but some part of me always believed he'd rally. I mean, it's Dad. He's too much of a prick to die."

The corner of Greyson's mouth lifted. "He's probably outraged."

Soren chuckled. "Think God knows he's about to get fired?"

Greyson smirked. "There's about to be some serious restructuring when the new boss arrives up there."

They both chuckled.

"Logan's going to be rough," Soren said, staring down at his shoes.

They all were.

"This whole situation sucks."

"Yeah." He agreed.

They stood in silence for a beat.

"I've been thinking a lot about Mom."

Greyson met his stare. "Yeah?"

"Remember how she used to make us those hot dogs with the spaghetti pushed through?"

"Octopasta?" Greyson hadn't thought about his mom's cooking in years.

"Dad hated it. Said hot dogs were nothing but trashy food for trashy people."

"He never liked when she cooked for us."

"Mom didn't care."

"No, she didn't."

"Remember when she and Haven took us swimming in the bay and Dad flipped out?"

Another lost memory surfaced. "He could never control her when Haven was involved."

"Those damn Wildes!" Soren mimicked their father's voice, and they both laughed. "I think he was always threatened by Haven's independence."

"She made Mom brave."

"Yeah. The more time they spent together the less she took Dad's shit."

Greyson grinned. "Wren's tough like her mom."

Soren met his stare. "So, you two are..."

"Yup."

"And it's..."

"Yup."

"No going back now."

"Nope." Greyson didn't want to go back. Only forward. "You okay with it? With me?"

His brother drew in a long breath. "It was always going to be you, Grey. We knew it when you were fifteen."

"Yet you still tried."

Soren shrugged. "Hey, if you weren't going to act, I wasn't going to let a fine piece of—"

"I dare you to finish that statement."

"Fair enough." Soren held up his hands. "I'm happy for you. I'm happy for Wren."

He wanted to ask if he was making a mistake. "Do you think we stole something from her?"

"What do you mean?"

"Do you think we disrupted her life or messed with her destiny?"

"It's Wren, Greyson. She was never leaving Hideaway Bay or Bodhi."

"I know, but... What if she was meant for someone else? Someone better."

"You've loved that girl since we were kids. There isn't anyone who could love her more than you will."

That's not what he said the other day. "What if I'm like him?"

"What if you're not?"

"But what if I am?"

"You're not, Greyson. None of us are. We might have his name and features, but he wasn't around enough for us to pick up his shitty traits. We choose who we are. Besides, you're out of your mind if you think you could ignore Wren the way Dad ignored Mom. You're totally whipped."

Greyson scowled. "I am not."

"Oh, please. You've been mooning over her for two decades. Disappear to the North Sea all you want. You'll still come running back at the slightest finger wave."

"Fuck off. I came home for holidays."

"You came home for Wren. We all knew it. Just own it."

The doors opened as other visitors stepped outside. "We should get back."

They both sighed, forcing themselves to face the inevitable. But this time the elevator didn't feel as constricting and he could breathe a little easier. When they reached the fourth floor, Wren stood, concern etched across her face.

Soren went in to visit their father and Greyson hugged her.

She eased back to read his expression. "You okay?"

"Yeah." He pressed his lips to her hair, not ready to let her go.

"Is Soren?"

"He'll be fine. We all will."

Her arms tightened around him. "Do you want me to go in with you?"

He drew back to look at her. "You don't have to if you don't want to."

She slipped her hand back in his. "I told you, I'm not leaving your side." They crossed the threshold as one.

CHAPTER 28

"Haul Out The Holly"

GREYSON MOANED AS WREN WORKED THE TENSION OUT OF HIS neck. Moving his father back home had been an ordeal. There was the coordination of his care, the arrival of proper furniture and equipment, but above all, the biggest challenge was meeting his father's unreachable standards. The man refused any additional care outside of his home, and insisted he would die in true blue blood fashion, dressed in a suit, broker on hold, and a fresh cigar in his pocket.

"You know, they say it's common for people to rally at the end." Wren worked the tendons of his shoulders and neck. "It's like autumn, when everything is crisp and at its brightest for one final hurrah."

Maybe that's what this was. They assumed the man was in the winter of his life, but he came out of that hospital like a tyrant, barking orders and making demands they scrambled to meet.

"Tomorrow he's having his portrait done. We had to commission an artist from Connecticut to fly out." Greyson dropped his voice to mimic his dad's imperious tone. *"Make sure you capture the defiance in my eyes. I'm not leaving without a fight."*

Wren chuckled, her fingers scraping deliciously over his scalp as he shut his eyes. The fireplace warmed his feet as his legs stretched across the floor, and he was perfectly comfortable sitting between her thighs as she rubbed the tension from his neck.

"It's all about control. He wrote his own damn obituary and called it in to the New York Times, demanding they print it above the fold."

Wren continued to massage his scalp as he vented.

"He's hitting up the private reserve in the wine cellar, flying out members of his board for meetings, and dictating his memoir to some ghost writer that traveled here from California."

"Shut your eyes and breathe in the lavender." She placed a cold, padded mask over his face.

He breathed deep, letting the soothing scent seep into his sinuses. "You know, I'd never let anyone else do this to me."

"I know."

She massaged the joints between his knuckles. Rat pounced over his legs, playing with some of the cat toys Wren bought. Greyson leaned back, letting the soothing herbs work their magic.

"What oil are you using?"

"It's a mixture of bergamot and ylang-ylang."

"I like it."

She massaged his back and shoulders for several more minutes, then moved Rat to the sofa and took the kitten's place on his lap, looping her arms around his shoulders. When she brushed her lips to his, he lifted the mask.

"Feel better?"

"Much. Thank you."

"Any time." She moved to rise, but he caught her hips. "Stay. I haven't held you like this all week."

She smiled and settled her weight onto his lap. "Is that your way of telling me you missed me?"

"It's my way of telling you I can't breathe when we spend more than a few hours apart. And that I'm sorry."

Her lips parted slightly. "Grey... we've been over this."

Stroking a hand down her thick braid, he admired the intricate twists. "The thought of anyone else kissing you or touching you... I can't handle it. Never could."

"No one touches me but you, Grey."

"Damn right."

She sighed and kissed him. "Besides. You were right. I think part of me likes your territorial side. I love your attention, even when you're in a mood." She laughed.

"What's so funny?"

"Nothing."

"Tell me."

She hesitated. "Once I..." She looked away, unable to finish her statement.

He caught her chin. "What?"

"It's silly. I was just remembering when I showed Keith Doble my boobs just because I wanted you to find out."

"So he's dead."

She swatted his arm. "He doesn't even live here anymore."

"You think I won't travel?"

She looked away.

"I should have stayed."

"Maybe we both needed space."

"Why didn't you date when I was away? I wasn't around to stop you—"

"You've met your brothers, right? They're just as bad. Besides, I didn't want to date. I was too sad, worried you'd fall in love with some sea hag and never come back."

"No escaping me now," he rasped, toppling her to her back so he could kiss her properly. He pulled back and framed her face. "Will you come back with me?"

Her expression softened. "To your dad's?"

"I know it's a lot to ask—"

"Of course, I'll go with you."

Relief struck sharp, and he pulled her close for another hard kiss. "Thank you."

Wren packed an overnight bag, and he carried it out to the truck. It had been twenty years since she'd slept over with him and his brothers. A teasing sense of nostalgia played at the frayed edges of his memory in a way that made him feel like a kid again.

"Remember upside-down days?" She must have been having similar memories.

Greyson smiled as he backed out of the lot. "Yeah."

Upside-down days only happened when his dad was out of town on business. Haven used to come over with Wren and they would have breakfast for dinner then stay up all night watching old movies.

"This reminds me of that." She held Rat on her lap with her little bag. "I brought my matching PJ set. I usually reserve them for a fancy sleep."

"A fancy sleep?"

"Yeah, you know—when you wash the sheets and make the bed all fresh. It's fancy."

"So you make your pajamas match?"

"Well, it's not like they're coordinated with the bedding or anything that extreme. But I try to put some effort in."

He chuckled. "Effort for who?"

"The bed, silly."

"Right."

When they pulled into his father's garage beside his collection of antique cars, Greyson let the engine run, everything inside of him hesitating. This wasn't home anymore. Hadn't been for a very long time.

Wren placed a gentle hand on his arm. "You okay?"

"Yeah." He sighed. "I keep having the resounding thought that I don't want to do this. Then I remember I don't have a choice."

"Grey, you always have a choice. But sometimes the right choice is the hardest to make."

He looked down at Rat and grinned at how comfy he looked curled up at the apex of her thighs. *Lucky bastard.* "Thanks again for coming here with me."

"Of course."

"Tomorrow, we'll do something fun. Soren's on Dad duty, so I've got the day off."

"Tomorrow's the Santa Fun Run. We could go into town and bet on the winners."

"It's on."

He carried her bag into the house, surprised to find it silent. Logan appeared in the hall. "Hey Wren."

She hugged Logan.

"How was he?" Greyson asked, peeking into the den to find his father resting in the adjustable bed.

"I think he tired himself out around the twelfth phone call." Logan glanced at the floral bag in Grey's hand. "You staying the night, Wren?"

"I am."

His brother's eyes lit up. "Like an old school upside-down day?"

She smiled. "Dig out the waffle maker."

She made breakfast for dinner for him and his brothers just the way their moms used to. As foolish as it was to eat waffles for dinner while dressed in pajamas, the act healed something in them and Greyson felt a closeness to his brothers and Wren that he hadn't experienced in years.

After his brothers left, Greyson led Wren to the second floor. The house staff worked quietly downstairs, as they did every night while his father slept. Any cause for alarm, and they'd come get him.

Greyson opened the door to his childhood bedroom and waved Wren inside. She stepped over the threshold and scanned the walls, as if entering a museum, slow and reverent. His heart thudded against his ribs. He could fix a busted engine in an ice storm, and drag a buck out of the woods with his bare hands, but watching Wren look around his teenage bedroom? That disarmed him in ways he wasn't prepared for.

The faint scent of cedar and damp earth filled the air. That coastal dampness never left Hideaway Bay, no matter how much furniture polish the maids used. He liked it more than the briny air at sea, because it reminded him of home. Of Wren.

Fishing rods still hung in the corner like sentinels. Lures were framed in shadow boxes, and old tide charts were tacked beside a bulletin board full of yellowed concert tickets and scribbled notes.

Her fingers brushed the edge of the small desk he'd built by hand the summer after the accident. Watching her reverently trace the grain in the wood where he'd carved little fish symbols made him feel like she was caressing etchings along his soul.

"Grey..." She breathed his name, but it wasn't a word so much as it was a feeling.

A lump formed in his throat as she turned to the bookcase and stilled.

She saw it. And he was going to own it.

"I couldn't let them go," he confessed.

Her eyes turned to him, then returned to the collection of treasures. Top shelf, back corner, hidden, but not really. The ribbon from the 4th of July sandcastle competition, which they won when they were young. A tiny photo strip from the boardwalk arcade when their moms took them to the Jersey Shore—her laughing, him pretending to look cool. A smooth heart-shaped stone she'd given him, *just because*. Her old senior photo—the corners curled upward with time.

She traced a gentle finger over the silver tray holding the dried lily petals from his mom's funeral. "You kept all this?"

"I kept the parts I wanted to remember," he said quietly.

She pressed her lips together, eyes shiny, then studied the wall above the bed. Posters still hung from thumbtacks—old rock bands and a boat schematic he'd drawn when he was fifteen, dreaming about starting his own line of high-performance skiffs.

A soft laugh passed her lips. "I remember this." She read the signed photograph of a local fisherman he'd idolized.

Pinned in the middle of all of it, right between the Eddie Vedder poster and a map of the Atlantic currents, was Wren's senior prom photo. Except the part where Logan stood behind her had been folded back.

She turned and looked at him questioningly.

"I was jealous," he admitted before she could ask. "It didn't matter that he was my kid brother. You were mine."

She didn't say anything, but she took it all in.

Lowering onto the old twin bed, her fingers curled into the worn patchwork quilt as the springs softly squeaked. A smile curled her lips as recognition dawned. "My mom made this."

He nodded. Haven had given each of them a quilt for their tenth birthdays.

She looked back at the prom photo on the wall. "You know, I wanted to go with you."

"I was twenty. You were still seventeen."

"People would have understood."

"I couldn't." He shook his head. "I thought about it—*a lot*—but I couldn't do it."

"Why?"

He stepped fully into the room and shut the door. "I didn't have the words yet."

"What words?"

"To tell you everything in here." He pressed a hand to his chest.

"I was angry. Grieving. Pissed off at the world. You didn't need that when you were grieving too."

"I needed you."

He shook his head. "Even then, I knew I'd want things from you that weren't fair of me to ask. You had your own stress."

"You mean Bodhi?"

"Him. School. Other guys."

"There were no other guys, Greyson. You made sure of that."

Again, he thought about their argument in the yoga studio. "I never meant to take it that far."

She reached for the framed photo of him and Magnus on the dock of the fishery, her hand coming dangerously close to the stack of old journals shoved half-heartedly on the shelf behind the nightstand.

As if sensing the one place he didn't want her to look, she paused and touched one of the battered spines. His heart stopped.

"Is my name in here?"

"Only on every page."

She took her hand away and tried to hide a smile. Then her brow pinched with what looked like regret.

He took a step closer. "I loved you before I understood what love meant, Wren. My parents...they didn't feel what I feel for you. I didn't grow up around it like you did with Bodhi and Haven."

She looked up at him, eyes glistening with unshed tears, and nodded. "My dad loved my mom so hard it broke him when she died."

Greyson understood that sort of love. Every time he tried to leave Wren, something inside of him shattered.

"If you would have told me how you felt..." Her words dissolved like missed opportunities.

"I tried. Every time I fixed a loose shingle or mended a step. Whenever I filled the bird feeders for you or patched a hole. I told you every way I could."

"But you never actually said the words."

"I was scared."

"Of me?"

"No." Was he really going to tell her the truth? "I'm still scared."

Her frown reflected some of her own fear. "Of what?"

"That one day you'll realize you could do so much better."

She lowered her gaze and shook her head, a gentle laugh softening the mood. "Greyson, don't you see?" She looked back up at him and smiled, fresh tears in her eyes. "You're the best man I know. There's no one *better* for me."

His throat tightened as he tried to swallow. "Life's about to get really complicated, Wren." He feared mentally checking out, like he'd done when his mom died. He didn't want to face what was coming. "I have a habit of disappearing when things get too...real."

"You won't."

"How do you know?"

"Because I know you, Greyson. You're not going to run this time. I won't let you."

Like an anchor stills a ship amidst a stormy sea , she kept him grounded in the face of the incoming storm. His father could hardly lift a spoon these days, yet he still intimidated the shit out of all of them. Not a single word of praise in over thirty years, yet some part of him still craves his father's approval. And he wasn't going to get it.

Hawthorne men don't complain!

Stop sniveling!

Toughen up!

Keep acting like a baby and I'll give you something to cry about!

Greyson's chest tightened. "This was a mistake. We shouldn't have come here."

"What? Grey, no. You need this time—"

"For what?" The walls of his childhood room closed in around him like a cage. "So he can tell us one last time how much we disappointed him? It's too late, Wren."

"Maybe for him, but not for you and your brothers." She pulled him to sit beside her on the bed. "It's important that you all go through this together."

Greyson didn't do togetherness. He preferred to drown his emotions out at sea or bury them deep in the woods—alone. "None of us want to be here."

"Yet, here we are. Think about how nice it was to have an upside down dinner tonight. You boys need each other. Those silly traditions are what make life bearable. They distract us from the pain."

"All of our traditions died with our mom."

"Well, maybe that's part of the problem. Maybe it's time you brought them back. It's like the song says, maybe you just *need a little Christmas*. You boys are long overdue for a real family holiday, one that's messy and chaotic, with presents and tacky lights and all the dysfunctional trimmings."

He drew back. "Sounds…horrifying."

"It does," she laughed. "But it will also be healing—for all of you. Trust me."

He did trust her, but he didn't share her faith. "It's a nice idea, Wren, but we might not have that kind of time."

"We'll make time. This year, Christmas is coming early. A good, old-fashioned Hideaway holiday is exactly what this family needs."

CHAPTER 29

"It's Beginning to Look a Lot Like Christmas"

SNOW DUSTED THE EAVES OF MAIN STREET SHOPS LIKE POWDERED sugar on gingerbread houses. Wreaths and garland transformed the town into a gift-wrapped wonderland. The blend of woodsmoke, cinnamon, and caramelized sweets hung thick in the air—a promise of comfort Greyson's uneasy stomach couldn't embrace.

Dread or hope?

The question churned in his gut with no relief.

Wren skipped across the snow-dusted square, her crimson knit hat bobbing like Rudolph's nose as the jingle bells tied to her boot laces chimed with every stride.

"I hope you stretched," she yelled, breath misting from her wide grin. "Because we're getting a holiday workout today."

Greyson shoved his hands deeper into his coat pockets as wind whipped across the square. "I feel the work part of it."

Wren spun to face him, clutching spiced cider like a lifeline. "Don't be a grinch."

413

"You knew this wasn't going to be easy."

"And you know I'm not someone who gives up." Her eyes sparkled. "We're going full-tilt, Hawthorne. Hot cocoa, mistletoe, all the trimmings! We're making memories, whether you and your brothers accept it or not." She pressed a cinnamon kiss on his lips and nuzzled him with her cold nose. "Trust me, there will come a time that you'll all appreciate having them."

He believed her, but that time wasn't now.

This was his fault. He'd asked for help. What did he expect her to do, nothing? That wasn't Wren. She saw a problem and put her whole heart into fixing it.

Drift & Dwell beckoned like a Christmas cottage, its window ablaze with twinkling lights and handmade ornaments.

Inside, cinnamon-scented potpourri and Christmas music bombarded him. Sugar cookies shaped like snowflakes sat beside a large carafe of mulled wine.

"First, a little Christmas fuel." Wren handed him a cookie and bit hers with a satisfied hum.

"Do you even know who made them?"

She licked sugar from her lips in a way that took his mind to a place it shouldn't go. "As long as they aren't Birdie's, I'm sure they're fine."

He followed her through aisles overflowing with holiday treasures, mesmerized by the sway of her hips as she piled their basket with beeswax candles, ceramic reindeer, and glass ornaments.

"How much are you getting?" The basket was already overflowing so he relieved her of its weight, but that only freed up her hands so she could shop twice as fast.

"We're hosting Christmas dinner, Greyson. A lot goes into that."

At the register, the proprietor showed them bone china plates painted with Victorian Christmas scenes in rich burgundies and forest greens.

"Oh, these are beautiful." Wren traced the gold-leafed edge with wonder.

"We'll take them." He didn't give a damn about china patterns. The pure joy radiating from her face was worth every penny.

"We'll need a set of eight."

"Eight?" His mind raced. "Last I counted, we were a party of five."

"There's you and me, your brothers, and your dad. Then my dad, Aunt Astrid, and Jocelyn."

"Jocelyn's coming to fake Christmas?"

"It's not fake, Greyson. Christmas is a vibe, not a date. And Jocelyn's my best friend."

He scowled. "I'm your best friend."

"Yes, but you're also..." She brushed close, batted her lashes playfully, and whispered, "My *lovah*."

They carved a zigzag path through town, hitting every shop. Hand-dipped candles, artisan soaps, and locally-made maple syrup in bottles shaped like Christmas trees. If Hideaway sold it, and it had a Santa, angel, or elf on it, they bought it.

Three trips back to his truck barely made a dent in their haul.

At the Christmas Market, Wren bartered like a seasoned trader. He loved when she got fired up about a few pennies, and found it irresistible when she got all huffy about not getting her way.

"Eight dollars for jam! Who does he think he is?" she griped, stomping away from a booth at the Christmas market that was apparently overpriced.

"Isn't jam just fancy jelly?"

"Exactly."

When they drifted back to the town square, her mood quickly lightened. An ice sculptor transformed a massive block into Captain Claws.

"Simon would die," Wren joked. "He's finally getting his moment of fame, and he's nowhere to be found."

"I'm sure he'll see it eventually."

Outside the Bay Roast Cafe, they were caught in spontaneous caroling. Of course Wren sang along without needing lyrics.

They grabbed more hot cocoa and a gingerbread man the size of a dinner plate. Wren bit off the head with theatrical relish and smiled up at him. "*Mmm*, so good. Wanna bite?"

"Any more sugar and I'll go into diabetic shock."

"Impossible." She laughed. "Everyone knows, calories aren't real in December. It's science."

"None of this is real." The words escaped before he could stop them.

She paused mid-bite, her happy expression frozen and then crestfallen. "You don't mean that."

Truth was, he didn't know what he meant. "It's just…a lot."

"It's supposed to be a lot. It's Christmas."

"I think I'm just tired. I didn't sleep well last night."

Her expression fell even more. "We can go home if you want."

"No." Despite his incomprehension of holiday cheer, he liked seeing her happy. "I'm enjoying myself."

"Liar."

He closed the distance, yanking the lapels of her coat together and also pulling her in for a kiss. Holding her stare, he whispered, "I'm enjoying watching you. It doesn't matter if everything else goes over my head. As long as you're by my side and having fun, I'm happy."

She bit off the arm of the gingerbread and studied him as she slowly chewed. "You're sure?"

"Positive. Let's keep shopping."

The next store carried quilts and other house-type things. Wren admired the detailed stitching of one blanket in particular, and he wondered if it reminded her of her mom. Weighed down by gift bags, he stood beside her. "If you like it, let's get it." It wasn't a Christmas quilt, but she seemed to think it was nice.

She smiled and turned away, moving on to the next display. "I noticed your dad likes the blanket I gave him." When he looked at her in confusion, she said, "The sapphire plaid one."

He hadn't realized that was from her. But she was right, his dad asked for it whenever his legs got cold. "How come you didn't tell me you visited him in the hospital?"

Wren shrugged and continued perusing the displays. "It didn't come up."

"Did you talk to him?"

"No, Greyson. I went to the hospital and just stared at him. What kind of question is that? Of course, I talked to him."

He frowned, trailing behind as she moved to the other side of the aisle. "What did you two talk about?"

"Reagan."

"As in Ronald, the past president?"

"Yeah."

"You visited my dad in the hospital and talked about Ronald Reagan?"

"Why is that so hard for you to believe?"

"I don't know. I guess I didn't realize you were a Reagan fan."

She snorted, a decidedly unladylike sound. "I'm not, but your dad mentioned him once when we were young, so I picked up a biography for him."

"You bought my dad a book?"

"Well, it was on the shelf at The Haven. A guest probably left it." She stopped walking and faced him. "Are you mad?"

"No. I'm just trying to picture you there, at the hospital, giving my dad a book."

"I also gave him a massage."

"No, you didn't." He laughed.

"I did."

Holy shit, she wasn't kidding. "You know my dad's made grown men piss themselves in meetings before."

"He's just a man, Greyson."

Just a man. That was the understatement of the century.

It was dusk by the time they drove home. As the sun slipped behind the mountains, the temperature dropped with it. Christmas lights blinked to life on every rooftop and railing, transforming the town into a constellation at their feet.

"Stop the truck," Wren called, and he slammed on the brakes. She unbuckled her seatbelt and leaned up on the dashboard to better see out the windshield. "Look how pretty!"

The Footbridge appeared through the falling snow like something from a Christmas card. Ancient stone arches spanned the babbling brook, every surface blanketed in pristine white. Glass mason jars lined the railings, each containing a flickering candle.

Pulling onto the shoulder, he flicked on his hazards so she could get a better look. He stared at her much like she was staring at the bridge.

Turning her enchanted smile on him, she said, "Let's make a wish!" She was already out of the truck before he could think of an excuse.

Was this his life now, foolish holidays and pennies tossed from whimsical bridges? He thought he hit his superstitious quota for the year, but apparently Wren wasn't finished.

He slowly followed as Wren's boots crunched to a stop at the bridge's center. She gripped the snow-dusted rail with both gloved hands, closing her eyes as if in prayer.

God, she was beautiful.

"I used to come here every Christmas Eve," she murmured, her voice barely audible above the water's gentle babbling. "Every year, I'd make a wish. Just one."

He came to stand beside her as their breath pushed clouds of vapor into the cool air. "What did you wish for?"

She gave him a knowing smile. "At first, I'd wish my mom was still alive. But when I got older, I wished about you."

"What about me?"

"That you'd see me—*really* see me."

He saw her now.

Her head lowered, and she continued, "For years, I just wished you would come home."

It was amazing how shitty disappointing her could make him feel. He wished he'd been stronger, wished he could take back those times he made her question or doubt herself. The truth was, he simply loved her too much and it scared the hell out of him.

He tightened his hand around her gloved fingers. "I'm sorry, Wren."

She gave him a sad smile. "We don't apologize, remember?"

In this case he needed to make amends. He needed her to truly understand how much he regretted ever hurting her. "I should've been there for you."

"You were. More than anyone else."

He couldn't remember how many Christmases he'd missed, because to him they were just another day. But to her, they meant something special, a day saved for those she loved.

He owed her and he planned to make it up to her any way he could. "Let's go home, baby. Show me how to Christmas."

She noticed the shift in his attitude, and her smile shifted into a happier one. "Really?"

"Really."

She bounced with glee, wreathing her arms around his neck. When his lips pressed to hers, everything inside of him shifted into a state of calm. He never wanted to let her go.

"I knew you'd come around." She turned to walk toward the truck, but he caught her arm, tugging her back to him.

"Wait."

Her blue eyes expectantly looked at him.

He wasn't ready to leave just yet. Maybe there was some magic to this bridge after all. "Tell me what else you wished for."

She dropped her chin and shyly looked away. "If I tell you, they won't come true."

"So some aren't finished?"

She shrugged. "Most are, but some aren't. A girl's entitled to her secrets."

"What did you wish for, Wren?"

"Grey, I can't—"

"If you tell me, I'll make every single one come true."

"No," she laughed and tried to walk away again, but he pulled her back. "That's not how this works."

"Why not?"

"Because it's not."

But she was wrong. So far, all of her wishes had come true. When she wished for him to come home, he returned. She wished for him to see her, and he saw her even when his eyes were closed and he was a thousand miles away. She wished for him to love her, kiss her, touch her… So far, every wish he knew of had come true.

There was only one more wish he could think of that she might have hoped for, and he never liked doing anything halfway.

He dropped to his knee, and her smile fell. "Grey…" Her eyes widened. "What are you doing?"

"Wren Wilde, I *wish* for you to marry me." He wasn't sure how this bridge thing worked, but he was pretty sure she had to say yes.

Her gloved fingers covered her mouth, hiding her expression as her eyes flooded with tears.

"Please tell me they're happy tears."

Pink stained her cheeks as she pulled her trembling hands away. But she wasn't smiling. She looked… heartbroken. Then she forced a shaky smile that didn't come close to reaching her eyes. "Okay, Greyson. I'll marry you."

He frowned. "Did I miss something?"

She sniffed. "No. I'm happy. I guess you know all my wishes after all."

But she didn't look or sound happy. Did he do it wrong? "I can get you a ring—"

"We don't need anything that fancy."

His frown deepened. "Wren, I'm getting you a fucking ring."

"Fine. I'll wear a ring. But it's not a requirement."

What the hell was she talking about? "Look, if you don't want to marry me, you can say no."

"I do. I want to marry you. It's just…" He waited, but she only shook her head and forced another smile. "I'm being silly. Ignore me. I'm happy!" she said with artificial cheer. "And hey, if it makes things easier for you, we can go to City Hall on Monday."

The world tilted and his heart stopped, restarted, then hammered against his ribs, as he suddenly understood why she was reacting this way.

He stood and cursed under his breath, "Mother fucker."

He wanted to take it all back. Of course she would think this had something to do with his dad. The whole day had been about him and tying up loose ends. He was pissed. Pissed about that stupid clause and pissed that she'd actually think he'd marry her for anything short of love.

Turning to face her again, he meant to say all of that but only barked, "We are not getting married in City Fucking Hall."

"I'm just saying—"

"Stop." She drew back, unused to him snapping at her. But he needed to make a few things perfectly clear. "I have…*a lot* to say and I need to get it out."

She blinked up at him with big eyes. "O-okay."

He pushed down his fury and tried to remember this was Wren. She didn't put them in this mess. She was only trying to help. "I'm going to marry you, because it's the one thing I wanted as far back as I can remember. This has nothing to do with my father."

"Grey, even if it does—"

"No! There's no *maybes* or *what ifs* about it, Wren. I love you. I've always loved you. How could you even think I had any other motive?"

"Whether it's your motive or not, the will is something that you'll eventually have to address. This fixes things."

His lips pressed into a firm line. "I'm marrying you because I fucking love you! I can't remember a time when I didn't love you. This month is usually the saddest month of the year for me, and it should be even sadder this year, considering everything my family's going through, but it's been... the opposite. I'm happier and more at peace than I've ever been, because I finally have you. You balance me in a way nothing else can. I want to marry you. Not because of any inheritance or any other superficial reason. I want to marry you because you make life worth living. When I'm by your side, I feel like I'm exactly where I need to be."

He pulled her gloved hand to his chest and pressed his hand over her heart. "You're my home, Wren. When I'm away, I feel sick because all I want to do is come back to you. Now that I have you, I never want to leave again."

She looked stunned. Maybe even a little afraid. That was a lot to digest, especially coming from someone who avoided talking about his feelings like most people avoided plagues.

He needed a damn ring.

Tugging off his glove, he unlaced his boot and snapped the string. "Give me your hand."

She held out a shaky hand, and he pulled off her glove, tying the tattered lace around her knuckle. "I love you," he said matter-of-factly. "I don't know how to stop, so this is me promising that I never will." He kissed the bow tied around her knuckle.

Twin tears fell down her cheeks. The makeshift ring looked ridiculous, but it was the best he could do in a pinch.

"Are you going to say something?"

She grinned, and more tears fell. "Yes."

"Yes, as in you plan to say something, or yes, as in you—"

"I'll marry you—"

He scooped her up in his arms and hugged the breath out of her. Pressing his face into her neck as he swore, "I promise to be a good husband to you, Wren."

"I know you will, Grey."

His mouth found hers. She tasted of sweets and tears. She tasted familiar, like she was already his. His home. His future. His Wren.

When he pulled away, she wiped her tears and laughed, then threw her head back and yelled, *"We're getting married!"*

Her voice echoed off the snow-laden pines, startling a pair of cardinals from their roost. The birds took flight in a flash of crimson. A perfect December picture his mind would never forget.

Maybe that bridge held magic after all. Not the hokey, fairy-tale variety the locals peddled to tourists, but something real and achingly human.

The rightness of that moment sank into his bones and he realized something. "You're right!"

"About?"

He finally had a good memory for this time of year, one he'd hold onto forever. "It feels good to make new traditions. I want to come back to this place every year with you, on this exact day."

She smiled. "It's a date."

He planned to grant her wishes every year, because making Wren happy somehow chased away all the fear and sadness. He loved her and he loved taking care of her. It was a privilege, one he'd honor for the rest of his life.

Closing his hand around hers, he ran his finger over the tied string and grinned. She was officially his.

CHAPTER 30

*"**WITH TERMITES IN YOUR SMILE, YOU HAVE ALL THE TENDER SWEETNESS OF A SEASICK CROCODILE, MR. GRINCH"***

PINE, SAP, AND FRESH SNOW INVADED THE HOUSE AS THE DOUBLE front doors burst open. Heavy boots stomped across marble, leaving wet puddles as Greyson, Soren, and Logan wrestled their prize inside.

"You're bending it!"

"Drop it down!"

"Not that way. The other way, dumbass."

Wren followed the arctic draft and the path of pine needles to investigate. "Did you get the—*oh*." Each brother gripped a different branch of the enormous fir, the tree bound in rope like a captive giant. "I see you went with the Rockefeller Center starter pack."

Pine needles scattered across the silk Persian rug in a festive massacre as they angled their kill awkwardly in the foyer.

Logan grinned proudly as he looked at her. "You said to get a big tree."

"I meant big as in normal-sized."

"Maybe normal-sized in this family is bigger than most." Soren waggled his brows.

"Oh good, more penis innuendos." She moved to shut the front doors, but froze at the sight of Soren's overcompensating—and extremely muddy—luxury SUV. "Car's a little dirty, Soren."

"I don't want to talk about it." He shoved the tree with renewed violence, muttering under his breath, "Two fucking pickup trucks and somehow we end up taking my Cadillac."

"Where are we putting this monster?"

Three sets of eyes turned to Wren. She pointed toward the den where Magnus had his hospital bed arranged. "In there, so your dad can enjoy it."

Soren snorted. "Yeah, he's gonna love this."

They heaved the tree into the den, propping it against the corner with collective grunts.

"What the hell is that?" Magnus barked from his bed, newspaper crumpling in his grip.

"Seriously?" The boys were dirty and in no mood for their father's unappreciative attitude.

"It's a tree," Wren said, rushing into the den. "A Christmas tree."

"Just what I want—" A wet cough interrupted his tirade, shaking his brittle frame. "A nest of ticks and spiders and God knows whatever else is living in that thing."

Monica, the housekeeper, materialized with water. "Drink, Mr. Hawthorne. You must have lots of fluids."

He gulped down several sips before continuing his protest. "How one of the filthiest traditions survived this long is beyond me."

"He loves it, Wren," Logan cheered, his cold sarcasm dripping like melted icicles.

Greyson stepped back to assess their handiwork. The tree nearly brushed the ceiling. "How are we standing this sucker up?"

Three expectant faces turned to her and she shrugged. "Don't you have a stand?"

"We haven't had a tree in years."

Greyson's fingers scratched his jaw as he surveyed the room, memory flickering in his eyes. "It used to go there." He pointed to the large bow window flanked by the grand fireplace and velvet wingback chairs. "We have to have stuff in the attic."

"The attic?" Logan whined. "You said we were having a party. This day's been nothing but work."

Wren smacked the back of his head. "It's for your father."

"Don't pin this nonsense on my account," Magnus griped.

"Yeah, he's thrilled." Logan rubbed his scalp.

Another gust of cold air cut through the den as the front door opened and Jocelyn's voice called from the foyer. *"Hello?"*

Soren stiffened. "What's she doing here?"

Wren shot Soren a warning glare. "We're in here, Joce."

Jocelyn swept in like a winter storm, kicking off stilettos and trailing a cranberry-colored fur coat. *"Glaðligr Jól!"*

Soren's face scrunched. "How are you a bestselling author when no one ever knows what you're talking about?"

"It means happy Yule, dumbass." She thrust a covered dish forward. "Wren, where do you want this?"

Soren eyed the dish with suspicion. "Back at your house?"

"Ha. Ha. Very funny, Daddy Issues. Just wait until you have a taste."

"What is it?" Wren lifted the foil, releasing an intriguing blend of sweet and savory aromas.

"Pork and apples—just like the Vikings ate."

Soren rolled his eyes, picking sap from his nails with studied indifference.

Jocelyn pivoted and noticed Magnus for the first time. The volume of her voice cranked up to a controlled shout, "How are you feeling, Mr. Hawthorne?"

Magnus's caterpillar brows collided as Wren grabbed Jocelyn's arm, dragging her toward the kitchen. "He's sick, not deaf, Joce."

"Oh. My bad."

Wren steered her toward the kitchen and added the dish to the growing collection of sides on the marble counter. "Thanks for coming."

"Of course. You know I always love to come."

Wren shot her a warning look. As much as she adored Jocelyn's unfiltered, colorful personality and inappropriate humor, today was about creating a healing, wholesome, holiday atmosphere, not a chaotic one. "Try not to fight with Soren today, okay? They're going through a lot."

"What are you talking about? I never fight with anyone."

"Oh, please, you two are always bickering and at each other's throats."

"Seriously don't know what you're talking about."

Wren rolled her eyes. "Just...behave."

"I'm always behaved." They held each other's gaze for exactly two seconds before Jocelyn's composure dissolved with snorting laughter. "All right. I'll try to be a good girl."

"Good would be a miracle. Just try not to fight with him. Come on. We can't leave them unsupervised for too long."

Magnus, in his monogrammed sweater, surveyed the chaos from his medical throne, micromanaging his sons. "You're getting needles everywhere."

"And joy, Dad. Don't forget the joy." Logan examined his sticky palms with disgust. "Hey, how do you get sap off?"

Magnus drew a breath from the oxygen mask. The blanket Wren gave him draped his knees with presidential dignity. "Try soap."

Wren moved to the other side of the room, where Greyson surveyed the designated tree area. He seemed less tense, but still reserved whenever in his father's presence. None of them chose to spend their day this way, but she hoped the forced merriment might help them face down their demons. Magnus was still an intimidating presence, but he seemed to be softening the longer his sons stuck around. At least she thought he was.

Grey's arm hooked around her waist, pulling her against his solid warmth. Gentle breath teased her neck as he pressed a kiss to her pulse and whispered, "What do you think?"

She tilted her head back to study the bound giant. "It's big."

"I know. But what do you think about the tree?"

She swatted his chest. "You're as bad as your brothers. Will you see if you can find a tree stand for it?"

"I'll take a look." His fingers traced the shoelace now wrapped around her wrist, their secret burning between them.

Their eyes met, and her smile bloomed. They hadn't breathed a word about the proposal. With Magnus's condition and the family drama, adding engagement news felt like throwing gasoline on a yule log. Besides, Greyson insisted on replacing the shoelace with a more traditional symbol of his love before they shared the news.

"Logan." Greyson pointed toward the stairs. "Come on. We're going into the attic to hunt a tree stand."

"And anything else *Christmas-y* that you find!" Wren called after them.

Across the room, Soren and Jocelyn huddled at the wet bar, their whispered conversation punctuated by sharp gestures. Rather than referee whatever battle brewed between them, Wren approached Magnus.

"Do you need anything, Mr. Hawthorne?"

His unimpressed, somewhat bothered disposition hadn't lightened much since morning, yet she believed he was secretly enjoying the chaos. He lowered the oxygen mask with trembling fingers. "There hasn't been a tree in this house since Sable was alive."

She followed his gaze to the wrapped pine. "Maybe it's time to bring the magic of Christmas back."

His sharp eyes dissected her as he drew a long pull of oxygen. "How long have you been dating my son?"

Heat crept up her neck. They hadn't bothered to hide their affection, so she'd expected him to notice, but his directness made her feel as if she were doing something…inappropriate. She suddenly felt like she was being called into the principal's office. "It's fairly new. But we've had feelings for each other for years."

"I assume you know about the will."

"Mr. Hawthorne, this isn't about…"

"Money?" His laughter crackled like dead leaves. "Everything's about money, Haven."

She stiffened. "I'm Wren. Haven was my mother."

"Right." Confusion clouded his features. "You look like her."

Despite his open dislike for her mom, Wren smiled. "Thanks."

Greyson reappeared, carrying their holiday haul of boxes and bags from the local shops. Logan followed with a tattered attic box that looked one sneeze away from disintegration.

"Where should we put them?"

"Over there." She gestured to the floor. "Did you find a stand?"

"We found something. I don't know how good it'll work, but I'm sure I can rig it."

Jocelyn wandered over, cocktail in hand. "*Oooh*, someone went shopping. What'd you get?"

Wren sorted through the various boxes, revealing the new dinner plates they bought. "This one goes to the kitchen. Soren?"

He retrieved the box of dishes and carried it off.

"That's a good pup," Jocelyn praised, and Wren rolled her eyes.

"You love to pick on him."

"*Meh*, low hanging fruit. He makes it so easy."

"You know, he took care of you a couple weeks ago when you were drunk. He could have left you there."

"I'm aware of what he did. I have cameras."

It wasn't like Jocelyn to cut her off so concisely, but the look on her face told Wren she didn't want to talk about her embarrassing episode at The Chowder House. It must have ended pretty rough for her not to make light of what happened.

Letting the topic drop, she revealed their treasures from town.

"Look how cute these are." Wren unwrapped the collection of ceramic Santas, handblown stars, and tiny porcelain boats with meticulously stitched Hideaway Bay flags. "Aren't they adorable?"

"There are more decorations in the attic," Greyson said, delivering the last of the boxes from the truck.

Logan was digging through the ratty box he'd found upstairs and Soren was speaking to his dad. She didn't want to disturb them, so she stood and brushed the glitter off her jeans. "I'll help you bring them down."

The attic smelled of cedar and forgotten decades. Wren shivered in the dry cold as dust motes danced in the pale light streaming through a single window.

"Watch your step." Grey shifted trunks aside, disturbing years of stillness.

Several chests bore labels with Sable's name in faded marker. Greyson avoided those and dragged the Christmas boxes into the center where there was the most light and room. The cardboard was too fragile to stack, and Wren worried moving them might do more damage than good. Maybe they should find a sturdier container and keep the boxes up here, only taking what they absolutely wanted down stairs.

Her fingers traced the tattered lid. "Can I look?"

"Go ahead."

The flimsy flap lifted to reveal treasures wrapped in fifteen-year-old newspaper. Wren touched the yellowed date reverently, imagining Sable's hands doing the same after her final Christmas.

Glass bulbs painted with winter scenes emerged from the paper cocoons, followed by ivory angels with tarnished gilt wings and picture frame ornaments. "Grey, look at this."

The floorboards groaned under his approach. She held up a tiny frame containing a faded photograph, Sable in a floor-length velvet gown, cradling baby Soren while leaning over Logan's bassinet.

"Wow," Greyson's voice caught.

"There has to be another one with you." She searched through the paper, unearthing frames with Sable and Magnus, more of Soren, faces she didn't recognize. Her hand froze when she revealed a faded photo of their mothers standing side by side, frozen in time and beauty.

"Look at them," she rasped, voice tight from dust and emotion.

The two friends laughed hysterically in ridiculous New Year's Eve hats. One with yellow feathers that contrasted her dark black hair, the other with silver sparkles that complemented her long blonde waves. They looked…timeless.

"They could make each other laugh harder than anything else ever could."

Wren's smile pinched as tight as her heart. "I try to remember her laugh…"

His hand warmed her shoulder. "I know."

She rewrapped the photo with reverent care. "You need to move these into plastic totes after the holidays. We have to protect the few memories we have left of them."

They found a bin and gathered what they could, selecting the items they thought the others would appreciate most. Downstairs, the tree rested in an outdated stand, leaning dangerously to the left.

"I'll get my drill and some rope," Greyson said, setting down the box from the attic and heading for his truck.

Soren used a pair of bolt cutters to cut the rope. Branches sprung free in a green explosion and Wren gasped. The enormous pine had a few blemishes, but it would look great once decorated.

"Don't scratch the paint," Magnus hollered, his gruff words muffled through the mask.

"We got it, Dad." Logan's patience frayed. "Soren, get over here and help me balance this."

Jocelyn perched on Magnus's bed like she belonged there, settling in for the show with her drink.

Magnus glared at her. "Who are you?"

She playfully caressed his bruised hand. "Mr. Hawthorne, it's me, Jocelyn Collins. You've known me since the third grade."

His brows knitted. "Of course."

While Jocelyn let him get away with the lie, Wren knew he didn't remember her. Still, Jocelyn played along.

"Are you sure you're not faking for attention?" Her friend squeezed his bicep playfully. "You look too strong to be sick."

Color bloomed in Magnus's cheeks as he chuckled like a schoolboy. "I've got a little life in me yet. Feel free to roam about—"

"Dad!" Soren's horrified face appeared from behind pine branches. "That's Jocelyn."

"I know who it is! I'm sick, not senile." He turned back to Jocelyn with a wolfish grin. "Far from dead, sweetheart, if you want to take a walk upstairs, we can test my virility."

Jocelyn laughed. "You're bad. I like that in a man. But, as fun as that might be, I'm afraid I can't. I've recently sworn off all men."

Soren's snort carried from behind the tree where branches jostled. "Yeah, right."

"I'm sorry, did you say something, Your Royal High Maintenance?"

He peeked out from behind the mammoth tree—no doubt to toss out a quick comeback—but Greyson pulled the trigger on his drill. "Soren, hold it still!"

Six hands and two bolts later, it stood straight as a soldier. Each brother claimed a tattered box from the attic, unwrapping ornaments while Wren wove lights through the branches. Every laugh made her heart swell. Whether they realized it or not, the holidays were already bringing them closer.

"I think we're ready," she said, winding the last of the lights around the lowest branches.

"Drumroll," Greyson announced, plug in hand.

Masculine hands drummed against denim thighs in crescendo. He shoved the plug into the outlet, and the branches glowed under hundreds of tiny lights, altering the room into something magical.

Silence fell like snow as they absorbed the transformation. She never knew what it was that made twinkle lights so enchanting. Maybe they were called fairy lights because they actually possessed magic.

"Wow." Soren came to stand by her side. "You don't even need the ornaments."

Logan joined them. "I thought they'd be colored lights."

Soren scowled at his brother. "Colorful lights are tacky. Mom liked a classy tree."

"That's the beauty of it," Wren said. "Sometimes, tacky is fun."

She glanced at Greyson, his expression a mixture of awe and stricken emotion. Of the three boys, he'd had the most Christmases with his mother and would therefore have the most memories to combat.

Sensing her stare, his gaze pulled from the tree, and he gave her a weak smile.

"All right, boys," she said, lightening the mood as she draped pearl beads over her shoulder and twirled them like a 1920s flapper. "Who's ready for some garland?"

They worked in tandem, the boys handling the heights while she and Jocelyn managed the lower branches. Compared to the dressed windows in town, they did a horrible job. But Wren decided all the cockeyed, crooked swoops and loops added character.

Stepping back, she admired the sloppy tree, proud of her boys and the effort they put into it. "Now, we decorate."

Newer ornaments went up first since the vintage ones required more reverence and care. As they unearthed the relics from their mother's boxes, they carefully handed them off one by one.

"That ornament goes at the top," Magnus's voice cut through the chatter. The room stilled as they followed his trembling finger to the ornament Logan had just hung. "Sable liked it close to the angel."

Wren looked at the crystal snowflake, and stretched on the step-stool to move it near the crown. "Here?"

Their father nodded, satisfied, but still scowling.

When the doorbell chimed, Wren handed off the next ornament. "That's probably my dad and my aunt."

Monica beat her to the foyer, and greeted their guests. Bodhi and Astrid swept in on a gust of winter air and patchouli.

"Will you look at this place," Astrid marveled. "Is that chandelier real crystal? Oh, Wren, there you are. We brought nut roast with turmeric gravy and reishi mushrooms."

"And I made my famous kombucha stuffing." Bodhi presented his creation like a proud alchemist.

Wren took the dish from her father and led him into the den. "Grey?"

Greyson turned and smiled as if relieved to see her family's familiar faces. "Bodhi! Astrid!"

Wren realized then how difficult this isolated time with his father had been. The boys might be paying a toll with each grumbled criticism from Magnus's mouth, but they were still gaining from the enforced togetherness. They were brothers, and they needed each other right now, no matter how much they fought it.

"Mr. Hawthorne, you remember my dad."

Magnus looked over his mask and gave a nod of recognition. There had only been a handful of times Wren recalled seeing their fathers in the same room. Unlike their mothers, the two had little in common and never passed time in the same circles.

"Wren, where am I putting this?" Astrid, still holding her dish, called from the doorway.

"In the kitchen. Follow me. Then you can help me with the centerpieces."

The maid fussed at the idea of letting others dress the table, but Wren insisted. Soren and Jocelyn bickered over candle placement. Aunt Astrid argued that the silver clashed with Greyson's aura. Everyone had an opinion, and Wren tried to compromise, giving up her dream of a centerfold-worthy outcome, and instead settling for a hodgepodge mashup of tacky meets good intentions.

Greyson, sensing her stress, took her hand and pulled her into the kitchen. He didn't give her a chance to gripe. Instead, he kissed her—slow and drudgingly. "Have I told you how much I appreciate everything you're trying to do."

Trying... That wasn't exactly a rave review.

She nestled into the shelter of his strength. "Is it working? You can lie to me," she teased.

"Depends on what you hoped the outcome would be."

She'd hoped for a miracle, but she'd settle for tolerance at this point. "Was it a mistake inviting my family?"

He drew back and frowned, holding her firmly by the shoulders. "Why would you ask that?"

She shrugged. "They're…you know…a lot."

"You mean weird?"

"Yeah."

He kissed her temple and hugged her. "You know I love Bodhi and Astrid."

"You do, but the others aren't used to them."

"Give them time."

"What about your dad?"

He chuckled. "He'll adapt. Your aunt settles in with the subtlety of an enema."

She laughed. "Your dad didn't look too happy to see my dad."

"My dad's never happy, Wren. It's easier if you just accept that he's a miserable man."

She looked up at him. "That's not true. I saw him…" Her words trailed off as she tried to explain the look in his eyes.

"What? Smile? Impossible."

"No, not smile, but I saw him get emotional a few times. He's not as unaffected as you all think."

"I'm sure it's a welcomed distraction."

Maybe her expectations had been too high. "How are you doing?"

"Me?" He smiled. "I'm great."

She studied his sharp blue eyes. "This isn't too much for you?"

"No. I can handle it." He swiped a fleck of glitter off her cheek. "You're very sparkly."

Rising on her toes, she kissed him. It was only meant to be a quick peck, but it quickly turned into more. When the kitchen door swung open, Greyson covered her mouth and yanked her into the pantry.

"My god, will you get off my ass!" Jocelyn's voice carried through the closed door and Wren's eyes widened.

Greyson slowly pulled his hand away, and continued kissing her.

"Would it kill you to ask for help?"

Wren broke the kiss, distracted by their bickering. They never stopped. Greyson, in the shadows of all the shelves and dry goods, rolled his eyes.

Wren frowned when he flicked open the button of her jeans. "What are you doing?" she hissed.

"Shh."

"Grey, we're in a pantry!"

Rather than answer, he sank his hand into the front of her panties. "You'll have to be quiet then."

His fingers pressed into her as soon as Jocelyn snapped, "I'd rather fall and crack my skull than owe you anything."

"That can be arranged."

Greyson tugged her close, distracting her with a kiss as he worked her into a tizzy. He guided her hand to the bulge at his crotch and pressed her fingers around his length. How far did he want to take this?

"Do you always stalk women who can't stand you, or did I do something special to provoke this sort of unwanted attention?"

"Don't flatter yourself."

"Oh, please. You get off on annoying me. It's like some sort of twisted foreplay."

Grey shoved down her pants and turned her toward the wall,

planting her hands on the built-in shelves. Wren's eyes widened as she realized he planned to go all the way.

His warm breath teased her ear. "Hold on tight."

She gasped, rising on her toes, as he gave her no chance to object.

"Shh," he chuckled, gently covering her mouth as he drew back and thrust hard. "You don't want them to hear us."

She whimpered against his fingers as he plunged into her again. Outside of the pantry, the two idiots continued to argue. A box of pasta fell with a *thud* and Wren froze, digging her nails into Greyson's arm.

"Did you hear that?"

Shit, shit, shit... With her jeans twisted around her legs, she couldn't move if she wanted to. Greyson froze, but didn't pull out. Wren winced, squeezing her eyes closed against the kitchen light when the pantry door opened.

"Uh…" Soren's voice was amused as much as it was confused.

"We're looking for nutmeg," Greyson blurted.

"Up her ass?" Jocelyn laughed wickedly.

"Seems like a deep inventory," Soren joked.

Greyson stretched and slammed the door in their faces. "Goodbye!"

Wren wilted into the shelves—death by mortification.

Grey only chuckled and continued on, stroking her back to life and not stopping until they discovered all the spice that pantry could offer.

When they returned to the den, Wren needed a drink. Jocelyn sidled up to her at the bar, smiling around the straw of some mulled concoction. "So… Come lately?"

"Please stop."

"Can't. It's a sickness."

It really was. "Please don't tell anyone."

"Your secrets safe with me. But can I just say how proud I am of you? Not only for getting it in public, but for holding that position while he covered your mouth." She tipped her head and sauntered away. "Nicely done, my friend."

Wren poured an oversized glass of wine and took it to the less judgmental atmosphere of the kitchen. Every inch of the marble countertops were covered with fresh herbs, cranberries, and copper pots as Astrid had now taken over the preparations.

"Can I help?"

"You can stir the gravy." Astrid handed off the spoon. "Heard about your little holiday foray in the pantry."

Wren stilled. "Who told you?"

"You know I have a sense for these things." When Wren gave her a doubtful look, her aunt confessed, "Jocelyn. That girl's lips are looser than tea leaves."

Wren covered her face and groaned. "I told her not to say anything."

"Sounds like you told her too late. Maybe by this time next year we'll be celebrating a New Year's baby."

"No," Wren laughed, but her hand stilled from stirring the gravy. It had been a few weeks now and she couldn't recall the last time she'd… "What's today's date?"

"The eighteenth."

"Oh, God." Her eyes widened as she did quick math. She should be safe, but they should probably have a serious conversation about children soon. Would he mind if she got pregnant? It wouldn't necessarily be a bad thing. She couldn't stop the smile that curved her lips.

Aunt Astrid nudged her hand. "Keep stirring."

Once dinner was ready and the table was set, Wren moved the guests into the dining room. Greyson, of course, noticed a shift in her mood.

"You okay?" he asked quietly as they took their seats, squeezing her thigh, his eyes creasing with concern.

She smiled nervously. If she was late, it wouldn't necessarily be a bad thing. Just an unexpected one.

"I'm fine." She pressed a kiss to his jaw. "Merry Christmas."

Crystal rattled at the other end of the table as Magnus wobbled up from his chair.

"Dad, what are you doing?" Logan sprung to his feet.

His father shook off his support. "I can stand on my own damn feet." He gripped the edge of the table with an unsteady hand, and pulled aside his oxygen mask and glared at his youngest. "I'm not dead yet." Their father took several seconds to continue as he struggled to catch his breath. "It's been a long time… since we…" He huffed as if coming off the last mile of a marathon. Defeated by his limitations, he gave up. Waving a hand in a way that showed no affection but some level of acceptance. He raised a crystal goblet and mumbled under his breath, "Merry Christmas."

"Cheers." They responded in unison.

Dishes were passed and the chatter continued. Wren smiled at the cheer emerging from the majority of the table, but never lost sight of Magnus's moody tells.

Magnus lost interest in the food when his hand trembled too fast to control his fork. He tossed down the silverware with a clatter, and the chatter silenced.

"Dad?" Greyson asked, as everyone stared at the patriarch of the family.

Worry tightened Wren's stomach. Magnus had too much pride to accept the help he needed, and she knew his vulnerability embarrassed him. All three sons watched their father with bleak concern, likely having the same thought.

Jocelyn, understanding her role as best friend, broke the silence and theatrically sampled the nut roast. "Sweet Oden, Bodhi, did you marinate this in despair?"

The table snapped out of its trance, and everyone laughed. Dishes clinked, and the happy chatter started again. Magnus merely sipped his wine after swatting away Logan's hand when he tried to cut his meat.

Conversation rose in volume as chaotic conversation topics shifted faster than the seasons. Overall, it was exactly how a holiday dinner should be—over planned, under prepared, and mildly off balance.

Magnus scanned the faces around the table and stilled when his stare met Wren's. His eyes narrowed.

"You okay, Dad?" Greyson sensed the moment she shrank in her seat.

His father called her Haven several times that day, and Wren wasn't sure who he saw now.

Magnus's glare snapped to the foot of the table where Greyson sat. "Where's Sable?"

Again, the table stilled, and the conversation stopped.

Magnus's cold gaze lifted past his son and his chin trembled. Everyone followed his stare except Wren, who kept her eyes on Magnus. His breath caught, and he abruptly dropped his gaze. "I've had enough."

Soren sprung to his feet as Magnus started to rise. "Take my arm, Dad."

His father shook off his help. "I can walk." But he couldn't, and when he realized that, Soren's arm was there.

The room seemed to hold a collective breath as the patriarch shuffled away from the table, grumbling and snapping, ridiculing anyone brave enough to help him.

"I said wait!" Magnus snapped, and Soren's patience visibly diminished. Leaning heavily on his son's support, he turned to face them one last time—not an ounce of kindness in his sharp gaze. "Your mother always hoped you boys would stay close. Thick as thieves, every last one of you. She always got her way."

Wren's breath turned unsteady as she realized what was coming. Greyson's hand clutched hers, tightening ever so slightly.

Magnus met her stare, then glared at Greyson. "You never wanted real responsibility. Always looking for an escape. The real work was a cage to you."

Silence fell like a guillotine.

Wren's grip tightened around Greyson's as Magnus turned his attention back to her. "Your mother..." He grunted a derisive laugh and scowled. "She was an ache in the shape of a woman."

A chair squealed as Bodhi abruptly stood, a look Wren didn't recognize burning in his weathered eyes.

Magnus didn't appear threatened in the least. "Haven taught Sable not to need anything from a man. Your mother wanted me to suffer." Eyes still on Greyson, his mouth curved with a wicked smile. "She'll never need you."

Greyson stood in one fluid motion and thumped his fist on the table with a hard, warning bang. Wren's stomach dropped as she felt all her hard work wither into ash.

"That's the difference between you and me. I don't need her codependence. I only want her love."

"Love," Magnus spat, as if the word tasted like rust on his tongue. "The prettiest lie ever whispered. Fools die under its spell. Real men know better." His cold gaze slid back to Wren. "Beautiful things hiding teeth. She'll eat you alive."

"That's enough," Logan said, standing from his chair. "Soren, take him to bed or I will."

His father laughed gruffly. "Well, well, look who grew a spine."

Greyson jerked his chair back and took a warning step. Wren caught his arm. Despite his hurtful words, something told her they needed this moment to play out. Her hope of ever redeeming Magnus in their eyes was now gone, so they needed to face down their demons together.

Magnus pulled the oxygen mask to his face and drew a deep breath, as if reloading a weapon. Wren braced for whatever came next. "I should have never let that woman into our lives. You boys were lost the day you met her." He angled a trembling finger at Wren.

"Soren," Greyson said with zero reflection. "Get him out of here."

"Can't run, so now you chase me away?" His cold chuckle was framed in a cough. "No need for old Dad anymore, eh? Got everything you wanted. Just like your mother."

The effort to stay calm radiated from Greyson. Tension filled the room.

Wren pried her fingers free of his grip and rounded the table, not stopping until she stood in front of Magnus. "Merry Christmas, Mr. Hawthorne." Despite the way she internally trembled, she rose on her toes and pressed a kiss to his dry cheek. "Thank you for a beautiful day."

He frowned, confused by her contrasting gratitude.

Wren didn't flinch or recoil from his bitter stare. It was clear, years of rotted pride had poisoned him. "You don't have to understand it," she said gently. "But this is what love looks like."

Magnus glanced over her shoulder at the table. She didn't look back to see what he saw. She already knew what was there.

It was not the image of greedy sons circling his deathbed like vultures, waiting for his legacy to fall into their palms. No brittle alliances had formed. Despite all of his efforts to turn them against each other, their bond remained strong to the very end.

"I love your sons, sir. All of them. And they love you. You can thank their mother, and mine, for that. They taught us how to love without expectation. The more you try to divide them, to divide us, the tighter we'll hold onto each other." She cradled his cold hand in his. "Can't you see? Christmas is grace unearned. That's why we're here today, with you. Our love might be undeserved, but we've given it anyway. And we expect nothing in return. Your legacy has nothing to do with it. We're here, for you, out of love. Just love. The kind, even death, can't destroy."

She released his hand and stepped back. No one said a word for several seconds, until Soren softly whispered, "Come on, Dad. I'll take you to bed."

When they left, she turned. They stared at her in shock and Greyson crossed the room, not stopping until he hugged her tightly. There were no words. There didn't have to be. After years of emotional silence, she understood everything he wanted to say.

CHAPTER 31

"SLEEP IN HEAVENLY PEACE"

GREYSON HEADED BACK INSIDE WHILE WREN MADE HER GOODBYES to Jocelyn, Bodhi, and Astrid. Rather than digest everything that happened, he headed toward the dining room to help clean up.

"Grey," a low voice hissed as he passed his father's study.

He stilled, wondering if he heard a ghost.

"Greyson," Soren hissed, poking his head into the hall. "Get your ass in here!"

He followed Soren into the study, where he and Logan hovered like vultures over his father's desk. "What?"

They exchanged a glance, and Soren pointed behind him. "Shut the door."

He wasn't in the mood for more family dysfunction, so he left it open. "What's going on?"

Logan spoke first. "It's Wren."

"What about her?"

"You gotta marry her."

The front door opened, and a chill cut through the house carrying Wren's recognizable scent. Greyson leveled his brothers with a threatening look. "Conversation's over."

"What conversation?" She appeared in the doorway, scanning their blank faces.

Logan opened his mouth, and Greyson shot him a lethal glare.

Wren turned her stare on him. "What's going on, Grey?"

"Nothing."

"We think you two should get married."

"God damnit, Soren!"

"What? We all know it's inevitable. After that spectacle at dinner, it's clear how badly he wants us to lose."

"This isn't a win or lose situation. Wren and I are out of it."

"No," Logan snapped. "You don't get to excuse yourself from every fucked up thing that happens to this family, Grey. You're a part of this. Wren is a part of this. And Soren's right, Dad did this because he wanted to watch us fail one last time."

"Dad added that clause because he's a miserable, lonely man who only knows how to push others away. I'm not lowering myself to his twisted—"

"We'll do it."

He spun to face Wren. "Baby, no."

She shrugged. "Why not?" Her fingers caressed the brown shoelace tied to her wrist. "We're getting married anyway."

"You are?"

"Wait, what?"

"When did this happen?"

She ignored his brothers. "If it fixes things, let's just do it. I don't want the three of you to fight."

"We're not fighting. I'm standing my ground."

"Against our interests," Logan barked. "What about us?"

"Yeah, what about the company and what we want?"

An argument erupted as they disputed the same old shit they'd been fighting over for years. Finally, Greyson snapped, "Did you ever consider I might not want it?"

The room silenced.

Soren scoffed. "No fucking shit."

They squared off for a long moment, and then Logan finally admitted, "I want it. There. I admitted it. I want the company. And so does Soren. Does that mean anything to you?"

Tension crept up his spine. "Yes, but that's not possible. The clause in the will—"

"Fuck the will! If you meet the clause, you inherit the company. You can do whatever the hell you want with it after that. You'd run the show."

When he hesitated, Soren scoffed again, "My God, Greyson, is it really so hard for you to put us first? We're talking about six months of involvement—tops."

"You're asking us to fast-track our lives. This isn't just about me. It's about Wren."

"Wren, do you even want a big wedding?"

"I…" She looked up at Greyson and back to the boys. "I want everyone to be happy."

Greyson's jaw locked. "Enough. I'm not going to let you make our marriage into some business deal. I've said my piece, and that's the—"

"Excuse me—"

They all turned to find Monica wringing her hands in the doorway, tears in her eyes. The world withered small enough to slide through a keyhole as the expression on her face sank in. All sound disappeared.

Logan rushed out of the study. Soren followed. Wren squeezed his arm, and the world shifted back on its axis, fitting like a shoe on the wrong foot.

"Greyson, I'm so sorry." She hugged him and his arms numbly lifted to hold her.

A chill rushed down his spine.

They were too late.

It was done.

<h1 style="text-align:center">CHAPTER 32</h1>

"We'll take a cup of kindness yet, For the sake of auld lang syne"

The last of the mourners shuffled across the frost-bitten cemetery grass, their black coats stark against the December snow. Greyson watched them stream toward the parking lot in clusters—some dabbing at red-rimmed eyes, others speaking in hushed tones that carried on the bitter wind.

Mayor Quimby helped his wife navigate the icy path between headstones. Simon Moseley actually wore a proper suit. Even Jocelyn Collins kept her commentary tasteful and reserved, not bickering with Soren once.

The irony wasn't lost on him. Half of Hideaway Bay had shown up to celebrate Magnus Hawthorne, standing in the bitter cold, paying their respects to the urn holding a man who'd never bothered to learn most of their names.

But that's what small towns did. They came together in love and support during the good times and the bad. And for the first time in a long time, Greyson felt the extraordinary affection of his neighbors, each one offering condolences and comments that reminded him their mother was still missed.

They didn't show up for Magnus. They showed up for Sable and her boys. That's how powerful his mother's legacy was. It outlived his father's fortune and stretched beyond his dark shadow. Her goodness was the real source of richness in their lives, and Greyson saw that today more than ever before.

Greyson pulled his coat tighter, watching his brothers outlast the crowd. Logan wiped his nose with the back of his gloved hand. Soren stood, statue-still, jaw clenched against whatever threatened to crack his composure. They'd held it together through the service, through the endless parade of handshakes and hollow condolences, but exhaustion weighed on all of them like wet wool. After Christmas, the three of them would take a ship out and fulfill the last of his father's wishes, scattering what remained of his ashes at sea.

Wren's fingers found his, squeezing gently through their gloves. She'd been his anchor through every brutal moment—the viewing, the eulogy he'd somehow managed to deliver, the final prayers as they lowered their father into frozen ground. Even now, she radiated the kind of quiet strength that made him believe he might survive this.

The funeral director approached with practiced sympathy. "The limo's ready when you are, Mr. Hawthorne. No rush."

Greyson nodded, taking one last look at the grave site. Magnus was gone. Despite everything—all the years of silence, all the ways they'd failed each other, all the words that would never be spoken—Greyson knew they'd been good sons. Imperfect, maybe. Stubborn as hell, definitely. But they'd loved their impossible father anyway.

The black limousine waited with its engine running, exhaust clouds rising like incense in the frigid air. Logan climbed in first, then Soren. Wren squeezed in beside him, and Greyson took the seat across from his brothers, needing to see their faces, needing to know they were all still here.

The driver pulled away from the cemetery in respectful silence, tires crunching over the salt-scattered road. Through tinted windows, Greyson watched the town scroll past, shop windows still dressed for Christmas, life continuing its relentless march forward while theirs had ground to a halt.

Love was a complicated son of a bitch, perhaps more so in death. Sometimes, there just wasn't enough time to figure it out. But he was learning.

His gaze naturally settled on Wren as she sat angelically in the dim interior. Light filtered through her hair. The gentle curve of her mouth and the steady rise and fall of her breathing settled him in ways he couldn't explain.

His future wife.

He knew, with bone-deep certainty, that what he felt for Wren transcended every petty thing that had come before. The thought still caught him off guard, sent something warm spreading through his chest despite the cold seeping through the windows. As long as he had her by his side, he could handle anything.

They'd figure it out together—the business, the inheritance, all the complicated mess Magnus had left behind. But first, they'd get through today. They'd stand in their father's house surrounded by casseroles and sympathy, accept more condolences, and somehow find a way to live in a new world without giants and tyrants.

The limousine turned onto the familiar tree-lined drive, and Greyson's chest tightened. Cars already packed the circular driveway—neighbors, business associates, distant relatives who'd materialized for the occasion. Smoke curled from the chimneys, and warm light spilled from every window, transforming the austere mansion into something almost welcoming.

Their patriarch and his legacy was gone, but the house still stood. The sense of family still survived. And maybe, just maybe, that was enough.

The car glided to a stop beside the front steps, and Greyson took a deep breath, preparing to face whatever came next. His brothers exited, and Wren waited.

"If you're not ready for this, we can wait."

He met her stare and nodded. "I'm ready."

She slid out of the car, and he followed.

The house buzzed with the peculiar energy of a wake—hushed conversations punctuated by the occasional burst of nervous laughter, the clink of silverware against china, the soft shuffle of feet across Persian rugs. Greyson stood near the fireplace, watching it all unfold like a movie he wasn't quite part of.

The dining room table groaned under the weight of casserole dishes and sympathy offerings. Tuna noodle, green bean, something that might have been lasagna but could just as easily have been cardboard smothered in cheese. The scent of comfort food mixed with the lingering pine from their Christmas tree, creating an oddly festive atmosphere for such a somber occasion.

Wren moved through the crowd effortlessly, accepting condolences with genuine grace, directing traffic toward the buffet, somehow remembering everyone's names and asking after their families. She'd changed from her funeral dress into something softer, a charcoal sweater that brought out the gold in her hair. Every gesture was natural, every smile authentic despite the grief shrouding the last few days.

How had he gotten so fucking lucky?

She appeared at his elbow with a plate piled high with food he didn't want. "Eat," she commanded softly, pressing the dish into his hands.

"I'm not hungry."

"I don't care. You need to eat something." Her fingers brushed his wrist, warm and insistent. "Please, Grey. For me."

He couldn't argue with that. He found an empty chair against the wall, settling in to pick at Mrs. Henderson's famous potato salad while keeping one eye on the room. Logan held court near the bar, regaling some old high school friends with a story that actually drew genuine laughter. Greyson scanned the crowd for Soren, expecting to find him working the room with corporate precision, shaking hands and accepting business cards, but his middle brother was nowhere to be found.

A movement near the hallway caught his attention. Jocelyn emerged from the powder room with the kind of expression that immediately set off alarm bells—eyes darting left and right, smoothing down her skirt, looking for all the world like she'd just committed some minor crime.

Greyson frowned, taking another bite of potato salad as he watched her slink toward the kitchen with exaggerated casualness.

A moment later, the powder room door opened again. Soren stepped out, and Greyson nearly choked on a lump of egg and potato.

His brother's usually immaculate hair stuck up at odd angles, his tie hung loose around his neck, and his shirt was wrinkled in ways that suggested it had been hastily tugged.

Pausing in the doorway, Soren straightened his cuffs and glanced up, his gaze freezing when it collided with Greyson's no doubt stunned expression. Color draining from his rigid face as realization dawned. He shot a quick glance toward the kitchen where Jocelyn had disappeared, then back to Greyson with the desperate look of a man caught red-handed.

Very slowly, very deliberately, his brother pressed a finger to his lips, his expression pleading.

Greyson shoveled another forkful of potato salad into his mouth to keep from laughing out loud. He gave his brother the smallest nod—a promise that this particular family secret was safe—and watched Soren's shoulders sag with relief before he melted back into the crowd of mourners.

Greyson returned to his potato salad, unable to shake the grin tugging at his mouth.

"The food must be good. That's the first time I've seen you

smile today," Wren said, handing him a rocks glass of what looked like his favorite bourbon.

He was tempted to tell her what he saw, but decided to keep his word to Soren. Jocelyn was her best friend and would likely tell her soon enough, if she hadn't already.

The house gradually emptied as the afternoon wore on, guests filtering out with final hugs and promises to check in soon. Greyson found himself stationed by the front door, accepting final handshakes and murmured condolences with the kind of autopilot politeness that grief demanded.

He was helping Mrs. Pemberley with her coat when he spotted a familiar figure in the foyer, bundling into a cashmere overcoat. Clayton, his father's attorney, must have flown in from Boston that morning.

"Pardon me, Mrs. P," Greyson said, exiting the hall to speak to the tall, silver-haired man who had handled Hawthorne business for the better part of three decades.

"Clayton." Greyson extended his hand as he approached the older man. "Thank you for making the trip. I know Dad would have appreciated it."

Clayton's handshake was firm, his expression genuinely sorrowful. "Your father was… an impressive man. Complicated, certainly, but impressive nonetheless. He built something that will outlast all of us."

"Thank you. Impressive's a kind way to put it." They both chuckled as if knowing exactly what they weren't saying out loud. "We'll call your office sometime next week to go over whatever needs signing." Greyson managed a tired smile. "I suppose it doesn't really matter now, since Dad changed the will, but it's a shame it couldn't go to my brothers. They wanted the company and deserved it, but..." He shrugged. "Dad was just that kind of prick."

Clayton's brows knitted together, confusion clouding his features. "I'm sorry, what change?"

"The clause he added. About divesting the company if one of us didn't settle down and get married before he passed." Greyson studied the lawyer's face, and something cold settled in his stomach. "The clause he added around Thanksgiving."

The confusion on Clayton's face deepened. "Greyson, I think there's been some misunderstanding. The will hasn't changed in years. Your father never contacted me about any modifications." He adjusted his coat, speaking with the careful precision of someone delivering important news. "You and your brothers will inherit everything equally, just as we discussed years ago. If you want to sell your shares to Soren or Logan, you have every right to do so."

The world tilted sideways.

Greyson's mouth opened, then closed. The sounds of the house —distant conversations, the clink of dishes being cleared—faded to white noise as the implications crashed over him like a rogue wave.

No change. No clause. No marriage requirement.

His father had lied. Manipulated them. Played them like chess pieces right up until the end.

"Greyson?" Clayton's voice seemed to come from very far away. "Are you all right?"

He managed a nod, though his knees felt suspiciously unsteady. "Yes. I'm... that's good news. Thank you for clarifying."

Clayton studied him with sharp eyes, clearly sensing there was more to this story. But he was too professional to pry. Instead, he clapped a gentle hand on Greyson's shoulder and offered a tired smile.

"Merry Christmas, son. Take care of yourself."

Greyson stood frozen in the doorway long after Clayton's car disappeared down the drive, his mind reeling with the weight of what he'd just learned. In the distance, he could hear Wren's laughter drifting from the kitchen, warm and familiar. His brothers' laughter followed.

In that moment, they won. Not because the inheritance withstood their father's games, but because they were happy, with or without it. Like their mother, they didn't need anything as long as they had each other.

He followed the sound of his family, finding them gathered around the granite island, completely unaware that their world had just shifted on its axis.

Again.

Wren smiled and pulled him close. He decided to hold onto this news until Christmas morning—a gift to his brothers. And giving it would be a gift to him.

CHAPTER 33

"HOME FOR CHRISTMAS"

ONE YEAR LATER

GREYSON ROSE from his chair with fluid grace, setting Rat in the warmth of his seat as he crossed to the wet bar to refill his bourbon. But instead of returning to his chair, he moved toward Wren, settling beside her on the sofa with the kind of easy intimacy that still made her pulse quicken. Rat, realizing his daddy wasn't returning, shortly followed, curling onto her lap as Greyson pulled her close.

"You know what I love about this story?" He set his glass on the side table and reached for her left hand, his thumb tracing the simple platinum band that had replaced his makeshift bootlace ring. "It has a happy ending."

"Does it?" Soren asked with a knowing smirk. "Because from where I'm sitting, it looks like it's just getting started."

457

Greyson's hand moved from Wren's ring to rest gently on the curve of her belly, where their child grew safe and warm, nestled in a nest of Maine coon fur beneath. The gesture was so natural, so protective, that Wren's heart swelled with the same overwhelming love that hit her daily—sometimes hourly.

"Any day now," she murmured, covering his hand with hers. "Can you believe it?"

"Yes, because I always knew this was how it was meant to be, but some days the reality still shocks the hell out of me."

"Get a room," Logan grumbled.

Greyson ignored him and kissed Wren's temple, his voice rough with emotion as he whispered, "You're going to be an amazing mother. Just like our moms were."

Logan leaned forward in his chair, expression softening as he watched them. "You know what's crazy? Last Christmas, we were all convinced we were doomed to be miserable bastards like Dad. And now look at us."

"Speak for yourself," Soren said, arrogance wafting from him as usual. "Some of us have always been charming."

"Right," Wren laughed, softly stroking Rat's long fur. "Is that what we're calling your behavior lately?"

Soren's ears turned red. "We agreed never to speak of that!"

"Speak of what?" Logan frowned. "What did I miss?"

"You agreed," Wren said with theatrical innocence. "I never promised anything."

"What did I ever do to you?"

"The pantry," Greyson said.

"The parade," Logan added.

"All right!" Soren snapped. "What are you two, her score-keepers?"

Wren dissolved into laughter. "I'm protected at all angles. You can't threaten me."

Greyson's arm tightened around her shoulders. "And if you try,

I'll personally send a detailed manifesto of every dirty little secret I know about you to Lady Lovewatch."

"As if you even know who Lady Lovewatch is." Soren crossed his arms.

"Wait, I'm still confused," Logan griped. "What dirty secrets?"

Wren and Greyson shared a knowing look, then sealed their lips shut with an invisible key.

"You both suck. It's probably dumb anyway. Soren's life's boring as hell since he became CEO."

Wren snickered. Soren's life hadn't been boring in a long time.

Outside, snow continued to fall past the windows, transforming the harbor into a winter wonderland. Christmas lights twinkled from the eves as the fire crackled softly and a familiar swell of contentment settled over her.

"You know what I realized?" she said suddenly. "This is the first Christmas in years where none of us are dreading it."

"Yeah," Greyson agreed, glancing down at his tacky holiday sweater *he* picked up in town.

Wren smiled, looking down at her matching one he insisted she wear tonight. "This is exactly how Christmas should be."

"Peaceful," Soren said, stretching his legs toward the fire..

"Together," Logan added.

"With those you love," Greyson finished, pulling her closer to his side.

Once her boys had permission to feel all the emotions they were warned never to express, they could grasp the true meaning of Christmas. Beyond the commercialism and chaos, was the truth. One day a year, everything paused so that feelings could mend. Families came together to prove, despite the ups and downs, love endures all.

Wren smiled. "We have one hell of a Christmas story."

Greyson laughed. "Too bad we all tell it differently. Maybe one day we'll get it right so we can tell the kids."

"What's left to tell?" Logan asked. "Boy meets girl. Boys fight over girl. Girl chooses boy. Boy and girl get married and live happily ever after."

"You're forgetting the best part," Soren protested.

"Which is?"

"Middle son and favorite future uncle becomes financial giant and global sensation among the ladies."

They all burst into laughter.

"No."

"Yeah, right!"

"More like the total opposite."

"You know what," Soren snapped. "Screw all of you."

Wren's smile lingered as she looked up at Greyson, her heart full to bursting with everything they'd built together. "Is this your happy ending, Mr. Hawthorne?"

"No. This is my beginning," he whispered, kissing her nose.

"Get a room!"

"Boo…"

The more his brothers grumbled the more he made a spectacle of kissing her. Wren didn't mind, because she'd waited a lifetime for his kisses and had a lifetime ahead of her to enjoy them. And she planned to.

The Christmas tree glowed from the corner under warm lights, its branches heavy with ornaments they'd hung together as a family—keeping their tradition from the year before.

Gone were the cold brass decorations that once made this house feel more like a mausoleum than a home, and in their place were personal touches like photographs and meaningful knick-knacks resurrected from the boxes in the attic.

It was perfect. Not magazine-perfect or Instagram-perfect, but real-life perfect, with all its beautiful imperfections and unexpected chaos.

Logan sighed and stretched his legs closer to the fire. "I love Christmas."

"Yeah," Soren agreed, staring at the flames as he sipped his drink. "Me too. Reminds me of Mom."

Greyson's hand pressed gently against Wren's belly. "Reminds me of you."

Her hand closed over his. "It's what brought you back, year after year."

He shook his head. "Christmas was the excuse I needed, but we all know I came back for you."

The fire popped and settled, casting dancing shadows on the walls. In the distance, church bells chimed the hour, their notes carrying across the snowy harbor like a benediction.

"Merry Christmas," Greyson murmured against her hair.

"Merry Christmas," she whispered back. "This time next year, we'll be hiding presents under the tree."

"I can't wait."

She never feared him running away again. Together, they made a home. A family. And it was exactly where the four of them wanted to be.

WWW.LYDIAMICHAELSBOOKS.COM

**Ready for more holiday fun with
The Hawthorne Brothers?**

Read Falling for the Enemy next!

FALLING for the ENEMY

ALSO BY LYDIA MICHAELS

BOOKS BY SERIES

Many first in series books are FREE

Grab them here!

MCCULLOUGH MOUNTAIN

Almost Priest *

Beautiful Distraction

Irish Rogue

British Professor

Broken Man

Controlled Chaos

Hard Fix

Intentional Risk

JASPER FALLS

Wake My Heart *

The Best Man

Love Me Nots

Pining For You

My Funny Valentine

Side Squeeze

CALAMITY RAYNE

Calamity Rayne Gets a Life *

Calamity Rayne Back Again

Calamity Rayne Gets Hitched

Calamity Rayne Over the Moon

Calamity Rayne Knocked Up

THE SURRENDER TRILOGY

Falling In

BreakingOut

Coming Home

Ruthless Billionaires

One Billion Secrets *

Two Billion Enemies

MASTERMIND

Blind

Untied

NEW CASTLE

First Comes Love *

If I Fall

Shattered Vows

Remember Me

ADDICTED TO YOU

Crush *

Bang

Throb

THE ORDER OF VAMPIRES

Original Sin *

Dark Exodus

Prodigal Son

Immortal Bastard

Primal Kill

Blood Moon

VILLAINS OF KASSEL

Hush Darling

Gilded Locks

Feast of the Fallen

The Rabbit Hole

STAND ALONES

La Vie en Rose

Simple Man

Sugar

Breaking Perfect

Hurt

Protege

ABOUT THE AUTHOR

To receive Lydia's Newsletter and 7 FREE Books, click HERE !

Lydia Michaels is the bestselling and award-winning author of more than fifty novels. She writes heart-clenching, unpredictable romance with dark elements and high heat. Her work is character-driven and bursting with broken heroes and badass females. With a sweet spot for overbearing, territorial types, her deeply emotional books are spicy, emotionally satisfying, and guaranteed to leave readers with many book hangovers.

Lydia is the consecutive winner of the *2018 & 2019 Author of the Year Award* from *Happenings Media* and the recipient of the *2014 Best Author Award* from the Courier Times. She has been featured by *USA Today*, *Romantic Times Magazine*, the *Women in Publishing Summit*, and more.

Michaels started her author career in 2007, becoming a recognized presence and advocate within the publishing industry. She is the CEO of LMC Consulting, a certified author coach specializing in character and plot development, and the founder of the *East Coast Author Convention*, the *Behind the Keys Author Retreat*, and www.LydiaMichaelsBooks.com.

She is happily married to her childhood sweetheart. Her favorite things include cooking Italian cuisine, hosting extravagant dinner parties, sipping espresso martinis, listening to her husband play piano, and escaping to her coastal home on the Jersey Shore. She's an LGBTQ ally, a BLM supporter, a firm believer that the patriarchy must end (women's rights are human rights), and an advocate for pediatric cancer research.

LYDIA

Follow Lydia Michaels on social media!
Facebook | Instagram | TikTok

THANK YOU FOR YOUR REVIEW!